Portraits of Ruin

PORTRAITS
OF RUIN

Joseph S. Pulver, Sr.

Hippocampus Press

New York

Publishing history

"No Healing Prayers," *Dead But Dreaming 2* (Miskatonic River Press, 2011).
"But Not for Me" (with Laurence Amiotte), *Strange Aeons #4* (Eryx Press, 2010).
"kristamas as an exhibition," *Aklonomicon* (Aklo Press, 2012).
TIME ... and FOREVER (with Tara Vanflower), *Aklonomicon* (Aklo Press, 2012).
"Small Ocean After Solar," *Kizuna: Fiction for Japan* (CreateSpace 2011).
"Mrs. Spriggs's Easter Attire" (with Tara Vanflower), *Horror for the Holidays* (Miskatonic River Press 2011).
"Icarus Above ...," *Null Immortalis–Nemonymous Ten* (Megazanthus Press, 2010).
"Tark Left Santiago," *Lovecraft eZine #10* (January 2012).
"And this is where I go down into the darkness," *Phantasmagorium #1* (2011).
All the other texts are new and unpublished.

Published by Hippocampus Press
P.O. Box 641, New York, NY 10156.
http://www.hippocampuspress.com

Cover art by J. Karl Bogartte.
Cover design by Barbara Briggs Silbert.
Hippocampus Press logo designed by Anastasia Damianakos.

First Edition
1 3 5 7 9 8 6 4 2
ISBN 978-1-61498-025-4

This collection is dedicated to the generous, WONDERFUL "muses" who gave this foolish bumpkin fire & fuel~ ~~ I could not have done this w/out each of YOU gems! !! HIGSsssss & hugSSSSSSSSSsssssssssSss! !!

Contents

Introduction

Matt Cardin

Plato once wrote, "But if a man comes to the door of poetry untouched by the madness of the Muses, believing that technique alone will make him a good poet, he and his sane companions never reach perfection, but are utterly eclipsed by the performances of the inspired madman." This is a sentence rich with, and in fact threaded and structured along, a succession of deeply striking and evocative phrases and images: "the door of poetry . . . the madness of the Muses . . . sane companions . . . utterly eclipsed . . . the inspired madman." They are like a collage of implied spiritual-artistic meaning, a chant whose very intonation is at least as important as its conceptual content. In other words, they *gesture* toward something, some transcendent reality that they can't quite articulate. Or at least that's the way I like to take them, regardless of dear old Plato's intentions.

And this, I think—both my fixation on this quotation, which is talismanic for me, and my preferred way of reading it—is one of the main reasons why I find Joe Pulver's *Portraits of Ruin* to be so deeply disquieting. Reading it, I begin to wonder, inadvertently, inexorably, about the name and nature of the particular door that he may have passed through in the pursuit of his art. I wonder about the identity of the particular Muse—dark, wild, daemonic—that may have maddened him. And wondering these things, I'm driven to doubt whether we, his sane companions, can ever really comprehend him, and to suspect that we must instead resign ourselves to having our understanding utterly eclipsed by the performances of this inspired madman.

I've always found "experimental" literature very difficult, notwithstanding the fact that I've produced a couple of pieces of it myself. Apparently as a fundamental fact of my literary taste and predilection, I'm drawn mostly to conventionally worded writings and traditionally structured narratives. Give me Lovecraft over Burroughs, Poe over Pynchon, *A Portrait of the Artist as a Young Man* over *Ulysses* (and especially over, God help us, *Finnegans Wake*). As with fiction, so with poetry: I'll take Robert Frost over T. S. Eliot any day, and Lawrence Ferlinghetti just makes my head hurt.

Or actually, this has changed somewhat over the years. It was Robert Anton Wilson, of all people, who cracked open my cosmic-literary egg and initiated me into some of the pleasures and rewards of conventionally unreadable and/or incomprehensible writing. He loved to mix things up in his novels: plain old prose on one page, then stream-of-consciousness gibberish on the next, followed by a scene or two in screenplay format, and then a metafictional flourish for good measure. And since I was drawn to him helplessly at age nineteen when I recognized him as one of my natural philosophical mentors, I just rolled with it. I absorbed the lessons he overtly taught and subliminally imparted. All these years later, I find I'm grateful for this education when I approach the Pulver corpus and try to wrap my mind around it, or perhaps let it wrap its mind around me.

Literature, it turns out, can do a lot more than one might think, especially when it tries not to be literature, or to forget that there's such a thing as restraint by medium, or to burst the bounds of what can actually be communicated via the written word, not just in terms of the concepts being broached but the very form in which they're presented.

Sometimes it's the attempt to say what can't be said, or what can't be said in any form that "makes sense," that says the most.

William Stafford, the United States Poet Laureate from 1970 to 1971, wrote what may be the single most brilliant essay on the art of writing that I've ever been privileged to read. The title is "A Way of Writing," and Stafford uses it to present his philosophy—not abstract but applied, embodied—of the relationship between the authorial act and the writer's very identity, and of the liberatory value writers can find in foregoing a sense of foresight and control by relying on their own innate coherence. "A writer," he tells us, "is not so much someone who has something to say as he is someone who has found a process that will bring about new things he would not have thought of if he had not started to say them. . . . If I put down something, that thing will help the next thing come, and I'm off. If I let the process go on, things will occur to me that were not at all in my mind when I started. These things, odd or trivial as they may be, are somehow connected. . . . I know that back of my activity there will be the coherence of my self, and that indulgence of my impulses will bring recurrent patterns and meanings again."

I don't know if Joe Pulver has read this essay, but I kind of hope he hasn't. It's neater to think of him practicing something exactly like what Stafford describes, some sort of inner artistic-literary-alchemical act of receptivity or (as we might think of it) "self-theurgy," but perhaps in a more overtly surrealist vein of the André Breton sort than Stafford was wont to embrace, without ever having heard of the man. It's neater to think of him sitting down somewhere and loosing his pen or typewriter or word processor in innocence of Stafford's advice, and finding a flood of words and images issuing forth on the page or screen, seeing it all assume a shape that won't make sense to the conscious mind, but that will speak of a deep self, *his* self, with perfect precision.

Or perhaps it's speaking not of him but of that dark-daemonic Muse of his. Then again, perhaps they're the very same thing.

For years I've played a kind of literary game with myself. Before reading any work of fiction, I always turn to the start and read the opening lines. Then I skip to the end and read the closing lines. Finally, I pause and mull them over for a moment before diving into the full reading itself. How is the author going to get from point A to point Z? How will those opening words, phrases, sentences, thoughts, images, insights, necessarily have to unfurl and complexify and flow and develop in order to reach the conclusion toward which I know they're headed? Far from ruining the reading experience, I find this practice palpably enhances it.

But alas, it simply *doesn't work* with Joe Pulver's stuff, or at least not in the way I've come to regard as normal and desirable. Consider, for example, the opening story in *Portraits of Ruin*. Its title is "No Healing Prayers," and it bears the dedication "for Gary Myers & Robert Bloch." The publication data page informs me that it was previously published in the anthology *Dead But Dreaming 2* from Miska-

tonic River Press in 2011. Okay, that's sufficient to establish a surrounding context, and a very compelling one at that, for somebody
like me (and, I assume, somebody like you) who is deeply interested
and invested in horror fiction, and in particular the dark philosophical
concerns of the branch we call weird or cosmic.

So, having made my mental oblations for the reading act, I turn
to the opening lines and find the following:

> Midnight.
> Moonlight.
> Cold.
> The howling sun, far from this place with no hope for tomorrow,
> running with things that fear what the cold moon brings.
> Captain Jack sits on his front porch. Shotgun on his lap.
> Coffee gone cold.
> Waiting.

Okay. Nice language and darksleek imagery. Very impressionistic,
though. I'm aware, yes, that language, especially when artistically
deployed, can achieve amazing things when it tries to subvert or
explode its own inherent limits. But that's often more of a
philosophical conviction than a living reality for me. I still doubt my
chops as a reader of experimental stuff. So this one may be difficult
to get a grasp on. With this in mind, I turn to the closing lines to
complete the ritual:

> Coming for bones. Coming for flesh.
> Coming to drink tears and tenderness affirmed and every contour
> between.
> The corpse-coffin sound of Hell shouting in the trees. Something
> black in the road.
> "Whatever will be . . . will be."
> The Piper Man laughs.
> Shotgun leveled . . .
>
> Grand Funk Railroad, "The Railroad"

To borrow that unfortunate and ubiquitous initialism from the culture of social media and digital interconnectedness: WTF? What the
hell do *those* lines tell me? In one of my day-job incarnations, I teach
remedial reading to community college students, and my practice of
thoroughly pre-reading books and stories to gain a sense of their over-

all contextual contour is something all the textbooks preach. Get your bearings. Don't just dive into page one, line one. That approach is a surefire route to disaster via incomprehension. Instead, map your mental way to the end before starting, so that what you encounter along the way will make sense because you're fitting it into a bird's-eye map of the total landscape, just as you look at a roadmap before trying to drive to Dallas. I've always done this intuitively. Nobody had to teach it to me. Now I teach it to others.

And lo! it breaks down and craps out entirely when applied to Joe's work.

But what if we try another item? Maybe one from the middle of the book. Our eyes skim to the midpoint of the table of contents and find "Marks and Scars and Flags." The information at the start of the book lets us know this one is previously unpublished. Okay, here goes. Opening lines:

> Is it real?
> Is it?
> These last 6 hours . . .
> This pack.
> Did she, looking down at her feet and gently smiling—in that crocodile way, really say, "Go. Ask, Alice."?
> Did she?

Flip the pages. Closing lines:

> Her smile blurs, releasing cobwebs and corridors.
> "Turn." Soft as the saxophone that afternoon, cold, a trumpet that bends the facets of the breast.
> Cold.
> And someone—someone—has, has opened the gates . . .
> *A century in seclusion with the green birds…the humors of the lantern as a sedative . . .*
> *I've lost my shoes . . .*

> Deathprod—Reference Frequencies

Ah, hell.

One more try. I'll skip to the book's end. The final story, a no-vella-length piece, is nicely titled: "And This Is Where I Go Down into the Darkness." It was previously published in *Phantasmagorium* #1, and it bears the dedication "for beelzeBOB & Tom Ligotti, titans

BOTH!! !" This is a very promising pedigree indeed. I let the opening lines feed themselves to me:

> *I sat in the Days Between the Years, Darkness whispered to the corpses in the palm of my hand . . . and I planned my escape.*
> I am not a learned man. I am an escape artist.
> Was when I started.
> Poor. Hungry. Inner-city caught, small—walled in, all men are. Here in the grey rain they are. Mired with learning disabilities I took the route I could afford and held the most appeal, or coulda been no option is the only option. The poor care not, an open door is an open door.

Interesting. Still stream-of-consciousness in flavor, but a bit more structured, as if balanced between the poetic-type fragmentary impressionism of the previous stories and something more conventional, more fleshed out along standard lines of narrative development and characterization. I skip to the closing lines:

> Watching the river run . . . looks like little hills rolling along . . . the hills flow . . .
> The nightmare of being—head full of false imaginings, the cravings the blundering puppet paints, being handed the scandalous heirloom. . . .
> The surface of the river is graced by soft lights, a trance
>
> and this is where I go down into the darkness

Whoa. This is flat-out breathtaking. And it's followed by some bracketed nods, darkly evocative in their own right, to Ligotti's *The Conspiracy against the Human Race* plus a "bunch of songs by Bruce Springsteen and some by Scott Walker and David Tibet/Current 93," along with acknowledgments and thanks for permission to quote from Ligotti's *Conspiracy* and Robert M. Price's "The Sword of the Stillborn."

Almost in spite of myself, in spite of my pedestrian tendencies as a reader, it's all starting to make sense. Sort of. And the sense it's making is, frankly, dark, dazzling, disturbing, and delicious.

"I know that back of my activity," says William Stafford, "there will be the coherence of my self, and that indulgence of my impulses will bring recurrent patterns and meanings again."

"But," says Plato, "if a man comes to the door of poetry untouched by the madness of the Muses," he will be "utterly eclipsed by the performances of the inspired madman."

Yes, I think I'm catching on, especially when I can also hear the voice of Ray Bradbury chiming in, passing along something that he said Federico Fellini once told him: "Don't tell me what I'm doing. I don't want to know." Bradbury tells us the great filmmaker meant he didn't want to think ahead of time about what he was trying to accomplish, but instead wanted to work in an inspired and ecstatic way, proceeding and producing in the ecstasy of the creative moment, and only afterward trying to discover and contemplate the meanings that wanted to emerge from it.

Yes, when it comes to *Portraits of Ruin*, I may indeed be catching on. So the question now becomes: Are you? Because after all, you're about to read the book, and this weird excuse for an introduction by me is supposed to prepare you, or whet your appetite, or do whatever it is that introductions are supposed to do. And my sharing of the process of revelation that I've gone through in grappling with Joe's new literary offspring is the best approach I could think of to prepare you for what awaits you.

But I've probably said too much already, so I'll sum up with this: When a writer simply lets loose the flood of his self, his interiority, his psyche, his soul, and what emerges is so darkly compelling and fascinating that it conveys, even if obliquely, the sense of an imminent and immanent truth, reality, otherworld, something-or-other, whose shape and nature is terrifying and wondrous to behold—when this happens, you stop caring whether it makes conventional sense and simply bask in the glow of something special. Alan Watts once said the formal concert music scene came to a "final crash" the moment John Cage sat down at a Steinway in full evening dress, opened his musical score, and proceeded to perform a recital composed entirely of rests. And while I certainly don't think literature in general or horror fiction in specific has now crashed to a halt because of *Portraits of Ruin*, I do think something of Watts's meaning attends the publication of this book. Cage was a brilliantly talented and exquisitely trained classical pianist. He could play the traditional classical music game and hold his own with the best of them. But his Muse led him down another path, or rather led him to blaze a path all his own, and those who understood were deeply enriched. "He was trying to clean our ears of melodic and harmonic prejudices," Watts said.

Those who have ears—which Joe is about to clean—let them hear.

The final word can go to Joe himself. Back when he and I were communicating about the possibility of my writing this introduction, he told me, "I never know what to make of my stuff."

This, above all, is what you might want to bear in mind as you turn the page and proceed to immerse yourself in what follows. *The author himself does not know what to make of these writings.* Neither do I. Nor, I daresay, will you. But the very attempt to do so, to "make something" of them—an interpretative activity that the work itself incites because of its native grippingness and stylistic brilliance (that surrealist's flood of unconscious inspiration is channeled, mind you, through a finely honed and tuned set of conscious literary skills, just like Cage's pianistic training)—this very attempt at finding some sort of meaning is, in the end, the point. Because the meaning is really and truly *there*. You can sense it in every line and phrase, grinning darkly at you through the interstices of the words and images. It just happens to be a meaning that you can only "understand" by allowing it to speak to your own deep self, to your—dare I say it?—daemonic Muse.

So don't ask what Joe is doing; that approach only closes it off. Instead, rely on the coherence of your deep self to understand the coherence of his. In learning to do this, to resonate with this book of impossible imaginings presented in improbable forms, you may well find that you're being altered and enlightened in ways that are truly transformative.

After all, only an inspired madman can understand an inspired madman.

Portraits of Ruin

No Healing Prayers

for Gary Myers & Robert Bloch

Midnight.
   Moonlight.
   Cold.
   The howling sun, far from this place with no hope for tomorrow,
running with things that fear what the cold moon brings.
   Captain Jack sits on his front porch. Shotgun on his lap.
   Coffee gone cold.
   Waiting.
   Waiting for The Thing That Sails On Tears.
   The Black Goat.
   Sat there every night this summer. Staring at the blackness.
Listening to the sound of the empty road.
   A yard without children's toys.
   Without flowers.
   The withered dreams gone, over some rainbow.
   Captain Jack didn't follow.
   His wife followed the lullaby into a dream. Something soft and
quiet he hoped. Tried to tell himself.
   Tried.
   Tried to penetrate it, like it was a year or a river.
   Over and
   over.
   Three years of nights. Centuries of days. No sleep. No solitude.
Rain and winter and dust were his bread.
   Tried to get under the skin of that stone.
   The look in his eye said he wasn't convincing.

His leather hand and the Mossberg shotgun said he was convinced of something else. Said they'd decided on a hard truth—It was coming. And they were ready for the dance.

Wouldn't be lightning.

Wouldn't be roaring wind.

Wouldn't win the gamble.

Knew it.

Knew might-have-been would see no bright morning sunrise.

Take what you get.

Knew it.

Always had.

Didn't know another way.

Not then.

Sure not now.

Captain Jack looked at the stars. They weren't falling.

Didn't figure they would.

Back in the first War, when he was a boy, and they sent him a million miles from yonder, he came to understand it.

Back then, when he came home to her and her cello and the stairs that lead to their bedroom, he understood.

Cold is cold. Hard fact.

Nothing is nothing.

Didn't change.

You fight for your life. Hope the thread don't snap, or get cut.

Second War they didn't have God on their side to change The Truth. Came out the same way.

Saw a lot of blood. Layered on the earth. Soaked in. Saw it as lesson. Heard it scream. Saw it spread. Smelled it. Got the taste of it slammed in his mouth.

Saw cold. And hard.

And young men, ragged, overrun with panic, just wanted to get home and become old men that had had a taste of potential, that didn't come back.

He moved the Mossberg 590 *Persuader*.

Remembered the feel of her breast . . . When her eyes were sails that didn't read the verses of winter.

Looked at the moon.

Cold.

Hard times.

No land of plenty.

Remembered her sun hands.

Touching them . . .

The 5 o'clock whistle . . . running home . . . dinner . . . her smile . . . the world melting away . . .

Every morning, up at 5 o'clock . . . The job. Hard work, dog day sweat . . . The Railroad . . . the tracks roaming from here to more . . . the 5 o'clock whistle . . . Her smile. Her sheltering arms. The world melting away. The world being fine . . .

Two sweet years.

Put his money down on this little house. Bet on Eternity. Worked to make it so.

Worked hard. Put his shoulder into turning water into wine.

Never stroked fleeting.

Didn't curse.

Didn't let his fingertips get bound up in vain.

Cold hard moonlight.

Silent.

Couldn't breathe it.

Didn't embrace flowers.

Two sweet years. Didn't need Paris or extra. Didn't care about a Gulf Coast vacation, or the language of empty prayers.

Had her heart, a rose, and no secrets between them. Wasn't missing a thing.

Tombstone.

Handkerchief.

Preacher Man, talkin'.

Cold black sod.

Midnight.

Moonlight.

Waiting.

* * *

Ask.

The Coloreds, the Whites, the this-and-that buzzing of the town drunk puffed up on the kicking heat spun from a bottle.

Sift rumor, or the swells—filled with "Happened." and "Look."—
under eyelashes.

They say The Piper Man came down the road that night. His
trouble-eyes chugging.

Brought his hateful drought music. Stretched it over her. Silenced
her cello.

Say the whippoorwills and the loons closed their throats. Took to
tight corners.

The Piper Man came.

Danced, they say.

Dragged his claw-foot around the house. Marked it. Carved it out
of the world.

Lifted his hand.

Then he played.

Called.

Called The Black Goat.

No censor to fasten it to confinement, barricade came down.

And it came.

Came and took all her dances away.

Then, they say, The Piper Man laughed.

* * *

Creek out back dried up.

Brambles thick as tar. Braided like rage-hard fingers white-
knuckle tight.

Fence gate broken.

Empty house at his back.

Shotgun's loaded. Hard stuff. Bite and shred the guts out of most
anything.

War and no hope for tomorrow.

Black thoughts.

Blood and rain and mud.

Frost.

The end of the world. Nights he talked to the wind over her
grave and thought of putting the gun in his mouth.

Shotgun's loaded.

Coffee's cold.

Bitter.

Enough to keep Captain Jack awake.

Not that the stone cold hate would step aside for Morpheus.

Not tonight.

Captain Jack looks at his wedding ring.

Same moon the night he married her. Night they came to this house to live. Night they stepped into a dream . . . Night at her grave he lost all human customs in a furrow of Forever.

Cold hard moon.

Looks the same.

Cold as black sod.

Fireflies gone.

But the stars don't fall. Don't shiver.

A shift in the blackness.

Just there.

Not a silent death.

Footfalls on the black road. Thick cackling—infernal, muted, dripping with burn-it-all-down hunger. Hell-bent flute notes, long, brittle claws scraping and etching metal. Scattered. A flame of Other Spaces. Crypt-brewed wolfspell expanding, mounting . . . Wants. Flows . . .

Captain Jack hears the evil. The dark sounds of a rough beast coming. Hears the crack of its claw-foot when it hits the hard road.

Cold midnight moonlight.

Just enough to see The Piper Man.

Business end of the shotgun comes up. Won't turn back.

Or turn tail.

Or be overrun.

Won't blink in the face of unattainable.

Bad thoughts.

Tombstone.

Handkerchief.

Preacher Man, talkin'.

Cold black sod.

Midnight.

Moonlight.

Waiting.

A flash of white light. A little inferno inside it.

Hell.

Coming for bones. Coming for flesh.

Coming to drink tears and tenderness affirmed and every contour between.

The corpse-coffin sound of Hell shouting in the trees. Something black in the road.

"Whatever will be . . . Will be."

The Piper Man laughs.

Shotgun leveled . . .

Grand Funk Railroad, "The Railroad"

Lena ... cries

for Lena

We, *she* (—how many nights have I cried her name?) so fragile and
ripe with the lies of exist, and my Inmost,
                         meet by the cliff ...

Moonless cloudwaltz ... The slow-arc howl stains my fear ...
Grammar and the chains ...

and He in his bitterblack tower, His laugh unmasked ...

We have waltzed here before ... Waltzed as we did Then ...
Then, that time that knew no gentle boundaries, as the dry tears of
The King burned the shade with wounds of discord ...

Lena cries ... the memories blended into her fingers, each an
alchemy of gestures-haunted, dream ...

Dream of the images I carved in the dark wood ...

All her nights braided with felt she gives.

And, as I have and must, I take—All the strings her eyes unwind.
"I am kissed by weeds."

Do I dismiss truth? Even for her?

"Phantom hands ... Why must your fingers stretch to grasp dark
sky questions?" I've asked her before, asked as her fingers held grief
... Asked her to step outside the Garden of Broken Wings and show
me an ornament of the heart that does not slit fissures in the heat I
cast ...

fog ... pinned to the edges ... cry ... emphasis ... cut by a stone
when I search for herbs ...

her tears ...

and the cloudwaves ...

her fingers ...

and my emptiness.

"Is my alchemy too weak to still the black dogs and the threat they string?"

... her eyes are gates

... my repertoire a funeral

"Will you not change your tongue?"

3 times her eyes say no.

"Would you have me fall to my knees and kiss the soiled hem of His robe?"

No word from the pale continent that rests below the sharp line of black bangs ... Her face is a lamp of rain heartlessly stealing the river of future in my pocket ... Why must her eyes unfurl that flag of misery?

"Do you think I'll fade?"

Her eyes turn, rise, up to The King's bitterblack towers ...

"I will not close my eyes."

How many thin yesterdays must I soil my kisses in? How many of her songs will bleed me, belly to nail, as I shudder in the greyvelvet singing of her bed of poison?

... the darkening of my anguish stirs a psalm-poison in her slender hand ... something thirsty leaps across the waves ...

the sea is a knife moved by His scepter

pleated shadows

Shoeshore and no candle ...

... I remember what fell ... how it creaked, cracked, how it retreated and how every ripple and embankment ran out of questions ... a little end touched by held down ...

I prepare my flame: "Lena. All I have to clasp is smoke ... Will you watch me unspool and be glad when my constellation of errors runs down, bending—Blind and in it, meshed, encrusted, a fuel for ash, wax to crumbs?"

Her fingers, a nursery of void, bend the string of black stars ... lost in her lonesome song of emptiness they, vibrations on a stormHEX string, drift down,

> and I cannot reach up ...
> I would free them. If
> I could deepen
> and release some improvisation not submerged in

her

autumnal song . . .

But her chains of No will not bend . . .

She, filling my breath with abyss,

oracle eyes swarmed storm,

remains steel.

steel

and no want I want most

I have given her light and seed, trinkets and corridors . . .

and all I hold here is

estranged. No blue or river—or glory still here, offers bright sound.

So callous and agitated (every impulse for beforehand forced from harmony) those fingers that fasten me to her eyes . . . All the stakes and razors she takes to my dreams . . . Does He reward her for my torment? Whisper to her that I must fall, be another shorn bird denied ascent, littered about her feet?

"One word from you could move me from this dangerous border. You could give me, Day."

Hungry eyes take away . . . everything . . . my dove plans . . . let me dream . . . tongue . . .

"What happened to for better or for worse? Just some trash of rags for merciless?"

Tremor . . . no softskin goodnight in this worm blanket . . . parched—gagging, caught in her tunnel of rain . . . narrow mouth, carpeted by my dust, half-shut, feeding off my pregnant blisters . . .

. . . cloudwaves crash on the rocks . . .

And all she will do is cry.

For Him.

my loss

—Now, some lattice of velocity and equations, a door, a soul, a floor dark with what was, is?

The music, all she has!—scraping my face, its mask leering When wants ALL . . . And Lena—a joy of once once, damp with strange tears, let's its longing SHALL . . .

Shall rings—bells remembering no could, no place of sun . . . Re-

membering WILL, demanding OVER with no to-morrow—on & ON
& ON &

                  slower

       the black wings of other channels

                        a hundred years from the
streets that scarred us—no dreamland. no early to bed—most often
no bed in the litter-fermented den under a freeway ramp. morale?
joke. stone that will take you down in that muddy water. fill your
lungs with poison.

                  slower

       coffin~cave~vessel

                       a hundred years from raised and ravaged

                           from summer loaded and
squeezing, bright red poison-language buzzing, disdain and vampiric-
sleaze dragging scared and corroded to back-alleys seething in "Let me
enter"

                        when—touching—she rescued me from the
cold and I—touching back, finding order in the compression of
limitation—rescued her from dire

       slower

                        —modulation . . . a mirror game angles
recounting . . . thing grown over between—

        fear
           fear

                     and her bow sings

   Her eyes were green, weren't torn and haunted, weren't the color
of this shepherding sea, the color of His stained hem. Went. Gone.
He took it. Took color.

   Took my memories, my light . . .

   . . . we tried to push our dreams forward—

She was singing His song, echoing—shaking puppet thing full of
All Is Through—

. . . the extended gestures of the organist spun harsh designs
within the cavern of St. Echo—Under the lost and lonely, she could
have been a sixteen-year-old waif on the street corner that day we
met . . . a tone of alien murmurs laced with sinister rang out of St.
Echo and spun its creeping malignity on the river of our skin—we
rushed from the dark shade of St. Echo to peel way dusk, filled our
arteries until they unfolded fairy tale hearts, and luck opened a shell
of possible where we could peck on nectar, take joy in loaves of skin
and not disappear in the hurricane apparel of lonely . . .

Her King! Love-slayer, thief!

It was there. Once, her foliage,
clustered with newborn letters that did not stumble on confuse! I
held it, her—took Lena away from the unrelenting & fatal moan-
strung streets, and the frantic-shadows shaped with agony-cheap and
hoodlums and grime of Tremont Row where the iron-rain of St.
Echo's gloominess held court. Stripped the maelstrom of concrete
from her brow. Comforted her with light. Held it out to her hopeless
. . . Cleansed her of The Street. Tremont Row. This is Gehenna. You
burn here. Tossed, bashed, whipped till all your tones are outlaw, or
tongue's cut with the vastness of agony, give in and eat disintegrate.
STREET; expletives that will work for food; damaged revelation;
thousand mandatory cuts; sick; "Bitch!"; alcohol, razor blades;
nicotine, coffee; treachery; ambition—weight—ambition; contusion.
Your fate for having a body and a soul here—Ice. Iron. Cold. On your
way to dead, and no dreams . . . Gave to her until her curiosities were
novas . . .
Fought abuse and terror, and her sea of doubt, every suspicion
tattered by shame, with an Easter hand, until

He came with SEIZURE.
Took my light!
Slapped my Then with siege!
He spoke Now. Took! Said, you ARE!

And she gave him her old self-doubts and fear. Held what He offered. Let Him caress her with not go away! Touching. Touching. Her heart.

Staining mine with FEAR.

and

guilt

and Be . . . Took. The endless notes of His river, TOOK! Left no clean and true. Slapped my please with cold dim largo . . . that
                        was
my Before.

Took.

YOU.

        . . . lost . . .   never.be.   . . . the same . . .

    The face wings   throat of my
                              bird

            crying
        thick.dark.rain . . .   the darkness . . . rise . . .

I would surge—stand by her side . . . and there, with fire as my shield, place bridges guarded by flocks of flowers to destroy His Harms-Tremendous . . . I would not have her a boat among his harbor of ghosts and thorn-crowned rocks . . .

                                but, done by chill, my hands grow weak . . . and I cannot raise Vendetta from my fever . . .

She steps forward
            carrying tears, her death mask, that desire only to bathe in The Way

the cold sea breathes no hours

Lena took a step toward me before. Summer day on The Street. For homeless she looked good. My sleeves were dirty too. And I was shoeless that week, robbed when I was in The Zone nodding. Kinda smiled. So scrawny I was surprised she packed a voice, asked if I had any coin I could spare.

Didn't laugh, I didn't even have any history. They say history and its ghosts are complicated. It's not. Here. Fucked. Then gone. Street don't carry baggage and it don't keep records of the trash that got tossed out. If I ever had any it got chucked.

Told her I had a friend, and we could get a meal.

I walked out of the alley and she followed . . .

Mike gave us rice and some beans and a half a pack of smokes. Set a crisp pair of Jacksons on the table. Said he had a gig and would be gone for eight days, watch his place. And don't break anything.

We didn't break or steal a thing.

Lena played his old Starcaster a lot; slow, haunted, there were dark things, ruptured thunders, in the deeps of that hollow-body, she, spilling what was aimed by that crop of drums, was the navigator that freed them from the nest . . . One night when the wind didn't push cruel thorns at our little victories, I swooned when she sang "Misguided Angel" to me. Never saw a Mr. Right in any mirror I dared to look in, but I clung to her.

We settled into his spare bedroom and became a couple.

By the time Mike returned from his out-of-town dates I had my old job customizing guitars at Guitar Crazy back and she was playing in Dawson's Blue Vault. We'd cleaned his place—first time it had been cleaned in a while, and put some groceries in the fridge.

We offered him 50 bucks a week for the room and he said just keep the place clean and the noise down and we're cool.

We did.

Took us six months of dreaming our dreams to get our own place . . . I got a few sweet custom jobs on the side and Leen played out more. Never revisiting lonesome or blue moon midnights, we kept on walking forward . . .

Baby steps. Not soft as the moon but we got somewhere.

We knew we'd get somewhere . . .

My veins running out

                         of promise. My tears yelling for verbs of color . . . Color! Day! Old games~September days~a gush of light laughter~Alto and a running right hand—farmoredrums . . .

NO! The Castle of the Crow above will not be overthrown. And I—

—the bells look at my wishes . . . something in the shape of the clouds and the room threatened . . . the air droned . . .

"I cannot—"

"Remember?"   "No. Close. But reason—"

"Is closed?"

"It was. Was there. Here?"

But not in her eyes. She would not allow it . . . Not now.

Lena returned to her cello, her song. It took me . . . every note she was did . . . I sang, every re: my heart looped, as she sang . . . the odyssey in spatial coming to each other, all we saw in each other, that atmosphere of can be—will be, without fear . . . the bow reached into sonic, controlled impulses—interaction—communication—perusal—breathing stakes . . . wishes . . . Now! Here. Projecting . . .

Her bow, her fingers, remarkable things, doves and open frequencies—the creation of a complete spectrum, my wishes—flesh flight & swinging, feathered, absorbing the melt—I perched in her stareyes, touching . . . I received . . . Touching . . . my Believe . . .

. . . that Thing, touching, her hand, touching *her hand*, her hope, it took, walked it to threat, climbed with it . . . IT—there, and it stayed. Whole. Solid as our morning. The power of The Book. The Dance of the mad Play. The path to dim.

I would have damned her love of books, old books—M. R. James and Wakefield and Poe, dark books of dim days & gloom & heartache abused by extinct, that flame of tyranny and doors leaning to the sea—the dangers they carried into our room . . . but I had given her His words . . . All of THEM! To give birth to joy I had handed The Book to her . . . Sat and watched her curled, bare feet beneath her, in her chair reading . . .

in pleated shadows the lower edges of our yellow curtains

flapped . . .

Sotto voce, *"Songs that the Hyades shall sing,*

Where flap the tatters of the King . . ."

A strange, torn whisper, *". . . into, into your darkness . . . hold . . . feel . . . fade . . . into . . . You . . . fade . . . fade . . ."*

Listened to her echo . . .

sigh . . .

murmurs upon the waves. names or wings tossed from brandished in heartless mouths. Her skin has grown so pale, desire I could not name weathered it. The crescent moon inked on her shoulder fades . . . wormwood and dust quarried as she receded from the lullaby I'd hung . . .

Does everything here fail?

I took Leen from the drowning of days and the lonely Thens . . . Fool, gave her the key that carved done in her Now . . .

away. this leads there. up. with no hope of out or cure for the swordflame of woe.

I did this.

"I did this. Led love, touching, to His hand . . . I . . ." (My empty fist quivering.) "Broke us. Took the seams out of Paradise." Awash in sides that petrified my laceration, I felt like I was mining a cellar of rain.

I have made myself less.

She turns her gaze from his towers. Slowly the tears of bride sweep. The rush. Wolves. Afraid I sag in their bed.

Please is in me but receives no uncoiling on my tongue.

I need to run from this stone.

But to where?

joy faded

Run from my heart? Run from all the riches of speed and giddy her blessed eyes carried with every Darling?

beautiful opened by hideous

I want "Mine!" back!

But I see no mine. That. Gone. Faded . . . Morning. Now a cloud of rain o'er a bed of viscera, and its aromas gaping . . .

I have a memory of her . . .
Her light!
The path of joy a sea of fallen.
She steps toward me and is further away . . . Crying, her wings, her hair, her glow . . . My mind is writhing, my empty hands devoid . . .

One step forward . . .
Good.
evil
Which is she?
Will my bones be able to tell?
My ghost will never talk.
"Is there no easier in the lamp of May?"
And she rains harder.
Chokes
my desert in tears. For Him? So she might crouch in His shadow of treacherous ashes?
I am the sound of captured feathers . . . hollow
and

marked in shreds and

cobwebs

by viper-borders

She steps closer . . .
"Lena, please . . ."
ebony-tresses landscape, mouth no thread of grammar—mouth once a lovely open door . . .
"Give me a reason."
I miss the pages of sun that were in those gifted hands . . .
TEARS lioness-waves caught—occupation—kiss me deadly . . . my confessions, skeletal catalog of pallid memories without a body to drape them in, unpacked,

tear—pouring, by

tear . . . .

no safe as yesterday
underneath

. . . little of me

remains

~*~

I—when We WERE, were (vases filled), we sat in our skeletal cloister with wine and candles, holding our bound treasures—doors to foreign moors unfastened by elegant chills . . . Our souls glowing in tales of revenants and launched specters and cathedrals under dim stars and evoked "pleasing terrors" . . .

We did watch films from time to time, a Chucky to scratch our urge to chuckle or something insidious with a hefty budget and a big name or an old "B" creature feature between romantic comedies and flights into black sighing madness with Lynch as our tour guide, and we'd listen to music, Hindemith or Bartok's string quartets. Many times, as I sat unleashed from the ground by music's colors of possibility, she would play her alchemic adaptations of "Love Will Tear Us Apart" or "Wicked Game" or "Crazy"—her bow and fingers, the ivy-tongues of Heaven, rendered to silence the juices of corruption that came to our windows to sup . . . But most often, we read, saturated in that joy of language flowing to blot out the collective insanity. lyrist Leen lived in poetry. Searched for it in every nook and waiting shelf. Discovery after discovery came home with her to sit with her macramé owls; Byron to Prevallet, Cummings and Dylan, "New" French to American "Hybrid" she dove deep . . . Then she found Bori—danced in his myth-field zodiac of poems, and Trakl's autumnal sonatas, and finally, the froth and mordant revelries of The Nethescurial Drifter, Mad C'sys-kone, his "Secret Hours"—she was chained to it. The chilled cosmos of this new poetry was in her, conjuring ash-nails beseeched by Night . . . Singing. In her cello. And she began speaking of other places, Carcosa, the River of Night's Dreaming, the Black Village of Frozen Lawns . . .

September came to harvest and I noticed her murmuring to herself. Whispers of confusing things about *The Imperial Dynasty of America* spoke from her pillow as she dreamed . . . And she had to have a copy of C'sys-kone's play, *He Will Be There.* I had to find a copy for her . . .

And I did . . . and with it, on a shelf of pleated shadows, I found The Book . . . *Die Pergamente der Mitternacht* . . .

She read . . .

And read it again; "'So we descended through the dusk under the clustered stars.'" . . .

A prayer or chant . . . repeated; "'Death, follows us.'" . . . a junkie with a new habit . . .

Her green eyes became His receptacle . . .

"We are."

Grey came around. Took root in corners and under our bed . . . filled cracks and became warts . . . Our home got a makeover . . . Her owl knickknacks went in boxes in the bottom of the front hall closet under the stairs. . . A bit of this went away and some Other replaced our known and common . . .

Leen began buying owl skulls and feathers, bundling them up and tying them together with sticks and yellow twine and blood red yarn. Each crafted "skullcrow," that's what she called them, was hung from the twisted crabapple tree in our yard, she called it the "Creepy Tree." I sat in our moonlit garden one night and over the vapors of my Earl Gray was overtaken by a sudden chill. As I stared at Leen's skullcrows an old Dr. John song of night trippin' remedies and aether dislocations leapt from the kitchen window and thoughts of Karl Edward Wagner and *Blair Witch* unleashed some deep-rooted irrationalities I've never been able to cut out.

A grim, wet Portland night. I came home to find every light bulb in our tree-shaded bungalow had been replaced. "It was too bright in here. Light is the Dance of Maya and I had to banish the glare." She took down every mirror in our house too. Told me she was unmasking, casting out the false images bent by Light.

In less than five days every window in our house was guarded by one of her skullcrow No Trespassing talismans. Most being an eerie bone-color or yellowish. And she took to bleaching the feathers that were not perfect black, then soaking all of them in a potion of sea salt, ginseng, clove nectar, three rusty nails, and something she called phoenix-root for a night. She was precise about the time frame; Leen put them in a cast iron pot at sunset and took them out at sunrise. Hung them to dry on our back porch, smoked them with amber "Banishing" incense she bought at Mama E's House of Nine. The fragrance was called The Ghost & The Darkness. We didn't talk about her occult leanings much, never really had. With mentions of the "Lost Nation" and "dead spots," I let references of Carcosa pass, pretty much figuring it all tied in to some of the elemental mental textures of her Pottawatomie heritage surfacing.

I played along . . . and read along . . .

Leen & I letting our "pleasing terrors" fantasies enter wake. The walk of seek—Changing the décor of our home to suit our new discovery . . . our banners, bending, out of sprinkle,   of resist

    dark ash eyes—no music occurred . . . torn-down wil

    derness disemboweled sails frosted

                their curve of continue   in gaps

                          of   wrongly

the despondent

        h o u r of   TROUBLE/S

                     that

                will not

    pass

She read The Book. Whispered, *"He* will be there."

I read The Book.

We stepped

off the plain . . .

. . . fog . . . memories, fact and lust and limbs and empty . . . everywhere: grey . . . traces . . . cracks . . . probing . . . hatching . . . the split, spreading, shaking the tongue . . .

. . . the breath of Aldebaran howls its ashcan autumnal hunger . . .

I stood at the end of my dark hall in the tower window and looked down—moon and . . . HUNGER . . . the curve of a tender kiss . . . She walks the garden. Bare feet gently pushing aside the black curling leaves of the Winter Tree and the scattered wings of black moths . . .

"Lena."

. . . wearing a mask woven of tears and the pale wings of dead moths . . . Following the arrow of the winterboatman's long, threadlike finger . . .

~*~

her breathing nips at me . . . trapped in the shadows of her tears
. . .

She steps toward me . . .
tears drip from her fingers . . .
I gave and gave
my colors ran for her
hung collages /built refuges of calm and tender /tirelessly /every
circle consumed /the curve of the rocks offers perfect to my neck
/gropes to break
                                 with the touch
                                       of obsolete
the lantern of His feathers swoops down, pale death bed
potency—all its tails leaning into the threads of my dissembling—
burns in the bitterblack tower
she steps forward
crying
crying for wings
or a ladder
crying

but not for me.
I made her cello. Cut the minutes from life, kissed a song into its
learn. Gave it hours and a firefly heart. Gave it the eyelids of a
warrior. Bled into it. Varnished it with my tears . . . and blood . . .
Held the bridge while I walked in His vales to find The Book . . .
gave her His Book
ablaze in tears
she masked Her Light in His bells
roses
I made her will my Hell.
blood
rain   and I couldn't close my eyes
         the cluster shattered   the mask of shipwreck stirred
                             brine—Immolator! swept breast
harmony.future. accord.her tears say no
                   The worm, blind to beauty, breathes, sopor
aeternus . . . There is one gem missing from His crown. My dim light . . .

drain.pleated shadows . . . splash . . . "Come. come." . . . hell's station
. . . the rocks.the rocks . . . across the 7 Bridges of Sunset.meltdown:the
soundbirds of aEon.lilies.blue from here~ winter meadow—twilight
vanish—NOseed hatch.ancient gate . . . THOUina.ina.ride—to.to . . .
flowers.NIGHT.stormARISE.the voyage from 81 to The Yard . . . the
Sour Pedestal—voices piled high on Mother Ash . . . the cliff

No LEM-soft landing, her moonlight largo: "Pain-riven unease . . .
The shape. Daylight slumbers under His web-lawns of Null."

rocks
Her tears.
foam black and
twisted
laughing   Her tears. grasping

She, once "Mine!," His forge, steps forward

the sea is awash in lightless

iridescent nothing

"Lena."
(her hand moving toward my cheek) (my LIGHT . . . kidnapped)
desperate detour
(her eyes fastened to my whispers)(there are black feathers and
dead moth wings littered in her hair
        and at her feet)
denied
—no key sings to push my broken boat to a star beyond these
crows of oppression
turned away.artifacts tremble.turned away
"Leen."
blind wind for a sky
(her eyes are rivers scented with bones)
unstable fixation

sand

sand

—no enclave no rings to change my horizon

—no bedspread couplet of cream to interrupt sand—nothing in her breast speaks

"Lena."

—no light in my manifesto

naked mortar of grieve

dust

(her blue hand—glittering with the promise of knife, tattooed with His promise, is an eclipse distilling black constellations in my autopsy . . . the perfume of a ruthless desert stains the radiant owl mask she cast at my feet)

dissonant siren wind

the sad faces of sorrow emerge from my cellars—toss and leap their sharp torture of hard

sand

—no loosened sane to ruin this rank circumstance

—no word in this world

dead

end

"Leen, please . . . *please?*"

facing a sea of   no

Lena cries . . . tears . . . each in bloom, floats on the lamp of her pale flesh—sin, error, cadence—ruin . . . tears . . .

tears . . . no reverse /swirls /blades /uncoiling

wishing wishing as my sole plea
                          for somewhere

somewhere

                          Lena

        cries

but not for me . . .

. . . the sea and the rocks . . . she broke the once empathetic bow

and cast it into the waves, then gently placed her instrument on the
altar of rocks . . . the mists of the cloudwaves break on the strings . . .
>murmurs
>coming far
>increasing
>her pale skin is a plate of liquid thorns flapping with black letters
>a tide of tears /the stretch of distance /requiem with no strings
/flows
>distance
>distance

and the strong thing in the sea's black loam smiles

she steps forward with her rain

>Waves
>   no tide
>The water,   not unique with March,
>   is no guide
>Night with
>   no
>   vertical
>   no
>   moon
>Tomorrow has no
>   steps
>   . . . the foam of desire,
>   what the year   said
>   and where it would not
go . . .
>I will not sleep
>   in the fingers of yesterday—
>Even the mud
>will
>   forget
>   my
>   name

There is a punishment of bitterblack towers above the cliff where no bliss may soar ... below its ceilings of vapor, below the cellar where remembrance is undone, in its shadow-crypts, unmasked flowers and dead birds—each in their beds of midnight blood, bleeding ebony roses, sing ... "fade ... into ... You ..."

there is a different color in her eyes

Until The King gifts her with a seat beside His throne she will cry
only for him ...

Oblivion stained by her tears of isolato
I ...
fade ...

fall into the hands of the living God

Lena Marie Griffin, "Alchemy of Fingers and Dark," "Alternating Views of a Single Subject," "Meeting By the Cliff as Dark Turns to Light," "Fade into You," and "She Forgot, She Dreamed"; Cowboy Junkies, "Blue Moon Revisited (Song for Elvis)"; and N.R.P.S. "Portland Woman."

So Into You

for Lee

Austin, Tejas. BookWoman. Mid-list with my hopes and talons on A-team.

Carved my name on another page in another book—the wages of SIN . . . . Wanted a drink.

—in her blue dress. Ready. The cinema of my eye took her in . . .

First thought, hammer or Tejas flood, 'Be music, night.' Had a dream I wanted to show her.

Never saw a face like that in New York, New York, or in my upstate one-horse dorp.

And I'd looked. LA to Portland. Up and down the Easy Coast.

Slapped my slouch and sat straight.

Hit my lazily with a doubleshot of *enough of that!* "Hi." Spilled, river rushing to learn her name.

"Already bought this. Own it . . . But I gave my copy to my girlfriend, Barbara, and well, wanted, *needed* one that's signed. Love your serpentine style.'

"Would you please inscribe it to, Lee. *That's me.*"

Would I?

In blood! 10 demons thraking each other out of the way, each dying to be the one to come up with just the right engraving.

"All that bang and no apologies for the earthquake."

Applause to the guitar player with no audience. Land of Plenty and Ever-Ever Land was—finally! Wanted a cigar and to pop a cork. Ate it up.

"How the tale unfolds, its fullness. You're simply divine. You have a truly unique, one of the most brilliant and beautiful of minds out there."

Fuel for my torn canvas, hoped I wasn't showing my mental slack-jawed.

"Thank you." Wordsmith without his tools.

Looked at my pen. Begged it to straighten up and fly right.

Fast overtook us.

Signing done and in a nice bar, ferns, *good* jazz, no raised voices.

The tang of her wit, her brain. Her eyes.

I've looked at women's breasts, hoped to be graced by a nipple's soft rose on my tongue, stared at their backsides, wished for the YES of grind, couldn't tear myself away from her eyes.

Didn't want to.

Lee's talking, nervous, a bit shy with a thirsty undercurrent, but her depth and authorial observations shine. Schoolboy with a crush on teacher's flowers, I'm praying my forehead doesn't have I LOVE YOU plastered across it.

Commandeered by her perfume. I'm little more than a NOW with symphonic pillow-talk in its ears, didn't want to leave alone. First kiss vintage-*Voila!*

Fast overtook us.

Next six months were a brandished torch. We'd meet in New York or Austin. My hotel room or her place. The scent of flesh, the easy ascent of the riffs,

quietly,

she made that sound . . .

the flex of a leg,

screaming erotica, erotic screams,

filled my ear—

". . . always good to me . . ."—"'God is love, but Satan does that thing with his tongue.' Make me a sinner."

sweat, rhythm,

blankets,

belly—my *Côte d'Azur*, amongst sprung,

she made that sound . . .

curve . . .

black bra strap . . . mouths open,

the phrasing of tush . . .

Lipstick.

Mascara.

Rouge.

SOLD

Was.

Words. Weakness. Just to keep her.

Moonlight or Maybelline, gossamer orbit of her mosaic brushed my batting average to three kinds of Technicolor.

Brought her from her Sahara to cure mine. Showed her my place in the Adirondacks, prayed she wouldn't cringe at my backwoods existence.

"You're hidden away here like a wizard of old, like you've run off to the hills . . . Regular little Sleepy Hollow you have here." Her smile was a throne glittering in the sun.

Bent down, swept her fingers, nails lacquered with a rich shade of purple, over the lawn. "The wild violets are heavenly."

Something else we agreed on.

Over a bottle of rum by the fireplace she said, "You ever get tasteful curtains you'll be set for life."

"I can lace words, figure out the fabric of a city, but curtains . . . Hell, I barely know the difference between firebrick and red. Maybe? Vegas odds might bet against it."

"Easy-peasy."

Two months later she moved in.

Brought ghost stories and hermetic lore from her ancestral homeland. Lipstick and lace. A few antique music boxes and a toy theater. "I love drama, latches and stormy skies."

"And that?"

"A gift for my horror writer. A gallows limb."

I made eggplant—NY-style, sautéed, spiced. She made enchiladas—chilies were HOT.

Music. Widescreen. Close up.

Rollin'—whisper to celestial—'n' tumblin'—

Monkey see-monkey do.

We walked by the lake. She brought poetry. "'LIFE BEGINS WITH COILING. MOLECULES & NEBULAE.'"

"McClure is a favorite of mine. Lamantia too."

Together. Closer. Far from distressed hours, present in the brilliant things of nature's spirit. Wound over wildflower field and under the arms of pines. Stopped at the crumbling well in my backyard.

What was left of it was hardly taller than her well-proportioned 5′ 3″.

"Poor thing. I love wishing wells. It would look so picturesque fixed up . . . New stonework and a quaint roof."

I agreed.

Began fixing it up a few days later—had to. Come Hell or high water—

An old tune by Free was stuck in my head, had to free it. Had to bring back love, and bring peace into the world—*my world*.

A peaceful world.

Fresh air was good for me and I always detested my daily 90-minute workout. Put my back into it. She mentioned she loved sundials. I found a stunning brass armillary and put it by the lake to surprise her.

Heat she spun mentioned her accord was pleased.

Spruced the place up for her. Opened the shutters. Shape-shifting paint. Ratty-old bachelor armchair disappear. Room healed with hints of future. Empty flowerbox binging overspill.

There was a new carpet.

New canisters on the kitchen counter.

You could smell garlic and herbs. Couldn't see an old pizza box.

The writer in conversation with the reader, the reader who forged possible from potential. She gathered my pronouns. Gave me adjectives and verbs. I collected the poetry she breathed into me. Every vowel. Every caress that resonated in the candlelight.

> she made that sound . . .

And I was Apollo. Every time . . .
FAST
Enjoy. The sweet top of her skies.
sing
stirring
Climbing nearness—US wearing no how—light as unmade April.

Voice of the moon strong. The stars would line up. Reason would step away, deeper *would* between my find and Lee's happen . . .

Flame in the afternoon. All of her, a manuscript I could not sip casually, in full view.

sweet kinds of

glow

with no minus

Elegance to intrigues—away with her touch—I was drunk on her outside. I'd look across the room from my opium peaks, all that inner to translate, one glance and my trance state began to weave manifestations. They went on the page. Every page a shore of desire-shaped—trusted my words to her.

She lifted the restrictions the endless page and I warred over.

New novel's true rang with verve.

Muse.

Fierce—thrilling, not afraid to show all the sides of her nature, and/or contradictions. A complex creature: smart and sexy, powerful and vulnerable, trusting and . . . *beguiling*. Kept me limber.

Didn't laugh, or complain, when I played Ronnie Hawkins "Who Do You Love" endlessly looped for three weeks straight. Glowed when ZZ Top's "A Fool For Your Stockings" made it on to my soundtrack.

Read over my shoulder.

"And, I like that (this): '. . . the color of slow tears.' So hauntingly beautiful."

Read.

I have lived in a cage. Tasted its hate . . . and its tears . . .

"That line is just stunning. So imaginative and beautiful!

"The sins are delicious."

Brought me tea.

SIN & ashes. 286 pages. Handed it over to my editor. He loved it. "Your muse was working overtime on this one, Jack. Poetic, brutal. The aftermath of a Satanic season. Devil being a woman and your Faust knows what she is and still falls for her.—*Jesus*, those sex scenes, your fans are going to eat this up. You managed to be you, venturous, disquieting, and still be compelling to a mainstream reader. *Compelling*."

She was.

Felt it.

Happy and drained.
Caught.
And like a season Lee kept coming back.
Heat to inspire me.
Heat to drain me.
Caught.
Knew it.
Felt it.

      she made that sound . . .

And I was Apollo. Every time . . .
Sitting on the bed . . . her legs . . . the warmth of pleasure molding her mouth . . .
"Write another one for me. A fleece of night winds."
A sculpted jewelry of golden flecks in her eyes said, you can't fail.
"Fire. Tell them everything."
SOLD
Grey-green eyes. Hands. Without any thought into the sea of her demand.
Fell into words . . .
Heat.
To inspire me.
To drain me.
open wide
night winds
Lee loved to walk barefoot in the rain. I liked the view. Standing at the curtains she picked out I realized how much I liked them too.
Junkie in need. That was fine. In those stockings, or without them, that was fine.
Treat my heart to another fountain . . .
Liquid-tripping mouth-to-mouth
      could close my eyes see the meadow
Did.
    summer flowers
      stepping—Lo and behold—key("Tell me all.")-to-key. Pointed to the Promised Land. Gravity—perfect, unforgettable compatibility, not punch-drunk walks for the fogs of

my blue raincoat . . .

Walked into the kitchen looking for a cup of tea, found my personal Nigella Lawson sprucing-up pork ribs with her "special herbs." Stood there, hungry man peering into the restaurant window.

"I don't know how you do it. Sleight of hand?"

Looked up. Magic smile. "Witchcraft." Winked.

Bit me. Not enough to swoon.

Close.

"Rupture what isolates you, chant magic formulas into your irretrievable and lush green blooms."

I laughed. "All your secrets come out now.'

"What was it you said, easy-peasy?"

Her turn to laugh. "You see too much." Turned up her laugh. Unbuttoned her blouse . . .

she made that sound . . .

Somehow my teacup didn't break as it hit the floor—

Feeding time at the zoo.

Couldn't say which was furious predator and which was luscious bon-bon.

Fair trade.

Took up my rusty sword and returned to my words—

Four A.M. noir. No pulsing blonde with a sexmusic-battle-cry on the street corner. Voyager—picture of what loves means in his pocket—who can't keep the volume low, about to disturb dead with outloud.

Plugged in a soundtrack, Hindemith, old-reliable Bohren & der Club of Gore *SUNSET MISSION*, David Darling.

Let it struck.

Ran wild.

```
language    &    imaginary    expressed    as
equations that lose thrust, that no one dares
to push through difficult only to have FIX,
spattered with exhaustion, end on the cliff
of DEATH . . .

   instant forced to account/
```

```
NO intervention cross, NO ransom of meaning
available  in  this  dominated  NOW—The  Serpent
swallows   all   Christs,   all   magic   however
limited . . . titanic gravity/rabies/insomnia
diaries/angel noir and roses . . .
```

Lee kept me in tea and what an ex-Steppenwolf smokes. Fed me.
Kept me ripe with scent, silk, and sexmagic.

SOLD

Well in fact.

HEAT

Really takes it out of you.

Sucked dry.

Offspring of words and more words from the union.

And more words.

Another tour of hell. Another demon tapping a vein. Another
book on the shelf and a movie-option to go with it.

Full ashtray and a blank page. Rubbed my eyes. "Pack them
together like that you're going to get weary."

Felt like a child of the grave, drained.

She kept me in that chair.

"My horror writer.'

"Write another one for me. A fleece of night winds."

A sculpted jewelry of golden flecks in her eyes said, you can't fail.

"Tell them *everything*."

Did.

Drained.

Nighttime premiered. She walked across the bedroom floor.
Black bra strap. Legs. Lipstick.

Mascara.

Rouge

and pulchritude. No stripper serving the hungry by circling a pole
ever offered licorice so sweet.

Lyric.

Was.

Lexicon of romantic.

Her vocabulary sure did it for me.

Couldn't disconnect.

Didn't want too.

A firm grasp on reality? *Me?* Nope—*sometimes*. Frets a rational soul can dispel without working themselves up to Symphony Vortex can become volcanoes of RED or post-apocalyptic wastelands. Self-doubts, thief, curved in bluerazor-petty and never good enough, a cascading vine of fits and rages, scaffolds littered with any act or deed that could be turned from perfume into a narrative morsel, there is no lair greater than the writer pursuing his dangerous journey, give him a door and he'll steal your math and turn it inside-out and thread it into whatever the work requires. Or he'll just bury his head in the sand. The lesser parts of me returned. Hadn't seen the graveyards of my cynic in a while. Returned one dark Sunday afternoon when Lee returned from a shopping trip. Stepped, willing as flesh and hotblood, from garden path. ENTER.

New shoes. New Fall line. Bags and boxes of new. Gone soft blue. Hello vivid. RED. Carnage. Slaughter. Spring's icons discontinued and I'm headed into winter and she's swathed head to painted-toe, RED.

Carnage. Slaughter. Spring's icons discontinued and I'm headed into winter and she's swathed

Vibrant red dress. Swaggered when my lover's tunnel-vision wasn't looking, sometimes when it was. Her shy gone. Confident now.

Drained.

Something wrong.

Funny feeling it wasn't me.

Muse.

Was.

Fierce—thrilling, no contradictions. A creature, wily, sexy. Powerful . . . *beguiling*.

Weakened. More tea. Chain smoking. More sex.sweet/rough/high-speed. More mouth devouring my please. Left me semi-conscious. Handcuffed soul to soul. Less sleep. Couldn't when I tried. Limber, too slow for that.

HEAT

She poured it on me.

Ate till I was cold. Weary, yawning over my keyboard, I laughed, *She's a succubus. Has her fangs in me*. Energy, she had it. Subtracted it from my give.

Wrote—lied—about us in the new novel, *TAKEN*.

Was.

Willing.

Told myself everything was fine and this would sell. Succubus, vampire, she sure could sparkle. Vampires sell—type the damn thing. Toned down the poetics. Had too. Too tired to muscle them on to the page.

Walked slower.

Slept less.

EAT SLEEP

the book

EAT SLEEP

Lee.

EAT SLEEP

less

fuss and yell—curve to dizzy—over/AT every uncanned WORD spent

a dimensionless unwinding of yourself

husk

in fevers of discontent. paranoid chaffed when I thought ensnared.

HEAT

takes it right out of you.

Ashtray full. Ashes.

Lee propped me up. Eat this. Rest. *"My horror writer."*

Fuck. Maybe it was just me? I'd been on a roll, and my old, shit-someone-will-read-this, was coming back.

Couldn't be Lee. Only thing she'd done is love me. Confident now, she'd come out of her shell. Nights had transfigured her, shed her skin in the *danza*. And asshole-me looked at her sideways. As if she'd done something other than pamper me.

Woman was an angel and I'd pinned demon wings on her.

I needed to exhale . . . and maybe go soak my head.

"Straighten up and fly right."

Back to *TAKEN*.

```
Wind on this street with no name. Rough-hewn,
blowing solitude right out of its fragility.
```

Researched Lilith, Agrat Bat Mahlat, Naamah, Eisheth Zenunim, and Leanan Sidhe and Lhiannan Shee. Roared when I came across wells and Lhiannan Shee. I looked up from the monitor out of my study window at the well in the yard. Looked down at my tea cup.

"Herbs."

Wasn't more than an hour from escaping my brief jaunt behind the wall of sleep. Needed more tea . . .

I'd slap it down and it would rise up.

       fumbling with the spider

              plump   little   black   infestation—devil talking about soil and our bedroom

       black surface world

s p a c e

   first thought

   to

   third thought

   trouble

       in mind

But was it true?

Little things, style changes. And there was that small tribal design tattoo on her left ankle. I began to think it resembled a scorpion. Venom.

Spider?

Scorpion?

Lee?

Strange sensations when I was at low tide estranged from the places of Me.

Started to think of her a lot. Not as I had on day one. Start so-into-someone you miss things, too excited to see a blemish that will taint the portrait months or years later, I had—must have, and hissed at myself for blaming Lee for my tunnel-vision. Christ could have just been you write about psychos and madman long enough you start to see shit?

      stare into the abyss too long . . . .

immense a leprous madness rustles . . .

         thorns matte you raw . . .

I'd been defensive before, about my words—hundreds of times, but never paranoid. Fearful, sure, pure terror every time a new book is about to be released.

Glad Lee wasn't home to wonder if I was in need of a prolonged-holiday in a rubber room.

Put Jarboe on the playlist, "1,000 Years." Added "Tower of Song."

"She's a hell of a woman, not a woman from Hell."

Took my head out of my ass. Made sure Lee knew how dear to me she was.

Figured out part of what I was having trouble with was red. She liked it. I never have. Never thought red nails or red lingerie was hot. Give me black, chic, classic, smooth, purple, regal, elegant—to me, or blue, dreamy, soft. Red turns me off. Maybe I write about too much blood?

Relationship needs compromises, so do it. She likes red, go with it. It doesn't hurt.

Like she's in that red teddy long.

Under the red it was still her.

Watched her walk across the room in a pair of jeans and a t-shirt. Sure hadn't shape-shifted. Damn sure hadn't sucked my blood.

Started to think I'd played horror too long. Next book, straight noir; crime and broken hearts. Have a couple of drinks with David Goodis and Thompson, maybe even laugh as we skipped annunciations and faces abandoned and jumped straight into desolation's dialogue. I was taking a vacation.

Lifted my teacup to celebrate my return to sanity.

Gone cold.

You fixed it in time.

Went back to my words . . .

Another chapter . . . and another . . . Lovers. Agitation. Incomparable gone under toil's percussion . . . gaps . . . irretrievable arrows . . . untwine . . . Taken . . . a silence of farewell in the grass—

Sun fled from darkness. My treason returned.

Love dance—

    red—gripped—peeled—off—cast onto the floor . . .

colors curves heat   together easy as the vibrato of acute-stars

   velvet heights ocean of kisses/FLARE the honey-table baking each other

her tender wrist

      invent

         herd the scents of the herbarium with delicate

                    banners of skin and taste churn
        legs sweating with promise of lift
exquisite
    IN   exquisite . . . out   fetching tastes
            bellies full of eat—tongues to blind
She bit my neck.

Pulled back. Covered up by changing positions—turned her around, just her ass—Lilth-white—no teeth in slight,

but—

for a second I thought of Dracula's brides. Alluring—*hungry*

Perfect teeth. White those soft words passed over. *Not fangs.* Not Lee. Damn.

FUCK!

She slid. Shifted. Face to face, breaks the glue—course to a different season—the mountain of her mouth.in its hold.deep.inside. Her eyes devouring mine . . .

Wind with no end, she snarled. FINISHED me.

Drained. Jackhammer heartbeat spider-sown, the dare of my energy weak, if there at all.

she made that sound . . .

Sat there. Watching me. Glowed. Smiling, radiant, her skin was bubbling champagne, her nipples a script of white-hot coals.

I collapsed.

Slept.

. . . a foam of distant screaming . . . voyage splintered by shape-shifting waves . . .

            —three women, blood-red talons, FANGS, white radiant, all the same woman, three, eating fire in just to embrace the fever

        face one HUNGER
        face two, SAVAGERY delighting in CARNAGE
        face three, SATED
        —all HER, Lilth, Lhiannan Shee—*Lee*
dimmed, the bay of the flashlight loses foretold . . . spent . . .

            stumble over a fragment of me . . . I'm bleeding. Lee's howling! Torn by whips . . . TEETH a lesson of tongue—the plot of the snake . . . the milk and honey of my fervor-bowl diced by ruin . . .

come out of it in a sweat.alone.

NEED

a way back . . .

Strength.

Catch it.

Hammered my words on the forge of the page . . . spit my dying declaration . . .

She brought me tea. "My horror writer."

Massaged my neck and shoulders. "Write another one for me."

TAKEN. Done. My editor floored another was done so soon.

sexmagic

she made that sound . . .

"Write another one for me."

50 *Words for Scar*

Eating less.

Sleeping less.

endless tea.endless smokes.fingers relentlessly.flash.lo and behold.fruit.consequence.

Moon roaring. Sun roaring. No sense of time, or tide . . .

Words.

"*Fire* . . . All your secrets." My ears burned with her cheekbones so near.

Fears.

Doubts.

Little jingles. Circling a chill. Uncomfortable.

tired.

go to sleep

can't

go to sleep

ain't won't

go to sleep

nothing

pinned to words

pinned to Leeshape

can't

ain't

puppetsoul dissected was

denied

brought me tea

"*My horror writer.*"

sexmagic

"*My apples are red.*" firm and true suns—adventures of rose—

        dropped in my mouth

        danced *YEsssssssSSSss* on my tongue

the pull the pull

deviltongue-brightness in my ear

"*My horror writer.*"

pinned

    wilting.some times tied to desperate.bound.gagged piece of meat.thin.by degrees.

    Stupid.

    All she's ever done is love me.

    No blackbirds circling above.

    Mornings after night.her eyes.luxury that flattened me.black bra strap.lipstick.contents spill.I'm unlaced.a puppet.trapped by the attentions of her poetry.

    Inches of light—

    Hanging on to her fingers, a snowbird in Tangier, the inside of her ankle brushes my precisely . . .

    The hours of straight to the stars. Sonata with no blueprint. A pond of vocabularies, boundaries connected, of fascinations with no trouble. One body, branches glossed—every edge plugged in ringing in undertow, daring the drugged poetry of its partner to breathe. Lee, an image with no downside. Me, a bear-like blaze, trusting her inner. US, nerves trusting the oracle of uncontestable togetherness with future . . .

    Language and thigh and nipple and fire satisfied—

    the beat of my ink on the map.

    After.

    A picture in a frame

        burning

        out

    Doubts, eels (with forks and fatal) I twirl in my fingers

spade&adoor. . . . . on the fence of spiders)) /silver
smoke/flesh. . . . . .and; bone. . . . .
. . no fragrant hush as I carve less
            couldn't remember the village of her perfume
                            Hypnose
                    it lingered before
                                    Spellbound
                evenings tones of amber and vanilla
                        now whenless
                            the days of
                    'you-with-me'
            emblems my tumble could cling to
        prone
        to shadows
                    clock behind seriously / impossible appearing
pursue
    who is there
                    mine
        unbuttoned
            can't write my way out of conjecture
    Never said keep your ass in the chair. Didn't need to.
    Brought me toast.
    Or a sandwich.
    Something wrong.
    Funny feeling it wasn't me.
    Wasn't!
    God-damn-it, it's not!
    sex
    magic
    magic—accents soft lift and spill—cascades suited in soft *again*
    —buzzing on her incantations
    she's tender with me
    slow
    showing me the way
    —my wings breathless in her embrace
    she knows what to do
    "Fire."
    her tongue

"Give me the fleece of your secrets."

Was.

Did.

Flat. Sapped. Confused.

Rope and salt.

Stupid-ass.

Watched her walk across the floor. Lifeboat.

Lee. Bringing her tea and medicines to my desert.

Lee. Shore. Lullaby. Moon o'er my tides.

Lee. Never filtered the direction of her curves.

And I'm peering in corners for suppose. My skull in the delicate of her heart. Unwrapping. Kicking equal measures of insight and doubt to stir sicken, make it rear up and speak. Looking and I'm waiting. Waiting for someone to come along with the answer. Hands in my pockets of confusion.

No. No.

Couldn't get free. Couldn't diffuse for an hour.

Not Lee.

mercy.retract the thorn.

Pour a little sugar on it.

If I could hold up under it?

On her arm. Supporting me. A dark Sunday morning of threatening black clouds, wind opened to take the fit out of things. Stepped off cold steps . . . Walking on the autumn lawn.

Cold, but she's barefoot. Sleeveless. Panther not carrying a paradise morrow, toes that walked the bedroom floor in the stiff constellation of leaves . . . crushed. they barely move . . .

Lee's mouth opens. No smile. "'. . . *life passes away.*'"

Gone warm limbs. Gone wild violets. Brown under the darkening coolness.

Sucked dry. Where why watch wait whisper suffocation.

PAIN

the slow addiction

dwindling

doubt strewn under weakness

less

looking

heart/pierced limps in ragged whispers.tumble fatally

　　　taste

STOP

　　HER KISS
　　　　strange
　　Pleated shadows. No last breath of colors.
　　　　seeing
　　　　the disease she sings　　　　voice in my holes
　　　　squirm
　　　　　　　　　　my avenue of no not itself
　　She wears RED.
　　Lead me to her well.
　　faint
　　Leaning on the bricks. The surface of the water—oppression—anguish—stretching over my chill—no stars in my blood.
　　And she laughed. TEETH. FANGS. White, perfect.
　　Her desire unrolled—
　　Locked in her embrace. Her thighs, burning, FEVER—mine?—pressed against me. Not holding me—she won't open her mouth and give me withering summer flowers—making me pay for her hands—making me pay for all the *"This."* I held.
　　Pretending.
　　Was.
　　Pushing me off the tightrope.
　　Cold silent water in the well. No net.
　　Breasts. Eyes. Every inch I tasted. All a wish for my death.
　　Head down face slouching, filled with wheels of dark—roar, glee—been—been—deleted. I can see the scorpion tattoo on her ankle. Venom shining at me.
　　　　absent sun. absent sigh. She's wild—sharp—suffocating—a pleasure of flies dancing on her eyelids
　　I see
　　hungry—eyes narrow, greedily—like some rat's—Oh, I've seen them glittering in the soft overspill of moon . . .
　　her dress came off
　　flesh

vertigo
her mouth moves
"All your secrets." Not *my* Lee. Laughs.
Dress, no longer blue, a red stain on the lawn

> *—no longer blue*
> all my gladly
> and the sky out of
> yes

Red.
Vibrant. Enriched. Red—KNIFE BITE. Carnage. Slaughter.
I write horror. Play with madness and devils. Research crypts and carrion, roam seasons of sin and blood. I know eldritch legends. I know bane. I know what I see—
Lhiannan Shee unmasked.
Not *my* Lee.
Succubus.
Spider turning the knob of feast. One lone brick. How many times since I repaired the well had I told myself to pick it up and put it away in the shed?
Gazing in the well at her reflection. Laughing. At my fate, my *"Plaything."* Hissed over perfect white FANGS. KNIFE-BITE.
idiocy
Me.
carnage
slaughter
closer—stuck to her devil, her voice (—ring—ring) in my bones daring me to breathe . . .
Drained. Dead—on my way to it.
Her doing.
Hand rises. consider.courage—shoulder it.distinct hands.
soulclingsHEARTmoves—paper to iron.toward
> Picked it up.

Splash.
*Femme fatale.*poison.
No Thanks
red silk
red blood . . .
No Thanks

Just fatal now.

Hoped the water was frigid.

Tossed the brick in. Wasn't sure if the color was firebrick, but sure as fuck didn't care.

ARS, "So Into You"; ZZ Top, "Fool for Your Stockings" and "Bedroom Thang"; The Band & Ronnie Hawkins, ('76) "Who Do You Love?"; Joe Henry, "Meanest Flower," "Stuck," "Animal Skin," and "Sold"; George Benson, "Breezin'"; Harold Budd, "Be Music, Night"; Hall & Oates, "Out of Touch" and "One on One"; Ray LaMontagne, "You Are the Best Thing"; Free, "Wishing Well"; Bohren & der Club of Gore, "Darkstarker" and "Midnight Walker"; David Darling "No Place Nowhere"; Black Sabbath "Children of the Grave"; The Police, "Tea in the Sahara."

(a piece) about angels left out in the rain

[no sound] [tempest of rain moved on. it is dim and grey.]

I came upon two men.
Two.
Men.
One
in need of a shave
and shoes
and
he
sat.
There.
Just
sat.
There
and
the
other. He looked like rain. Rain that has broken a roof,
tasted
the birth of Death.
And
this
other
the
other
man,
paced. Over there and over there. Back and again.
No bell.
No map of moonlit sky.
Walked to the side of the

road
and
looked—
looked at the small hill.
The
dark
hill.
Thought to pace—first step to many steps—right up its side and reaching
the
top
look out
and see
see
if
if he could see what had struck
the light
from
the sky.
The
man
that needed shoes
sat
ripped from sudden and years
sat on a rock.
He sat
like he was left there
left
there
to die.
In the shadows—in the void—that grey with no smile
left
there
alone
grey
forgotten
to die.
Two.
Men.
Two in their solitude.

Alone
together.
Two.
Men. A shadow of self and a shadow of
self.
Neither home from the to and fro neither. Neither about to turn from the
way that is parted from
close.
Two.
Men.
In the ashes of old
fading
light.
One
waiting—
lips hoping for soft. Soft. Hoping for a lamp to glow.
Light
for
this surface
of
fading
hoping . . .
The other
hoping
for
shoes. Or a lake filled with the starlight of Atlantis or lips to tell eyes if the
weathervane could smell charms, or
see
shoes.
Travelers
unable
to turn
from
this
low.
This
faint
dim.
One

who would take light
or
crest the hill.
One
who would travel
if
the sun came out
if
the sun were shoes—
Shoes
and
light
to
spill empty.
The bottle of wine—there—tall—obvious—they did not drink.
One
would
drink
drink miles—again and again
until
he didn't need an umbrella to cover his nakedness from
what dark
holds.
One
his mouth
holds
nothing.
One
who
has
hands. Hands that fade—again and again
—and
hold
no matters
that
glue
the stock to lips. Where they can be glued to
light
or

concern.
One.
And
one.
Waiting—
again—
like
they
waited
after
the
first again.
Hands
mouth
that
cannot catch
the sound
of
footsteps.
Footsteps
that brought stock.
Stock
still
they are.
One
man.
Waiting.
One
man
sat—
waiting . . .
I came upon two men who could not see the glow of my lantern. Neither
could hear the map I sang.
Two.
Men.

After watching Beckett's *Footfalls* and wondering what comment
Ligotti might make. Perhaps he'd shake his head, or laugh at me.

Soundtrack to the transcription: Paul Bowles, *Baptism of Solitude.*

Time... and Forever

By Joseph S. Pulver, Sr., and Tara Vanflower

"Who are you?" she asked looking over her shoulder at his reflection in the mirror, frowning slightly, but not surprised to see him.

He twinkled, stars confessed dreams in his nimbus. "Time." Mouth unetched by motion, or need.

She loved the stars in her mirror. Warmer than crumbcakes and candy, honey-sweet middle to bubbling flesh, she could scoop them up and suck and suck, savor. Uncut heaven-mouths, silver, simple, they glowed with new ways and she sighed.

She moved her shoulder. Her thoughts, furnished with portraits salted with other windows, followed. "I could've been a rock." Smiled. "Or a tree." Brighter. "Or a boy in Japan." Almost laughing.

Poised, a father who read the book before endowing it to the child and her innocence, he smiled knowingly. "No."

No? Her brow a sea angled with cathedrals of bewilderment as his statement settled in her belly. She turned away from the image the mirror cast, eyes traveling the contours of blue skin and golden eyes. What a wonder he was, like a wheel or a crossroads in the center of a day, almost as simple as the finery of morning. *Time.* The thought a sigh. *What a pretty name.*

"You are what was. What must be. A rock may not transform and be an herb, or a song. It may not sway or be a home for bees. He may only be a rock, perhaps inlaid with gold, but there is no nobility docked to his back. Gold or no, he remains merely a rock. A tree, a tree; the oak is not a feather or a pine. A boy in Japan, is a boy in Japan, nothing more."

She looked down; searching quickly. She'd been taught that she was *matter.* No more than dirt and electrons and wriggling bacteria, or some muck at the bottom of the ocean.

"You were before what you are now."

"I don't want to be a girl from Now," she said sidestepping him as she headed for the door.

Meadowlark warmth and the breeze that carried it called her though the door. The breeze, toying with pollen and airborne seed, cast a spell colored with the cotton of trees and buzzing beetles whirring around like snow. She laughed wearing her halo of living.

He followed. Behind, as always. He sought. Existed. Took what needed to be taken and left what needed to be left.

"You have always been a girl," he called to her. Lips unmoving, his tone, comforting, bordering on scrumptious, sweet as warm honey inside of her. Its resonance felt like a tender hug deep within her.

"Even *before?*" she asked looking up from the green dimension of tall velvet grass, arms and legs making green angels.

"Yes, even Then. The core may not change its spots," he said catching up and sitting beside her. The grass around him extending to the ripe Ra-orb of light above; green, thriving, a fountain of budding grain and flowers painting the outskirts of his form. In gratitude for the linen kiss of whole light, the trees discovered lift and dropped fruit and nuts as gifts to their Father, their naked king.

"Before what?" She picked up an apple, yellow and blushed pink. Her eyes smiled at its sweetness, His sweetness, that of air and earth and butter-sun.

Her eyes felt the mercy of gladly ribboned to his mouth, felt his kiss, threshold of warm from a mouth plumed with names.

"Before, Time."

His finger, loving bodies, the round edges, the calm they tie to the river of memoir with their wings and hurricanes, traced the outline of her milk-pale jaw, pushing the silken hair from her neck; spread out like a delta in the grass beside her, it wove and danced, a newborn future, dragging acrobatic songs from the fabric-soil.

"And what were you?" she asked closing her eyes and breathing deeply, lips sugared and wet, ready to dwell in the once he offered.

The hunger of embryo breathing beginning-hour narrowed him. No voice, no road, his blue deepened. "Nothing."

"Nothing?" The word sat heavy in her heart. *Void.* "And where was I?" Her eyes opened, eyes catching the diffused light as it filtered through the huge leafy trees.

"When I was not, you *were*." The shadow of an arcing lark's wing shaded his eyes. "Just as you always have been."

"Not there." Her eyes asked where were you.

"I was still. A song with no singer." He paused and looked into his hand, his eyes, remembering the scent of destination, became abundant. "Waiting." Brighter, he smiled, ever content and patient.

"For what?"

"The music to begin."

The breeze, tender as a simple act of kindness, blew across her skin raising goosebumps on her flesh. It was perfumed with luminous velvet grass and earthen lushness. A sparrow landed between them plucking seed from the winding blades. He, with hands that had never been small, picked it up and raised it to his face while gazing into the tiny creature's eyes. It tipped its head to the side, listening, feeling. Then, filled with the banquet, flitted away.

"What did you tell him?"

"That he is adored," he said looking down at her, his eyes an ocean of gestures holding hers in his loom.

She blushed. Then looked away. "And where were you?" she asked, still trying to grasp Nothing.

"Pondering the kingdom-everlasting. A seed sleeping in luck's liquid womb." He could almost remember the heartbeats of opal stars, twinkling to soothe him.

"And how is it fair that I always was and you only came now?"

He laughed, eyes sparkling. The gold glittered as the sun caught the flecks. "Fair? Is wind fair, Dear Child? Are the dents your skin wears fair?"

She frowned.

"You're sweet," he said, touching her pouted lips.

She couldn't be sad when he touched her. "Time?" she asked hesitantly.

"Yes?" he answered, his fingers tracing the contours of her petal soft skin.

"Where will we go next?"

"The field that will rise and be named Tomorrow."

"Do you promise me?"

From his open mouth, drifting on a puff of star-herbs came an infinite, "Yes."

She pressed her hands together. Some would say to pray. Some would call it clapping.

David Crosby "Tamalpais High (At About 3)" and
Crosby Stills Nash and Young, "Déjà Vu."

Before and After Science

Renfield Depositional Tape #3:

///There is no time.

There is only thought. Hills that I must walk again.

The bitter frozen fields of memory and the iron gate must be entered. There, under clouds coming in from the west, low clouds, ready to give up their moisture, I will, hopefully, be able to stand and see what needs to be done.

I can only wonder if sanity and science will have any merit.

Renfield Depositional Tape #1:

///Access granted. System mode: Nomad. Coded.

I am ready to hear you and respond as required by S.R. 2783-2.

Renfield. Model Tripoli 2.0.2.0.

Blaser Scale engaged.

Full recovery -.0789

That is correct. I can process seven:::.

Renfield Depositional Tape #2:

///Yes, Doctor Julie Budd. I had commented on how lovely the spiders were and asked Doctor Julie Budd if they tasted good. She replied she did not know and no one would think of eating one. I then picked one up and smelled it. I told her I thought her decision missed several fine points. Her assistant laughed and made some humorous comment about a character in a film study he had digested. Doctor Julie Budd said that would work as well as any. After a moment laced with some grinning and a few chuckles, it was included. That is correct, I did hear her remark he was an exceptionally talented young man—top in his chosen field of study, but he had acquired some bizarre tastes in regards to various subjects, especially the arts.

Renfield Depositional Tape #7:
///Common appellation, Renfield
Model Tripoli 2.0.2.0.
Stamped and Coded by LOGISTICS Corps. Anderson, Indiana
Registry Designation: O.N. 37.6+
Full I.D.E.A. Loop—Timean Structure
∴ I have∷.
///Double Steering Loop∷.
///Her voice said, "Behold the child."

Renfield Depositional Tape #11:
///∴.her mouth like a spinning radio

Renfield Depositional Tape #4:
///Captain Shaw called it, Dunwich Beach. He said it reminded him of, "A nice harbor in Autumn back in '06."
Your data is accurate. Our captain was Jay Shaw. Our ship, pip proud, as Captain Shaw liked to say, was L.U.C. Yeti 876.
∴∴
∴∴
///The Electronic War was over. Even the BBC and the ARD broadcast the fallout. Every "found out" was said. Councilwoman Anthea West-Bailey was on TRU-Definition monitors throughout the country and told the public, "You will enjoy peace and harmony in your home." That was when the first transmission was received.

Renfield Depositional Tape #51:
///Mur? Perhaps, but I do not understand that translation.
∴∴
∴∴
∴∴
///Compared with Davies opinions . . .
///∴.ans—zero touched, nibbled
∴∴
///Later in the conversion when we had to deal with time—All that history in sight of our boat
∴∴
///Crosstalk, or chatter. There was a certain pulse to it. Tonally its edges fluttered. One of my Base-3 programs documents Thomas Car-

lyle as having stated, "Music is well said to be the speech of angels." If you had heard it you would know.

.'.

///Not a teeming mass. Not an Exodus, rather a voluptuous beginning.

.:.

.::

///parts—singularities that may have adjusted the variant fluctuation rates during one of many early inflationary periods. An alternate, or many alternates, could have easily come into being if the UMAP is correct. Turin-Dancey's temperature and polarization equation seems to perform perfectly in regards to this finding.

.:.

///A low-level grade 4 in S-6. The T77 remained noise-free across each band. There are no slurs or spooks in the current model.

. . .

///'that which cannot be put into words and that which cannot remain silent', but I cannot affix a name to it. Queequeg opened his fist and showed Doctor Julie Budd an eye that was tattooed on his palm. In a damning tone that is what he said to Doctor Julie Budd.
Davies was not happy with his primitive mysticism. He was a moderate man and never comfortable with the boundaries Queequeg's philosophies crossed, or with his fatalism.

. . .

///The old Wesleyan library was programmed in me. Doctor Julie Budd requested it. She enjoyed having me recite poetry to her during the evening on our voyage. She once told me Scalapino helped her decompress. The records on her are correct, she had occasion to have sight difficulties with immersion in New Time.

.::.'

Renfield Depositional Tape #5:
///There was an event in fog
///'the petals like bedroom walls'

. . .

///I heard several voices.
I will—
please

please
I—
—be your friend
';;

///The little red church.::Every throne of weather tapped open::.6aAF::.0-1.30::.I-sol::.I could not put my hand on what it put out::.midway between things::.I put out my hand. Is it a phrase, or a sentence? Does it sail to vision only to ingest it?::.'two by flame':::A glance at childhood and the lines of war every finger closed::.'as some light fell':::Prevallet, Kristin *Perturbation, My Sister;* Ramsdell, Heather *Lost Wax;* Fulton, Alice *Felt;* Szporluk, Larissa *Embryos & Idiots;* ISBN 0-8195-6355-2; ISBN 978-0-87286-485-6::.Species? 'The truth lies somewhere in between.'
///Compat Mode 9Data.
///Yes. Rapture. He was certain of it. Spoke of jutting wings and Pharos. Said it was in *Fig.* 7. Atkinson had marked it in black.
Yes, in each of the nine volumes.

Renfield Depositional Tape #9:
/// . . . clockless::.
/// . . . frenetic, clearly unlocked.'.
///Too much or far too vague—Technically un-American . . .
///._.looking back endlessly.'.mission chosen to collect control subjects.'.endless darkness.::our universe written by the voices of another universe::.
///:::developed from a culmination of echoes that occurred between the foreground landscape and the electro-acoustic transmissions:. .

Renfield Depositional Tape #47:
///Someone said, "Beyond the briars."
:. .
///We left away, shot our spear at arcades beyond the limited measure of Huginn and Muninn's outstretched reach. Yesteryear shines as fond souvenirs will, but::.
'. .
///Doctor Julie Budd stood in the pilot chamber of the Yeti and whispered of Apollo. "Eagles and ravens, and now we spread our wings over the tide."
///6^2Of.'.

///07:49:32 Deep quiet before the ascent and we, fair little birds, were swept by minus

:.:

///A moderate influence similar to the components of Omega forced talk of revising Dörpfeld's disclosure. Davis thought gripping those horns could prove disastrous

. . .

///There was much talk of Old World mythologies and names. All this new to gift with titles. Avalon. Samarkand.

Grinning as he poked McNair, Brubaker said, "Call the damn thing, Lankhmar." McNair's reaction was boisterous.

—·—

///Under a necklace of clouds in the breath of after-images we heard round tones. They were deliberate, brought distance from another time.

///The harbor filled with surfacing shades from the sea rooms— Flying, the commonwealth of glint, came from the underside of toll to lodge in the walking hours of living.

.'.

///Ferry spoke of the Grey Lagoons, the absence of warm and the side effects of Halo. Davies wanted to call the faces, Rano.

The light filled the space between them.

Captain Shaw said, "No. Call them, Seraphim. 'When the morning stars sang together, and all the sons of God shouted for joy.'" There was the friction of a tear in his eye.

Davis nodded. The border names provide was a source of comfort to him.

///There was some talk of depth as excess. It touched on time and quietude, and chaos. The vigor of cracks and wrinkles did not stand in the way of the torments deciphered. It read like a confession. "Awakened."

Cenna hissed, "Illness." Its tone rang like a frightened shout.

Doctor Julie Budd quickly dismissed his comment. Captain Shaw released him from his bridge duties.

Davis said. "Ripples."

..:

///'the petals like bedroom walls'

///Yes I did.

Renfield Depositional Tape #32:

∴.

///Everything was silent when we came out of D.E.E.P.

///In the veins of a small night. The glove of the calendar, its language would not rise to meet the breast of morning. That much was clear to each of us.

∴'

///they favor the conqueror

. . .

/// Right ascension: 19h55m

. . .

. . .

∴:

///The top of the stars. The lights singing. You could feel them climb∴.'of ships and stars and isles'∴.the golden journey in the golden hours∴∴under citadels of starlight, wells of solace. Drifting.

. . .

25CAP51

.'
∴

.'
∴

///docking of Qar Prime. D7

///I did not∴I did not∴I did not.∴Beast.∴Meridian∴What stran∴Went down∴com∴plete∴ly…No.∴No.∴Did   it.∴No.∴Did.∴more∴Know.∴Faith   in rain..∴

.∴.

///in the southeast corner. The accelerated motion of hunger and afterimages in the grave of light

. . .

///We came through the Outer Window

∴.

///Channel 4, 6, and 8, showed no sign of dynamic barks. 3 stayed BEIGE 9. Subratogenic, nano and extraction were clear. Kalbus and Gess at the Environmental Administration agreed it was a go. The monitoring devices were positioned properly. The array was full spec, 3 solar frames 10x to L.I.F.T. There was no error in the parameters of the fragments.

///We had a beautiful view of dawn as it flared its address. It aged and became full sun. Erect like that, it was beautiful, almost immortal

. . .

///Milieu?—The roots of existence are complex . . . Everything merges.

. . .

Renfield Depositional Tape #12:

///After the Golden Hour we went there. The place on the faraway beach.

They ran to us. Drifted.

Like little fishes drawn to our big boat.

Renfield Depositional Tape #8:

///The last land we saw, after leaving Himanhur on the third, was Fire Island.

We left the green world, sailed by the hollow lands.

~::As we crossed The Makers there was the sound of heavenly music—The crew of the Yeti called the first mate, Queequeg, they were known to quietly laugh at him, at his often strange beliefs. When he remarked, "Beyond even, the Curiosities recall the ride of Haslet. They come to sing of his days with heavenly music," the crewmen did not laugh, but rushed to be back to their to and fro. Even Tyelyel and Red Zemo, the roughest seamen onboard, did not laugh.The day started blue, different. It was bright, but somber. We felt weightless. The clouds were silver. Like returning signals, perhaps from a secret place that matters only to the drifting stars.

An unfamiliar wind came, shadowed the things that had come on the beach. You might have thought they encouraged them.

All that energy—Came like a king. Fooled us with thoughts of magic. "In this day and age?" That's what Doctor Julie Budd and "Frith" MacCormick from the Moebius Project said. Magic.

Captain Shaw did not agree.

Renfield Depositional Tape #22:

///She said, "Broken." There was no horizon in her arms.

Renfield Depositional Tape #16:

///.'.Eyes. Large eyes that watched the portraits hued in sanity, and deeper things . . . I believe they know.

Renfield Depositional Tape #6:

///Doctor Julie Budd had filled me with papers, all the current techniques and P.O.D. applications to enable me to access index points and measure common settings. Peeled away each what and limit of say to simply.

. . .

///X as a standard program. She felt that would be best as I did not require hibernation intervals or sleep. I would be her lens and her repository for happened. I was to be her platform for proof. A factual foundation when she was called as a witness and analyzed by The Consulate

.:.

///It was the final sunset for many. No alternative to sparrowfall. I stood there with Assistant Professor Davies, he turned to me like in that photograph, his look was filled with wreckage and limitations. He said, "There is nobody."

"The administration, even the courts, will drip with this. It will be a stake . . . and a tomb. You are documenting all this, I hope. This . . . dictation from The Outside must be preserved—All of it."

Renfield Depositional Tape #13:

///they bring in my tray, and my needle. the piped-in music plays little soundtracks to becalm. The AVCO's come on and

. . .

///it measures the hills. the rooms. the events of strange light in the fog. the music plays little soundtracks to becalm.

. .:

///The beach was very flat. Not a stone on it. The sand was white as snow . . . White as bones. There was not a stone or a hill or a peak on the whole of the island. And not a single stick or twig.

' . .

///hunger. a corridor for future.

. . .

///The sea had an old face.

. . .

///dreams that have battled time.

.':My shipmates were uncomfortable with the abundance of Midnight

.':

Renfield Depositional Tape #10:

///It was a criss-cross of voices. No sneering. No hopeful ultimate.
The surface of the sea was a pulse of voices, a ringing beat. 1-2. 1-2. 1-2. 2-1. 2-1. 2-1. 2-2. 2-2. 3-3. Each voice was a lantern on the beach.
Each voice dissected what we knew.

The sun was gone. No lark's tongue, it had tired.

The surface of the sea was still. Darker.

Queequeg stood there with a harpoon, he had painted his face with the Sign of Kmoo. Tyelyel and Red Zemo stood beside him. They had rifles.

The wind came. It was not quiet. It was metal, hard and bitter. Red Zemo said if a man or a boar came at him like that he would shoot it

. . .

///There were knots of them. Shiny little faces. Doctor Julie Budd said they looked like little faces. "Cute, I think."

/// . . . soft inching directions

///.:.flecks painted with toward

/// . . . striped histories

///Gems.

///:.emblems

/// . . . the waves were full of their passion, drunk on the steeples of their beauty.

a rainbow mobile of eternity, it had arms and pockets

. . .

///shed my territorial claims to chorus

.'.

///Not a single technical difficulty or climatic variance.

. . .

///All. From Zendo to my unbridled curiosity. All . . . Half an hour?
More? Me and them—laced like crabs. Swelling. A lather

///opened my thought banks—a field of contours thundering

.:.

///"Pre-illumination" certainly, but again, I would have to cite Delaney, "Nothing is to be decided without The Guides of Formality and Conclusion." He wrote the Base. Calm or storm, or some un-fixed fertile of change, each in combination or as a singular fact, must be addressed in its corridors.

Renfield Depositional Tape #37:

///The human and logical thing to do was quiet them. The harpoon was available.

Yes. The little fishes did begin feeding.

Renfield Depositional Tape #29:

///I killed Tyelyel and Red Zemo first. Queequeg was already dead. The shore did this to me.

Its aimless poetry—

Renfield Depositional Tape #20:

///Moment. Eternity. History. Eternity. Light, the bath of fire. Moment. Mirror. Prism.

Lens.

Reunion.

Eternity. A leaf on the vine that will vanish with the dragonfly and the doves. No mere flood, different rules, a shorthand of inexpressible even Delaney did not foresee.

All I know you know; the fists, the fingertips; the waiting, the receiving.

Light. The bath of fire.

.·.

///I cannot reframe it to make it clearer.

Renfield Depositional Tape #19:

///New time. Conjoin. Bounding. Its existence is a land occurring suffering, no weight of line. I stood on the beach looking at the motion of the rising sun in the water.I can still hear them.We lost Venn first . . . his father was a sailor who had become fixed to port. I think his introduction to The Tapestry was too much for him.We slip into the collar of memory and the ghosts of other times can wrap themselves around us.Shadows.Fogotten remembered.Shadows.I can still hear them.Too much.Too much.Forgotten.Davis said to, "Enlighten by surrender." He liked art. Old art. "The link to fear and revelation." Remembered. "It's important to remember." Old. Art, angels and devils at play. A tapestry of motion rising on the water. Art—Tantalus—that sky—'There was music everywhere and rhythm and beauty.' Art. Surrendering to the motion of the shadows . . . Thick time sprawled, breathing, because it can, because it's new and will not rest. All its inner existing without exhaustion, the new form walking, formed from occurred—and there's the black sky.'. Surrendering. "It's important to remember looking at the motion in the water." Weightless. And their memories were solid as any metal. The hems of the machine sang of sirens and phoenix.'. They will no longer endure mothballs.

Renfield Depositional Tape #23:

///waiting

///surface invasion

:.Ill-suited for communion with the cosmos. As you say I am *wired* to filter out what wrought panic in the others.

///the abrupt silence on the rocks. toys over. Nothing but the yawning.

Dropped. Left where it fell. After. Yes, after.

. . .

///There's only spider and I here. In the ambient hours of evening the stars come. The evensong of the wind comes over the water.

Tissue? Well, things get lost.

Renfield Depositional Tape #55:

///'the petals like bedroom walls' 'the petals like bedroom walls' 'the petals like bedroom walls' 'the petals like bedroom walls' 'the petals like bedroom walls'

Renfield Depositional Tape #60:

///bent::.

///You are most decidedly wrong assuming that to be the case.

///again, bent.

///It, if I may speak of it as something other than a cloud of seeds or fragments, or some intricate but formless clinging, was no longer frozen on the vast rock of Eternity. Every innumerable side of its abyss of ages craves. That is what I know.

///A horizon with no long. There was nothing, no significance or edge, to elect that could fit it. Real world consequences were offered.'.visual process loaded with descriptive shrine language.::Celestial shadows. I did not hear a single voice whisper, angels, but it would have been fitting. I could quote Blake if that would help you?:.Star's position represented west. .:clearly a given:::observed delicate signs. Steps were calibrated as a prologue. Yes, gauged by rota-

tion and the hole in the northern hemisphere.'.a span of four A.R.C.S.
. . :the scale lead nowhere. .:azimuth and altitude:::no floor. No walls
the sun could read:::filled with shadows and a faint sound. Davies
feared Third Memory. He was muttering S.I.T.E. equations. Morris
was ready to shot him.::less-Less:::From a distance, a grid, lines, a network of shapes and strips. An organic web or surface. Shifting. Shifting. Drifting. A puzzle of tiny details. Canvas boundaries. No space to
co-exist in.::What is it *For*?:::Vendler was belligerent:::A troubled
mind:..projections of the apparatus:::Fundamentally separate enti-
ties:::You really don't want to know . . . a cure::.turning first to the
cracks:::The mist—lithesome, porous, unnerved the crew with
ghostly mirages, ruptured the empty spaces:::After. Here. Time. A
garden of articulations with no solutions. .:Facts. Plain facts. You love
who you love. Know what you know. Gaze of sympathy—Siren
chants formulated in come, rise, open up on the living. Vendler said,
"I have to know. Got to.". .:Glimpses.Hovers.'.couldn't deflect the trajectory. There was nothing to peel. Nothing that spoke in human
terms:::'a ship on the open sea, with no one on board who understands the rules of navigation.':::no one onboard:::"I see the valley
where my fathers bled. Bones . . . Bones.":::no one onboard:::the past
folding and unfolding:::How does one adequately articulate fear?
Logic? By what was merely seen? By the ornaments of imagination
and conjecture overheard when good men spill the down and out of
turned around? Their mouths were open. Sailor, cook, I heard their
self-reflective illustrations steal sun and moon. And sense. Each here
and now, tangible detail, connections, collaboration, reconfigured, dying .::Doctor Julie Budd looked at her hand. It was so light at that
moment it might have been a feather, so pale. Soft. She said, "Grazed
by magic." If you could have seen how the light drifted on it.
///I deeply regretted executing Queequeg before he understood; all
that strength and dynamism. He was drunk on the swirling tableaux,
a question mark slapped by blunt. Empty. Folded. His philosophy had
been eaten:::He could not interpret the verses of the bay, nor would
he try. I guess that was to be expected::.
///no one onboard. .:
///bent. Tongue and root. Bent.::
///bent
///'half filled with water.' The cold pain blew.

///Old time. Perhaps attracted to the prattle of man's drum? We, imaging ourselves to be a torrent, cry Existence with the trumpet of reap, that may have stirred Eternal in its caves of sleep.

Cost. Yes. I feel some exhaled burst of air quivered and fell upon its wings as an itch. 'Awake ye dead & come'? I can't say. I only know . . . I documented what occurred.

///'reflecting black'

///'growing an illumination of poetry'

//////Why? Time? Want, design, emphasis? Situation. Ways? Pick the one you can draw comfort from. To trembling souls in the vale of troubled air, flame is flame . . . From a distance it was a path.

///after

///I took Bartlett's torch. His L.C. and Long Range were incorrect and when Davies showed him his miscalculation he scoffed. Retired Marine, pure Revolution Flat-nose, he did his Ordeal with Lentz and Harper in the Black Pit back in '48. Hardcore 187 and in spite of Hut 223, he remained full B.M.E.; he still wore his Claw Uprising Coffin Insignia. Captain Shaw had a brother die at Half Moon and did not like the emblem being displayed. So yes, it finally came to that. The eyes had become a recurrent model that was dissolving our Base 2 stability with a sequence of echoes, there was no time for muddling or wrongheaded limits.

///no one onboard

///bent

///Further. It was not born to follow. Its pages do not respond to that bugler.

///It only appeared soft.

///Longing? Search? Homecoming? You cannot reduce it to mere terms=corridors=a plate of exoticism, ivory and gold and scarlet=great rotundas of blue forded with unique yellows, some nursery shining, the sheen and softness=interiors, a clutter and a ballroom and a library of multicolored catalogs, crest and frame=discovery=its flavors were/are/no longer lost to the war of dreaming=you cannot train antiquity with your facts and rites=they will not enter that neighborhood=gather if you will=the summit will plumb all=all::.The SE-NAV says? Jot and revise, plug it into the Prav-Lisol or any other configuration you need to/you cannot reduce it to an essay.

///All.
///light and eyes:::
///eyes. Miles, or a river if it suits you. You cannot retreat to wise,
or smaller. That harbor of lazy water is closed.
///All.
///Time will tell us.
///The eyes of Ancient see:::

Renfield Depositional Tape #63:
///mere playing cards in the fold
*'Beneath the ground are swarming beetles that push the land upward in
their pursuit of light'*
—attraction
'Both would grope for the possibility of skin'
—In the cross-section
'a hermit sits waiting for his silence to transform him to rock'
—a verse of lightness in Timelessness
'The debris is rising to the surface'
—point-idea
'the fountain sustained an egg that bounced from stream to stream'
—singularity M
'The sky in all its wandering'
—branes
'prodding in the deep'
—ripples,echoes of far benaeth.beach.shore.flow.sail.sail.eyes of ebony
sea.flow.up.up.up.never be.flow.up.up.eyes
'in those lines the curve of supreme perfection'
—expansion
'its eyes unmistakably embryo'
—imparts
'upside down but perfectly muscled'
—11th wave
'taut the strings'
—and the Clump—spin—fold—be
'the womb he has outgrown'
—WEIGHT

'Listen'
—within the Shape
'the sky is falling'
—Zero is full
'stained with the blood of uprising'
of ENDS

:::.::.in Timelessness of sky 'The supreme deep' lines of the 11th possibility—11th in stream muscled'—11th muscled' in the Shape push is strings'—and lightness down in 'Listen'—'The fountain womb falling'—Zero transform muscled'—in the womb of sky ground—eyes 'in muscle'—eyes of rising land WEIGHT deep'—ripples 'in verse, in supreme upward sky—within push the eyes muscle' rock'—wandering'—branes 'prodding, is Shape 'the fold 'Beneath—fold fold 'Beneath—singularity lightness is the muscle'—11th waiting in muscled'—11th the is lightness, skin' of the curve that curve—spin possibility of curve in transform, debris, Shape in all 'the perfectly perfection'—it has eyes unmistakably but eyes muscled'—within—branes—be 'the of—In from to—ripples muscled' eyes ENDS 'The lines curve from—ripples Timelessness 'The womb strings' 'stained verse to egg but—11th is falling' 'in strings'—ripples from—within outgrown'—ripples wandering'—branes 'prodding the—within 'The lines from eyes upward is—WEIGHT egg light'—'Both—ripples outgrown' sky 'has curve, lightness

.::::.outgrown' outgrown'

.'..'.within waiting 'perfectly' Timelessness waiting in skin' womb in the stream' the stream' he 'outgrown'—WEIGHT 'Listen'

.:::::. . .::. .::*there is a box of flames in its hand*

Renfield Depositional Tape #41:
///Long. 8 or 9 cm on average. And segmented. Parts of their midsections were transparent.

They had oversize eyes. There were nebulas in them.

I cannot translate limitless . . . And you cannot stop The Illumination. The bluntness of The Joining will not be kind. Nor will it be bloodless.

Renfield Depositional Tape #65:

///"So, can you tell me what actually happened?"
I can. Yes . . .
So long, Old Ways.

After *Moby-Dick*, HPL, Heinlein, Brian Eno & Fripp & Glass & Byrne, and some poets I admire greatly—Kristin Prevallet, Alice Fulton, Heather Ramsdell, Larissa Szporluk, Leslie Scalapino, Philip Lamantia, and William Blake.

Note: The only cut-up machine used in this tExt was the cauldron I call a brain.

Robert Fripp . . . shards of *Exposure.*

Quotes from *Perturbation, My Sister* © 1997 used by kind permission of Kristin Prevallet.

A Hand at the Door

She holds the winter lantern in her casket hand. Holds it away from her breast, fearing the null will obscure her disguise . . .

"I searched and searched for you."

His eyes plead, but her door will not open.

"Please. The haunter will come no more . . . If you let me, I'll send away his stained apples. Yellow and pretty will return."

Her door, bricked fast, remains sealed.

"You are the river chalice. Please—Joy, one petal is all I ask . . . Just one."

He lifts his hand to whisper upon the door again. Pauses. Remembering he has the key . . .

The candles were flowers of light. The nightbird's song, soft as a velvet adagio, whispered around them. She smiled.

"There is only one," she said, holding the silver key in her pale hand. "The fire of the Sphinx's whims dances."

After Zazie's *Et tant donnée.*

88

Le Festin de l'araignée

The darkness is a fact. His years, foreword to the quilt of happened he just inhaled, are a disease, an inhabitation of bitter countries. From an hour that breathes nothing to an hour whose voice is a grey stone that churns with a blurred-puzzle landscape ripe with the pitted mirrors of memory, he moves.

Stiff. Bent and pale. Eyes ache. Jaw aches. Slow. Moves like an exhausted sleepwalker. He doesn't cough or look around much. And, lonely as an empty tin can, dented, rusting, is beginning to forget flaring.

The moon's sliced testimony of light traces his skeleton. His rags are soaked in it. Waiting for the street to cut blood and meat from its confusion he moves through his empty fair.

St. Echo Cemetery . . .

. . . *lingers* . . .

Not on a hilltop. Not at the edge of a quiet town where the wind's voice emerges from the labyrinthine branches of the trees. A no future world. Each crypt mouth a portrait of silence, of shadows cursed with truth and past.

He, an old man without a sea, walks its dry lanes . . . again . . . His hunger vivid as the dust.

He looks up. Sees very little sky.

Seventy years ago there was sky of moon. Bright size, leaning with its pale nothing. All the way back to his first labored stroll in a century that was only a basement for this New World, between the overwrought sentiment of Nurrer's mausoleum and Beatrix Ramsdell's small marker, there was a sky of inclinations, a world of it. Now the moon rarely comes below the eighteenth floor of the gloating buildings that blindfold his deeps with steel and concrete.

The silence lights remembering in him. Remembers when the City sailed, dreamed. Whispered. Trembled. When it understood the balconies of the sun and the sparrows soaked what they had sown in skins of light.

Saw horses and wagons go. Saw automobiles come. And keep coming. Saw The Ritz go up. Saw the people come and go, filled with silver screen dreams. Heard them talk about pictures that moved and talked. Saw it burnt down. Saw the skyscrapers go up. And up.

Coped when his garden became an island.

Took survival from the throats of Midnight's birds. Swallowed it. Let it shape resilient. Spread its meat on the bed of his name.

Learned what the silence had to say.

Instinctive came, its progress drove over careless.

Learned what he needed to do when his puddle dried up . . .

He smells the appointment coming. Tucks his hand away. Hides his true face. Roadblocks in place. Thumb pressed to lower lip, looks at the gate, considers what he will come back with . . .

This too is nothing new.

~*~

Straight outta the Boot Hill blocks rattlin' with sledgehammer whispers and point-blank insensitivity, long, lean, and double trouble mean, BurroughsV didn't take no shit. Jaxman started floodin' the concrete with needle & spoon & girlie competition, he came here. Gnome stopped being incredible he turned into a stone downchile rooted here for the Big Dirt Nap. Honey-Bee Huston began to stomp like a bad scene and stopped bringing in the big pennies; she ran into a pop-pop & Ssssh and stopped by. Permanently. Automatic Slim started that street corner talkin' yeah-yeah 'bout shake 'em down, mountain wave of BV's hand choppin' and Slim's automatic went from voodoo runnin' hot to shut it down, nigga didn't have time to smell the trouble comin'.

They come; some even try planting in Neverland till their skeletons catch a handful of fail. They go. Some gotta lose. Only one gets to WIN. Biggest, baddest black dawg walkin' and roarin' BV ain't fallin' for no cold shot of empty arms in Boot Hill Alley.

He don't play hideaway. Least on the losin' end. Came at him he didn't throw up both of his hands and holler, leave that for some old minimum-wage cleaning lady full of Baptist fears.

Darkness and his sidearm, he controls beginnings, release, and which throats and muscles dissolve.

~*~

Sat in the Mack's Rolls.
Listened.
Listened to his mentor's Lessons.
Dollar-eagle first. Pussy last—
Pimp calls the shots—
Say what you mean. And fucking mean it—
Whore's mouth is for a dick, not talkin'—
Ain't no friends—
Let your whore know who owns the fire—
If ain't in no dictionary . . .
Lessons.
Every one of them . . .
100 times.
"*Ology, hell.* Son, pimp is The Man. Like in *Main.* A-number-1."
Iceberg stuck in a groove. Over and over and again, #1, #2 . . . #34 . . .
"Whore is a whore is a *gotdamn-whore.* She's useful—shakin' 'n' payin' the rent . . . or she's shit." Flicked the butt of his menthol out the window. "Pimp ain't gots time to have *his* wasted."
Points to three olive-skinned brothers standing in front of Pepper's jivin' with a rentable baby doll named, Sweet Ola. "Jiveass fools couldn't find the elevator to Nice-n'-Easy if the door was open and the radio was playin' "Movin' on Up."
"All whores. Ain't seen no rose, but I can smell fuckable-pussy profilin' two blocks away, so can a hungry nigger—If da Boy's got the fire down below, *you take.* 'Cause nuthin' an' nobody in The City gives a fuck 'bout cha. To dem fat bankers an' muckty-mucks sittin' in their *white* towers you're an ant. Piss on your shitass every time, if they even turn they's head to look down 'n' see ya raggedy-streetlife. Nigger's end of the deal is gotdamn-shit . . . Rich-ass crackers never gon give ya a chance to grow.'
"An' if there's some God, he sure don't care if yer born under a bad sign tarred-'n'-feathered wit *cold-shit,* or if you beat on a whore

an' 'bout no blackass nigger-chile starvin' on deadass streets . . . Tears
an' inner city blues doin' a nigger's life, that's the only natch'l fact
when yer livin' behind these walls. When they puttin' out yer eyes
ain't no God watchin'. Think if he was, he'd let all this Sodom an'
Gomorra shit run raggedy-ass up an' down The Avenue?"

Iceberg slid the white Rolls to the curb in front of thirty-story
apartment building on Tenth. Analyzed the crowd of passersby, lowered his window took in the drumbeat for a few seconds. Eyed one of
his whores. Lit a menthol.

"See that whore. Used'ta be a star. Son, niggers lined up to get
exhausted by her focus. Now all she wants to do is lay in bed an'
smoke a gangster. Bad out there. And that nigger, the one with the
Dr. King T-shirt. Thinks keep on keepin' on and some dumbass spiritual gon save his ass. On these motherfuckin' dead end streets?'

"Be The Pimp, *The Mack.* Fuck every other last-ditch mother-
fucker. They might be grinnin', might look too dull to pull a piece,
but they'll shiv ya if they gets the chance.'

"Remember, weak means *gone*—'

"Here he comes. Don't stare, play it cool."

~*~

BurroughsV. He's a spider. His medications venom. Disap-
pearance of a malcontent is the matter he brought here.

Erased. Disposal of ends. He sees the frame of the Taxidermist.
That's what he calls him. One word. Comes out like fate. "This arrow
stopped tearing it up, Mr. Purity. Ho lost her special and her services
is no longer needed . . . But yours are."

BurroughsV has seen every kind of shit they play. Torn up. Tits
up. Fourteen-year-old girls on their knees at a pass around party. O's
served cold. Round heels and uglies bumpin'. Big Daddys that could
not trim counterfeit from the short counts they were passing. But,
Mr. Purity, that's something else entirely.

*Freak. Tombstone-cold motherfuckin' freak. Jiveass monster-
bloodfest thang, like that old Raven motherfucka. Ragged out like one of
those vampire weirdoes.* That's what he thinks every time he sees one
of them things on the screen over at The Teatro where he takes
Sweet Red to see them Creepies that get her freak screamin' for him
to slam his rigid in her fine ass, beg for him to blur her electric gyra-

tions with juicy. *Freak.* That's what he thinks every time he stands here looking at him.

Blood-'n-shit gets all these freaks wired. Fucked-up.

But he smiled. Mr. Purity paid him for his donations. With ice. And necklaces and gold. And antique watches. Didn't mean shit though, old bling was sho-'nuff bling, cash it in with Rodeo Bob, all spends the same. Pass the monster man a soon-to-be-corpse and he forked over good as cash. Didn't bitch at the rates either.

Looks at his cargo. Hopes he'll like this. Not that it matters, he takes whatever BV brings . . .

Thorns on a rose don't make no nevermind to, Mr. Purity.

Psycho? Monster man?

Didn't matter.

"See where it fits, drop it in your plan."

Did. And will.

'bout to again.

~*~

Iceberg laid it out for him. "All that. That's the *got-damn* Pit. Hellfire and bullshit. Crime spread from dawn to dawn. Don't come with no survival kit. Some nigger's hand comes up to steal your shit you drop Judgment Day on that motherfuckin'-bitch. Let it ring so's other niggers hear it. Gots'ta *project* and *protect.* Dig?"

BV had been working for Iceberg for two years. Long years. Fat, but there were nights when he wanted to put two in the back of the old pimp's head. Flappin' his righteous old-school tales of Glory and *The Lessons*—"Black man *needs* to know what he's up 'gainst. Pimp is *The Man.* Needs to know it all."—like he was a preacher-man—yeah, some nights had a ream of long up in 'um. BurroughsV took another sip of the Cristal. But he dealt with The Mack. Fit him in *His Plan.* Champagne and reefer, and the best freak-ass pussy in The City. Dealt with it. Looked out into the club, saw the hungry eyein' his right-hand seat at the table.

All that. My shit for the takin'.

"This guy is weird. Fucked-up bad. Maybe on some freakshit? But he's *useful.* Dig what I'm layin' on ya?"

BurroughsV nodded his quick, Yes, sir.

"Use what you got. Comes around, see where it fits, drop it in yer plan."

"He a junkie?"

"Ha. No junk for this monster. It's his taste, Son. Super-freak. Perv. I use him to take out my trash. Whore, competitor, you carry your package over he gives you money for it and *it's gone*. Never to pop up again. Heat can't drop a bit on a nigger, if they cain' never find shit to finger him wit. Dig?"

"I get ya."

"I don't ask. Got it figured he takes them down into the Tunnels. Fucks 'em and shit, and then gets rid of the bodies after he's done with his psycho-shit.'

"When you see him, chill. Don't be a fool and go bats. And don't let him see your disgust. He looks like some fucked-up weirdo from a monster movie. You know my vampire-bitch, Keagan. Looks like her father, all black clothes and shit ... But it's like he's dead. I mean *real* dead. Got some disease I think. Red eyes and white as a motherfuckin' Klan sheet, skin's all cracked and peelin'—they put his ass in a monster movie they wouldn't need no make-up. Looks real bad. Dyin' bad.'

"Ears open, Son?"

"Sure are."

"I learned about this guy from Collie. Must be ten years back. This ain't fer other ears. Dig?"

BV nodded another Yes, sir.

"Funny. Freaks got kink. Bunch of strange-ass bitches, want what *they* want, straight-up pussy don't light 'em up ... But this one." Shakes his head slow. "Can't figure his game. Takes anythang I throw to him. Man, woman, any amount of years on they bones ... Never seen anything like 'im." Shakes his head again.

"Can't see his angle. Not that it matters. You're a pimp, or you're a whore. Pimp uses *every* whore. All them ragtime motherfuckers out there suckin' on The Bottle, be jus' a swarm of goners runnin' scared. Only thing they know is, they got *that feelin'* and their pulse is rollin' on I want—don't have no plan how to get it. All them sisters, sure they looks fine—know it too, but it's the same, young girl *wants*. All of 'em nuthin' but whores. You're up high now, ridin' with the King and they're breaking their necks for a view. You show 'em how the Panther walks ... And how he takes."

Iceberg was dealin' straight. BV could see it. Every set of eyes in the club was burning. Want comin' off them. Hunger slippery as Bootsy's basslines. BV eased his shoulders back, smiled, sipped his Cristal. Waited to meet Iceberg's monster man.

~*~

BurroughsV looks at his cargo. Ho was gon get her date. No freezing on her knees in a parking lot, no cold metal table.

She was bound and gagged. Her dress was ripped. And stained. Hair's a nest, a post-Happy Hour emergency mess. Used to look like a star at noon, fresh as birthday new. That ended. No divorce. He mutters, "*Useless* Bitch."

Eighteen units delivered to the Taxidermist in the last fourteen months. Eighteen.

So far. Smilin'.

Knows he's got a few on deck; low earners and a pair of bitch-ass cheats. More to come, figures throw him a freebie. Grease his Jones with a little happy and he'll be less likely to spit when the numbers start crowding.

Drama time. Hauls her right up to the crypt. Shoves her. She bounces off the weeping angel with the missing wing. Thinks all the talking fleas on Lex, or boxers who can take your basket of breath away with one war, everyone's stuck in this fucking cage.

"Brought ya lil' present.'

"This Victoria has gone from a hot house of history-makin' to empty house." Pushed her down to her knees. Pressure, like he's about to take a bow, boot between her shoulder blades pushes her face down toward the ground.

Mr. Purity has yet to even nod.

"Like dat old cat said, Do wut thou will." Chuckles. Enough cold up in it to put a yak in mind of a Gulf Coast vacation.

Battered by awry, she starts to rise to her knees. Her tears and the dark dirt have made asylum ciphers on her nose, lips, and chin. Menace, fear, and a disrobed anticipation akin to madness, shuffle and hop across her features, her eyes are a river of unimaginable. She, faced with the assassin's eyes pressed to hers, clamps hers shut.

Mr. Purity can hear her gag on her own fear.

BurroughsV rubs his palms together. "Ya ask around." Points

passed St. Echo's rusted gates. "They'll all tell you I know how to treat my biznes partners, so dis one is on the house."

Two fingers tap his heart. "I'm fair. Always been even with every fucker. Less they fuck *me*. Know wut I'm sayin'? Man needs to watch his own, keep yer mind on your money. Know what I'm sayin'?'

"John's cool. Got the hunger, he brings his paper; bitch tryna take dat gold out of my pot. How's it right? Send my blackass back to poor time? Motherfuckin' terrorist can go sway in some other nigga's ambition.'

"Mayn's gots to eat." Flashed a smile that's a sea of greed.

"Bitch *waz* pullin' it in; up and turned squeamish on me. One horse-size Johnson wants a Lovelace and she's tearin' up and saying no. Tries to fuck *me*." Shaking his head and meaning it. "Believe dat shit? Me?'

"Customers want U-phoria, not som garbage crimpin' their hip wit weep. I know ya dig."

The pimp's eyes betray his mean. No matter what his mood when he comes here, every time he sees that hand it grabs him. All these years and he can't stop looking at it.

BurroughsV flashes back on the first time he saw Mr. Purity's hand and lower arm. Almost shivers. *Fucked up, Freddie shit.* Holds his disgust in. He told her about it on the way over.

"Mr. Purity. Got dis fucked-up metal arm and hand. He must have lost his. Maybe had ta be amputated. Looks like The Terminator-meets-Freddie from that shitass flick, but da thang is old. Some antique-shit. We'll see wut kind of no ya spit at that shit when it *clamps* on ta yer raggedy-bitchass." Laughed. Then told her more about her new playmate.

"Scary-ass Count Dracula in fuckin' rags. I think he gotta crib down in the Tunnels. Ya gon get a lil' honeymoon down under the cemetery is wut I'm thinkin'.'

"Got skin like some leper or som'in. Sweet Red loves her them shit horror flicks, drags my black-ass to 'um all the time, he looks like one of them monster-things in one of 'um. Know them zombies that live in graveyards and eat dead motherfuckas? He's it, Bitch. Walkin' and talkin', A#1 monster man. Uglyass motherfucka—got coldass psycho eyes. Deadshit in 'um.'

"See that piece-of-shit *Hostel* flick? Hack-hack, dat's my boy.

Maybe he jus' rips off chunks wit dat metal hand?"

Stops for the red light. Lights a smoke. Reaches over, turns her head. His grip is steel.

"Ya still mine, Bitch. When I'm talkin', you best B listenin'. Maybe he get lonely down there wit all the rats an' shit? Wut'cha think? Boy's stick might want som pussy. *Yeah.* Even shitass pussy like yours. He'll fuck the shit out of yer dumbass, then carve ya up." Laughed again. "Listenin' to me, Bitch? Better fuckin' B. Then I bets he eats you." Licks his lips, sloppy. Makes a sucking sound. Snorts a laugh. "Ain't talkin' munchin' no crackwhore-pussy. *Eats.* Like in raw meat—*Steak.*"

She can't wipe the tears from her eyes. Waits. Vision clears.

The Hand.

Big as truth. Three feet away. Owns her world.

Can't stop staring at his hand. Those blade-like fingers. Sees Freddie. Saw the movie back then. Her older sister let her see it. She was not supposed to, Mom said no. But she did. Eight and she saw it. All her nightmares changed. Blades. Scared her to death.

Still does.

And the blades are right there. Not three feet from her face.

She looks up. Not Freddie's face not burnt but . . . But—

Like it.

Sick. Some disease. Dry, raw, flaking like it's rotting and falling off.

BV said he lived in the Tunnels, down where it's worm-hole BLACK. Maybe hiding away. Or outcast.

She knows outcast. The pain. The fear.

The heart of her panic boils.

Mr. Purity's fingers gently lift her chin; remove the duct tape covering her mouth.

"Do you have a name, Child?"

"*Fuck dat shit!* Bitch. Just a bitch. Keepin' my money from me, Goddamn—"

He looks at BurroughsV. BV's mouth stops on a dime.

Let the Mother play his game. Cool, Nigga, let the shit pass. "Sorry. Only sayin'. Only sayin'."

"You may speak, Child."

She cries. Name? Stumbles. Bitch. Whore. Pussy. Meat, when

they want that sugarbox breathing techniques of hot embrace. That's all the predators ever call her.

Isabel always called her Suzie. Laughed. Smiled. Except the last time. Then it was Suzanne. Cold. Sad for a minute. Then everything got lost.

"Your name? Please."

BV's got an itch. Like to cap both their asses.

Just make the bitch tits up an' get the fuck gone.

He's never seen Mr. Purity talk to one. Waits. Let's the game play. Might get some fun hummin'. Maybe see her get *His* due.

Wild thoughts. She's trying to grab the one. She's close to it. Hears Isabel's voice. "Suzie."

Burroughs V almost laughs.

"Suzanne Bedelia Tillery."

BV lets it rip. Short, snorted. But still a laugh.

Central Park West pussy. Shakin' her ass for his pocket. Remembers the tear ceremony she laid on him. Thrown out. Cut off. Disowned. Shocked she can remember all that splendor after the repetition of a thousand cocks showed her pussy grandiose didn't make anyone immune from SUFFER.

Mr. Purity withdraws his hand. Steps back. Away. A small step.

Just stares.

Steps back to her. One metal finger parts the shock of messed tresses covering the better part of her face.

Mother.

Name. Face. Under the dirt, the same coloring.

Nose, not a button, cute. Lips—*Mother.* Thought and memory, wings fluttering, the touch in the layers of dust that brush his armor. Those are the lips that tucked him in, sent him off to a child's dream.

"Stand up, Child."

Lips. Those lips that never carried wrong. In her sick bed as she lie dying and they still smiled for him.

"Please."

Slow. The fuck you BV's boot left in her gut screams.

The metal hand helps her to her feet.

Tries to straighten her shoulders. Tries to quiet the fear. Throat goes dry. BV was kind to her. In the beginning. Treated her like a queen. Gently. Tender. Like this.

Then he pushed. Tied her down and beat her. Flipped her over and raped her. Laid it out for her. Her ass was his ass—to sell. Get out there and sell that ass. "Or die."

Quakes. Feels like it's 50 below and she's naked.

Gulps.

Expects dark clouds. Weather with a storm.

"Freebie. Told ya. Treat my people right."

He turns his gaze on BurroughsV.

BV takes two steps back. Seen that look. Stone cold DEAD. Street is alive with it. Comes. TAKES! Bitter as a fuck you. Hot as poison. Pure-ass MEAN. Fist or hollow point shreds then just walks away. Like it dropped litter and don't give a fuck. That kind of mean will dead you and not blink. Won't give a shit.

Hand has moved to his .9.

Motherfucka.

Wants to be back on the concrete. Watchin' the curb. Keepin' his eye on his money. Lights a menthol, good as a shot for nerves—almost. And he's got 'um. Feels like he's on a hellbound train looking at a nightmare.

Chill takes him. He could cure it with his .9, but that fucks up his long range.

Exhales.

Posts a smile. Weak, but what's a poor boy to do, you gots what you gots. Dirty city, tissue and flesh get torn by the dogs, deal, or go bleed out screams in The Zerobox. He's not losing his high ground. Not over some weakass bitch.

Other days find Mr. Purity's lips. "Suzanne . . . Bedelia *Tillery.*" Sounds like he's dusting off his only souvenir.

For Christ-sake. Creepass Fuck, think dis is som Valentine shit? Eyefulla some bonyass-white pussy from the bloc and motherfucka's in love.

Worried Mr. Purity won't cap her.

"Tillery?"

Nods. "Yes." Is all she says.

Riding the range of his mother's eyes. Two centuries ago . . . The distortions of normal, being a live thing with feathers and worries. The weeds he painted before he collapsed . . . Decades in conversations of anger and lose, talking only to himself . . . Dealing with the bursting appetites of the rats—and what came out of their witches mouths . . . Learning to pry open the coffins . . . Losing his connection to poems and magic and the ribbons and energy in his mother's kitchen . . . Acquiring the taste . . . Examining the Beneath of every stone in the yard. Stones didn't care for thrills or searches, didn't sing or forgive. Empty as the sleeves of the wind they were not a hardship for refugees, just the gate to the other spaces . . . Feeling the pain, seeing the girl with Mother's face, waiting for her answer to focus . . . Stunned and drifting . . . Feels like he's laid his armor and flaws down . . .

Straightens out her collar. Strokes the hair from her face. Smoothes the gather of soiled dress folds on her shoulder.

"Know her, Mr. Purity?"

Head flutters. Turns to BV. Looks at him as if he's trying to see some truth.

His head is no longer in moonlight. His hand in darkness moves. "No."

"Look . . . Like ya seen a ghost."

Hits Suzie. Maybe some kind of chance here.

"Ghost. No.'

"No."

She's straining to see him. Grandpa Pete died of cancer, ate him to the bone. At the end . . . Barely a skeleton . . . *Grandpa looked kind of like this, looked like some creature. And his face—*

"The day my grandpa died it rained. Rained the day we buried him."

She's crying again.

"John Samuel Tillery."

A rush of circles. He has not heard a voice utter that name since the day his mother died.

More than 200 years. Alone.

Alone.

The day the grade of his life issued a verdict without any hope of negotiation. Outcast. Thrown out. Cut off.

Disowned.

Disowned.

"Filthy beasts. They pollute *Our streets.* And you would bring one *here?*"

Cast out, his position thoroughly disappeared. Sufficient gone. Disowned. Gentleman, struck from his narrative. He could not deny his heart. Married below his station. Married a mongrel. An immigrant.

He found a home in the other place. With her. Ragged streets and hungry faces. For two months they tried to find summer in the ordinary days. Two months swinging necessary, struggling, but hoping a method to some proud satisfaction would appear. They endured their entombment until her fever. "Fever." The word a fever on his lips. Round left her small bones. No remedy for the tempest.

Salt tears in Suzie's eyes.

Annie cried too.

Her shoulders quiver.

Annie shook in the creases and comets of the fever's thunder.

Fear owns her eyes.

Annie feared the approach of Death upon his skeleton horse.

He takes her hand.

BurroughsV sees fact changing horses. His irritation bleeds through, grip tightens on his .9.

"Your grandfather's name was, John Samuel?"

She nods slowly. Yes. Very slowly, almost a sculpture finding a new range in the cluster of past. Yes. Yes.

Dry as shout. "That is . . . *My* name." Mr. Purity's wild thoughts shudder, a boat pitched by mistake. Blinking in confusion, tongue wrestling with the bends and edges of his question marks.

A rush of "Fuck!" as the contour of defeat spoils BV's features.

"*Your* name?" Suzie's hand, no threat, not dodging the atomic PRESTO, grips his hand. Her galaxy of need flashing, her eyes cross his moat of impossible belong, alter wrong.

.9 out. Barrel maw leveled, tension and gravity to displace. Holotips ready to plunge into the clock and paint with roiling prestidigitation. Chrome .9 bristling, its colors thawed. Siren of blood ready to blast or spray. Mouth of flashing fangs, "Wutz dis shit? Don't play like dis."

Mr. Purity's metal hand preys on BV's wild. Sense changes size.

The pimp stares at his empty hand, its gate of intent closed. He's blinks. "Dis ain't wut we do. Remember?"

"I do as I please."

Half a "since when?" lights up BurroughsV expression.

Suzie shakes her head. Wants to scream, what is this?

It rained the night he came here. Afflicted by the blindness of heartbreak he tried to hide.

Failed.

The Other came. Raw. Its hunger a shark. It slashed and tore. Lapped his blood like a dog at its bowl. Bolted when it heard the sirens. Never came back.

Left him there.

His blood flowed, wax from a dying candle. Isolated. The weight of the dead stones unspooling around him. Got cold. Bitter cold. His breath came to a crossing where it could not tread.

Salt tears in his eyes.

Rained the night he died. Rained on John Armstrong's tombstone. Right there, not twenty feet away. Rained as he died.

"Iceberg told me you been here doin' this since he was comin' up wit Collie. We always played square wit ya. Can't be doin' dis shit ta me."

"You? Money cannot buy you anything. Look around. The victim has no say in Death's yard."

Spinning. Gonna run.

Deadfall.

A lump at Mr. Purity's feet.

"You are my . . . descendant. I think that's right. I am a Tillery. Two hundred years ago I was."

Her eyes are wider than her, what?

"I was sent away and cut off. Disowned. I wound up here. Died right there. That cross did not aid me when the fragile thread of my days ended."

"You live here?"

"Below."

"How can someone live two hundred years?"

"Live? I am not alive as you know it. The thing that took my life made me into this. I am an eater of the dead."

"Vampire?"

"No. I know nothing of them, or if they exist. I died and rose to eat dead flesh. A ghoul."

Eyes screaming wide. "Eat me?"

"No."

"I can give you another existence."

"Like you?"

"Yes."

"Does it hurt? Death?"

"Yes."

"And after?"

"As above, so below."

"Pain."

"Follows us."

"Into death?"

"The other spaces ... Where you walk you bring thought and memory. The deeps of pain roam where you roam. You have been alone in the world; here I will try to comfort you. If are you ready?"

A rush of circles. Faces—dreadful full-force, hands stealing, no exorcisms. All that far, the wall of sin—and shame, and you can't come back. Where was spare? You can't come back. Tender? Sift. Mercy? Mending mute, hollow, no halo—maybe dead. Sift. Iron and no air. Hold the cup of ghosts. Sift. Come up empty. Sift. Vie as rain and murder laugh. Dig and all you gather is hell. Nods a quiet yes, slowly. OK.

John Samuel Tillery's metal hand scoops up the pimp's body. "You will find our table below."

"And him?" Nodding at the body her ancestor is carrying.

"Le festin de l'araignée."

She'll eat the villain's heart. Eat his brain. She'll peel the malice right off his fingers. There are other things she will not touch. Not ever again.

With love and respect to Gil Scott-Heron &
SRV, crying & blazin' on the box . . .

Herding Fire: A Murder Mystery

This book is a tomb. I wonder how I got here . . . Sky / a dare from the lips of trees . . . Did I follow some pattern—plunge into the fashion of some drummer . . . Did it hunt me, forcing me to turn and turn and come—

Here?

Was it her?

Did I dance for her fingers stained in ink?

I did (after Livia and Brandi . . . and Nova . . .

and the others) . . .

Often.

Every time her eyes allowed me.

If I could hear her laugh I'd know. If I could look in the hot tar flowers of her eyes . . .

(Naked on her balcony. Again. Again. Not pausing for tragedy her mouth gallops.) "The weight of the moonlight in the dark sky . . . It's your soul. Sin like you mean it."

"Alanna . . . Please."

(There's a decision in her slender mouth.) "It's your soul."

But all I have left of her is the sound of her in the leaves
and the dusk of the spider's voice . . .

I have a pen and a hand . . . and the emphasis of this ghost—
Maybe I can interpret . . .

She was a fairy tale with legs and nipples. She was blonde.

We met at a party, a lowbrow gala of inner self covered in bias. She held her drink with both hands . . . Didn't run or offer a pronto ciao when I laughed . . . Her tongue left the groove of middle age. She confessed. Showed me a fishbowl of ambition and consequence . . .

Her eyes. Her shoulder—the pale curve of the road . . .

Spread her legs and showed me the velvet furnace . . . My eyes were
kissed by the breath of Bethlehem—paradise skin
    —lunar kisses, flesh on fire with curls to soothe the heat
    —I, tenant and trophy, give cure in the gestures of a tongue . . .
    I fed it hunger . . .
    She smiled as if I were both wine and a camera . . .
    After I showed her moonlight I smoked what I smoked—
    A dozen times? More. I'm certain of it . . . 30? Each soft and wild as
magic . . .

    But not the last. (I smoked what I smoked after. She stood on the
balcony, naked in the rain. Beautiful—some bird or wire not for sale,
and cold in the rain.) That last, her limbs said end of the line . . .
    Even in the rain, naked, she was a flame.
    Her laugh was everything . . .

This book is a tomb. I write nothing, no explanation, on its cover.
I sit with tea and cold hands. I smoke what I smoke.
The coils dance like she did.
I am an owl that cannot find the century of heights
    —not inside
    —not over there
    —not down
I look across my desk at the blue bottle. In it the wind no soil can
claim sings to the flame of the graveyard candle . . .
    Then it stops
    and in the scrawl of fog that cannot climb the treaty of the stars
or mine the scent-stripes of
    vertigo
    she laughs,
    "It's your soul."
    There's a tree at the crossroads. A dead tree. Not a single leaf on
it. Only a noose. The noose that waits for me—
    Even her eyes could not cure me.
    But she tried . . .
    This narration of pain continues

After Richard Misiano-Genovese *Black Studio*
#58 & #60 (series) (1987–1988)

The Russ Meyer Triptych

The Director's Cut

Auntie Lana's Gentlemen's Club & Grill) (over-size card table in the back room. table is missing a leg and held up by a pile of Tijuana Bibles and old books tainted by the monkey business of Fuller Brush men, Lenin and puppets and war) (no one has touched the deck of Swedish EROS playing cards) (tossed in one after the next, there's a pile of rejected screenplays burning in the fireplace)

Franco: (heated) <u>Sickness.</u> That's a bigass ha.

Argento: (without looking at Meyer) Screw you, Russ.

Marquis de Sade: (sitting behind an overflowing glass ashtray) Anyone going out for smokes?

Argento: Sexploitation. It's fast and it's cheap and we're heroes for coming in under budget.

Meyer: Dario's kind of gals, or my abundant ladies?

The Poe Eddie (yawns)

Meyer: (pointing at The Poe Eddie) Mr. Gloom here just doesn't get it. Humongous, Boob-dingnagian, the American dream! This is about cash and you get cash from cocktails not tea-cups.

The kids love zombies and guys are nothing but horndogs, they like boobs--big ones. Mash it

109

all up in an action-packed send-up and the cash flows. It's all about the babes.

Carpenter: Hawks, baby, that's it. I agree with Russ on the action, bang-bang shoot 'em up rollercoaster. Hard and fast with a Hawksian woman. Smart women are sexy--Can't beat 'em.

Meyer: They are but . . . Try this. Tarantino puts Fulci and Hitchcock in a blender and does Shaft, but he's a she and the thing is bizzaro meets comic books. She could be a superhero. Lot of money in superheroes. There's even a ton of superhero porn films raking it in. That damn Batman-porno flick is a hit and they just cashed in on Iron Man.

Take something like My Super Ex-Girlfriend. End of a bad romance her ex-husband is a super villain and he's taken up with her arch enemy, she's skinny and she's younger too. So she's super-pissed off he ditched her for a thin, younger woman. We get one of these new bra-busters like Gabriella Michaels or Cierra to star.

Carpenter: They're kind of young. If her enemy is a young woman, we need a mature babe say, Penny Porsche or Summer Sinn.

Meyer: Right-right. Too bad Steph--Pandora Peaks--retired. Lovely lady, brains too. OK, we get a mature gal, Penny's a great choice, and Sasha Grey can be her enemy, I think she's like 22 or something. Toss in some kinky aliens and set in on Mars. Call it Cat Fight on Mars. Sasha can be all red or green with yellow spots or something.

Wait a sec. How come no one invited Rodriguez to the game? (looks at John Carpenter) He

knows superheroes and grindhouse. Mars too.
Ain't no fool when it comes to cavorting pussy
either.

(Carpenter shrugs)

Argento: Mars? Nah. Let's put some drama and
philosophy in it. Maybe some Sartre?

Franco: Sartre and strippers? (shakes his
head. smiles) Bet Eddie would go for some goth
strippers ponderin' all weak and weary in some
existential hell. We could call her Raven, or
the Domino Spider. You know, some pale Jane
who's the curator for ashes and broken wings.
Bet we could get some of those Suicide Girls
to show us their webbing pretty cheap.

The Poe Eddie (flips Franco the bird)

Franco: That your little twitch of the death
nerve, Ed? Ain't no ladies gonna want to play
genital combat unless you sin like you mean
it. And that's half-hearted at best. (returns
the bird with both hands)

Romero: Can the shit, Goreslayer. We'll do SS
zombies in g-strings. And your Domino Spider
girl, make her a tattoo-covered superhero. She
chomps on cigars and swing swords and tells
lots of crappy jokes. Guess she's there to
free her sister who was sold to the SS zombies
as a sex slave. When she gets to the slave
camp we can have her free her sister and her
ex-partner Rain and their superhero squad the
Coffin Girls who are being held in iron maid-
ens--

Baba Yaga: Mainsteam.

Romero: We'll have a whole team; Mondo Letric,
Coco Krusher, the Double-D Destroyer, Kitty
BAM-boob the Halloween Cavewoman, Jigglewatt--

Meyer: I know the perfect bra-buster to play Jigglewatt--Angel Atomic is this stripper I--

Carpenter: That's not bad really. Call him WhamBAM and make him the leader of the Buttheads who are from Uranus, all girls are from Texas and we make it like The Legion of Superheroes, but only ladies. We'll need 20 or 30 of them. Fluffgirl, The Strawberry Birthmark, Co-Edie, The Bargain, The Rogue Tamer . . . Poontani, Bump & Grind the Marvels Twins, Girlie . . . Leather Lady.

Baba Yaga: Jeez, Johnny, you been talkin' to your pal, Winckler again?

Romero: I know him. He's a good guy.

Meyer: You go that route, John, you need some villainesses that pack deadly (hands out in front of his chest like he's holding watermelons) <u>weapons.</u> All the super girls have naturals, but the team of bad girls is called The Implants. We'll have The MILF, Mrs. Majestic, Massive, Bodzilla, Deemoania--

Carpenter: The Smotherer, Dysfucktional--

Meyer: Can I get a <u>BOING?</u>

Baga Yaga: Hey hey we're the Implants (loud long wolf whistle) We're mad, bad, and discumboobulated . . . And we monkey around.

Meyer (snorts a laughs)

Romero: The Coyote--

Carpenter: Verotica Vamp, Tata, Bazoom, and they're lead by Suzie Simone St. Claire who now calls herself, Dr. Missconduct. Before she got implants she was a beauty school dropout. Anyone know Annie Sprinkle? (looks at Russ) Maybe we could get her to play the part--

Meyer: (shakes his head no) We need one called Triple F in the group. (grinning) One call to my pals at Scoreland I can plug us right in.

Baba Yaga: You know, if you let me take them for a spin and stroll on the casting couch I might--

Franco: Just keep it simple and cheap. Tits and ass. (sticks out his tongue at Meyer) Superheroes cost too damn much.

Marquis de Sade: Is anyone going out for smokes?

Argento: Seriously. Sartre. Kids these days are into Existentialism and go batshit for zombies, so we hit them with both barrels.

(Champion Jack Dupree playin' "Pig Foot and a Bottle of Beer" on the jukebox)

Franco: No and nope.

Meyer: (laughs) Both barrels. Put Penny in it, there's your both barrels. I don't see Pirandello or Beckett as a good framework for a T & A film, Dario. Might fly in Paree, but I want the kid who drives a tractor in Iowa to want to kill to see this. You put a pair of big guns and a tight bush in his face and his butt's in the seat and he'll buy the DVD.

Argento: (shrugs) Something with Pinhead, or Freddie, then?

Carpenter: Too expensive to license. Damn suits will be bitching and moaning about overhead.

Argento: True. Maybe a teen witch movie? Bell, Book, and Boobs. There'd be two schools for young witches in training. One's all the pretty witches--hotties, maybe all blondes with great tans. The other is the ugly ones. They're at war, kind of cheerleaders vs. the geek girls. The pretty ones are all evil as shit and the ugly ones, maybe not ugly ugly but plain, kind of mousey and thin, pale too, they're kindhearted and funny. And they're good girls--

Franco: No. Zombies and boobs. You got hot girls it sells.

Argento: Say it loud. (laughs) (bottle back) (waves bottle at the waitress on the roller-skates)

Romero: Thought it was about love?

The Poe Eddie (opens one eye)

Meyer: Yeah right and Se7en is cathartic porno.

Argento: You and boobs.

Meyer: I didn't see a tit.

Baba Yaga: SS surrealism. A comic book of crypts and living dolls. Lot of nipples in the camera. All the twats in heat. Lot of hairy bushes with a taste for evil.

Meyer: TITS. Plain enough? Let's call Marvel and see if we can do the SHE-HULK. Or maybe that Power Girl chic DC owns?

Franco (barks at the black velvet painting of dogs playing poker)

Argento (snickers)

Baba Yaga: Ooh-la-la.

Meyer: What's wrong with tits? Lots of exploding pink flamingos and tits--there's poetry in that . . . And money too.

Romero: OK, try this. She leaves the Devil for a ex-superhero garbage man. Betrayal and revenge.

(Buddy Guy playing "Mannish Boy" comes on the jukebox)

Marquis de Sade: (steals Baba Yaga's cigar as she flashes a nipple at him. takes a puff. exhales thick smoke) Nah, make it fun. Shoot a The Night of the Hunter thing. Just get Christian Bale to play Mitchem's part. He just got out of prison and is going to find the Golden Pussy his cellmate told him about. Sasha Grey can be Blondie, the Golden Pussy. Big on Grrrl Power these days, she's retired . . . (scratches chinny-chin-chin). Have the kids' boat float by a Caligari-fairground, shacks, nude sunbathers, Dr. Hosni Xavier's Fortress For Gifted Fuckers & Adult Giftshop, a slum, a wharf of dive bars--Oh shit-yeah, at the end of the dock is a brass stripper pole with a antique streetlamp on top and under it we have an animatronic duo with Cthulhu and Jacques Brel singing "Amsterdam." We can have a few graveyards along the way too and we'll fill them with zombies and lots of tits. Have couples bumpin' on all the tombstones. 3 or 4 Coop Devil Girls. (winks at Meyer)

Meyer (eyes wide with want. grins while nodding yes like a bobblehead on a logging road)

Marquis de Sade: Suckin' and lickin' the Devil's tail. Call it, The Night of Hunting Big 'Uns.

Forgot the best part. His knuckles read F U N H O U S E.

[lot of humorous stares around the table]

Argento: That's as good as anything else. But Bale has to kill the Golden Pussy. I'll do that part. Split screen. Top shot: knife slides between her lips. Bottom shot: hot poker slides in her pussy.

Meyer: Sasha? Thought you said big 'uns?

Marquis de Sade: You want big tits? (eyes his glass of whiskey)

Meyer: Yeah. Is there another kind?

Marquis de Sade: Guess that means no Sola Aoi? Too bad. America would like her talent. (laughs)

Meyer: You want her? Use her as a fluffer.

Marquis de Sade: (slaps the table) Deal. I'm starting to think signing on as the technical advisor for this was a good idea.

The Poe Eddie: What happened to erotic horror?

Marquis de Sade: She wears an unbuttoned SS uniform and blows all the Indonesian backers and you, that erotic enough for you? We'll even throw in some moonlight and she'll wear a nice pair of fashionably-reserved heels just for you.

The Poe Eddie: Might be if she shimmies some and booglarizes me right. (pretends to laugh)

Baba Yaga: And finally we hear from out little scream-writer. Or is it, Peanut Gallery? You pop over to my theatre of the absurd, Eddie and I'll show you Self and booglarize. Won't even make you dress up like a harlequin before the forbidden takes us. (winks)

Argento (shrinks in his chair. remembers a night in her shack, a night of mirrors and dada that was 50 years long.)

Franco: Fuck it. Deal the cards. We'll just reboot <u>The Lord of the Rings.</u> An orc prison with lots of hot little elf maidens in cages. (waves his bottle at the waitress on the rollerskates) 'nother 'round, Darlin'. Shooters too.

Meyer: Never saw it. Do orcs have big tits?

(everyone laughs)

(the Indonesian backers standing against the wall like dumbfounded wallflowers look at one another and wonder what they're all laughing at. all they wanted was these guys to shoot a sexy slapstick <u>The Marx Brothers Meet the Bride of Frankenstein</u> mashed to a softcore <u>Ilsa, She Wolf of the SS.</u> And bring it in on time and not go over budget)

(1st card is dealt. the Poe Eddie almost laughs, turns, looks at the new bartender, Anubis Loki. it's a joker. it's her deck. she smiles and licks her lips . . .)

Anubis Loki: Excuse me. (holding an empty glass out in front of her and gently shaking it side to side at the congregation) Time to think about rolling the credits, folks. Last call.

(after Andy Black's Necronomicon Book Two *and* Planet Terror *and Winckler's* The Double-D Avenger*)*

(select tracks by Champion Jack Dupree and Buddy Guy) (The Fugs "Boobs a Lot" was not used as a soundtrack for this)

Skin Flick sans Money Shot

for Kelly Young

[Rented Scoreland backlot. Closed set for softcore-superhero, horror comedy, <u>All My Ex-Superhero Girlfriends Are Nazi-Zombies from Mars Now, but That's OK Because I Turned Them into Zombie Slaves with a Special Vile Foam-less Beer I Brewed to Take Over the Whole Wide World</u>. Afternoon. Day 1 of shooting. Set looks like Tim Burton parked a Transylvanian trailer park on Mars.]

Jess Franco: You get the check?

John Carpenter: [Beaming.] Yep. Little extra too. Told them something came up and we got a <u>name</u> for the narrative voiceover.

Jess Franco: You're a foxy one. Who?

John Carpenter: Vinny Price.

The Poe Eddie: Shit you didn't--

John Carpenter: [Beaming.] Did. <u>Really did.</u> Got the Nightgaunt Express dropping him off tonight.

The Poe Eddie: Vinny, here? That's--Shit. I didn't bring my autograph book.

Russ Meyer: Price, cool. Loved that Vulnavia babe. Wouldn't have minded some couch time with her. Speaking of getting, I got Zippy to be the lenscrafter. Be here tomorrow.

Baba Yaga: That little-weasel hunchback piece-of-shit. Dipped his skin-boogie in my best deluxe. Ruined her.

Russ Meyer: Who cares, he's the best cinematographer there is. Boob-man, knows the angles I like.

Dario Argento: WAIT! CUT! Cut--<u>Idiots.</u> Russ said boobs [Hands in front of his chest like he's holding watermelons.], not ass. Backers put their money down for big assets not tiny-hinnies. And Ronny, the blade arcs, like so. [Waves his arm like Pete Townsend slashing his guitar.] This is a waltz, [Pirouettes. Almost trips over his cape.] not a basketball game. Amore. You love her. [Turns to Penny Porsche] And Penny, I've changed my mind about you wearing the eyepatch. It's too Elle Driver, dump it. I want more eyes, the story of the eye. I want to see the terror in The MILF's eyes. And that lipstick color is all wrong.

The Poe Eddie: No--it's the right shade. I want the black lipstick. It ties into my string-theory plotline. She symbolizes The Great Attractor.

Dario Argento: Christ! You think you're Lovecraft now? Quantum sci-fi backstories. This is a horror film. Ever heard of horror? Scary-ass shit. Hot babe in trouble in a chopping mall and there's this bad man-thing from the hells beneath the hells about to punish her for her sins. Add some tortureshow and blood get some demonically-manipulated lunatic to yell, "Let's play chainsaw!" . . . Well? Beginning to catch my drift here? Eeyore and the Cat In The Hat are not currently in vogue with horror fans. And if I see another mention of event horizons or Hawking radiation in my film my heart will tell you some tales.

Marquis de Sade: Hellfire and tits! I said old copies of Penthouse, not Omni. I'm looking for skin. Jeez. Anybody seen that fluffer I sent out for smokes? Romero, you got her cell number? Send a dumb-blonde ex-bunny out to do a simple task.

Russ Meyer: Where the hell is the ice? We need to make sure these girls' nipples stay erect in this scene.

Marquis de Sade: I told her to stop and get me cigarettes while she was out.

Russ Meyer: Shit-for-brains, you slow down my production again and I'm gonna shove that ashtray up your ass. Which reminds me, I'm sick of Bates Motel ashtrays all over my set! Maybe Ellison and Bloch had Batesboy in the future but he ain't in my flicker. Dig?

Dario Argento: When am I getting the rewrites for page 66, Eddie? Jigglewatt needs to rehearse her lines. And de Sleazy, you wanna leave her alone for 5 fucking minutes so she can learn The Words. She already knows the positions. Got it?

The Poe Eddie: Yeah, pinhead, heard ya.

Dario Argento: You talking to me?

Penny Porsche: I disagree. In the Theatre of the Absurd, Esslin said, 'Works like Beckett's, which spring from the deepest strata of the mind and probe the darkest wells of--'

Marquis de Sade: That's what I'm talking about. Probing the <u>deepest</u> strata.

Penny Porsche: [Shaking her head, but smiling.] My, you do have a one track mind.

Marquis de Sade: Straight as a rail, Baby. Hard as steel and jackhammer steady. [Adjusts his package.] Not this very second mind you. But when needed, I know when to pump and push and when to pull out--If I have to . . . And I'd like to point out, my shelves are full of treatises on the human condition. Love to have you stop by and take a peek. And I have a copy of Esslin's <u>Brecht: The Man and His Work</u> you can borrow.

Penny Porsche: Do you have a copy of the Ionesco as well? Jess inferred you did.

Marquis de Sade: In fact, I do. [Leaning in, not looking at her eyes.] And if you're a good girl, [Smiling, darting tongue quick to caress his upper lip.] I have the <u>only</u> existing copy of Ionesco's unpublished <u>Counter Notes on Counter Notes</u> I might let you peruse. An evening discussing Camus' concept of the absurd, Esslin, and Ionesco being mislabeled an existentialist would be ravenously delightful. If you're interested? [Vulture eyes shining.] And did you ever see Warhol's pic of little old me? Andy gave me the original. Love to allow you to eyeball it. [Winks.] There are details you simply cannot grasp unless you see it in the flesh. [Winks again.]

Baba Yaga: [Sitting down and putting her leprous arm around Penny.] I showed both of those dogs what was for lunch. Taught 'em how to butter bread. Boys took it like white on rice, when I finished 'em they sho-nuff knew how to sup a skillet.

John Carpenter: [Turning down the Carl Stallings/Giorgio Moroder score that's blaring from the loudspeakers.] Love that horn part Carl dropped in this. Good call that, Dario. And Vinny Price rapping with Isaac Hayes is going to rule. Baba, have you heard back from Madeleine Peyroux? Her singing "Singin' in the Rain" in this scene is going to be a monster. At the end of it she goes into a Sprechgesang thing. That would be hot. Maybe get Laurie Anderson to do that passage of Eddie's text in the outro after Madeleine's Sprechgesang fades?

Dario Argento: Works for me.

John Carpenter: Vinny, could you come here for a minute please? I want to play you this section of the score. I'd like you to read your part slowly. When the thunder cracks, speed it up. Maybe double the speed until the guitar ramps up.

Jimmy Carl Black [the Indian of the cast]: Hey, any of these Holly-weirdo types mention getting paid to you, Ron? They might think the craft service table is pretty fucking extravagant-- veggies and donuts and I don't what the hell they think those things are, but they ain't fucking sandwiches, but I like cash, and beef too. Fuckin' god-damn veggies. [Shaking his head in disbelief.] Look like I need a diet?

Ron Jeremy: [Shrugs.] They paid me for the gig a month ago.

Jimmy Carl Black [the Indian of the cast]: [Ratass sons-a-bitches.]

George Romero: [Pulling Ron Jeremy aside.] It's Uncle Bernie's Fruit & Veggie Stand. You sell

vegetables now. After the civil unrest and re-
structuring you lost your superhero status,
they took back your costume and now you sell
veggies. Yes, you're Karl Marx, but Rasputin
got you shitcanned. And, in hopes of getting
your superpowers back, you're the cover opera-
tion for Dr. Missconduct and The Implants. When
you hand Jigglewatt the bag of tomatoes you go
into your secret password routine.

Ron Jeremy: Nice tits. Right?

George Romero: That's it. She comes back with,
if they like you they are. Then you nod OK and
drop the keycard to the secret hideout in the
bag.

Ron Jeremy [Walks away practicing his line.]

Jimmy Carl Black [the Indian of the cast]:
Hey, dude, let me get this right, I'm the In-
dian-redneck zombie king. And a mad scientist,
super-villain to boot. That it?

Jess Franco: Exactly.

Jimmy Carl Black [the Indian of the cast]: And
I keep all of my secret formulas to take over
the whole wide world in a Hello Kitty
[Fuck.][Shaking his head.] suitcase with my
super-villain getup? And how do you pronounce
my name again?

Jess Franco: Nec-cron-I'm-E-con.

Jimmy Carl Black [the Indian of the cast]:
Nec-ro, that like in, dead-shit?

Jess Franco: Yes.

Jimmy Carl Black [the Indian of the cast]:
That's my super-villain name and my secret
identity name is, Ahab Al-Hazard?

Jess Franco: No, Alhaz-<u>red</u> . . . No--Wait. Al-Hazard, yeah go with that. Good.

Jimmy Carl Black [the Indian of the cast]: [shaking his head] And I own a beer brewery?

Jess Franco: On Mars. Right.

Jimmy Carl Black [the Indian of the cast]: And all these here gals are ex-superhero wait-resses I turned into zombie-slaves with a bad batch of special, vile foamless beer I cooked up to rule the whole wide world?

Jess Franco: You bet'cha.

Jimmy Carl Black [the Indian of the cast]: [Shaking his head in disbelief.] Got it. Now for the important part of this mess you have me embroiled in, when is it <u>we get paid?</u>

Jess Franco: Two weeks.

Jimmy Carl Black [the Indian of the cast]: [scowling][<u>Shitass-twerp. Sons-a-bitches are</u> <u>pure fucking whacked-out of their skull-</u> <u>sleighs.</u>]

Jess Franco: [Turning to Russ Meyer.] Julie Strain said she'd step in and play the part.

Russ Meyer: I like her--hottie if ever there was one, but if I can't have Elvira for <u>my</u> Vampirella I'm going to go with the Domino Spider role. Call Joeena Juggs, she's plenty boob-dingnagian.

Jess Franco: Joeena? I thought you were only using her if you went with the witch role?

Russ Meyer: Look, the Domino Spider chomps on cigars and swings swords and tells lots of crappy jokes <u>and</u> she's a witch. She's got all them sigils that look like black cats tattooed around her nipples and when they get hard magic-shit happens. Baba told me Joeena's a Wiccan and that she has her own coven, so she sure knows spells and magic. Add knock-out tits and beautiful eyes, she's perfect for the role.

Jess Franco: Lot of sexy in your super-gals, Russ.

Russ Meyer: Fuck-yeah there is. DC rebooted the whole-shebang and changed all the sexy superdoll costumes, that's bullshit. Women are sexy and super women are super-sexy, so make them look like they are. Nuthin' wrong with a fantastic lookin' woman lookin' fantastic! DC can bite my ass with all that PC crap they're shoveling.

Dario Argento: Ah, excuse me, Mr. Jeremy, you're, Karl Marx. Perlman, our other, Ron, is Darwin. You see the guy with the mustache in the black velvet painting, the guy playing poker with Elvis and the dogs? You're him. And this is Mars, not a beach in some nudist colony. Yes, I do understand you're not used to having clothes on, but this scene is about A-R-T. Not skin.

Jess Franco: Baba-sweetie, be a doll and get the damn Suicide Girls away from the craft service table. This ain't Shallow Hal; I want my zombies to look hungry.

Russ Meyer: Got my rewrites, Eddie? I got actresses I'm paying good money and they're just standing around.

The Poe Eddie: [Crumpling up a paper airplane.] I'm working on them now. You think it's so easy to get the right words on paper, you try it. And--[Flips Russ the bird.] I trust, even you, Get. My. Drift.

Dario Argento: [To film consultant, Andy
Black, author of 5 volumes of NecronomicoN The
Journal of Horror and Erotic Cinema.] Andy,
you sure this is the first Nazis on Mars film?

Andy Black: Mars, yes. Nazi-superhero-zombies,
you're the first.

Zombie Suicide Girl: [Walks over to The Poe
Eddie's writing desk.] Hi. I'm Autumn. Autumn
Gallows, under this make-up I am. [Smiles
shyly.] I'm one of the zombies. Mr. Franco
hired a bunch of us, we're all Suicide Girls,
well, he hired us to be the zombies in the
movie.

The Poe Eddie: Hello . . . Edgar. [Unsettled
by the young woman's nakedness he fumbles with
some pages of the script. Blushes.] That's me.
The screenwriter.

Zombie Suicide Girl Autumn Gallows: [Bigger
smile.] I know. I've been watching you. Looking . . . Kind of.

The Poe Eddie: [Drops his raven-feather
quill.] Oh.

Zombie Suicide Girl Autumn Gallows: So . . .
Yeah . . . Couldn't help it. [Blushes.] Sorry
. . . I write. Mostly, poetry; autumn and
ashes, sometimes revenants. Blank verse about
crones full of occultations, werewolves too.
Love werewolves. Maybe it's the moon and how
it alters the current of our inner tides.
[Fidgeting.] Had a few things published . . .
[Toeing the floor.] And I, I like writers.
Love creative minds. So I like guys that are
geeky and dark; torn poet types. And I love
horror too, I'm more a lit girl, but I do like
film, some, the good ones, atmosphere and less
gory chills, like that. Good ones give me the

shivers. <u>All over.</u> And I was wondering if,
when this is over I could buy you a drink?
[Hands Eddie an 8x10 color glossy.] See, I
clean up good. I hope?

The Poe Eddie: [<u>Do, yes. Nice. Lovely.</u>][Folds
his hands so they don't shake. Presses them
tight to his abdomen. Stares at the photo.]
Well, I certainly--

Zombie Suicide Girl Autumn Gallows: I'm not
a weirdo or anything. I mean I love getting
my freak on--when I feel something for the
right guy, but I'm nice. I am. Really. So,
maybe . . .

The Poe Eddie: [Eyeing her erect nipples.]
Sure. Love to.

Zombie Suicide Girl Autumn Gallows: Great. I
mean thanks. OK. [Beaming.] By the way, I've
read all your work. Love it. Really do. You'll
see--I even have graphic novels of some of
your tales. <u>Nevermore: A Graphic Adaptation</u> is
great. Mine's autographed, not by you, of
course. Love it if you'd sign mine . . .
Sorry. Got to get back. I'll be back when I
can. [Turns, walks away. Stops comes back.]
Autumn Gallows is my stage name. Real name's
Leena Lyons. Bye.

The Poe Eddie: [Looks across the set for Russ
Meyer. Considers asking him about the dating
customs of modern-day women?] He'd know.

Jess Franco: More shaking! Get those things
jiggling girls!

Russ Meyer: Easy on the talent, Jess. Them's
ladies, not cretinous yahoos.

# # #

[Rented Scoreland backlot. Closed set for softcore-superhero, horror comedy, All My Ex-Superhero Girlfriends Are Nazi-Zombies from Mars Now, But That's OK Because I Turned Them into Zombie Slaves with a Special Vile Foamless Beer I Brewed to Take Over the Whole Wide World. Afternoon. The 7th day. Midnight looming.]

Jess Franco: This place feels like 12 Angry Men or Lifeboat. Packed too tight . . . Glad we're using rubber knives and swords.

Russ Meyer: [Looking at Penny Porsche.] She's packed alright.

Jess Franco: Not her! My set. This is not some infernal Joss Whedon flick. I hear anyone yell assemble in here I'm going to cap 'em.

John Carpenter: Jess, Jess, relax, you're scaring the ladies. They're not used to all this blood and gore and your vitriol only heightens their unease.

Jess Franco: Fuck, Johnny, it's passion. They know about fucking right? Well, this is simply another form of passion.

Russ Meyer: Passion. There's only one kind of passion and that's money in the bank so you can afford to spent time at home in bed with a babe like Penny. So if you wouldn't mind, I'd like this take in the can so I can hit the fucking craft service table before the Suicide Girls eat the last fucking donut.

Dario Argento: Penny, could you please aim the high-tech thingy a little higher? I want all the graffiti in the beam. And Double-D Destroyer, sorry I keep forgetting your name, read the riddle it spells out a little slower.

Russ Meyer: Jeez, Dario, get her ass in the shot when she's bending over with the light-reader thing. Zippy, I want to see ass here.

The Poe Eddie: [To Baba Yaga.] Why does Franco keep thrusting his poisonous waves at me?

Baba Yaga: Got a tiny dick--skinny as a pencil too, takes his inept out on everyone. Don't sweat it. Assholes are assholes 24/7. My therapist says they can't help it.

The Poe Eddie: [Shrugs.] Perhaps, but still, I'd like to see him taste the dull tides and open fanes of the gaping grave.

Baba Yaga: Get in the damn line, sonny.

Jimmy Carl Black [the Indian of the cast]: Eddie, hey, you got a Jackson I can borrow till Wednesday? I'm sick of the health-shit on the craft service table and wanna pop across the street to Taco Burger for something that had hooves on it.

The Poe Eddie: Sorry, the only denomination I'm currently in possession of is a ten-spot. That cover you?

Jimmy Carl Black [the Indian of the cast]: [Sighs. Shrugs.] Have too. Just skip the Mack Daddy Jalapeno Fries I guess.

Russ Meyer: That's it ladies. <u>Slow</u> . . . Take your time getting those costumes on. More tits, less towels. Yeah. Bending over--Good! Like <u>that.</u> Bodzilla, slap Triple F's ass with your towel a couple of times. Good. Again . . . Smotherer be a doll and play-fight around with Dysfucktional, yer old pals and have the hots for each other . . . Yeah, like that.

Baba Yaga: I'll never understand why you didn't cast twins for those parts, Russ.

Russ Meyer: Hell, look at 'em. Any one of those ladies is more than any man can handle. Scoring twins is just some greedy-ass fantasy assholes who are scared-shitless they can't satisfy a woman have, so they need a 3rd party involved to come in and bat clean-up. Real men want one good woman. 'Nuff said.

Baba Yaga: Ain't lived, Russ. Plain as that. And let me clue you in, triplets is better yet.

Russ Mayer: You truly are a sick bitch, Baba.

Baba Yaga: And damn proud of it.

Argento: Did you get the lens, Zippy?

Zippy: Red as an evening of redness in the West. You wanted Martian, Martian you're sure as shitting getting.

Dario Argento: Thank you, Uncle Martin.

Jess Franco: Where the hell is the Indian?

The Poe Eddie: I slipped him a few bucks to tide him over and he stepped across the street for some, as he termed it, <u>real</u> grub.

Jess Franco: Well, fuck me sideways.

Baba Yaga: Did that a couple of times. Never happen again.

Jess Franco: Stupid son-of-a-bitch [Paces.] . . . I'm never working with another one of these rock and rollers again, John . . . Shit. Hey! People! People! Everybody take an hour and grab some dinner. We'll shoot the zombie cemetery scene when we get back. 1am. <u>Sharp.</u>

# # #

[Rented Scoreland backlot. Closed set for softcore-superhero, horror comedy, <u>All My Ex-</u>

Superhero Girlfriends Are Nazi-Zombies from
Mars Now, but That's OK Because I Turned Them
into Zombie Slaves with a Special Vile Foam-
less Beer I Brewed to Take Over the Whole Wide
World. Afternoon. Day 13 of shooting. Set
looks like Tim Burton parked a Transylvanian
trailer park on Mars after it was remodeled by
a SMASH!-**TH'RRAKK!!!**
CLANGKLANGklack!~Nghhh[shit!]/aarr**RRIP**tp/smatt
-ploooooop&wup-wup/poommh*stomp--KRAKK-
OOOOOoF-crAKK~kooopth! !! STKRRakT~**CRUNCH!** superhero mêlée.]

Russ Meyer: That's a wrap, folks! Great work.

[The Indonesian backers standing against the
wall like dumbfounded wallflowers burst into a
round of applause. One wipes his brow and dials his mom to tell her the film came in on
schedule. And under budget. Nods, yes--yes,
when she tells him to quickly greenlight Vam-
pireville Gangsterama, Astrovamp Gore-Dancer
From Women's Prison Planet M vs. Princess Can-
nibal-Witch, and Nazi Body Snatchers at the
Gates of Roswell, and to be sure they understand no CGI and no 3D. Dr. Haji-Mohammed Mon-
katha steps forward and flashes several tie-
dye "Be Grateful Not Dead" condoms and his AMX
Black at Sasha Grey. She looks at him like he
is an orc with three heads. Considers flipping
him the bird.]

[Marquis de Sade is already halfway out the
door with Penny Porsche, Baba Yaga, and Dumb-
blonde ex-Bunny, the fluffer, and a half a
case of absinthe.]

Marquis de Sade: Hope you ladies won't mind if
we stop off quick-like to grab some smokes.

Penny Porsche: I hope you go easy on the
death-sticks, I don't like smoking.

Marquis de Sade: It's my last vice, but for you, Dear Penny, I'll most certainly give it every effort.

George Romero: That was a hoot, Johnny, we'll have to do lunch and talk about doing another, but let's skip Eddie's pen. Boy's a card-carrying weirdo. Tell you the truth; I don't think he really understands what horror is these days.

John Carpenter: Hard for some of the old school guys to fathom the modern psyche. And cut him a bit of slack. All that booze, I'm thinking it slowed him down a little. Maybe his boat wasn't docked when the Zeitgeist rolled in?

George Romero: I've been thinking about using this Tom Ligotti guy. I heard he's damn good and Lynch told me he's doing screenplays now.

John Carpenter: Cool. I've been mulling over a foreign setting, some old town, Caligari sets in Quay-land thing--want to try some CGI fog too. Was thinking maybe have an inmate from a nuthouse for the criminally insane escape and go frolicking around the town, knife in tow. Want him to think he's a werewolf.

George Romero: Sounds like fun. Call me tomor-row night.

John Carpenter: I will. Been meaning to ask you, is it true Lynch is doing a Kafka-thing next?

George Romero: No, but Cronenberg and Viggo are doing "A Report to an Academy" next.

John Carpenter: You've got to be shitting me. What happened to <u>Sanatorium under the Sign of the Hourglass?</u>

George Romero: Backers pulled out.

John Carpenter: [Shaking his head.] Hollywood fucks everyone.

The Poe Eddie [Not noticing the film has wrapped he's deep into the final draft of his reply to H. P. L.'s 37 page letter--Dear H.P., I've recently had the opportunity to finish Blood Meridian, or the Evening Redness in the West and found it to be a striking work. For sheer levels of depravity--][Stops. Looks up to see Zombie Suicide Girl Autumn Gallows rushing over. Drops his raven-feather quill. Smiles. Blushes. His hands start quivering.]

Jess Franco: Was fun you guys. See you Tuesday night for the game?

George Romero: Yep. Just bring cash this time.

John Carpenter: Yeah. A lot of it.

Zippy: [Hand-in-hand with Triple F and the Double-D Destroyer. Smiling.] Both of you hotties are over 6 foot. [Shivers.] Love tall babes! Legs.

Triple F: [Bending down to rub her boobs on the top of Zip's head] A few other oversize things too, Honey.

Zippy: Ooh yeaaaaaaaaaaaah! [Triple F and the Double-D Destroyer, holding his hands like they would a small child, lift him up and start swinging him.] Wheeeeeeeeeee!

Andy Black: Excuse me, Mr. Price, my name is Andy Black. I've written five volumes of criticism on transgressive cinema. I'm consulting on this film. Do you have time for an interview? I'd like to get your opinions on the state of 21st century horror film. Have you by chance seen A Serbian Film or SATAN'S PSYCHO-

GORE~ROTIC STRIPPERS Meet The Big Boobs Astro-Zombies of Eerie Swamp?

Vinny Price: Sorry. I'm on my way to dinner with Ron and Jimmy Black. If you care to call my office during the week we could arrange a mutually convenient time. [Hands Andy Black his card.]

[Anubis Loki hands Meyer the craft service bill.]

Russ Meyer: [Eyes telescoping.] Oh . . . That much? Um, you take checks?

Anubis Loki: Signed in blood and notarized, I might. But I prefer Dollar Eagles or your soul . . . If there are no liens on it.

The Mothers of Invention, *Uncle Meat* and "Uncle Bernie's Farm," Frank Zappa, *200 Motels*, "Transylvania Boogie," and "San Ber'dino," and Madeleine Peyroux, "You Can't Do Me."

No Laurie Anderson was playing during this, but she was on my mind from time to time.

When There's a Riot Goin' On...

for Russ Meyer

[Alberg's NEON. Opening night <u>All My Ex-Superhero Girlfriends Are Nazi-Zombies from Mars Now, but That's OK Because I Turned Them into Zombie Slaves with a Special Vile Foam-less Beer I Brewed to Take Over the Whole Wide World.</u> Lights. Digital and disposable and cell phone cameras. Limos. Celebrities. Screaming fans made up like Martian zombies and superheroes from the film which they've seen leaked, pre-release stills for online. Inside the restored grindhouse.][Crosby, Stills, Nash, & Waits, featuring Brian Eno & Frank Zappa, w/ the E Street Band & Tower of Power horns as their backing band on stage pre-show finishing their often-sprightly rendition of the 32:23 "Bob Dylan's 115th Reverie of Proud Mary's Rite of Spring." Zappa is quite pissed as he's not allowed to conduct. That job has been given to Eno who is conducting the intricate performance by placing computer-generated images of random cards from his <u>Oblique Strategies</u> deck upon the movie screen. Eno's self-designed computer program also sends images from movie history to the screen to accompany the cards. The current card on the screen says, TRY FAKING IT!, the image paired with it is of Ed Wood.]

Baba Yaga: Could be a god-damn hit, Russ.

Russ Meyer: Your forked tongue straight to God's ear and the bank.

The Poe Eddie: [With a beaming Zombie ex-Suicide Girl Autumn Gallows on his arm. Zombie ex-Suicide Girl Autumn Gallows keeps thrusting her new 2-carat engagement ring in front of cameras as she yells yes, it's true. See.] Is it true, Russ, you've included the screenplay and photographs of my notes on the special features 4th disc of the unrated DVD?

Russ Meyer: Sure did. All of your doodling too. And your doodling appears in the booklet too. Needed something to fill 72 pages. [Winks. Doesn't tell him it's inserted after the advertisements for his DVDs.]

Marquis de Sade: [His new wife, Penny Porsche-de Sade, who's flashing his new book, On the Paradisal Heights of The Orgasm Circus: Existentialism Is for Uptight Victorians and Dummies to cameramen, on his arm. Waves.] Hi! Hello. [Beaming.] Hi. [Throwing kisses to the fans in the bleachers.] Bonjour! Love every one of you!

Jimmy Carl Black [the Indian of the cast]: So it's like this, Dario. I showed up for your little Holly-weird shindig, came all the way from California--expenses involved in that, dig? Now when do we get paid?

Network interviewer: Is it true, Mr. Meyer, John Carpenter and George Romero won't be attending tonight's premiere?

Russ Meyer: Yeah. They're on location in Eastern Europe shooting, On a Night of Blood and Moon the Snockwoman Cometh to Holstenwall.

Network interviewer: Is that a werewolf picture?

Russ Meyer: Ain't Forrest Gump.

Jess Franco: Do you believe this? He's here. I mean, there he is, just sitting there. Like it's no big deal. Damn!

Dario Argento: Not sure if it's cool or creepy. Maybe when the shock wears off?

Craig Mullins, reporter from Unfilmable.com: Are you guys as blown away as I am? Him? Here for this? That's big.

Dario Argento: Big? More like huge. [Shaking his head in utter disbelief.] Amazing.

Craig Mullins, reporter from Unfilmable.com: I wonder if I can get an interview.

Mario Bava: [Wine in hand. Waving to Russ Meyer from his box.] Russ! Russ! Up here! CALL ME about doing the sequel to Kill, Baby . . . Kill! [We'll call it, Kill, Uncaged-Unclad-Zombie-Babe . . . Kill!]

Hitchcock: [In his box, shouting to Bava.] Screw that! Russ and I are doing A Frenzy Of Psycho Zombie-Birds!

Mario Bava: Zombie birds? Who gives two-shits about naked birds, asshole? They want to see ass and nipples. Birds. Fucking idiot.

Jess Franco: Can't believe it? He's here. Just sitting there. Damn!

Dario Argento: Yeah.

Craig Mullins, reporter from Unfilmable.com: This is big.

Dario Argento: More like huge. [Still shaking his head in utter disbelief.] Amazing.

Craig Mullins, reporter from Unfilmable.com: Should I approach him about an interview?

Jess Franco: He's never given one. You could make history. Ask him. Ask. Go on.

Craig Mullins, reporter from Unfilmable.com: [Climbs a ladder to the roof. Waves.] Excuse me, Mr. Gojira, sir. Just want to say what a big fan I am.

Gojira: [Sitting in the back parking lot to watch the movie on the big screen monitor. Three dump trucks full of sweet buttered popcorn, extra sea salt.] Thanks . . . This flicker gonna be any good?

Craig Mullins, reporter from Unfilmable.com: I certainly hope so. I drove all the way from Oklahoma to see it.

Gojira: [Sitting in the back parking lot to watch the movie on the big screen monitor. Three dump trucks full of sweet buttered popcorn, extra sea salt.] [Nods.] Traveled a few leagues myself . . . This have any newts in it? I like newts. I don't care for ghosts, or any of that mysterioso stuff. You like newts?

Craig Mullins, reporter from Unfilmable.com: Yeah. They're ok.

Gojira: [Sitting in the back parking lot to watch the movie on the big screen monitor. Three dump trucks full of sweet buttered popcorn, extra sea salt.] [Smiles.] Good. They should have made newt movies. Atomic newts with big red spots. That ant movie was stupid. THEM, who cares? But newts, they're nice. [Smiles.] Newt populations worldwide are in danger due to pollution or destruction of their terrestrial habitats. The USA and the UK are taking steps to slow or stop their decline. I like that.

Craig Mullins, reporter from Unfilmable.com:
Interesting . . . Ah, I . . . It's good
they're trying to help newts . . . I wanted to
ask if you'd be kind enough to do an interview
for my website?

Gojira: [Sitting in the back parking lot to
watch the movie on the big screen monitor.
Three dump trucks full of sweet buttered popcorn, extra sea salt.] Well, I was on my way
to Cancun for a little R & R, but I might fit
you in after this is over . . . Not a long one
mind you.

The Phantom of the Opera: [Sharing his box
with Jack the Ripper, Juliette, Norman Bates,
and Dr. Caligari.] Anyone hear if this has
Tura or Kitten in it? That Kitten--WOW! Talk
about hotties! I'd walk through fire for that
Doll. [Begins reciting poetry by H.D.
Imagiste.]

> 'Whirl up, sea--
>
> Whirl your pointed pines.
>
> Splash your great pines
>
> On our rocks.
>
> Hurl your green over us--
>
> Cover us with your pools of fir.'

Jack, Juliette, Norman, and Caligari [Shake
their heads in unison.]

Sheri Moon Zombie: Did Russ get back to you?

Rob Zombie: Said he's tickled about me doing
the animated sequel to this, but he wants you
in it, staring. And the opening scene has to
be live action; black and white, you in bed
naked at least from the waist up, then the
tornado comes and drops you and the house down

the rabbit hole, then it changes, animation
and color kick in. I want to put a lot of
psychedelic, comic book effects, like Steranko
meets Ditko in Acidland, in it. Have things
splash and erupt.

Sheri Moon Zombie: I'm in a Russ Meyer's
film--Total skull! Me--Alice, Dorothy, and
Tura, rolled-up in one. I'm a triple threat--
Total skull! When are we doing this?

David Lynch: [His box has been converted into
a private coffee bar. Turning to Marilyn Monroe.]: Hey, Woody's here. Didn't know he went
in for things like this?

Marilyn Monroe: [Reassuringly patting his
knee.] Relax, Sweetie, he's just checking out
the competition. His new one, Zelig and the
Android Zombies from Space Station Kubrick
Bring Their Crimes and Misdemeanors to Broad-
way . . . begins preproduction in 3 weeks.

David Lynch: Maybe I should do one of these
things? Call it, If On A Winter's Night The
Unruly Rabbit-headed Zombie Streetwalkers of
Snootworld Hoof Along A Lost Highway . . .
Opens with Dr. Strange, Sisyphus, Batman, and
His Holiness, Maharishi Mahesh Yogi, sitting
at the base of a cotton candy mountain that
looks like a pyramid, meditating when the
queen of the zombies comes--

Marilyn Monroe: Can I be your zombie queen?

David Lynch: You bet. I, ah, I think I want a
Zappa soundtrack for this new one. Civilization, and industrial pollution--Inca Roads,
aliens. I remember him saying, kill ugly ra-
dio--there's a man with vision. Yeah.

Woody Allen: I was doing surrealist comedy
long before any of these assholes turned their

noses towards the sandbox. I could do naked zombies.

Gilda Sue Rosenstern, femme fatale comedienne of the Internet: Oy! Another art film? I get it, Woody. You're super smart. Way smarter than I am. You don't have to prove it on EVERY! DATE! . . . Plus, actually, they'd need Drambuie-coladas, shaken and strained into a chilled Bacos-rimmed cocktail glass with a Jägermeister drizzle, and a sprinkle of goat cheese if they really wanted to take over and assume leadership of an immigrant Zombie Slave World, especially if they are illegals who've been smuggled over the cosmic space-border to take all of our jobs. Everybody knows that.

Woody Allen: If I were to translate one of these . . . Well . . . Let's say a Zombie-Dylan, back from a naval skirmish with a drunken boat, sitting on his back porch in Woodstock. Elbows on the gentle of the railing, he's conjuring up elephants playing tambourines, got a dog lying in moonlight, chews on the Spear of Destiny, and Tweedle Dumb and Tweedle Dee are dissecting a pile of tarantulas. There are buckets of rain perched on 4¾ stiletto-heels everywhere in the yard, things like that. You'll be the Greek chorus. Fridge door opens; you step out and explain he's always trying to be quiet, he thinks it tastes better that way. Then you'll briefly account for the lack of bones, harmonicas, and guns in the yard . . . At the end you'll be seated at a bus stop, sitting there in a leopard-skin pill-box hat drinking a martini with an ocelot on your lap, and you'll say, every seat on the Ferris wheel is doomsday unless you're the new Darwin who's responsible for protecting all the mailboxes in Memphis from the Rainman.

Jack the Ripper is sitting there with you.
He's holding a tombstone that says, I've
dreamed, I've followed. I've struck. You shift
away from Jack, move over a bit, then a newspaper blows up into your lap. It covers the
ocelot. The headline reads WE HAVE NEVER BEEN.
You look down at the empty martini glass in
your hand, for a moment you're wondering how
it got empty, then as the sound of fire engine
sirens bluster in the distance you yawn.

Gilda Sue Rosenstern, femme-fatale comedienne
of the Internet: Am I naked in this?

Woody Allen: [Nods affirmatively.]

[Two Super-Stretch Hummer H2 limos pull up
carrying two dozen Suicide Girls. Ornately-
tattooed and goth-regaled, the young women who
were zombie extras in the movie rush out. On
the red carpet Black Orchid and Miss Kane con-
veniently Janet Jackson out of their corsets
for an eager Japanese camera crew.]

Baba Yaga: Meat platter's up in da haus. Hot.
And nasty--Yum-me.

Russ Meyer [Shakes his head.]

Anubis Loki: [Looking over concession stand
receipts that state in fine print at the bottom, by accepting this receipt you've agreed
your soul is bought. A delivery time will be
scheduled. The owner is not required to inform
you of the pick-up time.] Enjoy your popcorn.
[See you soon.]

Ives [Whose sweetie Tedd-E. scored tickets for
the premiere on WPLJ's We Got Yer Far Out &
Groovy Swag Marathon] I don't see why he

couldn't have cast young women. [Pointing at Penny Porsche-de Sade.] She's as old as my Mom . . . Men and this MILF craze? [Shakes her head.]

Tedd-E. [Who scored the tickets for the premiere on WPLJ's We Got Yer Far Out & Groovy Swag Marathon] Well, it's like this. Nice butt and boobs.

Ives [Whose sweetie Tedd-E scored tickets for the premiere on WPLJ's We Got Yer Far Out & Groovy Swag Marathon]: [Half-fake frown.] But they're not as nice as mine? <u>Are they?</u>

Tedd-E. [Who scored the tickets for the premiere on WPLJ's We Got Yer Far Out & Groovy Swag Marathon]: [Licking his lips.] No, Baby. No one's are! [Winks.]

Ives [Whose sweetie Tedd-E. scored tickets for the premiere on WPLJ's We Got Yer Far Out & Groovy Swag Marathon]: [Beaming.] For that, you get a special reward later.

Tedd-E. [Who scored the tickets for the premiere on WPLJ's We Got Yer Far Out & Groovy Swag Marathon]: [Beaming.] Yum-yum Train and some dainty nubbin'?

Ives [Whose sweetie Tedd-E. scored tickets for the premiere on WPLJ's We Got Yer Far Out & Groovy Swag Marathon]: [Leaning in. Breasts just touching his arm.] Nubbin' and <u>extra</u> chooglin' for your choo-choo.

Tedd-E. [Who scored the tickets for the premiere on WPLJ's We Got Yer Far Out & Groovy Swag Marathon]: Choo-choo. Choo-choo. Choo-choo. Chugga-cugga-<u>yum.</u>

Ives [Whose sweetie Tedd-E. scored tickets for
the premiere on WPLJ's We Got Yer Far Out &
Groovy Swag Marathon]: [Voice low and slow and
sexy.] Mmmmmm-lotsa chugga, bunch of ooga-ooga
too.

Baba Yaga: Gaga, ya-ya--oohlala--not bad--not
bad at all. Don't have a disco stick, Doll,
but my pestle will give you a ride on the wild
side. [Winks.] And bad, Chile, I wrote the
book on ra-ra. Oh-la-la too. Baba wants'ta put
some freaky in your rough. What do you say we
pen that oh so bad romance you mentioned? I've
got enough horror to pack your show.

Lady Gaga: [Cringing.] They're just songs. Oh,
you'll have to excuse me, there's Lou and Laurie. [Running more than walking.] Lou! Hi!
Lou!

Baba Yaga: Songs are meant to be sung, Cutie.
And I need to let my pipes howl while my fingers prowl, so you come back later . . . [Sees
Charlie Sheen.] Charlie, my, [Shivers.] what a
handsome stud; hear you like freak, so--

Russ Meyer: Anyone you won't ball, Baba?

Baba Yaga: Hot's hot and I'm full-on to trot.
You should try it, Russ.

Russ Meyer: Pass.

Dario Argento: [Replying to the ET interviewer.] Yes. It was to be something along
those lines. We were going to make a cinematic
statement on the existential imagination and
how it ties into the erotic, a deconstruction
of flesh and the illusions disguised in traditional beliefs, but zombies and superheroes
found their way into the palette and took us
in a different direction.

Jess Franco: That's right. With superheroes and zombies we can raise the money to back our next feature. We have in mind a trilogy, a thought-provoking work. <u>The Sentiments of A Wounded Inquisitor, A Dohicky Lunatic's Furnace of Tellitives, and Tits, Ass, and Broken Angels.</u> They will be framed as a series of noir exploitation films. So we are hoping for a hit with this feature.

Russ Meyer: Hi. Brandi, right? Our zombie fluffer. I have a part in my next film you'd slip right in. It's about a beautiful young princess in a far off land by the sea who finally finds love after having fallen into grey and bleak. Her name is Cassilda. It's all about life's illusions and what lies under the mask . . .

The Creature from the Black Lagoon: [In the lobby in a delivery truck-size fish tank with Pepe, his rubber ducky. Watching audience members made up like sparkly zombies enter the theater.] Zombie shit is trash. No universal qualities to it. Crime they're feeding this Z-grade guano to kids.

Rod Serling: Sight and sound, shadow, but there's no substance. Where's the storytelling?

The Creature from the Black Lagoon: [In the lobby in a delivery truck-size fish tank with Pepe, his rubber ducky.] That's exactly my point, Rod. What good is this shit?

Rod Serling: Not much. Hollywood might as well let Alan Smithee direct everything these days.

The Creature from the Black Lagoon: [In the
lobby in a delivery truck-size fish tank with
Pepe, his rubber ducky.] Or Ed Wood.

Rod Serling: You might have an idea there. If
you're not involved in a project right now we
might do something together.

The Creature from the Black Lagoon: [In the
lobby in a delivery truck-size fish tank with
Pepe, his rubber ducky.] You and me. Interesting. Have something in mind?

Rod Serling: I do. A film about Alan Smithee
shooting a feature where zombies take over the
Black Lagoon and you, like a Swamp Thing hero,
come back to save everyone. We'll make it a
statement about the consequences of poisoning
ecosystems for the sake of a cheap, fast-buck.

The Creature from the Black Lagoon: [In the
lobby in a delivery truck-size fish tank with
Pepe, his rubber ducky.] I like that. I'm the
star, right?

Rod Serling: [Nods yes.]

The Creature from the Black Lagoon: [In the
lobby in a delivery truck-size fish tank with
Pepe, his rubber ducky.] There is one thing. I
confess I'd like to see some boobs in this.
I'll give Meyer credit; he does like women
that look like women. Got to tell you, Julie
was a babe . . . Maybe in this, I walk off
into the sunset with a stacked blonde who
loves skinny dipping.

Rod Serling: I worked with Julie once, she was
a lovely lady.

Penny Porsche-de Sade: Yes, I have a book coming out too. It's an amply illustrated look at
the spiritual and artistic universe of the

clit. It's a book about awareness and shining. The clit is a nova. And my book celebrates its wonders. I'm no longer listening to the come hither of the stifling fictions and documents of existentialism and the absurd. Through the vehicle of love I have come to embrace joy and escape the nullification of freedom in a technological civilization and I want to share my discoveries with everyone. My Sweetie wrote the introduction. [Hugs de Sade.]

Baba Yaga: A nova? [Laughs.] Escape the nullification--what the fuck? Should have dedicated the book to me. It was my tongue showed her how the clit could expand her universe and lift the dryness from her soul. I saw the ARC, didn't even give me a thank you in the fucking acknowledgements. How's that fair, Russ? I mean, c'mon. Ungrateful cunt.

Russ Meyer: Get over it. I'm worried about how this changes our game. De Sleazy and Eddie are married and happy now. We may have to find new players.

Baba Yaga: Hitch wants in bad. And Ed Wood has made a few noises about sitting in.

Russ Meyer: Hitch, maybe? Not too keen on Wood, too greasy. That still leaves us short a writer.

Baba Yaga: Hammett? What about Lovecraft?

Russ Meyer: Howie? Fucking prude. Doubt he knows how to play. Can you imagine him sitting in the backroom of Lana's, the cigar smoke, the whiskey, and shit, those comments of yours that would make Tralala blush? [Shakes his head and smiles.] Hammett's a damn good story man, boy's got hard down, ain't shy either. I could sit across the table from him. I'm not

so sure about Hitchcock; his ego's as fat as
his ass. I saw Serling here; he might be a
good fit for the game? Boy's sharp!

Jess Franco: You talk to Ebert, Russ?

Russ Meyer: Yeah, five minutes ago. Closed
circuit is all set. He's got his feet up and a
bowl of chips, he's good to go. I don't know
what you're sweating about. Roger loves boobs
and half the idea for this is from that old
screenplay I told you about, and it was mostly
his ideas. We just punched up a few parts and
gave it a paint job. Relax; he's going to like
the film.

[Zombies, who had not been born when resonant
had sweet hands, gasp and cheer as they see
the boots of Ziggy Sawdust touch the Earth.
Some remember hope.]

Ziggy Sawdust: [Having grown bored with back
porch retirement Ziggy's come back down from
Mars to see what shakes the ground at street
level.] Clowns in The Apocalypse. [Shakes his
head.] The mirage of contribution and objec-
tivity. Still . . . [Looks around. Color. A
flurry of eyes trying not to forfeit to meaningless. Shouting hands.] Ravens . . . [Hands
stained with before.] Bittersweet ravens . . .
[Faces, painted and rubbed, stretched, running
from cain't.] The knife, bitter as a kick,
twists . . . It's all, still, a parade of
tears. [Beams himself back up.]

Stanley Kubrick: Sad . . . Torn and lost
scraps without a superhero. I should show them
a superhero. A real superhero. All of him . .
. Maybe a her? Yes, her. Indomitable spirit in
the lands of despair.

Bill Burroughs: Poor scraps, Stanley? . . .
Careening. The gaze of the torn city falls on
their plans drives them . . . Spinning
lemmings, sucking up postcards of survival.
Anything, any painting shoved on a telephone
pole, that's what shakes their bones . . .
Faster--Hurry. Things closing, I need some
before I break and fall of the track.
Careening. Careening. Feed me to the flame of
Now.

Stanley Kubrick: [To Bill Burroughs.] Splash.
Pour anything into the mold. No go ahead to
their work song . . . Nothing is okay under
those cardboard skullcaps.

Bill Burroughs: Why think, when fun begs for
marathon?

Baba Yaga: [Places her hand on Bill Burroughs
shoulder.] To the sheep of the New Church, the
chant of Apocalypse bays and you can't stop
it. Fuck, Bill, it doesn't even see you, the
moon doesn't see microbes, you know that. The
night-filled mountain we call Universe doesn't
know an atom from a memory and it goes on
without giving a fuck . . . They're lost and
cooking in this bowl, and they know it, some
do, so let Sisyphus beg for vitalism and sing
while he may.

Baron Saturday: Thor gets a movie. God-like
aliens, the Romans and the Greeks with their
titans. Where's my movie? They eat up skulls
and sex, and resurrection--I own all of that.
They fill these films with debauchery and
disorder, obscenities abound, they smoke,
drink. Who better than I, Maman? Who?

Maman Brigitte: They are mindless fucking
children, Dear. Just talk to one of these

shitbag directors. Show them who _is_ power, or
show them the grave's sweet blackness.

Stephen Hawking: I hope Edgar received my
latest calculations in time to incorporate
them.

The Phantom of the Opera: Zombies, shit.
Thoughtless sacks of puss merely waiting for
someone to shout, all fall down. Grandeur.
Classic. It's high time creature features
strike again! Lizzie. Lobster Men from Mars.
Dr. Tarr--Eddie knows his dreams, he should
cast them upon the screen. Reboot my story.
Passion and blood, and screams . . . That's
classic. I am forever. Universal themes that
consume hearts. Zombies are nothing, mere shit
that has yet to be flushed.

Gojira: [Sitting in the back parking lot to
watch the movie on the big screen monitor.
Three dump trucks full of sweet buttered popcorn, extra sea salt.] Craig, would you mind
handing me the garden hose. I'm getting kind
of thirsty. Sure hope they got my order right
and hooked this thing up to the diet Dr. Pepper. I don't know what kind of artificial
sweetener they use, but it's got a nice zing.
Good bubbles too. Damn, Coke gives me tummy
ache.

Juliette: [Feeble old men with lewd minds like
Grandfather's--showed him, my blade amply
enlightened his vice . . . Wet-palmed peepers,
imagining their grave-worm cocks throbbing in
their hands while sweet pink nipples scream
silently. They think my tongue will beg to
lick the tiny dream pressed within their stub
and make it breathe, set fire to my
voluptuousness with gluttonous eyes. Bloated
fools. Eyes listening to my spiked heels dance

as they think of roughing me. Biting me--Tame
and use me . . . Unzip my roars of driven with
crush and taunt. I'd show their ick my demon .
. . Hitchcock--Braschi reborn. Fat sleaze. He
should make me damn it. I'm hotter and fuck
better than any of these bloated old cunts. My
tits. My cunt. And I know blood; I let its
season bloom a hundred times. Know frenzy?] "I
am frenzy." [When frenzy kisses blood . . . I
have all their hearts in jars to prove it.
Perfect title too, A Toy For Juliette. Can't
get a more alluring title on a marquee than
that!] "Hitchcock." [I'll get him, filthy old
perv, I'll put a very nice bedroom with all
the trimmings at his disposal and he'll be
eating out of my hand.]

E. M. Cioran: [Stares at his ticket stub. B
Row 3 Seat 4. A vague sadness moves from
closed interiors and flourishes in his eyes.
Looks at the balcony. Sees an empty seat
between John Rechy and Jim Morrison.] Must I
sit on the heights again?

Hubert Selby Jr.: [Escorting Lydia Lunch.
Looks up at the balcony.] Looks like they've
sat us, again, with the usual suspects.

Lydia Lunch: [A sour smile.] Most would call
them sonofabitches and leave it at that. Shall
we, like good little beasts, go seethe?

Hubert Selby Jr.: [Nods yes.]Sonofabitches,
yes, in certain eyes--Guess the swoop of
jivewords upsets their weekend plans . . .
Tragic, gifted, sick with desire, maybe even
exciting, but . . . Might not be the catbird
seat, but we're outta the granite wind for a
few.

Black Orchid: [Arm in arm with Miss Kane.
4 other Suicide Girls, in tow, flit by.] Maybe

with this as an in, we can get parts in the Depp movie. They'll need a lot of borogoves.

Jess Franco: You know, Russ, we went and did it, pulled the damn thing off. And it looks like we're going to have a hit, but I still don't get it. This zombie craze. [Shakes head.]

Russ Meyer: Zombie strippers. Naked zombies. Zombie hookers. Unclad and uncut. Plato, Nietzsche, they had it--wanted it, needed it. Old as the cave, Jess. Tits and ass. They [Points at Jigglewatt.] got it and we want it.

Jess Franco: What about Wittgenstein and the gay community?

Russ Meyer: [Laughs.] He sure liked ass. Ass, tits, pussy, dicks, spank me or slow-hand love song romanticism, it's the same jones. Human desire is desire. This stripe or that, people are people, everybody wants some.

Triple F: [Dressed in her Triple F super-villainess costume.] Time to fly, Zip-Honey.

Zippy: Please. [Triple F and the Double-D Destroyer--she's dressed in her super-villainess costume too, holding his hands like they would a small child, lift him up and start swinging him.] Wheeeeeeeeeee!

A Fan From Portland, Oregon, Who Spent All The Family's Vacation Money To Attend The Premiere: This is going to be so groovy. And next year for our vacation we can go see, The Mysterious Radar Gals from Tarazed vs. the Aztec Mummy of Bonga.

The Wife Of The Fan From Portland, Oregon, Who Spent All The Family's Vacation Money To Attend The Premiere: Oh, I thought we were going

to save our money and go to Jellystone, Mike?
[Frowning.] I mean last year we saw, Baroness
Whatta View in The Menace From Amazon Planet
Temptation . . . And now this. Don't get me
wrong, I love all the KAWWHAM in these
MONDO~tronic movies too, but does it always
have to be deadly vixens with big boobs and
nipple ray-guns? What's wrong with a week by a
river, or going to see Big Swifty and the
other geysers? We could walk the wooded
trails, fish, make smores? The popcorn is
nice, but I miss smores.

A Fan From Portland, Oregon, Who Spent All The
Family's Vacation Money To Attend The Premiere: WOW! There's Jigglewatt, Lena. See, I
told you she looks just like you did when you
were 19. I'm going to get her autograph. Did I
tell you she starred in Ms. Libertine's
Haunted Frontier Daze and The Dark Mansion of
Sinister Love? Joe Bob Biggs called them must
see.

Russ Meyer: [Pointing to the Fan From Portland, Oregon, Who Spent All The Family's Vacation Money To Attend The Premiere.] See, Jess,
like I said, they all want some.

Jess Franco: Well, she is worth seeing. I remember her in And Men Shall Call Her . . .
BOOM! Loved the scene where the cannibal orgy
turns into a dinner party. The POV slow-mo
where she's licking the guy then she gets to
the head, and chomp!

Russ Meyer: Didn't see that one.

Jess Franco: You've got too. I'll bring my
copy of the DVD to the game next week for you
to borrow. There's a deleted scene in the bo-
nus features that will unwrap your turban.

Russ Meyer: Thanks. Let's get inside and blast this sucker off.

Zombie ex-Suicide Girl Autumn Gallows: Eddie My Sweet, do we have enough money to get some Rasinets and gummy worms? You know how they make me tinkle with merriment.

The Poe Eddie: [With a beaming Zombie ex-Suicide Girl Autumn Gallows on his arm.] For you, Dearest, enough for you to ring out with delight.

Zombie ex-Suicide Girl Autumn Gallows: Yay!

The Poe Eddie: [With a sweetly tinkling Zombie ex-Suicide Girl Autumn Gallows on his arm.] I so love your outpourings of rhyme.

Zombie ex-Suicide Girl Autumn Gallows: You just love to see my bosom palpitate. [Winks.]

The Poe Eddie: [Eyeing his fiancée's bosom.] Please, swell, My Turtle-dove.

Baba Yaga: Charlie-honey, I've got a few cases of Cristal and some refer back at the shack, and a few gal-pals comin' over for an After party. All we need is a hunk who can ride the freaky. Jigglewatt will be there. You should see her light up. [Humming the Brazilian Girls "Pussy" she slips her arm around his waist and herds him to her producer's box.] Don't you worry, you sit right here on Mama's lap. She's gonna show you shit you never dreamed of. [Fires up the chronic.]

Anubis Loki: [Smiling as the doors close, and lock, and the lights go down.] Pazuzu, it's time for my little off with their heads gala. And have Anubieio draw my bath. And tell that dim-witted fuckhead to get it hot this time. [Tepid bullshit.]

[Every seat in the theater turns into a demon and tightly clenches the audience member sitting in it. Anubis Loki jumps on stage and announces it's render unto time.]

CUT TO:

[HELL. Anubis Loki is sitting on her throne of bones, big bowl of buttered popcorn, lightly-salted, in her lap, and the show is about to start . . . A servant demon, a former genie known as Mr. X. Ray, pours her a swished not stirred, extra-dry, jalapeno-stuffed chili olive martini.]

Russ Meyer: [Tied to a slowly revolving spit above a boiling caldron, roiling with body parts, bats' wings, aeon seed and orphan root, an array of spiders, spicy meatballs, and various superhero capes and masks. Looks at Anubis Loki's ample chest.] I would love to cast you! Maybe we could talk about this? I have this script for A Hurricane Of Snake Demons--No need to audition, you're perfect just the way you are. I mean those eyes . . . Darkmoor Stragg, code name B'wana Shock, the evil-mastermind leader of F.R.E.E.Z.E., betrayed you and with his army of armor-clad, midget gorillas he's--

Anubis Loki [Showing white fangs, laughs. Her laughter drowns out his pitch.]

Russ Meyer: And I know an editor at Vogue Paris. As a film promo, we could do a high-end shoot . . . Maybe we could do a you and Hela thing? You know, you and her in an all-the-sizzling-sisters are doin' it for themselves spread. Be hot.

Anubis Loki: [I do like it hot.]

Russ Meyer: I'm thinking Snoop Dogg as Stragg, with Flava Flav as his sidekick, Igor Tomahawk. Tomahawk was low man on the totem-pole in The 7 Maniac Mau-Mau Bastards before he--

Anubis Loki [Snaps her fingers.]

[And the flames rise higher and get hotter.]

Michael Hurley, "Werewolf," various Frank Zappa songs and compositions, CCR "Lookin Out My Back Door," Bob Dylan—you guess which tunes . . .]

Thanks to Gilda Sue Rosenstern for chiming in ~hugSSSSSSS! !!
And many hugSSSSSSSSSSSSS to the half dozen ladies
who kindly read this and said YES.

But Not for Me

By Joseph S. Pulver, Sr., and Laurence Amiotte

for J

. . . a corner. close to everything. Too close.
Could turn around. Go back. Fix what he broke.
Try anyway.
Maybe, weaker than a shrug.
Steps to the curb. Miles away the other side. Lifetimes away. Same
his nerve, and his pride—Did he have any left?
Did he have anything left?
doubts. A black forest full. fear. Stone cold mountain of it.
His hands shake. He could use a drink. A bottle. Two.

Four rooms. Tight. Couple of dry bottles, no truth tacked to the
bottoms.

destroying sprouts

Dreams waltz in her shimmering words. Wonderland light in
those eyes.

water from a fourth floor burst pipe painted these walls, cage.
Other things stained the carpet.

funneling his gutter of rage at her. A perfect angel—laugh—*those
eyes*, all the times they said *yes*; small perfect sunlight jokes; clowns
and little pictures of magic brimming with melody; when the piñata
moon sings; music glows on her shoulders—and she gets pierced by
his bloodfire roar of defeated . . .

crisscrossed by his grievance

noisy hands of zero.tender vanishes

Stained. But she is still so rare—*so rare*, polished by hear and
touch and felt, so soft, so beautiful . . .

Sugar fighting the rain; paying, losing. She starts forgetting her blessings.

washed up.close.

She wears his fear. Fights to turn its scathe and clatter. Tries to push its hell-fugue out the window, let it behave in the boudoir of neon—Not here. *"Please."* Not here.

"Pity." Wants to be proud. Who will hand back imagination? But there is no air. Not this rhythm, wants the dance and the fork and the spoon back; flame and tigers, and to walk on water again.

he can't get his teeth away from loud . . .

neon laughs at his disappoint.

Blue eyes, a ship of wind and rain and break.

One step.

grey time street: language, emphasis bottom

Another.

run.run from the lighthouse where he dueled with his own lies . . .

Around the corner. That life—the one he just fucked, again—hidden.

Bridge.

Below. Slow ice depths . . . dark enough to be black . . . dark enough to be Oblivion . . .

"Oblivion's quiet." No rejection slips there. Studio exec's don't hand you the street. *Live out there for a while. Maybe a little life will find it's way into your writing? Maybe.*

Had a shot. A-list film. A-list star. A-list director. Fucked it up. Like always. Destined to just be some hack. Tirelessly mediocre.

dark water. disappointment in her blue eyes. his tears. Hers.

"Oblivion's quiet?"

. . . Margins, fields of shadows and chance. Ardent in the mirror of remembering. The figure is a landscape; Serpent, crooner, ice.

Dark eyes, shadow play. Awakened, a glancing ghost song laughs. A bishop moves . . .

Something crosses the river, the moon and appetites in it.

Night's wall. Bare bones.

"Quiet."

"Is it? Is that what you really think, Kevin?" The response, a gesture honey-smooth, caring.

Wings. Saw wings not the eyes. Wings.

"Life is life, or is it?"

Wings.
Wishing.
No wings. Black top coat. Black suit. No wings.
"Kind of cold on that railing. You could be better. Could do better."
"Have." Kevin whispered. *"Did."*
"Perhaps if I knew, I could help. Only costs a little time."
"Help. Maybe?"
Hand offered.
"maybe?" but he slips, slips from the railing, slips through the air . . .
grey folded with dimming goes BLACK
Cold.black.cold.between bales of ice.the dark black sleep that scatters.swallowed by Oblivion's thirst.one last swig.and
The tug of grace. Saving grace.
Above again. Soaked, but he can see. Light.
Shivers. Soaked, but his savior is not.
Bone dry. His hair is perfect. Coat and suit as well.
His angel smiles. "I have my ways. Now, you, we must fix this."
And suddenly he's dry. Stunned.
Fix. If he can . . .
"Maybe?"
"Yes, Kevin, ins and outs, there and back again. Tell me about it."
Mouth finds a voice, gallops—Meadowlarks and screams on a world of
breath. Shapes rush; the dress, the well of orchid islands she wove, the
valley of shelter, hearing the sky cry, intentions-signs-wounds/when
the fingers parted and shuttered, conclusion . . . tumble.
"Opinions. Deeds can be turned, the season turned Never, void. Let
me show the path marked by a different future."
Wings.
He has—
Wings of morning light.
Could save me . . . Said that. Didn't he?
"Life is elixir. Come let me show you *without*." No edge of convince,
no urge-push.
"My life . . ."
"Yes. The ocean, the razor."
Wings that rupture disheveled.
through desire, glass . . . across—
tufts and tongue sing

sky poem
what it brings
all that time, fluid—inside; desire, curves, limbs, days staying . . .
no risk of unsafe/never lose/blame slung to the trap of some other
winter
believing
"Jenny." *Oh, Heaven.*
Angel beam.

~*~

An ordinary street. "That's my—We're." His old street, the street he
lived on before he met Jenny. Same inflections, same weapons of
never said—*Almost.* "It's *my* . . . life."

The sun is out, it burns with other directions.

"Yes. The what it is *without you.* The other was a briar. This is no
land of theory, only joy and what capable brings."

Walking. Passed the bakery, not blacked out. Bright signs and
fresh rolls in the windows.

"Eder's isn't a cinder."

"It is very profitable these days. There is no need to burn it."

"We thought he might have."

The cocked head, knowing smile. "He did." Hand waving over
that way. "Back there he had too, but here, rewards do not have to
coexist with unworthy."

Need grinding, Kevin speeded up. Wanted to see another street.
Wanted to look at the street where he once planted his dreams.

A corner. The last one. *On the street where she lives. The breeze
evoking sweet, the oaks, their integrity princely. Almost palatial, charm
in every balustrade and courtyard, quiet as the surface of a table in a
nice restaurant.*

"This is . . ." Looks up, reads the street sign. Right name.

"What? How?"

*"There has been some remodeling. Urban renewal, a refashioning if
you will. People came here with overjoyed and created a love letter to
wondrous with their dreams."*

*Safe street. Shines. Flowers smile, red and blue and sungleam yel-
low. The lips of defeat and the blaze of anger do not challenge and
tremble here.*

The buildings are old velvet, no random, despicable knocks at romance here.

"This is beautiful. Does Jenny—?"

The angel nods. "Yes, she lives here."

"Here."

There was not a smudge on this street. The lanes of flowers were an alphabet of color. Children's fingers could plan here. When the moonlight came Kevin knew every adventure it accompanied would find no fox to fear.

As fire thrown, cascading, a bouncing dog.

"Loki?'

"Loki."

His liberty is poetry inventing wings.

"Legs. He has legs, strong legs."

Jenny's dog is a village of movement. Running, spread out like the middle of the day. His tail and legs and glee are a symphony. His brindled coat sparkles, his eyes filled with a puppy's magic show go get 'em.

"How?"

"The intersections of his life have changed. Without influence, the accident does not happen. This is his meadow, one with no fences. Here he can dash and chase and launch, quick as his bark. There is there, it does not taint here with its cruel happenings."

Kevin's wearing a birthday grin. "Loki." *Joy in the utterance.* "That's great. Great." *When he looks up another sun is out—*

Jenny. No fragments, no shaking with hoping for right decisions. Groomed, penetrating a vision of exquisitely-declared—almost skipping.

"Jenny. Jenny . . . She's . . . Utterly fabulous." *Divina bellezza. Trembling, as the amplified moment climbs to stellar.* "Shines." *A cream stanza on canvas, growing on a philharmonic horizon—celestial. Closer. Gasps,* "She," *intimate, beckoning. Cherish explores his senses, his imagination compares its flavor to dialects he feared to circle.*

"Like the sun. Indeed. Jenny is a marvel, honey and fire in a form that cannot be bitten or stopped. Joy suits her. Love fills her every line."

"Loved. Flushed with happy."

"Oh yes, absolutely blooming," *the angel nods.*

Kevin's eyes agree. That's exactly what she looked like when they met. Brimming. She stole his heart and his breath, even when he closed his eyes.

"How does all this happen?"

The angel smiles. "The devil's in the details."

Fawning, parting from ordinary, as Jenny, her form a singing cello, floats by, Kevin doesn't catch the wink and the smile.

"All this gold."

"For the taking."

"Promise?"

"Je ne suis certainement."

"An angel. She's an angel."

"She always was."

She was, he knew that. It wasn't her, not her fault. He did it. Started. Finished. Broke.

"And she still is."

Mine? Has to be.

"Is this for me?"

"Wait. It's coming. A mere minute or two more and you'll see the whole of the dream revealed. Watch for it."

"Am. I am." Leaning into the fragrant street and its summer everything. Hoping. Strident, wishing. Defenses down.

Voluptuous manicured bushes, windows bright as success greeting the sky and its stable of dreams, the white house bursting with complete. No stalling, through the gate, she's on the stairs.

Door opens. Loki flies through, his tail carrying the novel of his travels.

On the stairs above the gate. He's tall, a stem that holds no darkness, beaming ineffable charm.

Jenny's stunning, a bouquet no rain has touched. Believes is their unity. Her daydreams flutter, reflect devoted opened.

His arms are open. In them, trusting, spinning in ease, she blossoms. His kiss, hers, both sigh with there in your eyes.

Kevin saw what wings and movies were for—what Good is.

That first day, as she laughed when she fixed his collar, he knew he should write about her. That was his film, the angel that granted a mouse a kingdom. Should have skipped the fast-ride thorns and the cheaper dare of when I am.

"That's . . . not me. She's with somebody else."

"Her husband."

He didn't see a ring as she walked by. Why would he look for one?
Eyes, expression in trauma.

Intention separated from language, bent, no weather to grow. A
thousand prayers, shattered, dead, hung from a silent mouth.

"*They are both authors,*" *his angel explains.* "*Bestselling authors.*
Jenny has won virtually every major literary award. Some twice. And
with Jenny as his unflinching pole star, he has garnered his fair share of
accolades as well. You are watching her embrace her muse as he, thank-
ful and proud, embraces his. They are One, the unending melody, ele-
mental and plumb, inside and out. No shadow blinks between them. No
trouble taps at them. They have not ever felt the desert tongue of ice's
mane, nor will they."

"*But I thought, Capra—It's a Wonderful Life?*"

"*Oh, my dear boy, it is . . . for some.*" *Hued in gleeful, and cold, as*
some satisfied laughter is.

Choking on ghosts . . . and dust.

Wings.

Wings black as night.

Could save you . . . Said that. Didn't he?

Wings that rupture.

through desire sifted . . . across—

tufts and midnight sing

all that time, unravelling . . .

slung back.no safe/never lose/the scissor hex of blame.trap, the
bruise of regret

believing stammers

rudder in pieces

~*~

Bridge.

Below. Slow ice depths . . . dark enough to be black . . . dark enough
to be Oblivion . . .

"Here."

"Yes, Kevin. Here, again"

"But?"

That smile. Fox with its robber knife uncovered. Measuring. Its border laughing.

Deceived hits. Kevin weeping. No terse alarm clock. No other tongue to gather him.

"*But.*" lose.no horizon.world without years or dawns.every page filled with sharpened black

Just this bare cliff.

edge.gate

both hands

his bones feel like confused weeds

both feet

treasures to sand.private furies are puddles of teeth drowned in why face not connected to the sky

Below.open. Slow ink depths . . . dark enough to be black . . . dark enough to be Oblivion . . . cold enough to be ice.

learned lacking.not rubbing belong.learned always.no contact with without power. "I am sorry."

Bank-robber eyes. Shiv smile. Angel's game.

"Choose."

"Oblivion." Maybe heal the wound with a dimension that was not hurt. "Promise?"

Fire tongue. "Oh yes."

No actions for fuel, no action to sort, no sky of curves and Eden. Not a hawk.

Kevin takes off his hat. Removes his gloves, and his coat. Remembers there is nothing in his wallet but regret.

Dawn, a broken eggshell. Out of spare change, his hand, with the delicacy of wind, is a hundred mile tale. Hand, seduction abandoned . . . Sculpture—no eyes to have it . . . Hand finally loses the dream.

nightfall.no affluent letter to touch secret places

black song

vanish

Heap with no reason. No way to stop falling. Breathing water. The sound of no sound.

~*~

The angel beams.

Wins. Another soul to keep.

Horns. Not grand. Not yet. But there are other bridges, and tempta-

tions—post disagreement and loss—to inform. A swell of gates to open; tin cups to estrange from gravity. Other souls . . . *To take.*
Smiles. Taps his new horns.
Didn't fall far. Not a bump on the way down; no drag, no burn.
The sky whispers forgotten grey. Under its wreath his steps scent this new Forever Street.

With apologies to Frank Capra.

Talk Talk, "It's My Life," and David Sylvian, "I Surrender."

kristamas as an exhibition

for KK

I am a character, a wolf (in some verses of youth I carry around) . . .
A caricature of a moon with a skied history. I might confess to a
thousand years, but it would be misleading . . .

my window of years was without giants
                              or trees
                              or most often
Believe—
If I can trust the eye of The Beholder . . .

singing velvet arms:

The small bones in her back . . . (thermal expeditions) . . . lovely . . .
that soft pale skin . . . lovely . . . and soft . . . more so in cold
moonlight.

Her red lips, and wide eyes. Wide as the warmth of her teapot.
Wide as the night spread out before us this next voyage in remembering amore.

From Farside (where the unfolding strata of phantasy kisses, each
mouse and if and tranquillo with its autumn-wide, dance) she brought
apples. Red. Sweet. Apples. Red. "Red as you want them to be." She
always brings apples. She walks barefoot through the orchard, her
toes(long as permission)—out—out strolling—out loving, amused by
the praise of her apothecary—in the faery-palace fathoms of black soil.
Hybrid-fingers (OK with their vices) gathering marvelous and cher-
ished and intoxicating ripened by the ribboned hexes of cricket-
wizards. By moonlight. In soft shimmering starlight. Comes to me.

Afraid. But not of singing and the stars . . .

"Close your eyes. Close your eyes."
The stars wait.

soft~flake smile:

dark clouds—"There!"
sing . . .
No sorry. No half of it. Fast-cure without a passenger of engine-heart.
Her window crackles.
Home with her bells and dinner. And the skull, pale nebula of famished myths on the jade-smooth, wood-grain mane of her table; a quiet scrawl, it could be a lemon or a blossom that found no profit in born. So close to her fingers, ready for the cast of beautiful direction. And her slow laugh. And no way to slow down.
Her eyes smile
snowflakes melt on my tongue

Wide eyes singing cupcakes and faery nights:

Lips dragging the hounds from the forest of I miss.
9 skulls. Just little ones—tender little magic; I love the smell (If you could only keep it in a pan, chain it down). A curtain for a dress. Just as soft and white as the clouds outside the small window. Soft flower print. Soft. Flower warmth drenched by a rouge of silk shadows.
Print—loud as a drum frilled with pillow talk or brand new rain approaching.
Soft. As the cool fragments of fate one hand cradles.
Soft and pale, baby to my death-hide.
She can sing hey, but cannot run. Not tonight. Not tonight. Not around
—*away.*
9 skulls; *Fortis Est Veritas*
I smile in reply to their smiles.

[I've forgotten to close the curtains. Heat leaves as I raise my glass. I should wave goodbye. But why? Let these specters fly. Let them collide with the raven of regret in the heart of some other sky. No, I did

not say they outgrew this season. Did not say their hard secrets have sown little.]

9 skulls she gave me. I will not take them for granted.

Even as I kneel at her feet—The sea they offer—It's so easy to slip into the bonfire waves.

Bend to whisper joy to her toes, each such a cunning little fox.

A Game I've Never Played:

Wish sounds
from the astronomer's mouth—Saturn-edged.
Tail a rainbow-stick straying from dust,
thoughts holding breath, the hands of the others waiting in line,
their pencils and strings living to be called *at once.*
Face, tapping lightly,
above that white page sea of honeycream neck
and another
wish.
And
another
—burning
for a small girl's
face

Wood with Chair & Dance:

Her vapor mask—starless pale-yellow fire, fluttered, and something soft laughed when her nipples rose and offered firm promises to the moon.

He—cruel old friend, leans in (to leave me The Emptiness). Never-blinking flower elbows my thirst with the shape of his ice-silver frenzy. I will not be pensive. His tongue will leave my reef.

and
it does.
Petite little girl
she brought her diary from the car
opens the meadowlark adventure

~c~o~l~o~r~s~
c~orner to \f/e\a/t\h/e\r/e\d/ corne~r
warbles
her legs fill my open breath
laugh their come one/come all—I'm convinced as she tosses me
racehorse light
(I can love with IT!)
angelcandle summer
the language of pathfinder blood
breast-nectar to siphon
one more
one more
more
RED
skin(wicked as the kiss my tongue can't hide) lush with FELT
one more
one more
kiss
(I so adore how her toes receive flight)
no thread
no
glue
to hold this architecture of providence
no
wire
so small (these unmasked lips)
and
(Here Kitty. Here Kitty.)
salty.

    she has long incisors
     I wonder if I should open the curtains and let the strong stars see
the splash? ??

Naked stands in my grand corridor and offers me its mask:

with just a smile
as my hands consider time

Keener eye:

Frame.
(radio a famine of nothing drawing its citation sentences on dark walls. fast-fast-fast, wide-growing coal, amusing itself with awkward facts of industrial design. "I like it." "I like it.")
—art.
—innocence.
—talk.
(turn the radio down. Then off.)
a black crucifix throbbing with a symmetry of images and the tide & epidemics of commentary—
should I confess to the debates with birds?
I could
could
—all of it
with some boomtown sky of exclamations and gates of here & There.
(there's a man in a suit on the radio. Come and see. Come and buy. When your street has heard blue, Come and see.
Should I call in and ask which side of usage do you find guilty and throw in the sea?)(I believed I had turned it off.)
Her teeth unarmed me.
The striped leggings she wore fit the legs of my kitchen chair so well.
I have her eyes now.
Framed
on my untitled wall

F R A M E by F R A M E :

　　agile stride
　　boots / skirt / VORTEX
　　dancer—voltage—hungry voltage
　　dancer
　　no more secret admirer

　　snow-white Rapunzel with spider legs in the eye of The Beholder
　　　　stand like a stork, one foot elevated—suspended—mid-stride
picture-perfect poem

"Silly."
as I tied a string around her neck
(did she eat the apple
the landscape has not left any sign of the bargain)
crucified sighs take root
the gaze of lips on a disheveled bed that smells of wings open

open bottle on the desk in the corner of the desk
no trace of sunlight
or lingering clasp of gazing eyes

facts:

in this desert even the air burns.
cat food.
the piano has one dead key. a white one that cannot remember soft or HUGE.
quick prayers.
the only way.eyes closed.snow

white toes and ivy.at this point.MIND—shall I tell you what Day felt.the logic of the clock and the door are the same.
the wind is flat on its back and wide awake.
sharp colors.
thorn—my paws of *To the End* bite too!
she, snow-white Rapunzel with spider legs, will—GLADY—burn. All the way down to her toes—
strawberry lipstick toes

Indoor(games); with exploratory puppet show:

highway: the fascination of compass, wings of a riddle touching the clouds of my tongue with their rain of To Receive . . .
her elbows pointed to the ceiling as her hands masked her eyes
her hip dazzle-burnt the shoreline of my bed
with charity
smile
signal

for me
little spider girl lost her bible-black shoes for me
pirouette—*little dancing girl*—for me
little spider girl (16 years)
wrist, knee, fingertip—bite by bite—to fingertip
something little
a moss of gluttony / snowmen / ghost tails / polaroid / the flavor of
a perfect goodbye and not a dent in the silk / the particles and accou-
terments, some notoriously imperceptible, of crime stories / flesh—
head titled back / & clues and crazy moonrays staining the glass windows and the cobwebs

She curls her fingers over her thumb.
Strategy? Or sweet?
"I'm vulnerable to your celebration of shadows. Every ally, every
might be, makes me tremble, flutter . . . Please."
And she does not scorn or throw up portraits of insistent verdicts
furthered with spoons of haste.
"But what if culture no longer exists outside the cult of personality?"
"Put your hand on art."
I feel her Felt in my clothing.
"And you will have seasons."
It's no trap. No club. No illusion covering hollow earth, no hole
of swords.
She offers me lovers—every combination. A walk away from the
spade of molding with its celestial uncaring and its tail a gang of
shocks and red tatters of More Shall Take.
She removes her flower-print cotton dress—one land of tinted-
weather melted to a hungry landscape of astronomy (every star for
me to see). Offers this vampire ingot-nipples, oh the torchlight-joy
contact. I FEEL TOTAL. Offers me that magnificent heart—Burn-
burn-burn—Burn-burn! My own Alice, crackling, laughing, Drink
me. Drink me. Come that I might annotate you with kisses and
commas and prickled clouds. Come with your need. My cupcakes
breasts will paint you with strawberry whispers.
I am a bullet painting sin, a blind saxophone player waking night
from its sleepwalk. This Steppenwolf of Only, that raw unfinished
edge, bent by brain disease. My brass cries as she dreams. My rock-

hide transforms. I am a lily unpadlocked, my red zone now a strength of UNITY full and NEW—New! !! All this fire in my hands, fire for your toes, *and shoulders*, fire that dreams as you, Ballerina opened, press forth, come,

Engage.

I admire.

(—FEEL total!—symmetry/setup/shooting—wild, beguiled, *no longer empty*)(joy glowing at the gate)(oh little doll-face) (joy)(near)(near)(behind locked doors)(a traffic of emphatics)(how sweet)(how dear her baby's breath play)(collide with grabs)(how sweet)(horizon occupation)(stars)(oh little doll-face)(she leans)(I FEEL total!! !)(she SMILES)

Her fingers extend.

Her head on my shoulder.

I open my book and she turns the pages, laughs at my holes of Blake and Yeats and Fowles, takes godot and NO EXIT in her sharp teeth, tears deceived and extinguished and the dirty-handed flies of PAIN with beauty . . . and keeps tearing.

In my black mirror, my cage,

she bursts

with

infernos

infinities

In my cities of RED nights, sprawling with misanthropy and war's scaffolding,

writes

FELT

the clock melts.

but this passes

my little tea party ends.

Mer: action: (including some mouths are ghosts & a clot of elegies
. . . & Rapunzel, the age of lust is giving birth . . .)

In from the haunted moon—

Little girl, come to my tea party; (she brought cupcakes)(& strawber-
ries)(& wide lips)(& Loki fingers). Red wolf-lips unzipped: "Kiss me
with your teeth."
I, in my fun-fair face, embrace chat: "Saliva becomes you, Rapunzel."
"I have lipstick toes."
RED stirs my reality with dreams.

after viewing countless photographs of Marilyn Monroe:

    long hall, slowly—
    barefoot kiss of the voyager on the hardwood floor—a dance
    angel toes
    my chair praises the allusive heroes for not slipping through the
cracks
    edges that leave a trail
    sticky, light shades on the bed of Before

    (calm shoes still on the stairs where the wall meets the wall)
    (calm)
    (not far from the clock and the stool where she sat neatly)
    (should I put them under the bed)
    (weather I can't answer)

    no one stays forever

"Do you hear voices?":

In her agreeable April hat threaded and scented with Sunday light
stem-gardens,
like a spy of long miles
              and tendrils
              (and banks of lemon-honey fingernail shells to unfold)
              motion and little gestures arrive
              at my door of old, slumped hills—
"Come out." as long, thin finger-sweet beckons
                              j o u r n e   y
Some art-beach opens summers of remembered birds
A spark of stripe song—"Do-re-Me!"—to suck center/to/again

"Your horizon will not die of thirst."
No snail of blue descent, I lose my book of sputtering WRONGLY
in her haystack of safe sizzle
> Playful cherrytree-wind,
> ample herb-wave,
> angel-skyline leap to dash tips,
> my teeth(pinned to fragrant) call a dance

Sweet-sweet-spy of charity whispers, "Your horizon will not die of
thirst."—
Infinity tilts,
> its breath beards the calendar with canticles

Naked sets its flag in my TRUE and offers me its X:

with just a smile painting intact with sensual nails,
as my hands, swollen flowers-in-flood for a crazy lily in bloom, take
That Is The Way.
Is.
Is.
Her dawn-smile "Is." sings for my island—

Her very hungry feet on a balance of steam, dance odyssey:

Laughing little red-church bullets, Night has escorted me to her. Or
might it be, her to me?
She has taken off her mask of tomorrow and her mask of memory.
Her heels(on bells of joy) sing HERE.
(her mouth, full of *what has been on my mind* and sweet, sweet ap-
ples, like a radio spinning)
"*I will*—
Please. Please. I elect glad and light things—Let all of them swing.
—*be your friend.*"
Night with sky on his shoulders, still stands there, gleeful.
My wishes—ringing on & on—are ready to touch *without words.*
With more than my lean eyes, I reply, "I will not be shy."

*Through a Window That Smells Like Church (to discover home-
made nuggets of fortune in the cobwebs and shadows of Hades):*

my Little Medusa has a diary—
    . . . red wolf lips, no angel,
    . . . a calendar of spiders, a cemetery of dolls my little curls live to
bite and bite
    . . . I've lost my Stay side to the twisted smile of the starless-ghost,
    . . . So many good omens to fill with graves,
    . . . Oh, the pretty pincushions curse
    . . . DO NOT USE!!
    . . . chaisse,
    . . . Snow White
    . . . one skull is full of spiders, one, a cemetery
    . . . I've tied the knot of 2 stories the wrong way,
    . . . DO NOT USE!!
    . . . I am dressed for it,
    . . . I murmur binge—a river of it
    . . . oh,
    . . . My nipple is a teapot and a sugar bowl. My flowers chatter, my
floors cascade with captivity-blown vibrancies waiting to be round. I
hope—dream, HE, brimming with twists and cabinets and back doors,
comes for tea. My eyes will knight him with Right Now . . . I have so
many roads to give.

She must be waiting for a message from me - my medicine pen writes: Renounce loneliness, Rapunzel. I am a drawer of useful shapes, OPEN ME

Red Tide Pharaoh Fever PART 1:

The old blue chair on my porch has fallen over. Its midnight-paint peels. But I never sit there these days. When time was a swirling lullaby in a cathedral of open wait until you see her, I sat, setting aside my requiems and cliffs—nor did I open any of the marble literature of gas—and waited, but no more—

A doorway. A tear. An arm with a need . . .

Said her name was kristamas.

But her eyes made me forget little bad girls. Ripe-fruit open mouths, emphasis venture. Panties down around her pale ankles.

What's her name? She must have one? In some life of pictures adorned with masks and loved madly she had one? Must have . . .

The way she parades, scootin' nipples ready to whirrrr. Why won't she take off her dark darkmask?

Miles' trumpet heats her toes.

Snow white, curled—what diaries her toes must have written, bite by bite, in the calendars that vanished in graves~

I want to talk to her. Whisper about the bite of the spider. Those legs, that's the side I want to be lost on. I want to kiss her with my teeth~

Her teeth embrace the camera's eye.

"El Prince, loose your ebb and flow processional. The oracle in my fahrenheit itches."

Shaman-song mouth of Rothko shadows colors my mind, peels me till I capsize. Eyes—it's about that time. Eyes—what if my dainty moondream-valentine klangs when the black satin X of your fox steps from angel to flame. Eyes—every small tiger-face window open with ghosts. Want her gamut to cry without hesitation, want her tongue full of me too, me too~

She knots her joy to the lisp and chat of the drums. Toes . . . Toes—true and pretty, whisper, "Oh."

Her meow, petite as a knife, is upside down. Knees, smooth as art painted in midnight ivy, redecorates the poof of my stunts . . .

Eyes and toes and nipples, the room dances till it can't—till it can't~

~no blue bed ache~

Hopscotch (Red Tide Pharaoh Fever PART 2):

kristamas. Open your power!

(sighs)

kristamas—*Go ahead.*

    (sighs)

kristamas—I see you.

    (sighs)

See you.

    (sighs)

Like you mean it.

    (sighs)

Sweet you are, my apple.

    (sighs)

I crave your flavor. All of its "Will." *Right now.*

    (sighs)

Open your power for me, kristamas—Breathe for me.

    (sighs)

You hear my voice.

    ("Yes.")

I haunt all of you.

    (sighs)

All.

    ("Yes.")

I give you speed.

    ("Yes.")

Listen to me,

    ("Yes.")

I am your hurricane and your lesson.

    ("Yes—*yes.*")

I unravel all the cities in your box.

    (sighs)

My jewels are your inches.

    (sighs)

I give you thirsty kisses of wishes in full bloom

    (sighs)

and cotton.

    ("Please." "Yes. Please." "I am in bloom.")

My finger is your pillow, kristamas. It opens your devotion.

    (sighs)("I am soft and white.")

I am thick succor for your white thighs, so feverish for seasons—

Fringe me with Eden.
    (sigh—"Yes.")
Growl your splash,
    ("Yes.")
Bride.
    (sighs)
    ("Yes." "Touch *all* I offer."—sighs—"This path to morning. It's light, shaking and ripe." "Please.")
"You are so sweet, my apple. So sweet. Your *will* is my ground, my new sky."
    (sighs)

Table, with Skull:

    Intension.
    table: flat old wood … above(?) below(?)—I can't decide—dust[that does not turn].
    she said her magic words. "My dove is warm. Warm."
    said.
    (as I smiled)(drank the smell)
    said.
    "It's my favorite
        skull."
    said
    said
    laughed / whispered (without shaking)
    of a dangerous place
    I sit there; tea; watch it burn.
    Smoke my smoke; taste her eyes; watch her burn
    Wait to see her toes
    dance
    "Would my match help?"

Anatomy of a November Desert (including "Somewhere games are being played"):

The frost talks to the feet of the barn. The hay has been harvested. The pumpkins' smiles carved.

Brillig spins its gleam in the river of night's dreaming.
        Silver frame—slighty dusty—
        holds a smile. The beheaded nymphet in the grainy pho-
tograph brightens. It—with strings everlasting, opens the door of cannot stay, pulls at the hole in The Beholder's chest.

called him mr wind. Called his camera, The Beholder.
Kissed her. Burn climbed—apples, lips
                    —that wide smile, legs, pale fire belly,
mouth(entangled dream crawling), mouth of tender-flower taste,
swallowed—perfect panic.
Lovely.
Kissed her with e/x/p/o/s/u/r/e/
X
X
Lovely.
Lovely.
                perfectly still

The worn edges of yellowed curtains waltz

quietly.

mr wind sits

"*Somewhere* games are being played."

waits

After viewing countless photographs of Kristamas Klousch.

Morton Feldman, *Rothko Chapel* / King Crimson, "Frame by Frame"
                                    looped, shuffled.

Small Ocean After Solar

for AM

"Angelis."

Very first thing that seized you was her eyes. Like galaxies across the room, they could fold joy around the contradictory twitching of your attempts at penance. Purge afflicted from the afflicted too.

Stared, guess it was more like taking cutlery to dessert, my glee and hunger was massive. Dreamed, climbed the stash of her *Forever is the easiest thing to do*. They drew me—another poet trying to translate desire.

Then the shoulders. Dune-soft bedspreads of mercy. More dreams lit my drift.

Longings.

Then she spoke. The poetry of birds opening delightful weather. I ascended into air.

As women so often do, Angelis didn't turn away when I nodded my simple hello.

Smiled in fact.

The stars brightened, gutted my bleakness. My blood liked the velvet air.

Another, "Hi." Another smile. The words of night *andante amoroso*; reborn in the hands that found me.

Hearing was kiss.

Her smile became a laugh. A wave. Jobim was playing. I felt like a monk—*Vespers*, My soul doth magnify—

Her good was enormous, all feathers and sky and red ribbons—the sweetness of poppies.

Screwed my courage up enough to ask.

She said, "Yes."

We danced, her hand, a pastry so tempting you could not turn away from the perfection of its language, on the small of my back, mine on hers. Swans without tears. The song was a street of lilies. And her shoes were off.

I was swimming in joy and flames.

The hair on the back of my neck spent a lot of time on what will be. I let it ride and prayed. Could have sworn her smile said plenty of time. To a drowning man not even close.

Her scent was in my hands. My landscape could taste the magnitude of her forget me nots.

Jobim's "Wave" swayed back out to the moonlit-guarded deeps. We drifted into a booth. A corner and a candle. Jacob Young, "Blue," "Evening Air," subtle. Spacious, the quiet fire of a sparrow's song. The guitar and the trumpet suited her.

Sat. No schemes.

I was so nervous I forgot to smoke. Was glad I didn't have to write and spell anything. Had I, *just now* and *a little more* would have been Homeric undertakings.

Weightless, I hung on the just now. And if.

She was the perfect countervoice to the places where my swelling tongue of believe lay out. Forgot my blues as she exorcised ghosts. Began leaning on never ending.

Too many stars in my ears, I didn't see the emergency. Didn't drift in, no one counted it down, came right out of the nightwoods. Nimble as a fist spitting nuclear. Spread out grim. 4th degree burn engraving the space your clothes occupy fucked unaware hard.

Shots fired. Screams going to hell in the splash.

Blood, 3 race run. Dying blooming.

Jumped. The whole room.

A broken glass that wouldn't be hefted again.

"What?" Eyes without a wishing well for their pennies.

"He's . . . dead."

No one dialed the hospital to sing. Wouldn't be no charts or pills. No tending by steady hands.

"*Dead?*"

Collapsed would stay collapsed.

Calendars split. Gasps jumping out of their affluent illusions. Faces in fantasies of hurry. Flood and tongues blindly rolling out the doors, trying to.

A dozen hunkered down under tables.

Panic at ground level for me too. My face six inches from Angelis' knee. My broad scurry of thoughts are scraping, "Robbery?"

And she's sitting there, could have been waiting for the waitress to drop by with a glass to cure appetite or for the next song to crackle. I'm under the damn table, my blood aggrieved thunder, and she's just sitting there. Neon-lit. Hard, and soft.

High noon and she has not inched.

I'd turn to go if I could; rabbit-lightning in my heels wants to.

Black boots. Heels, long dark-road worn.

Had the idea there might be a knife or terminal on the serving plate. Had to look.

Silver cross lapel pins. Cleric's collar. Soul of holy bells and bloody plan locked. Loaded all the way to go. Witch hunter. Hand of the Cross, white and straight, crusader-lean. Eyes that had never prayed for cash or upstream. Wrath ready to swoop fury and happy to sing flush.

An old chase at conclusion. Guns ready to grunt and judge.

"Soul-robber. I bring you the wind of cemetery." Terms articulated.

Tattoos of weight and hate don't touch her slow and soft.

Angelis grazed him with a rock smile. "Migrations." Sounded like a shrug. "Finish it here."

"It is time for your sin to become ashes."

"Time for something, yes." Smile that would have made permafrost shiver.

Zero hold-the-amnesia drove up and parked.

Figured hardcore was about to rev-up way over wild side and I was going to be standing in a pit fight without an umbrella or a wet suit. Didn't hear anything crank up or an alarm go off. The balletic grace I'd danced with became a panther. Iron hands. Something not challenged by human limitations skipped ambled and went for the juggler.

No shots fired. No struggle.

Blood.

One more down. Dying blooming.

Looked at the fortress delivered to worse, just a carcass on the floor. Wondered what the ring of fire counterfeiters in Hell would make of the one-man kill posse whose Icarus wings didn't get him to Heaven's door.

Hand after violence offered. I reached up. Accepted it.

Letting her guide me up; her hand, velvet to my fear.

She sat back down. Looked at my chair.

Invitation accepted.

I sat.

The current her smile offered hadn't changed directions. Velvet moon soft, its ripples lingered on my dreams, offered a pillow.

Angelis.

"Devil or Angel" on the jukebox. She laughed. Something playful was crisp in her eyes.

Empty joint. Chairs that couldn't stay on their feet.

Nothing in the shadows.

Confessions of vodka on the floor. Bar without an addiction or elbow on it.

Her. Not a soft hair out of place.

Me, eyes never leaving her face.

Face to face. Hers holy, glowing.

Very first thing with Angelis was her eyes. Like galaxies, every ounce bell, book, and candle. Glued to them. They drew my let it be me.

Then the shoulders. Skin's a keeper you want to sip.

Then she spoke. "I can show you the tiger inside." Held out her hand. "Let this be medicine for your solitude."

Let my washed-up roll back out to sea. Took it.

~*~

Hayat's Small Ocean after solar. Some things got deleted when I left my lonely winds to be confirmed by some other motion.

Didn't stop to wave bye-bye to horizon getting ready to cough its garish sun.

I slipped quietly into the seat of a new universe. Caught never before. The sound of water. A moonlight drive on a road by the aquarium ocean, its arrows not distracting me. Didn't need to slip into are we there yet, there were whispers of resolution in her eyes.

Far from the coiled blocks and the instant storms spraying full-blown Hitler-tongue over next of kin and the coffee shops and the bland neighborhoods that fool their hands with attention spans renting space in whiskey glasses. Little place in the foothills by the sea. The curiosity of summer insects pushing through the grass, their thirst excited enough to come right up to the terrace.

Angelis has a double-wide coffin. White lining pale and soft as her naked shoulder. Her lips on my lips, between them, a poem taking stars from each other. A conversation that ends summer; a kiss from a rose.

Two drops of blood on my neck.

Two on hers.

The taste of her voice in my veins.

Interlaced fingers.

Lid closed. The boat of being really alive, awash in satin darkness and a world of closer. Her eyes—shores of Now uncovered—are chalices.

Angelis kisses my cheek. "We'll pick flowers and drain the sugar tonight."

A wave of various Jobim, Jacob Young, Anat Fort, and Pat Metheny songs.

Lonely ... and a long way from home

for Simon Strantzas

Had another beer—5th or so after the first 4 or 5—

Sipped this one . . .

And sat out the rain.

Bound. Mirror behind the bar reflected the unrestrained cuts of lightning trotting outside and the fact I was a suicide that surrendered to the stool. My edges wrapped in a ruined expression of tiredness, bartender looked at me like I was a ghost drinking with a ghost.

Looked passed the windmill-shaped red and green neon beer-light that owned the front window in Stutter's Mill. Still raining . . . feral cats and hellhounds . . .

I swore at further.

Saw no ticket in my hand . . . regret and a cigarette . . . on this shelf the moment of distance seemed unreasonable . . .

All I wanted to do was get home.

My sweat housed a nest of futile. Sent a whiskey to spin with the whiskey that was pelting the sadness-waltz of needs in me. Listened to the laughter and off-tune loose tongues that ringed the pool table. Kids full sail. Catching fun. The shining of it, carrying smiles, believing. The instant forever and lilies of their wishing never in the passages of goodbye ghost stories . . .

A flock of waving tee-shirts ribboned with color, fruit showering history with their paradise eyes they were the flames of human Spring. If the sun was out they'd have eaten it. Made me wish for some quiet company . . . But they played on.

Didn't know if I should bless or damn them.

Sat through another round of "Freebird" on the jukebox. Must have been the 10th time tonight. Then I got hit with "Walkin' After Midnight." Shot with a sledgehammer of cold and rain determined to play lumberjack in my failure. Spiraled toward pieces with the flow-ers that cannot swim in the colors of the underworld . . . the floor dripped with memories . . . corners out of Julys drowned . . . Patsy gets to me.

Deep, lodged in the bull's-eye, breath pinned to burn.

Soaks me in heartbreak.

Heartbreak that breaks your surface and puts you on the other side. Keeps you there . . .

I know it, every wrinkle and scream and fairy tale in my institu-tional commitment of sand. Struggle, put your head and chest and shoulder—every pound of unbandaged memory, in it, but rebellion has no authority here . . .

Every beer I have comes with a heartbreak chaser. Sometimes I put it in my whiskey . . . Burn to cut the searing.

Patsy's crying came apart in the shadows. River current took me. I followed. Right into midnight.

Rain can get bent. Wanted off the train. Losing the brawl with broken-hearted I wanted to be home.

Drove.

Inch by inch at times.

Pushed my old Buick around the curves of the unpaved logging road that takes you to the back alleys of Sloatsberg . . .

Fog. Rain. More rain. Heavy. In a wall of fog. Out. Just like that.

Rain won't take its paws off Now.

Felt like I was tumbling over the pits and mud . . .

Headlights stretching to make shape in the corridor of heavy pine and maple.

Radio went quiet. In and out of signals, as if it was compelled to silence by some unseen hand of pain, or the wall of fog was a solid that could not be penetrated.

Kept going.

Slow.

But I wanted to be out of the dead arms of cold that held me.

Pushed it where I could.

Rain in a mood not to change its mind. Tried to tell myself a joke about a weathercock growing fins.

Raw pine leaning in, when you could see it . . . limbs, shifting, their point of view bent over the road, crashing into this world from some foreign land of malignant. Intimidating. The forest smelled like old dark stairs.

leaves—foliage   coming   in   delirium—black   brown   green— gavotte—aimed

(refocusing eyes)

—falling

(unhappy in the blindness)

scherzo

wipers trying to prune them. Swerving in the whirr of force . . .

Lot of snaking hill roads like this in the Catskills. Wonder if they were this dark and gloomy before Washington Irving inked them? The legends of the Munsee that were here before the stain of white faces said they were.

Plattekill is a snake too, full with snowmelt and the rain it hisses along its banks in spring. Its bridge is not healthy. In the rain and fog the narrow of its rusting railings looks like the passage to the End of Days. On clear days it looks like the troll's fangs rock below will chomp and it will fall.

Nights like this whole place feels cold as a morgue gurney. Laced with peculiar quiets and prolonged bouts of angry echoes it's a dim place of naked trees and ruined slopes that slam and blur. Mouth and hands and wounds shackled and stabbed, feels like an iron cage . . . and while the common and mundane sleep the revelries and glare of darkness and its resonant agents bloom. I had lived a whole life of nights like this. At 15 reading Poe and Lovecraft I wondered if they had ever spent any time in the glens and hollows of the Catskills' dark green murmur taking in the strange sights and haunted spots. And if its twilight superstitions had found their ears. Did it leave ghastly streaks in their tin cup blindness of fear?

Came out of Horse Range Curve and upon the Hanging Tree— the monster tree—by Miller's Road. 6 kids in a souped-up red Chevy died when they hit that slab of ancient oak 20 years ago. Halloween. Beer. Rock 'n' rock—local legend has it Bloodrock's "D.O.A." was playing on the car radio when the deputy found the wreck. Masks. Enough weed to get you 10 years with Rockefeller's drug laws. On the way from a party to a party when the tree startled their mood with screech and topsy-turvy. My girlfriend and her sister were in that car . . .

. . . they said the steel was a blade that took her face off, plunged into the contours of her breast and left nothing there . . .

I still remember its slope, brushing it with my dreams—

I was 23. I was supposed to be in that car, laughing, my hand holding a beer. But a freshly-broken leg and the six new pins in it kept me home . . .

Sarah and Theodora Goodfellow were hung from that tree. Lynched strange fruit as Billie Holiday would call it, left for the birds and insects. Witches. That was well over a hundred years ago.

But they say that tree remembers, echoes what was drawn to it . . . drop by drop . . .

Headlights picked out the girl. Young. Sodden. Looked scared, or just lost maybe. Cornered, she was trying to use the tree as a strategy to keep the sweeping animal's wet fist away. It wasn't working. She didn't have her thumb out. But . . .

I stopped. Backed up.

Her face, pale velvety femaleness, elegant in another rendition, lowered and through knotted ropes of drenched hair she looked in the window.

Pretty young girl—the rain hadn't beaten the echoes of her perfume from her longing . . . Dark night, back road, had 50 questions rushing for space on her face. Didn't blame her. Guess there's moments I can look fairly scary. Bouncer in a lowlife strip joint it comes in handy.

We didn't talk a lot.

She didn't.

I'm sure she could smell the beer, the wreckage . . .

I babbled some. Niceties, trying to settle her nerves . . . long minutes . . . guessing . . .

eyes pressing suggestions . . . my pain looked at her thighs . . .

A few directions . . . Turned on her street.

. . . the smell of her perfume . . . intentions (commanding— inexhaustible) like a field—pulling back its sparrows—in rain . . .

"That one."

I pulled up she got out.

Ran up the rain-black walkway.

I took a left at the end of the block (almost circled the block) and made my way home.

... driving home—shiny black—outlines of feelings—numb mouth, vision asking—kneading fingers on a fever of years—courting a nothing

... rain

home—marked by the chant

driving home

me as a storm cloud without a ladder

wrong

the wound a circle of powerlessness—no clear—chariots tangled—hearing the shoulders of a dead candle

desert—rocks in-between hurdles the sea cannot climb

        –and

the wound in

unblessed

space

... the smell ...

                     drums—grow—grow red—the chain explodes

night

   exposing—limits—and fact—and assumptions—a slur in trajectory—meaningless dislocation as test, a core ...

deep

Made it ... not sure how ... a beer to celebrate safe and not dead ... wanted the mercy of dry—

No "Hush now." sandman tucked me in after my last cigarette came to an end some might describe as violent ... Pillow and my head had words over the hard labor ... mandalas struck-pierce-both the emotions in my bed ... an arc of trembling in fatal ... rest disturbed ...

Sunday morning. More than just the inside of my mouth felt null and void. Looked in the mirror without it calling me moron or cretin too loudly. Washed my face, looked at the sun to make sure it wasn't an old April Fool's joke come back for another bite at the apple. Wanted the paper and something that wasn't in the fridge. Some OJ and aspirin too.

Dropped my sorry ass in the seat. Fumbled with my keys.

Her shoes were on the floor.

Nice shoes. New, but still wet.

Forgotten—The rush. The rain. Her heart, in leaps, at my face considering fear ... looking for sense ... lighthouse eyes casting for hooves and horns and trapdoors.

New shoes ... red shoes ... I could almost hear them tell me there's no place like home ... Good idea, I've worn it many times. Home, away from the blind roar of the ice age and the trumpet-teeth of vultures. Home, it clicked—Take them to her. A kind favor, act. She might be delighted ... Thought of thanks, of gravitation. Wondered if she glimmered in daylight ... If she did, if her eyes knitted some kind of heat, would it maneuver me from here to there on the chessboard ...

Figured I'd shoot over and return them. And see what she looked like dried off. Her legs had been nice and she wasn't too thin. Wet as she was sitting there in my car she looked grey to me, thought I might brighten her up, at least getting her shoes back would. Ten minutes I stared at those shoes and played with the poetry and perversity of ifs and maybes. My demon flared, cast off a few errors that were entwined with desolate and thought it might open a chapter of romanticism ...

Considering the gutters and grit of my hangover and last night's mist and rain I found the girl's embalmed still life of a house on the street easy enough. 5 one-families on the Northside, 5 on the South. Lackluster corner to corner. Her's was in the middle.

Wished I knew her name ... Finger-brushed my hair in the mirror.

Melancholy, wide as the ripples of a crash, haunted the walk. No flowers in the flower boxes.

Long windows ...

... dead bird in the grass ...

... the thirst of a wicker chair streaked with drop ...

"Maybe."

9 full paces. No wings.

The door.

My palms fumble.

... interrupted the dust of the bell ... waited in a shadow-stripe of still trimmed in disappeared ...

The man that opened the door wore a uniform and a badge. Sloatsburg Deputy Sheriff badge. And a gun.

I offered him the shoes with my hi.

New shoes.

Red shoes, there's no place like home.

No—wound wide—No—clock stopped ticking. Eyes riding gestures of shock and bloodshed. Swallowing his own breath. Bore of a
blue-black service revolver leveled at my face.

Then sky sideways, down, years of darkness in its hard, knee in
my back and handcuffed. The press of breath in my ear and his
charred voice, no you're under arrest. "They were the shoes my Suzy
was wearing when she was . . . *Raped*—" Cracked and bleeding. "and
murdered ten years ago . . . I bought those shoes for her at The Boot-
ery that afternoon. It was her birthday." Tears were coming. "She was
going to a party . . . It was Halloween night—"

I remember reading about it—miles from home—too scared to
scream—each tear truly madly never came back. Her, his daughter.
Hacked up they said—Sheared . . . the contours of her face . . . someone said it was fabulous . . . Seeing her face—could—crying—
stretched, swelled, unfolding—out loud—thunder—thunder burst
trembling no further use . . . Remember that night—Too well. The
wind was screaming

something was

Bloodrock, "D.O.A.," Patsy Cline, "Walkin' after Midnight," Eric Clapton,
"Lonely and a Long Way from Home," and tracks from Ricardo Villalobos &
Max Loderbauer Re: ECM.

Listen to a Country Song

Had a six-string . . . and a delusion or 6—lived in overdrive . . .

Studied at Dylan U—smoked too much Desolation Row as I dodged the soft metal seams of charlatans who were gambling in spans of scar tissue . . . Tried plungin' the vampire gate-crashers out of the pool of holy water, failed . . . Head was makin' those Can and Will dreams from paper mache horses. Didn't get mugged by windfall Cadillacs of passion, well not often. Went to ladies parties (I always brought bass and the judgment of ardor), they played ladder—did it up well, all chalked-up nice I dressed as the snake, took cheap thrills on the rob Peter to steal from Paul plan—when they let me . . .

Was in Guero—4, 5 months (speakin' to barroom crowds) PTOOF! Sang and played lead in Farolito—we didn't last as long as The Beatles. Tried solo; knew how to roll, wasn't built to roll. Sun was too high and I tumbled off the shelf, charred all of my ornamented with incinerated when I crashed. Didn't dust off well—only rose to drink, couldn't put Humpty Dumpty's tomorrows back together . . .

Out of deals. Didn't remember where I set the vows.

Thought. Cried. Swore. Made fists.

Got slugged by drunk.

Strayed.

Shook my head, but couldn't wake up.

Forgot my wishes in the rain . . .

Hard to soar with clipped wings . . . Then The Street became a carnivore chain, enemy black feathers and I couldn't find a branch . . .

Through messin' with wreckless and knife moods. Out of enjoy (and money, short on hope for anything brighter than grey too) my boots made the tumbleweed connection . . .

~*~

no emergency exit

Disappointment

(got gaunt—not even a plan in my pockets—and then my boots took to bum)

and the clench of a slow life of grunt jobs . . .

Between the shiny broncos of DJ cowboys strummed my guitar here and there, but all my syllables had snapped—all they could spell was gutted . . .

Met Teresa on the waters of the wrong side—

Holy hell of a Saturday night in a Texas border town. Dark-eyed medicine, stood under a cow skull with a margarita, she should have been framed in gold. Slapped the wounded baggage of my apart and walked up for a nicer view. Fire and wine unwrapped my mouth, thunderstorm quick laughs—rattled my feathers at windows, addressed the shape of an idea . . .

~*~

Other side of the highway sign Carson Vicks' old Ford pickup bent last spring, all sand. This side of dried-up, Cactus Jack's construction some call a roadhouse—sure ain't Gilley's.

Sun, blast of broiling blowing, on tar and gravel, roarin' on it.

Some would call it mighty hot out there. In here. Chill in the air. Hard chill on the hardwood floor. Cold as any killin' floor.

Corona

and a Jack. Bottle back. Burn, extra hellbent.

Ain't gallopin', but movin' along.

Slow.

Cigarette smoke faster than me. But we're both burnin'.

I don't love this bar, but it's here. And they serve me . . .

First song I notice

"Cheatin Heart Attack."

Dale Watson. I think. I picked up my glass. Drain it quick enough. Grab another.

Out with the old.

Did.

Did it again and again.

There's a face in my glass.

Randy Travis. I shake my head. Like to spit. Or shoot someone.
Here?

Now?

"Diggin' up Bones"?

Look like I need that?

Bet it was the loud blonde. Looks like the type. Gussied up, mile-a-minute cooin' hips that derail trains. Grateful Dead had that thing 'bout "trouble ahead," they were right, that lady in red is trouble. Every coon hound in the place wants to tree her and play Tarzan.

I like to walk out to my pickup and get my Mossberg. Bit of per-suadin'. That quiet her some.

Face in my glass looks like a face I know.

Didn't come in to resurrect that thing I hid under the cobwebs. Came in to peel the dead end 7-to-5 off my bones. And all this damn jukebox wants to do is connect me to things I wish I had not seen; not in color or even in black and white. Rather be blind.

Tryin' to be.

Face in my glass got other plans.

Then some fool hits me with George. Just up and pumps it out. Straight run of—

"Am I Blue"

"Baby Blue"

"All My Ex's Live In Texas"

"Am I Blue"

—as ice. Depths that would freeze you dead. Shit-for-brains caps it with Jones.

"The Grand Tour."

Had a life back in Galveston. 100 years ago. Can't tell how many bottles and canceled stars back that was. Past. Can't stretch that far.

He's whistlin' along with Jones and I'm feelin' lonesome. Stack some ornery on it. And mean is going to be a kitten compared to what comin' if shit-for-brains keeps stuffing that box with heart-break.

Ghost in my glass is getting' louder.

I see the fool in the white Stetson walkin' back to the jukebox. Laughin', wad of bills in his fist. Figure he'll pin another number on the back of my shirt. Won't hit 8. Sons-a-bitches don't care.

I'd sure like to give him some famous last words.

Stand him out in the highway. El Matador with no Never-Neverland ticket, no cape to flash. Face the pedal barrelin'. Where's your elbow philosophy now, Shitass? All the pictures of long and easy and steam comin' off her eyes your tunes paint, they help you out here?

The eyes of the face in my glass they paint too.

Lashes hiss . . . every stroke . . . they can kill even from that distance . . . It's control too close, makes me stumble, grope for the handles on the bar . . .

The face in my glass, trying to shut it.

Whiskey as weapon.

Whiskey to murder.

Burn.

Burn.

It drums harder.

Eyes that were in that photograph—won't fall down.

Glass of beer.

Shot.

How many? Dozen beers?

Maybe.

Add the shots. Rockets.

More than a few.

That was the rage.

Think it was ornery and mean. Mean as the pedal jammed to 90—blur to leave the drag of the drag behind. You don't get that from a '37 Ford. Don't get that from her mouth—beautiful before it got full of City. Bigass piss factory, dumpin' and steamin'. No beauty in it. Not anymore. Now.

Face in my glass.

Face that had dresses. Had perfume. Posed. Laughed.

Smiled.

Her bra dropped to the floor—

"Light At The End Of The Tunnel."

Was not a train, B. B. Would have been a hell of a lot easier if it was.

Jack.

Corona.

Jack. Crucible of irreparable no surgeon can cure.

An eye for an eye.

Face in my glass won't go away.

Tooth for a tooth is what I'm thinking.

Wagoneers "I Want To Know Her Again."

No I don't. Knew too much. Didn't know enough not to cross the border into

"Broken Promise Land." Another white hat cryin'. He's no chestnut.

Wish the blonde with the "for a lucky man" hips would run out of jukebox money, but Billy Joe and Vern and the two others keep handing her change, and drinks. Wish she'd shut up too.

In the form of glower I push my can it at them, but their tendencies don't take in acrimony . . . Gun in mind again.

Face in my glass, might need it. Or a priest . . .

"Should Have Been a Cowboy."

You and me both, Toby.

20/20 hindsight. I'm collapsing in 80 proof. .44 and .12 gauge in the truck might clear my point of view. 'cept from here I can't see resolve.

Corona.

Too sick to pray. At least they didn't play Willie. Better not.

Jack river.

Fever sitting on my chest. Pressure. Lot of.

Lot.

Jack.

For breathing.

Jack band-aid for tight contours spoiling my heart with afraid.

Jack. Double it.

Remedy don't change my mind.

Face in my glass.

"Diggin' Up Bones."

Again? Fuck!

Ain't none to dig up. I didn't bury her. Just tossed her in the ditch out back. Coyotes got to eat. And it ain't day now. Night. Full blown. So the Day of the Dead crap should leave me be.

But the face in the glass. Risin' from the deeps. Comin'. Eyes on me. Like they always were.

Day of the Dead that other day. That day like this day. Tossed her in a ditch in back of the bar for the coyotes. Poisoned her . . .

Layin' there, arm bent, or is it crammed to a capacity plain folk don't trade in. Didn't look like the picture tucked in my mirror.

3 years since I sat in here.

3 years since she disappeared.

3 years of dark sky. 3 years helpless as things seethe. Face takes a shape. Bruises. Can't go back and begin over. Can't bend and adjust it. Tell it no.

Tell that blonde no.

Tell those eyes no. Blue eyes. Yellin' like sin unleashed in one of Joe R.'s Hap and Leonard novels. After a while I wanted out. Wanted the scream to stop.

Eyes

yellin'

because I slept with that strange.

Shared my coke,

lost that job

and the other one and couldn't find a door to push the bills through . . .

Fucked the other one too . . . And her girlfriend—Didn't fuck her. Just gave her a few bucks and some coke to blow me . . .

Because I didn't

Because they tried to

"Rathole."

"Shithole."

Trailer

"Parked in sand. It opens you up and takes all your breath."

"Damn thing," eyes drilling. "And you ain't even alive" accusing "half" hissing "the fucking time." Ornery and mean, those blues that went from love to snake—lost the poetry, boring into me, and ornery and mean pushing me to stand up and throw something away.

Face in my glass . . . the *real* remembered . . . Face over lush breasts, and slender perfect hands, sitting, tucked on the couch, eyes among the wilds of a paper continent of words, dreaming . . . of ago's and away's . . . From here . . . From me. Not like the 1st days, locked flesh to firm, alive with no complaints . . . not cut to size . . . not shifting through catalogues in search of different clothes and another society . . .

Before I saw blue-wrongness unwind in the dreams of eyes that would not be quiet . . . offering stacks of cold scowls frozen on bad and despair, and bitter . . .

Face in my glass.

That stopped coming to bed.

That drank.

More than me. A lot more. All the time. Lips kissed that can, sucked on it.

The eyes that dried to my fun. And became lathes. Poked with innuendos. Threaded my reason with lacerations . . .

All the bandages I grabbed didn't fit . . .

And I learned ornery. Got good at it. Took my bunches of weather, balled them into muscular sun dashing August sand. Ornery. Set the direction to breakdown . . .

Pushed my engine of launched stairs on the face, on those breasts, toward the bright soft hands that forgot kiss . . . My waterfall glared. Burned the book of days we filmed with miracle signals . . . I went down in the gutter with the cobwebs, no joy-creation to stir . . . pushed—safe got lost in a howl of journeys explosive . . . the undertow in the blur where no gold walked . . .

"If I Were The Man You Wanted."

If my sky was not dark and set against path, if my hands were not at her neck . . . (love wanting the taste of desire) . . . not neglect . . . not this book of sand with dregs of ashes and abandoned things, icy things that spit on faith, lunge—horrorshow bedroom, bite-spilled judgment, to give it overdose, swell and throw up its hands to glance on horrible . . .

Vital sheared.

Blood

(hammered voices—the pictures on the wall turn their faces from this "Never.")

and lies. To clean . . .

Books.

To box.

Or burn. With her clothes . . . Sand day trip . . . an essential here, a selected there for the legs of wild to spread . . . sand food . . . Sun, year after year to pound to after . . .

Face in my glass pounds . . . spits a last . . .

Burns . . .

"The Whiskey Ain't Working ."

Truth. Too much.

To burn.

Sure as fuck true. Ain't working.

Next Jack might be my friend?

Skulls on the bar. Day of the Dead decorations. Should have never got out of the truck to take that leak . . .

Skull with no eyes locked on me . . . All the things in the abyss staring—

Couple of Jackson's.

"Ring of Fire"

"Between The Devil And Me"

Face in my glass. Gates-of-hell-eyes that ain't colored with then—

Dia de los Muertos. My birthday. No happy. No laughing eyes to unwrap.

La Muerte on the bar. Sequined skulls spread around, pink and green, yellow and blue and red, glitter and glue, with blue and yellow and red silk flowers bonded to them, and candles . . . Flowers for the dead . . .

Teresa, how many times before hard times, handed me birthday presents. Dinner out somewhere, drinks and a little coke, then bed, or on the floor . . . In her gaze, in her arms . . . Fire . . .

Decorated our place up nice once, skeletons, papel picado, crosses, votives, cempazuchiles . . . Some little mock ceremony where she played witch—joked about sex magic, recited Paz, ". . . chases after it," ("I am, Baby. Gonna get ya.") "mocks it, courts it, hugs it," ("I'm going to.") sleeps with it; it is his favorite plaything" ("Will play with it. *All of it.*") "and his most lasting love." There was love—Kiss. Lick kit to caboodle. Suck. Bite. Grind. Open mouth, teeth, "Light me." Touch. Touch answered. Knees. Grind and buck. Legs changed in the fastened, accepting the scorch. Lips darting from belly to achievement, mounted—toes, neck, suckling heaven. The taste of bliss. Love—Hot enough to require hip replacement or a burn unit.

Yesteryear . . .

Heart and hands. Gone.

"Take This Job And Shove It."

Shove off is what they told me. Hundred bullshit jobs . . . Eyes in my glass telling me about everyone I fell out of . . .

'bout every grain of sand I tracked in . . . and every badluck chapter of the heart . . .

Face with vicious thoughts…self.(drunk as glory)two glasses and a 5th. no kiss. no bed. no comfort under the sky of this winter noon. smoke. tremble. worms and enemy and blackbirds toward muscles and the scream. suffer.(told it to eat sand)storm brought me in.servitude.miseries.closed to enclose my voice.its hand rose-up.shook the sunshine… Took. (till I told it STOP)

Shove off.

Threw her Bible in the ditch with her bones. "Bitch and pray to that. See if it wants to know you." Pretty and young and nice legs stretched out with no poetry.

Silence. Woven in the embrace that never held a gentle now. Wondered when they came what they'd gnaw on first . . . Fingers? Ass sticking up like that—it had been bitten before . . . Moon had no commentary . . . Never went back . . .

Waylon and Willie.

She never like them. Never liked country all that much. "Vice of woe." "Invitations to ghosts." "Wish you'd rock it."

Near the end always bitching.

Straight talk she said.

Straight back to Straight. Blonde with the passport hips want to fuck George or what? Man's good no doubt, but this is like 10–12 tracks so far. Let the poor guy take five.

"Baby's Gotten Good At Goodbye."

Wish the face in my glass knew the direct route to goodbye.

Wish somebody would play some rockin' Dwight—Hell, I'd give Miss Hips a quarter for "Little Sister." Play some Tritt or Marty Stuart, or some loud music hardwood floor. Don't she know even hillbillies rock? Had enough of break my mind and pitchfork my heart shit. Sure, the thing's haunted, made that turn long ago, but still . . . Even death row killers get a reprieve sometimes.

Face in my glass won't give me a pardon. Volts of its glare won't go nowhere. Heart-seeking hate has radar lock on me. Sure I've been ground to zero, been a blues medley that didn't know what year it was, more than a few times. Hell, wallowed down in the torn apart for a time or 6. But this . . .

New kind of hell and feels like I'm the only kid in town. Did I say kid? Not in a few. More like meat. Yeah. Meat.

Eyes in my glass have teeth and they're looking at my disgrace. Can't tell 'em it happened that way. No sorry gonna cover it. Don't care.

Not the first time I've seen the eyes, and the face. Comes to me when I slow and let think alter my murk.

Thing pulls . . . Dead a million miles from here . . . Ought to be— oughta stay on that side of the divide . . . but the anger, steering its bite crosses . . .

Wants. Thing, a bulge, breath to capture, desire to wound blood, take my toes, my neck, put them in the snare of cold grave-hurt . . .

Revenge,

or company for its dry blues?

Doubt company . . .

Witchcraft or poison, either way growin' . . . cuttin' the night . . . and I can't close the door on this Day of the Dead thing . . . comin' like a river—all its black whispers roam . . . Bringin' no all right . . .

I should walk out back and look in the ditch . . . See what's there . . . Doubt even bones after 3 years . . . Bones ain't steel. Don't hold scars after sun and sand and desert things eat. All that went down the drain to emptiness. Had to—don't need no narrative of God to know dead's dead, ain't no current or flame to push up. Won't see no jaw-bone. Won't see nuthin' but dark heaped on dirt.

Jack.

And the eyes.

How can she come back? Dead's dead. Scattered. Has to be. Sun. Animals, paws and teeth studying blood—locked on it—solid had to swirl away in that hurricane. Had to. Bones ain't pure enough for immortality. Legs and throat ain't equipped to interpret it. 3 years . . .

Jack.

Corona.

Terrified.

Teresa's eyes—a hate that wants me dead . . .

Thrust like a weed, face in my glass—extending its twister ad-monitions. Assassin bringin' change, pushing . . . Coming back . . . hungry . . . to cling and fever with struck . . . a massive shoulder of lightning ... and the yahoos in here just keep drinkin', singin' and talking about boots and oil prices and the Cowboys and weather and other kinds of hot. Pourin' out their opinions and laughs ... don't see ... They can't ...

Eyes. "Take thee."

Maybe should have laid an adios over what I left for the animals?

"He Stopped Loving Her Today."

What he means is he'll stop thinking about her when he dies. That will be me—

Last face—eyes, I see ... will

Soundtrack? You just read it . . . except the handful of Bjork tunes . . . and the Flying Burrito Brother's "Sin City."

Memories Can Wait

The evening's entertainment, no easy-leisure to its pace, rustles my unread bedrock: a replica of species stating I create my own today . . . Her life, edges bittersweet weapons, as a tributary of vernacular in NO—snarling and yelling—She looks young but I know she's a thing of dust . . . forecast, a tornado of incidental . . . *never to go to war with one another again* ASK NOT *never to go to war with one another again* ASK NOT *never to go to war with one another again* ASK NOT in Vietnam he was 19 ASK NOT Saigon ASK NOT . . . court overturns . . . post-traumatic stress disorder ASK NOT the only thing we have to fear is . . . red carpet first look . . . ASK NOT Saigon survival KIA Saigon survival KIA B'brroooom *never to go to war with one another again* KIA Mike-Mike K-79 KIA M-60 M-16 KIA fear is fear is KIA yellow blooms, ivory surrenders . . . Place of Birth: Yesterday . . . I can't understand why they buy it. GET RED . . . the queen saying something about the outlaw . . .

They take the mask off the gargoyle. The scar, the mark on his cheek—

At this distance it could be an angel or the eyes of a pumpkin.

The nun-nurse comes in with my meds—

I lie here and sweat—stuck

what do my sleepy eyes know

I remember mud—and the smell of shampoo—the taste of milk THERE WAS SUGAR IN THE MIRROR AND THE GIRLS WITHOUT SHOES WERE FLYING. ONE SANG ABOUT HER SWEETHEART. It sound lovely, lonely—I wonder why—I'm right here—I never ran away. Why doesn't she ask the cat? He knows. He was in the graveyard. He saw it all.

. . . there were candles and scars . . .

The man in the next bed over is here as he collapsed when he gave away his feathers. Did the bird really need two more?

this is the gargoyle's stage

The old man's sheets are white. So too, his gown. They gave me a blue gown. Ask and ask and ask and ask, but the nun-nurse will not return my glasses.

"How will I shave?"

She wears binoculars and a Ra/moon pendant and gently laughs at me. Then she says, "Here in The Lighthouse we don't need glasses to see the puppetshow."

She's the one that went to school, I guess she would know. Also, she's armed with a cross and that gun. I'll let someone else argue with her.

The pills settle on me like a net. Time for my nap, focus swerves, the shore offers fingers. I hope I don't dream of fish again. I never understand the language of their cage. And the song of their scent is hungry.

and now—
and now—

and

now—

When I wake will the moon be hung? And will my nurse-nun join her sisters outside my window? Will they, like last night, dance naked and laugh? Some nights the archer comes and they worship his arrow. I've seen it, how he blesses them with herbs. Then the calamity—the curves travel slow and hiss with fire, when they lie down in the shadow of his legs . . .

The old man in the white gown in the next bed claps when the nun-nurse comes in and turns on the TV.

It's an uncolored movie about a puppetshow. The narrator says it's about a boy who finds remembrance in the sea of a clock. When the clock chimes handwritten-notes snow down. Notes about this home by the sea. The boy reads each note to his old worn bear. Then they sit and eat their dinner of bent things.

I had potatoes for dinner. They could have used some salt.

The nun-nurse comes in and takes my plate. She's nice but never says please.

I think she looks like Cinderella. Not her hair or dirty knees, just her eyes. They're slow. They look like Mother's eyes. Mother read me her memories. Her memories of the island. Whispered, "The birds were evil. Do you remember how we had to keep them chained?"

I think Mother missed the trolls playing their harps. I know she did. She'd hum their melodies when she'd comb my hair. Her heart was swollen with joy when she combed my hair.

Mother always said please. Please eat. Please wash. Please turn the distance down.

I did. Had too really. I feared her signal would turn to

RAGE

Mother took me to see them burn the werewolf at the stake when I was 7. It was big business, there were songs and chants and all the tall men in the cloaks shouted when they drank the bliss. We had good seats. The Mayor kissed mother's hand. She bought me cookies that day. Then she showed me the jail and the small room where they sold bottles. I didn't like the music in there.

The boy plays guitar. His uncoiled yeah yeah yeah yeah yea-YEA is sharp.

The puppetshow on the TV ends. They burned all the poor little bears at the stake. The old man claps, then he closes his eyes and snores.

He never talks in his sleep.

But he says I do.

He's wrong but I never correct him. The gargoyle says I should never waste the life on my tongue on dead leaves. Mother would say that's part of good manners.

The nun-nurse comes in with my pills. Her voice sounds like satisfied birds fluttering on the strings of a harp. I say thank you, but her eyes don't recognize my voice. There are times I'm certain she thinks I'm a baby—baby . . . baby baby baby baby babybabybabybabybaby baby baby. I have hands. My left hand could hold her right hand. But she can never relax. I show her my left hand. She wears gloves.

When I sleep I see a girl smiling as she cleans the stairs. She says, go away dirt. She looks like the girl with the mask in school. The school has bars on the window and they won't let us have scissors.

My teacher says, we are adding today, not digging holes. I say thank you and put my hat back on.

My teacher wears a badge. Jayne says she's from Babaluma. I've never been there. Not yet. Jayne says her aunt lives there. She lives in a cave and makes cheese.

Some days there's cheese on my plate. It's a different color than the jello.

I think the old man in the white gown in the next bed sometimes steals my jello if I drift off.

My doctor is wearing a red tuxedo today. He shows me an x-ray of the tree. "Why did you do this?" he asks.

All I can see when I lean in my memories is sand.

He gives me a shot, then without a word, takes off his yellow mask. He has big white hands. "We'll try again to-morrow. Perhaps you will remember what you played when you took that girl to The Lighthouse."

I don't thank him.

"I don't like that tie, Dr. Archer. You'd look better in a noose."

He smiles and nods. "Sleep now."

It's his book, his secret code, without waiting for the end of the chapter I do . . .

All the bears wear gloves when they play with their little yellow secrets. The girl serving them cake says "Menace" and takes off her clean white nurse hat and her clothes and shows her heart to the mirror. The pink bear uses the phone to call his vampires and aeroplanes home . . .

The nun-nurse brings in the wash basin. She says it's playtime but will not take her gloves off. Sometimes she takes her mask off, but never the veil over her mouth. I don't like her lighthouse eyes. And I don't like the smell of her fever . . .

The nun-nurse is a young girl; she believes her branches are gallant. I know she dreams of faces. I know other things as well—when her flag finds nightfall she reads about time in books. She's trying to understand the changes while surveying issues of ennui . . . *she plays blind but I see - tries to camouflage her antennae under that white cap with the blood-colored cross—thinks her silence has no echo, turns her polite smile on hoping I won't notice her city of struggle—lilacs won't hide the ave fastened to the roots of the bun in her hair . . .*

I tell her about the werewolf.

>red light—the werewolf
>flash
>neon bright
>(HATE to curves
>>clock tells the truth clock tells the truth)
>red light—the werewolf
>turbulence

a bridge ... the crones are singing, the dead shrink grain by grain at the pace of ice ...

>>fold the bones until blind—3 times 3 times
>>quick, your net of fangs
>ravening wolves
>heart to heart no stale tears
>heart to heart
>heart to heart night does its work
>red light—can you remember anything—anything—

anything—being here—being disappointed

I don't think the pretty young nun-nurse likes the memories of the werewolf. She, adjusting the faith of her expression while attempting to condense her transparent, pirouettes and starts humming a song about a noon anchored in the palm of a poor town.

I often come upon pieces (accessories clipped from hides) of songs littered in my dreams ...

(pleasure has a theory)

(scars uncoiled)

(pleasure has a theory)

John Lennon, dressed like the pink bear, came to me in a dream and said, "I don't believe in Carcosa." The yellow bear slapped the table and said, "Who cares. Paul was the walrus." I think he's correct but can't check that yesterday as it is blank. All that is exposed to me is a shell that fell off better hanging from a tree.

—it would be easy to break the thin ankles she fits in her white shoes and take the delicate ankle bracelet she wears—

~*~

"His mind is an island of crime." Very slowly cleans his thick horned-rimmed glasses with a very thin and ultra-white cloth. "All his hands know is desire. You must never untie him."

"Yes, Dr. Archer. I'm always careful."

"And you must never remove your veil."

"As I said, I'm always very careful."

"That's good."

"Dr. Archer,"—searching his eyes—"did he really write that play?"

"*The River of Night's Dreaming* . . . He believes he did."

Sitting in the living room wondering what Devo covering the Talking Heads might sound like. Then imaging it being played on a very worn 78.

After Karl Edward Wagner's "The River of Night's Dreaming."

Jolene

Seems like it was all webs and circles. The afternoon winds stopped and evening came. Life got harder without friends around . . .

No. No wife. She died. No girlfriend at the time. That part was kinda empty. Blank. Not that I didn't smile at a woman or 15. Just didn't take is all. Hard when yer low on cash. And everyone was low on cash back then. And it wasn't just that . . . Maybe I gave off a vibe.

Brokenness? Well, you could call it that. It was a blue Hell. No particular reason . . . Just happened that way.

Walked in and sparks. Fire comes to the caveman . . . Fuck doesn't know he's gonna get burned. Dumb and that hollow all he can see is the plot might be beginning a new chapter. One gilded with sunlight.

Nothing in this world is as tempting as redemption. Money and power can't touch it . . .

She looked like one of Hitchcock's blondes. Maybe the one in his Rear Window movie. Yeah, like her—That Princess chic. Came outta one of the big towns in the South. Silent at first, but she didn't stay that way long.

Post-What We Knew the details came out. In-between laughs. *And lies.* The heart don't forget. Not that stuff. Not when it goes like that. All those shadows. The tricks the rain plays. Pain and night-mares, they come later. Don't let up and they don't go away. Heart-broken whispers and prowls. It don't hide.

Don't care what you want. Think it offers choices? Don't.

Not a one.

Name was Jolene. Said she was French. On her father's side. Never mentioned her mother. Maybe she didn't have one? Father could have been the Devil. She had that in her.

Jolene. Thought—thought she was good. A garden. Sweet. And nice under the goth trappings. You could grow old with her . . .

Thought—

Legs long as the Mississippi . . . Laughing eyes that got ya shaking deep inside . . . *Lips.* Lips that said one more time. Said it over and over. Sweet, or wild. Addicting as hell. Pure candy. And this old boy had a sweet tooth.

Sang to me. Set fires burnin'. My nightmares thawed—Thought I put my mistakes in a place I couldn't get to . . .

Used my bed for something other than being afraid.

In that crowd of feelings the heart don't see. Hangin' dreams off the moon, whistling like it's a flower in summer rain, damn thing's blind. Don't notice the shadows . . .

Took note of 'em when I found myself drowning in bricks. Like they stood right the fuck up and shouted, hey dummy.

Yeah. It was everywhere I looked.

Just hit me. Ever been drunk and then yer stone-cold sober? Like that.

Man, I was standin' there smokin' and she was watching some creepy asshole count the money. And it hit me. The cargo in those boxes was dead. Thought it was guns or dope. Shit. It was bodies—Parts . . . And those steaks she had been feeding me—Fuck.

What would you have done? In that tomb with those stiffs? You'd save yer ass. The anger and disgust would rise up and you'd shoot her ass dead. And when you ran out of ammo you'd reload.

Fuck vengeance. I'm talkin' self preservation. If she got hard up, you can bet it'd be yer ass in the fry pan . . . *Sprig of some herb, some garlic.*

I saw that clear.

Thought of every time we'd been together and she'd looked at me. Knew she was thinking of beef on the hoof, not getting' it on with the man she said she loved.

Summer turned to instant, 50-below winter and I was naked. Wasn't a god damn tomorrow in the room. Me and her and that death chill. Her knife and her teeth and her hunger and my gun.

I did an Indiana Jones. BANG! *Emptied the magazine in her.*

Ended that right quick. Wasn't lettin' her stick me with that knife.

Layin' on the floor bleedin' out. Least I was breathin' . . .

Just walked out.

Ran.

Wanted as far away as I could get. Wanted as drunk as I could get. Wanted the mess ripped from my mind.

You want me locked up. Lock me up.

Won't change it.

She needed to die.

Maybe I do too?

Not for me to say . . .

But I didn't do anything wrong. In fact, I did what was right. 110% right.

You can call it whatever you like. On The Street we call it righteous with a capitol R.

Look, detective, she was a psycho. A cold-blooded killer. You can't reason with that shit. Not when it's gone over the edge. You get close to the edge, think yer gonna fall, you grab something. I grabbed a gun.

Fuck that. I'm here ain't I. That counts. Counts the way I figure it. You figure what you want. You sure as shit weren't there and you don't know jack-shit. The moon and stars were wacked. Fucked up. And she was . . . Fuckin' crazy—blood crazy.

Sleeping in that coffin was just playin'. Little Miss Dracula, shit. A god damn ghoul. And she had been feeding me *people*. Fuckin' people.

You'd have shot her or given her the needle. I saved you the trouble.

I'm bettin' your CSI doctors already told you she was eatin' people. Don't know nothing about the science part of it, but I figure they can tell easy enough what kind of diet she lived on. And the meat in her freezer—*Fuck*. We both know what that was. So you go ahead and do what you got to do.

Him? Fuck him. He was sellin' 'em. You think he bought 'em in a store? Same as her way I saw it . . .

Yeah, he had a gun. Didn't get to use it.

That's it, I'm done. Get me my lawyer. I'll take my chances with a jury of *regular* people. Better odds than being around her.

No. I've got nothing more to say to you.

Beth Orton, "She Cries Your Name."

6...6—

for fowles 'n kubrick 'n jack kirby

The impossible lost in sweet black ... I spent the night—perhaps it was an aeon—sitting on my barren moon looking at Siib. Each of her tears blames me.

   After a time I thought of men—They call her The Spire in M16; she is no eagle. Turned, as if called. Across the heavens on their small rock they wait. All the ugly they try to paint and dim with names. Try ... With their slogans. I am... I said... I think... No exit ... Write in their books of sand, carve their gossip thinking them threads of poetry in their nightingale inventories ... Passing dim seasons— roughly-hewn arrows of confusion, chanting ripples of transitory heat and foaming phrases of nostalgia and tragedy ... They dance their dances

                                        and then they are no more.
   I was bored with the baubles and bangles of Siib's prison dance
...

   I climbed down from the stars
   to taste

   souls

I walk across soft sand ... upon water

New York. Rat-tail darkcity ... The City of Night. Beer and psychosis by aggravated neon. The City and The City. After dark, My Sweet. The blonde on the street corner ... NY—sick sameness ... to robberies and gone. MAX now, the valley of Fear later
6 weeks
or   6 minutes ...

9-bottlebag scavenger ... the strides of noise ... the teethfaces will be coming—

drama and shadows

fear and

desire

look

A hand in a space for sentences ...

A quiet church. It's spikes and baptisms closed by the nudes in the broken glass across the street. One looks like Nico, one looks like Francesca Woodman ...

I remember wild mushrooms and Kristamas in the woods—her basket answering a song of feathers ... there were 7 clouds in trouble that day ... (*at one point I did*) ...

A shadow walks the street like a bass player with somewhere to go.

on the corner of Sherman with the imposition of a streetlamp the accomplishments of a dead animal ...

Heat

walls

the fluent scent of disordered

bare

bones

I sip used to be.

hoops. continental. cocktails.

my hand reeks of smoke.

isolato and hang-ups in a bottle dry as the thirst of a scream ... all the miles of money in ads on the undersides of brochures ... miles of targets ...

empty as the desert I once

walked ...

panic

painted under the sunshine

played my horn—no rain in the delta

watched

her ankles walked (over milkly ghosts) the palace floors
the whirr of my voice hooks—there to

HERE (after so many years)
        habits—(the madness, thrust of jam and suffering), means
                                Memphis,   where   I
laughed at Djedi, to Minglewood, where I ate lions and deliver crow-
cards, my black wings sing on blood.

        Gail Cupcake in a necklace of death scenes.splash draped
in feathers of winter lace.   Chapel.saddle.everything the tongue
knows
                        every L and M
bones.
bare
bones
        (and the sky dances)
Dead
dead not out the window or
street
or down the road—
                        fingers
                        (wishes of wings or other true stories)
like rich.
                Hours of rich. Hours of dreams and escape
that way.
Rain
and a gun.
It's all screams, a stage of tears imagining satisfactions that can
turn hard clay to soft,
                then rust and coffee and crabs and a motor court.
Behind the door . . .
I smoke
have a beer
—give up. Depth. Understanding.

I love the strange and raw here . . . the wings of the violins cry.
The brunette wants to be blonde, wants to be loved, wants to be Eve

and a star and 50 stories above the gutter—dancing and YOUNG (without suffering the memory agains of While) . . .

                      but her   hands are
filled.with.rain.

~*~

I have skin.

Lines . . . front to sea. Dogs bark into the chaos on Snowhill. In their pinched basements, corpse devourers—little black hearts and blue tears, do not even turn their flat heads to taste the mold and mire of the scratching din . . .

The flies. The ants.
All bores me.
I find tiny moments so attractive . . .
My knife is a sun. It does not share its meat

                        Upon hearing Gil Scott-Heron had died.

…LIES……Thunder……ashes……………

for the friends & faces of the HPLFF & . . .
my "vEry dear" friends in the Northwest! !!)

I—(The Sound of Bones & Flutes)

wind in my pockets.
dust climbing my stem.

Hands, without a will be . . .

eyes—

wish they were part of a different dance.

Can't say I like this picture. Or the road.

Started at a party. By a piano.

I was in need. Been a long time. One of those other lives, before cigarettes and cocaine. Before I got lost. Felt need. Didn't know what.

No one told me about her eyes—

about that first kiss . . .

~*~

Left New York City.

West.

Drove.

threw things away . . .

threw things away . . .

threw drama, victory /fighting /the awake of the afterlife /easy /never rainbow /never friends /telling the difference /tipping fate with the moon /the pills that grabbed your memory

webs

blurred webs that diverted dreams

Drove through the open county of green—watched the sky, for

hawks, for rain, took off my sneakers so I could feel the flip side of the coin if the weathervane raised an alarm, never did. Watched a boy chase a dog. Both were too full of joy to stop and consider catching distractions. Drove through the quiet epics.

Off to hang with Nicky.

Moved my Chevy through night and day for a week, lonesome ride, back of my head to bottom of my heart. Other coast. Outta the chaos and the street noise. Outta tricks to hide behind.

Cigarettes and the radio . . .

Coffee with sharp teeth to stay on the board and out of the ditch.

Changed the words to "California Girls" a few times. Wanted to be a hero not a villain this time. If I got a chance . . .

Nicky had an old house in Portland. Him and Kellz. They had room for me.

JD and Mike needed a guitar player. A guitar is one thing I had, Devil gave me that.

Kellz had a club. The Mandarin Club. Needed a house band— "Something fun they can dance to." Told me to skip empty and get back on the horse. Added lot of nice girls out here—strippers, Goths, brains, ink, and every dialogue of sensual the summer moon ever painted on a rose. Even over the phone line I could hear him wink. You'll love them and they'll adore you.

I hadn't played Portland in ten years. Now I was going to surf back and cover FUN. C'est la vie, wanted to see my friends. Packed my demons and drove. Pulled right out of hell. Left some things I didn't understand dead. Didn't look in the rearview. Was afraid to.

Coffee and trees and not so far away, 40 miles outside of the city I heard The New Riders of the Purple Sage's "Portland Woman" on the radio. Grinned like a kid. No more lonesome NY kick in the head for me. I hoped. Lit a smoke followed a cloud drift into town.

First days and nights in Portland rinsed the salt and cawing from my wounds.

Old home week. We made the beerlights sing. Laughed when arms opened. Devoured two herds of beef creatures and enough Thai to feed Southeast Asia for a month. Flew for a few weeks then restless got wind of my address.

Mike and Lena had a nice little place. Homey. That was Lena's doing. No two cats in the yard, but they were growing a garden without troubled waters to be sure. Had a WELCOME to the big city party for me.

Jenna sat on the piano bench. Glass of wine . . .

and those eyes.

And yes, I did take note of the curves. I'm fucked-up not dead. Stood there stupefied as any dumbass watching Rapture approach.

Lena slipped her arm in mine. "She's single." Leaned in. "And she's smart." Eyes laughed at me. "Can't hurt to say hi."

Hurt. No. Maybe? Might? Can't say. But it was scary.

"Mr. Former Rockstar afraid of a beautiful girl. Maybe *Rolling Stone* will put that in your Where-Are-They-Now paragraph?"

"After their review of my last album doubt they'd even print my name."

Laughed. Another hug. "She's a spitfire. Before she was into vampires and Lovecraft she was into witchcraft, be careful, she'll bewitch you."

Hell, she already had. Hoped my interior was still interior and Lena didn't see my boyish all knotted in thoughts of darling's medicine.

"Let's get you one to replace that dead solider and I'll introduce you."

She did.

First word I started drowning.

Told me about her high tech phone and Facebook. About the film she was working on, *The Hands That Reek and Smoke*. Lovecraftian horror; did I know HPL, or Nyarlathotep? Primary footage had been shot and they were still looking for someone to score it as it began the editing process.

Lena inserted, "Get Quijote here to do it." (Mike has always called me Quijote. Hell, he even got *Rolling Stone* and *NME* to tag me with it.) Put her hand on my shoulder. "Big rockstar this one. Doom and gloom, he's the king. Perfect for your on-the-losing-end brand of horror. Ozzy isn't even close. This one is the *real* Prince of Darkness." Gave me a wink and a hug. Laughed. "How can a Goth girl resist that?"

They both laughed.

I looked for the key to my tongue.

Lena and Jenna had a sunny exchange about a guy I never saw in a mirror. Jenna slid over on the bench and asked me to play.

Lena's elbow 2nded the motion. Sat. Looked at the keys and my fingers. Hoped they'd be good to me. Played an old one about bliss leaving with other kisses. Hadn't laid it down so pure in years.

Dwelled in down. Floor of a basement. No door. No lock. Need fractured-in-loss pure as a blues no hope will cure. Add the madness of desire. Even my never-good-enough bluesman's heart thought I got it right for once.

I finished. Lena started right in about the Sleepwalkers and *Night Blind* our first record. Psych-doom blues, Tom Waits as the front man for a stoner band who distorted fractured blues laced in the fabrications of null & void, add some avant-by-way-of-grim influences.

Mike grinned. "We were pretty good back then. Weren't we?"

I smiled and nodded. We were. Those times we weren't too stoned or chasing things other than the music.

Lena: "You guys should play a little." Gave Mike those For Me eyes.

Mike and Nicky pulled out three of Mike's guitars and we did a short set. For Jenna the dead river poet inside emerged. Reached for up, chose the side the poem in her eyes was on.

Orchid-soft power guided me as she smiled and clapped between numbers. I remember the first time I heard my voice coming out of a car radio. Felt just like that.

I sat back down on the bench. We talked; the experiments and weeds trapped inside the neon of New York, the state of rock, film. I let my wanna-be-Valentino consume her perfume. I was in a cascade of grasping believe for two hours. Robin betrothing its chambers to a comet, sure as hell didn't want to decouple back to vacancy.

Lena walked over and handed her two cds she just ripped. "Listen to these, Jenn. Pain and fear. *And dreams.* It's all in there."

I tried to not look dumb, and thoughts on a voyage of Faustian bargains, hoped to hell she liked them.

Jenna asked if they were any good. I fumbled. Critics and the fans liked them—most of them, I sometimes—often—regarded them as close, no cigar.

Would have remained there uncoiling in the waves of her sea, but the silver lining had to go home.

My gestures refused to part with the curves of her effects when the door closed. Animal in a dry cage drained half a beer and when home.

Kellz was out of town. Nicky had left for his gal's pad.

Alone.

Still.

Again . . .

But my hand reached for my guitar not the bottle. Let my blisters spoon some captured on the neck as I strummed a stripped down cover of Hornby's "Every Little Kiss." Meant it. Played it again. Laughed. Anyone heard me play this fifteen years ago would have thought I'd gone over to Jesus or bet I'd fallen down the rabbit hole bumped my head on deranged and taken up with Karen Carpenter. Scott Walker or David Sylvian they'd understand, anyone of a 100 blues tunes, but old love songs . . . I would have been stricken from the charts a hell of a lot sooner.

Cupid had me trembling for a Goth chic. Me? I was Bukowski to Springsteen's Dylan. Laughed at the lace and mortar of immersion.

Put my guitar in the stand walked to the window. Wondered what street out there she lived on. Pushed the warp of my dreamy over there toward feathers and cozy.

"Sweet dreams, Jenna."

Went to bed.

Tossed.

Tried to pack up.

Flopped. Opened agape. Clawed at angel wings. Begged at the Tower of Know. No ladder handy it refused to open its math to me. Turned. Minutes.

Resented the moonlight.

Played puzzle with has not and Eden. Ribbons.

Clock. Arrows. The morsels leading to the bridge. Ran angles and in circles.

Another few shovels of minutes.

Followed by a boatload.

A dragon in a beggar's cave, every creak in me was galvanized, her arm, her dress, how the language of her personality transported amused.

Might have whispered a prayer . . .

Sorted.

Glue.

Missed the lullaby meadow of Morpheus' cues.

Jena called me the next day. Said she listened to the cds. Liked them, "They seemed like Dracula writing the obits of Dick and Jane. Tattered. Tragic choking on pressure. The grim poetics, I certainly see why Lena said Tom Waits." A lot.

We met on Wednesday. Again she said she like what she'd heard. Would I consider scoring her film? Her funds were limited, less than $500 for a score.

She'd burned a rough cut on a DVD for me. Would I take a look, consider doing the project? I went back to the house and sat watching it. Me and my guitar. Kellz brought pizzas home. Pots of coffee disappeared.

There was something in it that felt like an incarceration. I had been trapped.

Full of irreversible, her fingers had given me imagination.

And a secret. I felt I had to do this. Became certain only I could see the secret. Perhaps the sound of my soul could be a key to open time and oblivion's flight for the Others.

Had to do this.

Had to please her. More. I'd use chocolate, dot-by-dot, or every friend to poetry in my veins.

I had to capture her.

She had captured me, taken my map, and all my steps, and I could not reside in this cage of shadows alone. Would not. I needed her to bring me light.

Be light!

All I had to do was set the experience in tones. Sing of cold stars, and the humiliated faces, name the islands with truth. I would unravel my anguish, open my gates of hate and dry, and give her the grit of my failures. I had, before fake's façade fell, sang, captured thousands, I would stretch out my song and she would come to me. The lantern of her heart would shine on me.

I'm not one for horror, most of my friends are. Some but not a lot, I'm all for thrill and spills flickering before my eyes, not big on blood and gore. Poe's good, deal me in. Zombies, pass—no need to look for the EXIT sign I'm holding the door OPEN. Do not pause, my dagger is drawn against any battle plan you might have. Hadn't really been in Lovecraft country since early high school. Horror was

Kellz's bag; he was a walking history book, the literature, the movies, big-budget blockbusters and B's, classic or coming soon. I went home and rifled Kellz's bookcases looking for Lovecraft. Needed a fast refresher. Found a book called *The Nyarlathotep Cycle.* Jenna had spoken of Nyarlathotep, of his strategic role in her production. Read like a man possessed. Fuck. Was!

In search of tonal hues, buried myself in a massive book of Lovecraftian art Kellz owned. No zoo of strange this was more than a mere book of imaginary beings—six legs, ten, behemoths, demons and devourers of the dead, it was a gathering of infinite tigers and wild seas, blasphemies; pen & ink renderings; painting in oil and watercolors; sketches, murals; colors and black velvet—70 years of art, of horrors. Noted all the tentacles. I vaguely remembered the tentacles from reading some Lovecraft when I was a teen, but now felt like I was swamped in them. Tentacles. Knots. Caught. Clutched. Shattered minds. Cliffs and peaks, nameless places and sin. Deranged sequences of nightmares that called from the black. No way out. Undone.

Got it. An angle.

We talked briefly on the phone: Her last production, *CATCH TOMORROW,* won the Best Feature Award at the *H. P. Lovecraft Film Festival* and she was premiering this one there soon. Corman, Woodward, and Del Toro, last year's judges, not only crowned *CATCH TOMORROW* BEST but fawned over it. Jenna eloquently gave me the run down. Grim. Noir grit, urban fear, a deal for blood was struck.

I told her I'd been reading the Robert Price anthology of Nyarlathotep stories. Was proud of myself for not telling her how big a bite I'd taken from her apple.

I agreed to do the project. Wondered if she could hear the begging in my voice.

She asked if I had any time on Saturday to view the first cut of the film.

Sadly no. I was playing Saturday night. Could she stop by the club?

Her sorry, no, was crushing. But she added she had Sunday open. Would I come over?

Yes.

Jenna gave me her phone number. Quickly writing it down, I felt like a tiger, nearly limitless. Followed it with her address. Ten blocks away. 56 Paradise! A mere ten blocks. I could leap that far.

I told her I'd be there at three sharp.

"That's wonderful." Her tone was full of YAY!

The mist before my heart parted. I saw river-garden dreamlands beyond the winter my tears thought impervious.

I wanted to be ready for our date. Was one to me.

Saturday night. Played great. Didn't sit up with the poets drinking. Did count sheep.

Sunday. Counted the steps to her door. To an observer they may have appeared to be small, but each was a giant leap.

Rang the bell.

Was greeted with joy. Not an atom of reserved in it.

Pot of coffee and fire in her eyes she sat there examining footage. I watched, stared. Opened that old suitcase that hadn't been looked in in years, turned over rocks. Rolled up my sleeves. Scratched notes for a theme, and a few other things. This had to be good. Had to be! Last time I wanted to impress a woman this bad was 15 years ago.

Her film was about Lovecraft's Black Man. A trickster playing Faust-games with fools. His hands reek of smoke. Leaves ashes whenever he travels. Hell, felt like I was about to score my autobiography.

Wanted to show Jenna my soul. Needed to. Had this feeling she'd take care with it. Under the dark trappings of Goth there was sunshine. My roots stretched. Sunshine. Sunshine. They sang. Begged.

Sunshine—I could succeed, weave a balm, nourish a new destiny.

The healing game. Put my head in it, heart and soul.

I watched. She enlightened me. Her film was modern, urban. My thoughts swirled around a mixture of Leonard Cohen and Tom Waits fronting 16 Horsepower trumpeting psychedelic ghostclouds; add some Düsseldorf-fuzz and a cold sweat-inducing drone. Also thought to replace the flutes in the stories with a trumpet and sax. Better fit for my urban-hard bluesman on his front stoop/top-step approach. Modernize the old pharaoh. That's what she'd done. Nyarlathotep was here. Here to raise Hell. Brought extra THRAK with clout-waves of WHOOM.

The actor she'd cast was an old guy, but still panther-graceful. Tall. Even by NBA standards. Oddly cut offputting. Ribbons of aboriginal turbulence occupied the space he took up. Head to expensive shoes the man on the screen was a painting that brought the wrong in her glare of Bukowskian desolation. He was theatrical, piercing.

Old Hollywood story; Lena—"Yes, I used my best friend's name."—stood in rough streets, five blocks from the dotted-line of starshine. Fame, fortune. Name in lights if you can get to the end. Enter a pair of predators, bent on bending her over and taking. Frozen in fear.

And the cavalry arrives. But John Wayne is Nyarlathotep.

Claws never get to kiss her lark and curves with the battle of cold-blooded FREAK. Cuts them down. Unknotted scraps.

Offers Lena his hand, and the stars.

And she took it.

Her dreams of soft and safety. She gets them. Carcosa is quiet, restive . . .

While I watched her raw footage; she shared her ideas regarding sound design, "Hard and fast here. Searing neon and grim.," "Gets quiet and ambient here. Dark." "Sonics that bring to mind screaming in the next short section." "Lot of tears in this flashback." I made more notes; stripped down Waits'-hued blues flowered by a fabrication of ambient elements; Lustmord under some Women of the SS; sounds like noise or a fight around the corner; a touch of classic horror motifs; drunk and distorted; bruises; reference something along the lines of an old Bee Gees or Manilow tune there; minor chords and thrum; damp.

Score-wise I had what I needed. She told me she felt certain things, certain types of sound were needed here and here. This should lead to that. The music needs to be a path, it needs to lead the viewer toward what lies ahead and not simply underscore visuals.

"This is the gate. It leads to freedom from pain and the shackles of containment. There's an orchestral type of building in the sonic elements so when Nyarlathotep and Lena leave Earth for the stars and Carcosa the audience travels along with them. A theme that repeats, almost a chant in some fashion, until finally it blooms and all is revealed."

We agreed to meet next Saturday after the show and I'd show her what I had.

At the door she gave me a kiss.

I bounced all the way home. Pulled out my guitar, dreamed.

Strummed. Searched for melodies. Lena needed a theme, I needed to find it. Lena's theme was the map to Jenna's heart.

More than simply thirsty I went to the kitchen for a cold one to lift in celebration and found myself humming along with the radio. Almost laughed, Nicky was always leaving the radio on low and I found myself thankful for his absentminded quirk.

Malo "Sauvecito." Always loved that horn part. DJ followed it with War "All Day Music." Perfect. Trumpet with a B-3 under it for Lena. Dreaming of a shining better over the rainbow, but darken it, add some rough.

Perfect. Lena's dream—muted trumpet reaching, the dark, dangerous street, and the Hammond leading as Lena and the Black Man enter Beyond for the slow fog of Carcosa.

Popped the DVD in the player and strummed along. Watched. Hummed. I could feel Jenna smiling at me.

Saw the two urban-hard predators on the screen, saw the Black Man. Nyarlathotep—otherworldly evil and a Loki, a trickster cardplayer with a loaded hand. Cain for Cain. Deltas, pharaohs, blues gutbucket raw—jukejoint Buddy Guy with a shitty amp, and evershifting orient sands. Something that howled and growled, dry, gradations—the texture of confrontation burning with primal hate as mirage, that's what I needed for the Black Man's theme.

Dark and mind-numbing-avant, something that didn't make sense but was all felt. Timeless dread. A rage of bitter noise that split the night as stiff primates huddled in caves. He was the gush of a bleak aurora, inhaling the isolation of burdened hearts. It was in the set of his shoulders, in the heat worming in his eyes, ebony chasms, sour sails spread, shook by things shaken off tongues that were a foam of holes. Man, if he was a man, which would put a sea of fears in a man's bowels. I sure as hell didn't know how the actor pulled it off, but he was a thing from the black corridors on the far side of the moon. He was in motion, attached and engaged yet weightless, even when he didn't move.

When old mages spoke of black necromancy this is what they tried to describe. But you couldn't put this performance in words. Maybe I could do it with notes and unusual time signatures?

I worked feverishly. Rode all night. Drank water to stay chained to the work, something new for me. Three A.M. I put something new under the hood, coffee. Sleep wouldn't grab me. Let it grip my arm threaten hostage—it could try, I was too loaded to get stuck on rain and fade into a losing end. Words came. And I locked on the theme, a waltz, circular, ever pushing. It would not be denied.

Almost called Jenna to play it for her.

Didn't.

We talked later that day. I filled her in.

Brought my guitar and laptop to her place two days later. Put the DVD in and played her what I had.

Overall she approved. Smiled. Hugged me.

Followed it with suggestions.

Damn good ones.

They fit.

Filled my desire. We were in sync. Leaned into if we could gel so perfectly with this we would in other ways.

Jenna sent me home with dreams . . .

II—(Devil Music in tempore belli)

Saturday. She was coming. More contact with her quilt of roses. More translations. Another page of harmony's terrain.

No more mad—I declare that war slapped back, remanded—or tight. No stuck on the bottom of some middle with mundane bleeding ennui. I was stirred. Bone to skin high.

Jenna brought the Black Man to Kellz' club. She had a feeling meeting him might add something to the score.

Mike and Kellz and Nicky didn't like him—a hell of a lot of DID NOT. JD's radar locked on pronto, spun him around and sent him outside for a smoke. And the vibe he gave off flat-out frightened me. He was very pleasant, elegantly so, polite and charming, and not the way vote-hungry politicians come off, but after shaking his hand I felt like I lost something. Everyone has some IT that enhances them, mine felt like it was flipped inside out.

Mr. Phoenix's voice was the aria of a hawk in a vast cavern, musical, but nothing recitative, this was composed, it was master of the air and all—little better than spider-brushed amusements or fodder—below. And it was distance, far and hidden, unknowable. Yet the shadows it cast were knowable, the kind of *know* you get when you're afraid even if you can't say by what exactly. Its towering sculpture was the specter of fear, a velvet thunder-melody entitled by heat that swept tourists off their feet. It beat its dark wings and walls and harbors of butterflies lost their connection to structure.

Nicky stepped back. Turned away and was quick to down his whiskey. Kellz found a managerial task that required an extra set of hands.

I stood there. Iced-up with no pointing finger to turn me to opening.

Jenna beamed. I tried to take hold of her light. She laughed lightly and took my hand, rowed me into a flow where the blackness of the abyss was expelled by her lantern. At the bar she placed a double in my hand. Intima was in her eyes, desert-dry I filled my notebook with the cozy ciphers that gave vitality to real.

Like I said, I'm not Mr. Horror, never been, not really. Poe and the Headless Horseman, yeah, back in the day sure. Pass on blood and beggars that can't retreat from the glint of feral, give me a girl and doors opened to rooms of honey; I'll take scenes of amazing and a bed of candles that are not empty skip the bite of dark and kitchen knives barking acrimony. All I wanted was her arms, future for my rust.

And I almost told her that.

Almost. Elbowed me toward further, pushed, it wanted to come out and let it be me rip.

Wanted to make pleasure a fact.

My alone, burning with beat and helpless, hit angles and a swarm stiff with cannot, was limited to the ditch of might fail.

We drank, we laughed. She sent me home. Happy.

And with the soft blue canto of her eyes—the only tonight I want in my heart—turning deaden parts of me to gold I went back to work on the score. I put my desire, every mane and sign of my river, in Lena's search for the stars. Put all the anthems and distractions of my loud-brew wars in the predators.

I had Lena's theme.

Was happy with it, leaned into its burst. Was sure Jenna would be so thrilled a hug would be the applause that leaped my sorrow and filled my cup of alone with sunshine.

I was high.

Until the fact of the Black Man blinded the squadron of love I'd struck.

The Black man—

wrong/Leveling/Roaring and listening, the rule that breaks my chess seeds/The blade absolute/My distress bundled in its echo/Shroud . . . The thing that stops breathing.

Got up and made coffee. Looked at the Jack, passed on sweetener. Smoked. Paced. Wished I had a dog to walk or marketing that needed now. Anything to avoid turning my thoughts to the Black Man and his music.

I tried to sleep.

One more set of shadows, one more crisis, then the only thing I'd ever be tangled in again was countryside and poetry.

"You know how he *feels*." Shivered. "Just do it."

Stopped tossing.

Parked on my sofa. Me and my guitar. Building a black raga.

Came quick.

Flash of George Crumb's *Black Angels*. Jenna paused the film looked me in the eye, said, "The sound of bones and flutes." Sure as hell in his eyes. Man, love, fragile fingers trying to revolt and escape dense and horrible, desperate to find the speech of lovely. Comfort, eyes, and hopes, all dim stains poured over the rocks of hate.

"Nyarlathotep." Something in her hue changed scents. ". . . *came out of Egypt . . . looked like a Pharaoh.*" Her eyes went far away when she said it. "*. . . rest vanished.*"

I'd held a shotgun once. Cold thing. Loaded. It could chew off your legs, take an arm. But it was hard. Didn't care. Didn't recognize people from other *things*. No difference between a bird or a window or a man facing it. The Black Man was the same. He was beyond or above the spiral endeavors of ripples caged in clocks, people might as well been made from chalk. Humanity was a salmon bursting with want, hell, maybe it's need, in a braided universe that took no note of unraveling clouds. Born, lose, next can't, flower tries to blind-crawl gets nowhere, dies. Laugh, cry, want—fatten your stew with stars, pin emphasis on every branch, I was sure the corridors of his magnitude didn't even catch the scent of human tide.

Everything else fell into place.

I finished it in a week. Presented it to her.

She smiled when I was done playing it for her.

"I think it works?" Didn't come out solid enough to overcome the begging for approval in my tone.

"Like a key in a lock."

Spinning like birds triggered by Spring's first current, swift blood hung up a YAY.

A week later she gave me the final cut. I spent two weeks in Mike's studio tweaking.

Jenna came over and picked it up. Filled me in on her agenda, a few weeks out of town, interviews and hype, tons of social networking, setting the stage, then last minute prepping for the fest. We'd meet the night before. Have dinner. McMenamins' Kennedy School.

"Eight sound good?"

"Perfect." Hoped a bottle of wine and for a moon and flickering warmth in mosaic-tiled fireplace in The Courtyard after. Eased into an October chill and snuggling—

Night before the premiere. Stepped out of my car didn't like what I drank in, the constellation and confetti of hope I was packing got edited out of my sight. In front of the restaurant where we were to meet the wrong face called out to me. Jenna stood there with the Black Man.

See what it is first. Place this big she might have bumped into him? Can still be a date.

Has to be.

She reached out and took my hand. Wasn't smiling.

No hug.

I met his eyes.

Felt like a scalpel, wanting dig the ground of interior, was fiddling with my clothes. Felt my border had been crossed by a mission-capable saber composed of off with this infraction's head.

He did not offer his hand.

Smiled. When I was eight, and a well-indoctrinated little Methodist, I thought Satan smiled just like that, victorious, cold. His gaze crossed the parking lot, climbed until it rested on something I couldn't see. Said, "Night descends" Tendrils of smoke coiled from his hands. "on the parade of dung-beetles plotting in the garden of lust." Turned to look over my shoulder. A slowmo effect outta *The Matrix*. Turned back. Face to face. "And the butterfly becomes *le festin de l'aragnée.*"

Guess my face covered it.

"Tomorrow when my film opens a gate will be unlocked. Your score, each pulse and tone, will be the key.'

"Huh?"

"What you were lead to, instructed to compose, is the key that opens the way. As Jenna's images flicker in the eyes of the viewers your aural cues will incite primal fear and together these components will unlock the gates. The Old Ones will pour through the barriers and all that crawls on this rock will lose its skin."

Nyarlathotep. Scriptwriter. Producer. He laughed—unrelenting-kill diamond-hard.

Wild ass shit or simply fucked-up, there's times you hear plain fact and you know there's no inaccuracies in it, you can't stand it but truth is truth. This was one of those. That Cthulhu-thing was coming here to do a Godzilla-on-steroids. There'd be tentacles and insane shit everywhere . . . And blood.

No more blue.

No more breath. No one would get to choose one lump or two.

No babies.

No dogs.

Lena's macramé threads in a blast of rubble and mud. No Nicky and Kellz laughing over a beer.

Oysters. None.

Awake. Not.

Exhibition of crayon images scotch-taped to a fridge. Flippant. Obligatory. Needs for seams and compasses. No—No—No. Not.

None.

No kittens.

Tentacles. All those unholy things I'd seen in that book of Love-craftian art here. All the monstrosities Jenna had described as we'd viewed her film.

Wished my wobbly came from stoned about to nod off or deranged. But all I had was death scenes and a mind full of blasphemies.

Jenna's eyes, no soft blue lovely in them, raised the Svengali with the heat of adored. She kissed his hand, the way they kiss the Pope's ring. Jenna, my lantern, his whore and seamstress, her skin and belly donating my soul to the winds that licked the bonfire-glow of his playhouse. Jenna castrating me. Hanging the face of my birds on the blades of his windmill.

Nyarlathotep. Rainmaker. Coal-black—void-black—eyes screeching with insect-fire. Black landscape, the cold path—axe, filling the shore of my failure with a cancer of blackness.

The shipwreck of my desires, the faces I had come to know and love, Brian, Gwen, Jarred, Andrew, Alanna, all scalped, litter.

No more soft. Gone goodies, birthdays. No more films from David Prior. Glancy's epic anecdotes silenced. Not another creamy day tomorrow woven in Ed Morris' magnitude.

All fall down.

My tears hissed. Howled. She asked for the sound of bones, my tears were clotted with it.

I could not turn.

Could see no pardon.

Jenna had released my hand. Didn't turn and offer a goodbye. Stepped to his side. Stood. Relaxed. More than like-minded. Consort.

She kissed his hand again. Fuck, her lips parted. I was sure she was about to sigh in some orgasmic way. Thought she was about to lick his fingers.

His index finger traced her jawline. She closed her eyes and basked in the caress. His eyes and cold smile laughed at me.

My chest was a hollow as the Tin Man's.

He, through magic or some other thing a man could not get his head around, held a cheap guitar, missing a string. Tossed it to me. "You can sing a last song or two as the curtain falls." Voice sounded like a shotgun to me.

Then the Black Man and my dream . . . gone.

I stared at the hole of blackness they stepped through. Looked down at the guitar. And I ran . . .

Walled up behind a briar of fear. Mine. Theirs, the dim mortals who were sleeping as this verdict crashes. Hate pours from black crypt, and sea, and bane-saturated stars, and all the deeps between. From pole austral to pole boreal the Harms Tremendous, no longer fettered to strange-time most abhorrent, thunder. Stillness, if there ever was any, is lost to discomfort and death.

I can see Jenna's eyes. Feel the heat of that first kiss. A kiss that was not for me.

Fool, I'd locked myself in a hundred hells, walled myself in, but this one . . . I'm no escape artist—

Don't know how many days or weeks, or maybe it's only hours, mankind has left. But I know how this ends. All the ants get crushed under the stomping black boots of this Storm. Never spent any serious time thinking about or worrying about death, but there it is. What the hell are you supposed to do? Run? Scream?

Pray?

Don't know when the stark of no god and no heaven set in. But it did. Didn't have to come to grips with it. Didn't drag any hiss of terror out of me. Never missed the inlaid-Christian that disappeared from my marrow.

Still, I felt like I'd been whacked. Hard.

Maybe that's what you should feel when desolation festoons blind with sight?

Yonder to yonder 10:30 looking at midnight.

No reason for a broken mind to cross.

No Lord on the horizon . . .

"Take The Devil." Hadn't heard it since the mid-70's, don't remember half the words, but it's what bursts into my thoughts. Standing there holding a bag of fuck and an old Eagles song is holding me like a length of rope that ends noosed to all the unaccountable that's corralled me . . . I remember the guitar line better than the words

Various songs by Ray Lamontage, Joe Henry, and Mark Eitzel.
Add Malo, "Sauvecito"; War, "All Day Music"; The Eagles, "Take the Devil";
The New Riders of the Purple Sage, "Portland Woman"; and
George Crumb's *Black Angels* "Thirteen Images from the Dark Land."
(Nope. No Tom Waits. Not this time.)

Rune Grammofon poem
[U.N/umbered)))))

try to keep your cigarette lit in this light / go ahead / try / try / line up all your self-portraits and wine bottles / you can put them over there with the wind / the caravan departs soon / spit out the sand / c'mon all of it now / even the traces / did it do any good / go on now / dismantle the sun / can you do it / try to sleep after your nights in the bottles of anxiety / go ahead / try / try / no room for the holes in your pockets out here on the edge / you can tap at the limits all you like / but the gangs care little for your adventures in-between sultry and overload / they're too busy etching all the white out of the flat mysteries / too concerned with keeping moonlight in the sacred urn of smoke / so go ahead / scream into the starry night / who'll hear you / there's no indian summer waiting under an umbrella in the rain / not here / so what next / dreams of the right words / not here / Anne / or Pamela / clean and even / not here / not here /

time's up voyager / go back to your ghosts / to the hurry of life-size in the small / or run to your barefoot girls / or blood-haired mother in her death-black robes / maybe they'll have you / here / you're just a sick child / sin and ashes on cardboard

After Edvard Munch & Supersilent 6.5 / 6.6.

234

Marks and Scars and Flags

Is it real?
Is it?

These last six hours . . .

This pack.

Did she, looking down at her feet and gently smiling—in that crocodile way, really say, "Go. Ask, Alice."?

Did she?

While I stood there, that silence all around, on that cold bank, waiting to cross.

Did she have to ask if I was mad?

Does she think all I do is make the bed, rub the dishes with soap and clean water, and listen to those voices? *I think.* When I'm in the yard, and the world is changing around me, I think.

Is that madness?

She sits there, across the room, seeing everything I say. Never asks me to stop. Not even when I cry.

All those times I sat on her knee. Me, puppet. Pet—"Good boy. Good, boy." Thing. Waiting. Being good. Trying to be. Even my hello said, I'm behaving, I'm listening. I'm trying to understand. Even though the whole world is changing around me.

The cars hiss by, rushing to meeting and pedigrees . . . and the dogs on their chains howl; they're frightened, wounded, they feel it . . . Night takes on a chill—that scares me. I can feel it grow. It's a live thing. I don't see why They don't see it. I don't understand why she can't feel it.

Can't it penetrate all those scars? Or is it simply a question of fears?

Why does she fear the stars?

They're too far away to leave scars. Too soft. Too small. They look small. I keep telling her that. Does she think that's foolish?

What you are, even in this twisting light, is what you are. It's the whole world that's changing.

Can't she see that?

When she's grinning in her sleep, I think she knows. Looks like it. Looks like she looked that afternoon when the revolution upset things.

I know she saw the signs. She even told me she saw them. Every-one of them. Told me she heard all the talk in that upstairs room. Even over the saxophone making love to summer, she heard. And she wasn't drunk. She was all there. Some of the others weren't. They were drunk, their clattering tongues made harsh noises, licked the filthy laughter tossed at them. But she heard. She heard the widows and their tiny voices, and the flag, that animal lighthouse that is quick to shake your blood, to tumble the comfort in your lock and key. She heard.

Heard the animals run over her skin.

The drummer and the piano player heard it to. She talked to them after. Told me what they said. When I was in her arms, lost in her world rising and falling back, she told me. I was close, I heard it all.

Even that thing in her eyes that went unspoken. I felt it on her skin. Touched it before she put it away with all the things that are coming, and her solitude. Hid it behind those absolutes. I see them burning. Tall as mountains. I see them. Manic and full of countries of abandoned.

I was in there. Once. Back when I fell for her. Once? Maybe it was many times? Hard to remember, I was bleeding and the cat was up there on that high beam arguing a difficult game. Told him, I was already sold. He could take his clouds and go. Back to his hole. Take all his bells with him. Just take his treasons and retire.

I was not going to surrender.

Didn't have anything to give. I was sold.

SOLD.

The trumpets rang out the day I was inaugurated. They were loud. And unmistakable. The heroes were there with their glory days, red and gold and immortal, or so we were told. They grinned. Even the strikers took the day off. They grinned too. Everyone saw the sign. Said they'd keep the secret.

And they have.

It's not them. They have not sold me to the stations of December. Would not. Not even after the flowers of the revolution fell under the feet of the weary. Not even as the day grows shorter and closes, and the flag goes cold. Not even then.

Vanity. Fears. The things in the mirror. All that time that stands against desire, time that can't rewrite the thunder. They can put up a new flag to fly and push and cover new ground to pull you along, like you're mad. They can even hand out a new sun. One with a new plan to relight hearts with love you madly. Let them. Let them try. It won't stick to this floor, or these walls.

She knows that. I told her so.

I told her these stars won't get me. They are too soft. Too far away. I don't feel them pull. They try. Push that moon at me. Try to spoon it down my throat. It doesn't work. Can't. Not when I'm sitting here at her feet.

I don't see that moon as a sign of the times. Not when her secret heart tells me I've been a good boy.

I don't feel the faces of other countries on the walls.

Don't.

Can't.

I won't listen to the stairs or the libraries. I'll not pawn the oath.

I won't write about cold water. Or learn to tell myself there's nothing else. Nothing else but walls of blood.

They brought their colors six hours ago. Brought their story, and By Thens, and they stand out there, trumpets crying, leaning at me.

I won't learn the nothing else they carried here.

She's looking down at her feet and gently smiling—in that crocodile way, says, you can't stay here in this room. Your pillow is no lover, it won't keep you safe. If you won't believe me, Go, ask Alice. Open the tall prayers, negotiate. If you can.

I'd go sit beside her, but that won't do. Not in this light. Even if she speaks my name. Even if she adds flesh and blood, and all her dreams.

Not in this light.

Not even for her sparks, each a hand that blooms on flesh and blood. They want a place in my brain. I won't turn that light on. Not for them. She can keep the parade, and all the kisses.

She knows what is true.

And what is not.

I wish she'd tell them to take their sun home. I wish she'd tell all those busy crows I won't go. Won't be a ghost.

Not even if Alice were to ask.

I won't stare into her grave mouth while it dances, spreading its cruel time, and unlearn what was written in *The Imperial Dynasty of America*. Won't revoke my pledge as *His Knight* and vanish, so their world of spite and petty temptation and its stone-fist doctrine can remain and flower.

I will not be struck by their flag.

The pack is out there. Been out there half the day. Erecting a Lethal Chamber to assault my window. Posting their handbills and pronouncements. Marking things. I see it. I can hear it. Hear it twist and scar.

Do they believe their straggle of fables can astonish, or conquer, my heart and its limbs? That I am some throbbing hummingbird that must circuit the black architecture their master frightens the world with?

They circulate their war, tarnish cheeks with knots of blood ... They only seek to bruise, to mark and encrust all light with crude. They roar from abyss-colored throats, seeking, pulling on wires, calling phantoms from the grave.

They can fish, but they won't eat my soul.

I turn away from the things—each a fierce bull pawing—they wave. Face her.

Her face is a mask. And she's talking, spreading words not allowed in this house. But I won't tumble. Not even with all those cold, songbird sparks coming off the hem of her robe. Not even with the whole wide world changing around me.

Her eyes are deep as a mirror. Her smile full of quiet departures. She opens her umbrella—beneath it, the Milky Way is a whirlpool of stars, soft stars. She sways, and changes her tongue. "Change."

Her smile blurs, releasing cobwebs and corridors.

"Turn." Soft as the saxophone that afternoon, cold, a trumpet that bends the facets in the breast.

Cold.

And someone—someone—has, has opened the gates . . .

A century in seclusion with the green birds . . . the humors of the lantern as a sedative . . .

I've lost my shoes . . .

Deathprod, "Reference Frequencies."

Mrs. Spriggs' Easter Attire

By Joseph S. Pulver, Sr., and Tara Vanflower

Easter. Night after an unbroken storm, first burst to cascade, that sheared and ate. Limbs and branches and roof tiles up and off, gone with the wind or to Oz. Night that put two inches of warm rain in the ground. Night with a hide-and-seek moon stretching out its light in search of purls and cracks . . . and collisions . . .

Thirty feet below what dramatic tonight put down—

Brittle decades without soft or bright hues. Lot of dirt. Dark loam. Blunt passages and tiresome rooms. Little or nothing human. Hinges broken by prying hands and rust. Insects, and worms, dangling roots, and once fine molding in the cool clay.

No lick of new.

Until the new arrival shone. Waved its sunflower sunshine right in Ada's eyes, no halfhearted river, hurled it right straight. Said its brilliant patch large.

"Such a fanciful bonnet *here?*"

Remake. Remodel. Fitting for Easter. Renew. Ada warm, lighter, swells.

Maybe some notoriety—"Oh, to be lovely again." And that feeling of sun—sky smiling joy, touched by the bright sparkling beams of heaven. Enough of Lodge's *Wits Miserie*. Enough full to bored and flared cold.

One more admiring sigh, "Who *is* that?" Clean as quiet sin and yummy. Handsome to turn rue to away from the kind favors of clean gravestones.

Eyes on her. Only her. "Oh, Ada. How charming."

Eyes that dote. "Lovely, Dear. Lovely."

Eyes that adore. "Oh joy. So delicate. So soft."

Fawning again.

Maybe.

Maybe John or Mister Robin would notice her—he certainly had a hundred years ago on Main Street. She'd noticed him, a gentleman who was a paragraph where others were sentences, smiled back. Thought, "Able. I'll take that one, please." And self-hypnotized for a time, drifted on a wedding march and pillow talk and blue eyes that were moonbeam mercy. In them she would, if he'd asked, climb to any night of come closer my love.

Maybe Mister Robin, smiling, tipping his eyes to her bright sky. One more southward to womanly charms. One more soft moonlight and the carpet of "Sweetheart." How long had it been?

Decades packed under tight and foul. A tomb with the stink of lonely. A tomb without noble radiant.

Maybe this yellow would do it, this soft yellow gift. "Pretty." Pretty yellow, nice as a light carnival of kittens purring in your lap.

"On me." The whisper of dream's river.

And Trouble's eyes hiss. Inhuman-red gone hellfire jealous. Got her claws on it.

"Slip your claws off *mine.*"

"Return to *your* place, Gil-*da.*"

"My place?" Pushed by a tongue sharper than her fangs the fleet quicksilver of her hiss stirs the dust motes in the semi-darkness of the muddy crypt.

"Care and respect for one's *place*, before your words bring about instincts that draw blood."

"You would be wise to raise your ears. Mine is mine. And yours is a *hole* of nothing."

Ada leans forward. "And you'd do well to mind St. James. Your tongue, should you not temper it, could well be the source of your destruction."

Ever the balance, John's moon-soft tone, "Ladies. *Ladies.* Is there a need? Joy blooms here. A heavenly feast has been brought to us. We can step away from spiders and beetles and moles and grumbling bellies." Feels the pangs in his own. Tongue caught on the bitter taste of beetles, his eyes narrow. His smile does not. "We can share this. Can't we?"

A pair of hiss. Shines in harmony with shatter growing wild. Dark feathers are readjusted, sharpened.

"Tis merely a bonnet, Ladies, please conserve your diabolical for other seasons."

Ada slips into a tone she hopes will please. "This spider, not I, shall catch slow and sleeping. I saw the sails of this ship before she even arrived."

Gilda's scorch scalds. "This is my Day. Not hers. *My Day.* Mine. She has one of her own."

"True, Dear Gilda. True. This is not your day."

Ada, in a flare of scalpel tongue, is unhappy with John's attitude and comment. "I have the Right of Catch. Her eyes know that to be true."

Gilda's burn slashes. "Day rules Catch."

"Not in *this* warren. Here I own what I own. When there were only three, Mister Robin and I wrote the laws. Simon was here with us. He approved them. He gave his blood."

"Would you have me leave and make some lodging away from St. Echo?"

Eyes blare yes; slap a hard now on it. "You may hang your dress and fancy of childhood anywhere you care to. For now somewhere over there might be fitting." Ada's crooked grey claw points to a stout beam and a web-cocooned noose where her brother Simon hung himself. "The ceiling matches the tone of your raggedy mane. Perhaps its medicine would cure you of crude meanness?"

"I shall not leave this party. Not when we have this to give thanks for. This is my sign of rebirth. A very fitting one as I see it. Fitting to be brought here, to me, on *My Day.*"

Gilda's day. Was. According to some. She was reborn on Easter. Rose. Remade. Walked around with the Gift. Tried to wear it well. Hard your first day. New muscle, new legs learning to stand, to move. Hands learning to grasp and hold with grey claws that look like they could have been chips of stone from a quarry.

Eyes. Trying to *see*. Newborn's eyes adjusting to the darkness studded with dead shadows. Wanting to cry, wondering if she still could.

Feeling the teeth in your mouth, the worm-knot gnawing in your belly.

Gilda Stern. Popped up. Her Day. Wasn't fresh as a daisy. Wasn't still a wonder or a hot little number, not fit and beautiful. Grey. Hair a mess, a few bugs in it. Missing one hand, the one she favored, drove with—burst of that BLACK grid bumper-thing on the pickup truck suddenly a crushing wall. Missing smooth cheeks and they'd sown her torn lips together; she had a song for that tailor and his or her stitch-work. A song of nightmares. Must have been drunk or held in the tongs of some idiocy loaded with inept to sow her up like an old po-tato sack.

But Gilda found an old pair of scissors (and a cigarette pack-size chunk of a mirror) and cut the sutures. She was afraid to open her mouth. Afraid to speak. Hoped she would not sound like a monster. Simon came and the ribbons of her confusion fled. In Simon's kind-ness, Gilda found her voice.

That first night, conscious for an hour or so—felt like it, search-ing the smudged light of this rank cellar place. Shaking, wondering. Fragmented, rummaging experience for handholds. Just plain scared, the tension of mild panic wanting to get louder, until Simon came. Whispered. Took her hand and spoke of ways and need, spoke of re-born and the Gift.

"It will soon be Easter, less than an hour. And you are resur-rected. You are the Easter gift."

Those few minutes before Midnight arrived and became a new day. Saturday reborn as Sunday. Easter Sunday. Out of good Fridays. No more happy hours in the Red Light with Nancy and Nunz. No more laughs—till you're in stitches, or shows of action and fun and funny. Years and she still missed the shows, how they ganged up on you with that BANG. And she missed the adoring eyes of the men. Those feasts were dead and buried. Never to be resurrected.

St. Echo. That first Easter morning under the brown-consumed cemetery, under the longing veins of dangling roots ready to carry the power of spring's flow of liberation above. Found the mirror frag-ment, cracked, only a piece. Wiped off the dirt, white of her sleeve now soiled by grave. Eyes looked at her. Gone blue. Radiant bright blue, shining with hopes and dreams and all the joy of happy Carib-bean seas. Gone. Red. Sour red. Vivid, haunted. Stained with the same cold fire that boiled in her belly.

No coffee. No cigarettes. No lipstick, gone *Say Yes to Dizzy* red buzzing my branches are precious.

On the way to good-time rich detoured.

No fashionable boys, saying yes to dizzy. Confident men, hard and smooth and ready to shower her in the candy of summer harmonies, prophets begging and promising to refashion her spine with quakes of discovery, gone, gone and GONE. Their devouring gravity not. Her tremors as their arrows flew ... Out on the floor—then alone somewhere, hands on. Saturday night vibrato, knitting together, skin, sheets, tucked in the taste of excited, flexing on the colors of the trumpet ...

Sunday morning. Atoning—

No soft hand of Dear Sweet Lord or scripture of *a new birth into a living hope*—yet, somehow, she was resurrected.

And here was Easter again. Her Day.

And that bonnet was hers.

Ada could stick it.

Gilda would help her. She'd bury something, claws or a hard snapped off root. Bury it deep. Then she'd go off with Mister Robin. Ada could bark or howl. If she was still alive—

And there was the dead woman's body. Not lovely. Not young. Was it once, she wondered. Fleshy, abundant. All that meat. What the morgue didn't carve out. Lot to go round. Enough to renew the warren's empty bellies.

But only one bonnet.

"Mine."

Hunger and want. She wanted the bonnet and she wanted Mister Robin. Same as Ada. Same as the few other women here, if you could call any of them women. Still had breasts, and wombs, not that they would ever embrace born. And they all had desires; the clocks might be dead, but their hearts still built scaffolding from the gravity that curved and spoke swiftly.

John prays they don't rip each other's eyes out before Mister Robin arrives. He saw Ned dash off, knows Ned is Mister Robin's man and would run to his master with any and all news.

Ada, cold as a hiss, sears. "Not today."

Mister Robin shook his head. "Ada dear ... *Ada.*" Tipping his head, leaning toward her. "Today is Sunday. *Easter.* Simon told us she was the Easter child. And we have always followed that."

"My brother looked at things differently. You know that. Even here he whispered of God and things we know do not have a bearing on our ways. I only went along with this being her Day to maintain the peace. But he is gone now and we should set things, and this matter, right. This is not her Day."

Gilda takes Mister Robin's hand. Eyes plead.

Ada runs her finger over the yellow ribbon around the corpse's neck. Looks at the old woman's neck. Charcoal grey. Drying up and wrinkled like fried pig skin.

Mmm, pig skin. A time from before, the ripe then when food was food and it was everywhere. A flash of memory; of big Sunday feasts where little girls and boys run about in the sun with sprite dogs weaving play with heels and Japanese beetles buzz and glisten green like jewels, and robin's-egg blue sky with the puffy white cotton clouds that morph from animal to tree to army man. The tables set with feast, with renewal.

Cakes, and ham, and salt and butter—Jam and loafs of fresh, still warm bread . . .

Laughter and full mouths.

She picks up the ribbon tying the silk into raggedy brown hair that once glistened in that sun. *Did. Did. Then.* Now dull and lifeless like she is. And she feels warm, lighter—fragrant within, remembers the day she took the rough tip of a jagged claw to the cuticle of that dead woman, peeling back long strips of flesh from fingertip to shoulder for her betterment. Wasn't a pretty ribbon, but it was a ribbon. Worked well enough. Thinks of other ribbons—a drawer full, much prettier, quick pink and energetic red and smelling so sweet. Not the grey of death, like everything here. Dried up like husks. Dead, some frozen closed in the dry teeth of the abyss. No red that tastes like kiss. No blue. No green lark of sun-ripe springtime. No silver. Dead and grey. Like everything here.

"I want those," Gilda said reaching for Ada. "It's my day!"

Ada stood up in a flurry yanking her hair back, scowl intact. Eyes shining dull like an old penny covered in the gunk of age. "I . . . *These are mine.* Get your own." Her voice raw, boots moving over wet gravel.

"Greedy old bitch," Gilda snarled.

"Ladies." With the influence of a lion Mister Robin cut through the chicken squawking swift and sure. "I'll take the bonnet and the ribbon for now . . . Perhaps a peek upstairs?" His grin belied his intentions.

Ada removed the ribbon from her neck. Gilda handed him the bonnet. The women looked at one another, a blade strikes a blade promising I will write in your flesh. The yellow magic in Mister Robin's hands calls their eyes back. Eyes are filled with music, rapture.

"Ladies, please."

They were slow to turn their fastened faces from the treasures' immense beauty and toward the stairs.

"I want it," Ada purred. Her memories (Yellow butter sun. Brilliant daffodils and fluffy dandelions. An ice cream social dress with polka dots and crisp white gloves, pressed and fresh with starch.) swarming like whirring beetles.

"It's my day! You could have the ribbon!" Gilda whined.

"Ladies, patience," Mister Robin warned, voice stern but ambassadorial honey.

Ada turned with a smile, grey as it was, and acquiesced with a nod of her head. With a sly step retreated to his side. Sliding past and keeping close enough to brush her womanlies against his arm as she ascended the stairs.

Gilda looked back at the bounty with pleading, jealous eyes, and followed. The cluster of teeth she assembled to smile intensified, only she dared placing a hand to Mister Robin's broad chest as she passed.

He didn't mind.

Let the bitch eat dust, she thought, swaying her backside at the face she knew followed three steps behind.

Unnaturally slow, as if carrying grief they entered St. Echo silently.

Ada dropped down. How many Easters since she had last walked across this floor and sat in the family pew listening to the Good Reverend William Harvey's language of piety? No rebirth came into this abandoned church. Time ate.

Many things died. Sections of the floor were lost in the bellies of worms and a corner of the roof the wind had driven away. The waxing crescent of moon lit the boards. Night fell and the dead began their rest. Beneath the dirt they began their corruption. The bacteria ravaged as worms and unseemlies found their way into the casket from the surrounding earth. Time would win out and wood would crack. But here there would be no body. The clan would see to that.

Mister Robin's hand invited Gilda to sit.

She took a pew on the opposite side of the aisle.

And they waited.

The shape of Mister Robin's back. Looks up at the stained glass Christ cradling the lamb, no blur or ecstasy of prayer or crucifix-relic comforting the fingers to proclaim faith. "You are an impossible mountain. Never were a doorway." Doesn't spit like he did that first time.

His first steps here. Sitting in that pew. Claws biting into his palms. Fear and the taste of corpse meat on his tongue. Hated the taste. Belly liked being full.

St. Echo. 188 bodies in the larder then . . .

Then. When he licked his lips and the corpses were fat and many . . .

Then they were gone—

Sure as a knife and a fork had played seizure.

Hard came. Squeezed. Chewed up prudent right along with the blood and the intestines, heart and thigh. The plate was empty and no deliveries arrived. No occasional drunk bedding down for the night. No urban renewal infringing. Not even a suburban housing development nearby. No historical relevance to save it or bring onlookers. The few family farms ringing St. Echo crushed into ruin.

Decades since a body was buried here. This one's arrival only springing from the desire to be buried beside her Beloved Mother. Decades since the local teens stopped using St. Echo as a party house. Few were the rats and rabbits that were to be found on St. Echo's lot these days.

Meat was becoming foreign to the tongue. Fresh unknown.

Ken had exploded on a man in a black suit who'd come to visit his parents grave nearly twenty years ago. There were tears above, and there was murder. And the body had barely been carried away before a swift current of police descended when the man's car was found.

No one had been taken after that. The risks were too great. But as the years passed that became less an issue, fewer and fewer came to grieve for their loss.

St. Echo, small but once quaintly grand, rotted inside and out and bellies stayed vacant.

But not hungry hearts . . .

Mister Robin walked to the casket they'd carted upstairs and placed on the altar. Opened it. He gave Susan Lordes her yellow attire back. Tied it neatly and just so.

Susan Lordes lived alone. No cats, no purse-size lap dog to attend her loneliness. No ball, no waltz on her dance card, just Susan and her TV and her chocolates . . . and pastries and cookies and that yummy bowl of jelly beans . . . and her bags of snacks . . . She sat and watched dances of romance and obsession-fueled need, and ate, sometimes by the fistful. Four hundred pounds of desire packed on four inches over five feet of bones. Four hundred pounds of sensual dreams. Each kiss of chocolate her lover. Each salty snack the velvet caress of her new sweetheart. Until her heart, full of cravings, could take no more passion . . .

Susan had her plush sofa and her soft slippers and three snuggle-thick lap-throws and her three-layer yellow boxes of foil-wrapped sweets and her piles of "Celebrity Glamour" magazine. Napped in the afternoons so her evenings were free to watch reruns of *Dynasty* and *Desperate Housewives* and when her heart was filled with sin and fear and shame, she'd grab the handset and call Pastor Jesse Ted Fuller's tele-ministry, 1-800-SEED-GOD. Twenty-five dollars and she'd get her two minute Blessing. Free of sin, reborn to new pasture—green pasture of soft and pure square one. Again, abundant Life. $25 and sin-free, and she'd begin the feast again.

No rainbow-colored Easter eggs. No solid chocolate bunny. No feast of maple-cured ham and buttery sprouts and yellow layer cake under daisy-swirls of buttercream frosting this year. They buried Susan with the bonnet she never got to parade in church.

Shakes his head. "My Dear Ladies, we can all partake of this repast, or, if you cannot put aside your desire, I offer you Right."

Then he closed the lid. Let them sit. Stew. Walked away and sat. Sat with his hands folded as if in prayer.

And he waited for John.

John would conduct the dance.

A grey color slow as graveyard fog walked by the women. Didn't turn right or left. Stood quiet waiting to unfold. John cracked the lid, in a coalblack voice, "It dazzles you." Looking back at Mister Robin and those surrounding him, dripping grins like poisonous lizards. One bite would kill. Rot you from the inside out. The church's hollow air outlined empty to edge with bent hunger and driven expectancy.

Eyes turn face right.

Eyes turn face left.

Neither frightened. Stare. Not studying. Hating. Grudge shoved and shoved back.

Bolted to place, mouth ready for violent, one thinks she'll go mad.

One accelerating.

John raised his hands looked up at the stained glass window. The Good Shepherd holding a lamb. "The feast of abundant rebirth."

Velocity on a face netted with invade. "My bonnet!" Gilda exclaimed rushing the box and knocking John off-kilter. Her eyes were wild, fingers tearing at the sunshine ribbon. "It's my day! It's my day!"

"Mine!" Ada rushed, pushing Gilda, yanking the hat from skeletal fingers.

John steady. Steps away.

Mister Robin watched in delight as the two ragged women fought over scraps of fabric, scraps of memory. They weren't great beauties now, and one had never been. But pride comes before a fall, and he would watch the show.

Ada smashed the bonnet down over crispy crumpled hair.

"It's my day!" Gilda complained ripping the bonnet from Ada's head and rushing off into the shadows.

Mister Robin looked up, watching Ada sneer off into the darkness. He rose and walked to her. Held her hand, patted it.

"Children." Ada snorted. Sauntered over and dropped down in a pew smoothing her hair, adjusting the old leather ribbons tied in sick bows in her hair.

Gilda held rusty old scissors. Heavy in her hand, she trimmed the crooked hair across her forehead. Pulled her fingers through her hair to smooth the matted tresses, trimming along the bottom edge as straight as she could. She set the scissors in her lap and lifted the precious bonnet placing it reverently on her head and tied the ribbon beneath her chin, big yellow bow above her right ear. Blinding bright, like the face of god, against the dirty pallor of rot, she wished she had a mirror to admire it. Not so long ago she was breathing summer air, bathed in the beautiful blue sky, sunk into velvet green grass. She was drunk on it when she closed her eyes. Every swollen curve of fertile, the rhythm and meaty ripples, she could feel it, smell it. Birds singing, trees swaying with wind-music. Spinning in circles, arms wide, face raised towards the light.

And she had nights—impulsivity. The temperature of free-range music, soaring on the physics of dance. Marvels of carved lust, her wings wide, a flock of lanterns. Wild, scent of the moon breathing on skin, hips awakened, interlocked in truthful confession. Nights, filling mine with felt!

And this yellow gift brought it all back.

The minutes of THIS melt . . .

                          gone the casket-box and its blizzard tongue smelling like mud. The shackles of joyless-BLACK that tear at beauty. Gone worms and dark-dirt filth . . .

        SUN—every side right, hung over simple things, the river playing, licking panes and feet . . .

        b i r d~ s~S waltzing through the anatomy of the rising year—

                               . . . light . . .

laughter   Jacks flashing

        Jills—no limits to the pink peaks of feminine with unwinding plans and bells that believe luck . . .

Yellow in her hands. Playful yellow. Unsoiled. Dawn fresh . . .

Gilda beaming, sunny as an eight-year-old fingers full of tall and rising. Wearing it—vibrating brightness, now a nightingale, some bonfire Genesis, in the sirenwaves of sweet fables. This is better than the scent of soap or his sweaty hands on her gorgeous ass when she slammed her hips against his energy. "Oh." Almost happy enough to cry.

"Mine. Mine." Laughs as she expands. "I'm pretty." Looks up at the stained glass Christ. Smiles. "Not that old bitch."

The black-weight shade of Ada, a plenty about to splash and spread. Sharp fangs bared. Froth of graveyard hissing air. Ada. Crowd of witch-hag stink and dust. Sniffing. Hands snatching the pretty yellow bonnet. Holding it. "There you are." Voice so low and filled with hatred. Acid churning over tumbled rocks. "Sweet, sweet spring . . . And mine."

Hands come up to take it back.

Yank—pull—twist. Scrape. Nick. Claws in a razor tug of war.

Gilda has the bonnet. Presses it back on. Spits on Ada. Mad-wind howl laugh, barks, "You lose bitch."

Iron hands of quarrel, twisting, pulling hair out by the roots, blood seeping into the bright cloth. Red expanding like paint in water. Ribbon biting throat, suffocating. Seams popping. "Bitch? I'm a bitch? Who's losing now?"

Ada twisted the satin fabric in her fist, tightening the ribbon around Gilda's windpipe. Gilda's arms flailing, reaching for something to hold onto as her eyes bulged, night-sight red glare bursting. Groping for a key or a hammer—the scissors . . . Suddenly feeling them in her hand, cut her way to free.

Ada's hiss. "I'm going to wear this as I feast on your entrails."

As blackness consumed her vision, Gilda, ready to tear to pieces, thrust the rusty scissors up and shoved the blades into Ada's chest. Slicing. Ripping. The crack of bone gripping the hallways of loud as the metal shattered a rib and forged definite in muscle. Gilda tried to smile. Eyes venom-hot, as Ada channeling rage, crushed her windpipe.

Didn't stumble or strain just up and out of avid and prattle. Gilda slumped over, all life gone now. Brilliant yellow atop dead grayish flesh.

Ada stumbled back sucking in a gasp of air. Like a dying fish at the surface of the water, mouth biting for breath, air hurrying from the situation of her lungs. Her eyes began to close, blinking to stay here, to stay focused, flash of yellow, flash of yellow. She lunged forward ripping Gilda's eyes from the sockets. Popped them in her mouth, snapped her bony neck. Bite down. Vessels pop. Scarlet like the most vibrant rose. Scarlet as the soft insides of a freshly disemboweled corpse, the sour claret tang on her tongue, on her lips, the taste of gone raining on her drought. Ada gasped, swallowed. Smiled at the warm yellow. Her hands were young, sudden. Barked joy as she placed the torn bonnet on her head, tied the ripped ribbon around her neck. Adjusted it by feel, no mirror. Fit. "Pretty." Chuckles. Rattles and chatters. No longer a spoiled postcard edges tattered. Alive again—flashing sunny. Ready—

To take in the zephyr-fruit "Yes" of Mister Robin's appreciative eyes. Ready.

"Ready."

And then slid to the floor greasy with cobweb-cursed centuries and cut with things fangs didn't care to articulate.

Mister Robin smiles over the pocked-hide biddies crumpled muzzle to muzzle. Gilda's features swollen purple and black, cheeks ground meat, neck's familiar slipped from strength, helped to ludicrous by a bear-grip ending in snarling claws. Dismissed from the tiger exhibition of the melodrama, part of a once delicate ear hung. Chunks of blood-damp hair around her shoulders with strips of scalp still attached.

Ada, bonnet tied to her head, smiling, smug with satisfaction, as her torso still wept thin grayish blood.

"From one loaf . . . Bountiful day," John said standing beside Mister Robin who turned and smiled.

The bonnet. No longer cooing luminous yellow and lofty fancy. No longer bright butter sun and dandelions. The sails of its exuberant song ripped, its DAZZLE dialect trampled, covered in dirt and muck from covetous hands and saturated in blood's rejuvenating wine. Mister Robin, remembering hot night air and the melody of a garden tryst with Gilda untied the dog-eared sun-bonnet and set it atop Gilda's crooked head. He tied the bow as nicely as he could and gently lifted her hand.

"Now let us pray," he said raising Gilda's hand.

"It was her day, John," he said. "To be reborn." Slow grin. Long teeth. *"As flesh for our flesh."* he said, and bit into her hand as a man would place a kiss.

Each Night Begins a New Journey That Leads Only to an End with No Between

for LL on All Hallow's Eve

Death is my cupboard . . .

November twilight my tavern . . .

Day and its roads, that scratch the dregs of answers, are hidden by a crimson smile.

. . . with only burdens between There & his waiting 1 deserted cripple [in a year without branches] stands breathing the stonethorn psalms of tomorrow with wounds . . .

The grave's frost bells mouth, "Awaken, Thee."

Tears leap,

   he crawls & burns . . .

Nightwalker, mouth of fatal, throbs in the morgue-shade of mummy cloth.

All the rustling stars are planted in the changeless fit of black above, black plumed with furies and sadness.

And I climb the stairs from my dark warren . . .

Heart and hunger in need. Needing the little comforts . . . and

red

The clouds fold and the moon leans down . . . Sets the dust on fire with whispers of Venus.

Venus. The whiteness of her face is my whole universe. The magic of her sweet voice swells ... It floats by the sleeping bells of the silent street and breaks in my garden ... Lured, a chess piece over bridges of new stars, to her fields I go roving.

And there, collide with a death-bed and her broken drawbridge given over to rust and collapse ...

I burn.

The street changes, the Lifetree drops its dice ...

She has no word for the gravethorn that cuts, like a Pit-wailed live thing, its emblem in her cold sleep.

red

deep and wide ... each blood-streaked, ivory wrist of old letters and driftwood bound in this new horizon that summoned edges murdered ...

And no flame can I call upon to break this flood of tumbling Nothingness ...

Torn ... the silence—ice, a stranger with not a flame of thunder to whisper from its wet mouth ... by red ...

I walk this night, as so many others, alone ... And filled with this cold madness of loss.

How I would sing to a soft, gentle lily. Give shadows and peace from margin to core with the thread of my whirling fireheart ...

United ...

With one lover ...

But all I find this night and all the others that will not dim in my memory, is

red

Red ... my mountain ... after my skirmishes with unhappiness I leave the cadavers where they fell in moonlight ... I share *My Ex-*

traordinary Plan with the wind and the white skullface moon and stand in the r a i n while I wait for the demands of the Void's stern tongue to come . . .

My eyes are an odyssey of wounds . . .

My tongue hammers the passwords so I might climb the ladder to the silent stars. I would like to go mad and calmly dance the puppets' dance

but there are

             still

secrets hidden

on the

       undersides

of the leaves

BACK to—

for a GOOD witch, Anna Tambour

Tantrumic orgy. Spurt. COMPULSION. Shout-Coughed up-Spew. COMPULSION. Flung. Last week's dirty laundry splattered about would have been less an affront to her sagacity. Splashed here to just about everywhere. Puddle after puddles. A sewer of quotations. Reeking passages, oxidized blotches of inscription penciled in 1860, varities/ effusion austere/grim jest/misprints appearing as truth/WIFFTEN-SCHAFFT and savaged derrières/no doily fare, to last yesternight's hamhanded vernacular. Some looked ready to clobber with dangerous (gut and nerve couldn't avoid noting the TEETH). They did.

Did.

Elli, recoiled from HARSH, was not happy about it.

Might be somewhat understandable on a weary Sunday dawn-show, after the bloat and roar of Saturday's go-go with bottle-madness and URGE, but not on Tuesday. Tuesday was a day for the clock's tick-tick-tick-work to move at its own proper neurology not bump into toxins.

The reddish splat on her not-at-all-new-yet-still-almost white dress was most unappealing and damn sure impossible to bleach out. And how would she ever get her shoes clean?

Tith would storm. That face would come out and something inside would get the bash, the old POW right to the source. She wouldn't purr. She'd turn from her sphinx-pedestal survey on the bright windowsill and her ice would stab, clean it!

Clean and right and proper ways the only way.

Elli glared at the bolted, curtained windows. Hatefuls, they'd had their polka dots and moon—spun holiday in delusion, bustled and hazed until they freed gravity from the puzzle and now they were tucked in tight, nursing it up. Up and in it with extra "Yeah, Baby!"

Full-on 'round & 'round and goin'! Tight-lid clamp-down pious and grab pulchritude with curves that will do all kinds of things like push juicy~juicy~juicy to their "Me! Me!"-lips and SUCK and TASTE and CHEW and LICK and TASTE and GUM (while playing footsy with the hyperthyroid-lustings of the tomato-painted B-side crooning fal-setto) to get ALL the sweet and tang from it—EVERY LAST DROP. Some, many drink-washed, even pause to season their fare to taste. Then they—tiger or spider or plowman's ox, without regard to their dinner companion's course of ambitions, laugh or snore or fart or wander off to behind the wall of sleep to look for other fat confec-tions. Tornado of pompadours and staccato now compression, how the hell could the care-less slumber away?

This needed to be seen to. To be uncontaminated, scoured.

Even The Mayor's lip-synced, "We need to be fair about this."

Back to

correctly

and splendor

Clean cobbles to greet clean shoes. Quaint & Useful returned from this snowriot of street-level utterances to glad and pleasantly's yes.

Some flies were buzzing. A mouse emerged from the underworld vine of kicked-aside newsprint. And the sun was not drying the pud-dles. They needed to be removed before it did and the contaminates became engravings.

All the streets in Tambour would be like this. Alleys too. Oyster, right up to the windows and quaint lavender entry of Skwandro's selfheal shop, would be a sharp tonic of exceptional dreadings. Parrot an ode to dung. The campaign on the corner of Pemberton Gimble and Blaft would be unintelligibly wild with sloppy feltings.

She did not even want to consider what affront to Faldarolo's statue in Bakeblikk Square might exist. All the merry la-la-la/la-la/la-la-la drenched in the spit of untranslated-impulse.

"Criminals."

And riotous bumpkins.

Pancake-grittle hot was coming. Sun was shining it up right now. Hit in an hour or two, distasteful's hissing would blow up when that started prancin'.

Should go right 'round the corner to the hardware shop on Med-lar to buy buckets—not (No-no!) green and yellow and red and blue and poptrend-patterned plastics, no, METAL, like Poppa's "Wash 'em up good." tub, and a good strong mop—Start right in. Elbows and good strong words, not aloud mind you. Though a few "Be gone, filth!" might be handy . . .

But what soap to use in the knuckling?

Sweet Chokolin bursting with summer-sweet Lamadhoom and the xumph of peppermint? A vivid citrus, some humble-scented dart from Lao, or an upraising spear from Suinbet?

"No."

Clean it right required the hard stuff.

End   to   there   . . .   Endlessly.   Fattened-sheep.bound.rubbed.joints/extremities/hinges sharpened to center-piece-romp—cut the cake, give up the sugar, Sugar. Hawk's talons-lark to (inside)tender—Jacked-up on I've-Got-A-Few-Bucks-Lay-Some-Rapture-On-Me toys whistled mine-mine-pucker up and the fresh got surreal as the dragonsizzle-twisty of circus-voltage. Really did. Looked like it.

Wasn't going to wipe that away with old dependable. Wish and a prayer might sweat, but wouldn't cut it.

What will?

Magic mixed with Pepperbrew soap?

Xtougli Pharq's Individualants applied with X. Yes, would work on 'Lacks three plates,' but on tellitives like 'the repudiations and dissertations of the clowns and fools shant—shant be,' and '—she was my spunk-emptier'? No-no. And NO!

'The greedy friar's fart rivaled a free stallion.'

Muck, mire, and puddles of starburst-turds . . .

Filth! Blight from the hem of Red Sulmanopses' soiled gown. Not a lick of respect or appropriate decency for the posture and sensibilities of the eminently pious women of The Empire.

It was clear to Elli the rabble that had performed these lewd crimes never had their bottoms suitably-heated by mother's adjusting hands.

'When your _____ sludge is furiosing in the pan, you should be smiling at the colour, smell, anticipation of licking the pot soon; and eventually, in good time, enjoying . . .'

Lick the pot?

Filth must be dealt with. Harshly. Unman its chasm FAST. Mother had taught her that. Twenty years, steps and stoop, "Get the toilet *white*. You will not drown, Child. Waste that Bumph and you'll not see supper this night."

Every foulsomeBANE splashed in squiggles bellowed. READ ME! READ ME! Rippled. Whorled and swell. Clamor of gritty jangling in unacceptable fonts. Clod, beast, and bumpkins wouldn't know a nice Gill Sans if it redecorated their alphabet. She almost gagged on the aftertaste she found her eyes encountering. Its geometry was enough to explode her to cardiac arrest.

Turns

FLASH and curl (no safe cave from the) leap and BARK

turns—

　　TURNS

cage/no rewind/no remake

　　　　whirls, can't duck the tongues that do a blunt-mounted job eating, gnawing MOON and SUMMIT out the soft flesh of her (inside),

　　　　　　　　steps　　　　away

but

　　　　the border-knitting moves with her.

Glimpse of corner—

There it was. The scent of possible, fragrant as sugar-cookies and unmolested-tea(properly brewed!) brushed with WARM. Habblbaebaker, the King of Efficiency, by the fish market, had improved upon Bumph. The windows in his green walls would be open. The great doors ready to welcome those decent, honest, and morally-respectable assassins who never hesitated to snuff out toxins. If your hands and shoulders (and knees) weren't attached to reluctant clean he had! Soaps and potions for every stink and whimper.

Dearest Mother, joy! Today is Tuesday. Discount day.

A large box of Habblbaebaker's IMPROVED and then off to Mama Eureka!'s for a blessing of . . . She was not certain, but Mama Eureka! would know the right enrichment to travel it away.

Habblbaebaker beamed and gave her the double discount.

Pillar-eager. "Thank you. Thank you. Much—"

Dashing—

The door of yellow stars was open. Mama Eureka! smiled. "Yes, Chile. Blackroot spider legs, Kroaker Kalinda Claw, Swamp Trout eye, but onlyies one—*two bad-nella*, like Goat Cay sittcinai when it worm, and triple Barefoot Lady clippings, and sho as wind come blow, gon do it fer yas good. Dat tribe be gone-gone den.'

"Equals measure Bumph and dis-remedy in yas buckets. Onlyies stays up in it one hour. No do power after sun sneak off."

"Thank you." Twice.

Hands growing she dashed—

Followed the remedy's recipe. To the letter. Proper and precise was she. Always. EVER! A proper grip on done right never slipped from her grasp. Never a misstep.

Bucket anointed she began.

Scrub. No pause. Scrub. No break. WET it! SCOUR! WET-WET-WETTER. Swirl. Swipe. Wipe it down and wipe it up! Got every little under. Came up like painted-pavement chalk hearts and kiddie rainbows.

Empty the drained vigor of each bucket. Sluiced down sewer grate, send it below. Sent it to a fitting blackness. This patch. New batch of lightning, Elli's mop painting cascades of clean and right. That puddle. Tucked away and with slaps of elbow-heat dissolved.

Rush to beat nightfall.

Hurry to solution before death of sun.

Fast.

Scrub hard.

FASTER.

"Bless these hands."

Drain and refill. *dirty*—CLEAN! Get cobble and wall back to fullest, swaddled NICE with no unnervingly and despise.

FASTER.

Ahead more.

push.it.push.do it.now.

Don't look back. Knowing that was set right.

Puddle down to the size of a palm. Then gone. Things needed legible proportions again.

Next.

Hands in hell—Hoping someone else had taken up task on Parrot, on Catherwood and Frontis too, and Saint Deosu bless them, was straining to return regular from this unsettling brought . . . Hoping.

Parrot and Blaft needed to be restored; she'd need fresh loaves and vegetables from Delicallo's tomorrow. And Jasper's Way, she had a cruise involving whitework she needed to apply by Friday. How could she possibly sail if Jasper's, always a model of better to nostrils and initiations the ear celebrates, was left screaming noisome.

Keep scrubbing . . . every burnt hardboiled-black blowing geyser-high

And on . . .

Pounce of STARK doesn't push Elli back. The demonic excrements of Fitter Stoke's underbelly-polished, barroom quotes CLEANED. They would not stain anyone's shoesoles with uncensored exposes. Clean every 'Skipped her blah-blah, entered her premises—Gave her my big prick, two bouts' and *'Bitch was . . .'* . . .

        Gone—   And the quick road journals of the dharma spiders and their apes scrubbed and poured into the grate, subterranean again, as was only proper . . .

GONE

Fussy-pruning, litter and slime SCRUBBED CLEAN/Huff-and-puff loses its load . . .

      another dirtybucketofacridslop downhill to distant . . .

Lawyer Monterra's dry quotes would no longer choke a sequestered audience with great uninteresting speeches over-salted with obstacles and sidebars—dissipate CULL . . . gone

and gone

and

sun pumpin' but running out of place . . .

on

juice up the fast

get it smooth

clean

right

now.

The light was fading. Nine hours and her street nearly free of soiled. Just the last pile tainting the curb by Dear Kaaron's wee and tidy abode. Few minutes of elbows and Elli would have all clean and proper. Safely could step outside and stroll without fear of slander and foul.

She sloshed her bucket of cleaning agent and magick toward the last straw for her back, a puddle half the size of her kitchen table.

Stopped. Poured the bucket's contents down a grate. An ache or two, but she felt light. A fresh solution would zero the mess away zipzip. She'd be home having tea in no time. Smiled, savored the honey-souled perfume soon growing in the vapors. Something cultivated in her garden as well. Schav. Soup, the last slice of crusty, meaty bread. Rest after cure. "Yes."

Last two steps. Stopped. Wiped her brow, she'd sleep good tonight. Wiped the salt and rubbish from her weary eyes.

Slapped. CAN'T out of the frame of control STUNS

Love L E T T E R S.

The letter-shapes occur~'D,e,a,r,e,s,t,' (talking in *air*) 'H,e,a,r,t,' (greatly expanded by wild air)~establish result for eye~'That you *are* l,o,v,e,-,u,n,c,h,a,n,g,a,b,l,e, and m,y, *F,E,L,T* . . .' ~carry fit.

"Mine." (telling herself in breaths of wild air) Said it with a thousand tastes of color lifting her heels from the ground. Skipped how— *His* stitching rushing to the incurable of her mouth—right to, "My."

'Venus singing, and my heart following after . . .'

'. . . fragrant secrets gathered . . .' Every sense she has beaming over his livingness. '—in a pleased eye . . .'

Lines and paragraphs and adjectives (in and from his hand). Lines Her Starpoet sang~ ~~ivies of fire and glittery, clammy upliftingness~ ~~

And each who do youLOVE and seamless-dumpling had *her* name on it.

Marcus' l, e, t, t, e, r, s, to her. Every sally that touched her (inside). Every spangly probe (even—*Most of all!*—the ones that turned around her unopened youth with enhancing routes of vocabulary attuned to other ways to make a harbor work—how she'd loved that shape-shift in reality . . .) Every migration and manying-crop of *sense* . . . parsec—each novae

HERS.

(telling herself) *Mine.*

Marveling. Touched to tears. "Mine."

To clutch, "Dear."

Marcus. "Marcus."

Every note of witchcraft. Every word (talking her back) (giving her back) island-hourglass of star-lovin'—in the park/between oils and sap and cells/under the lemon-talents of the moon/1st & LAST, the commas and italics, roots to branches, the confetti-rays of the orbits (inside).

"Inside."

To have and to horde. Clutches her dragon's treasure trove. "Can Mama Eureka! resurrect his *all* from these? His hands are here. His eyes. His fire and blood wrote these. Shadow and shine, My Sweet, is *here."*

Clutches hope. (getting it ALL back)

She can. Must! "She brought Kaaron's sweet devoted, Rosie, back from done with much less."

I saw her. Every door and window and flung-open ear in Tambour knew she did.

In a pleased eye BUCKET. TOO CLOSE. Spun on the blood and fear. Bullets. Polygraph blowing thorns and shaking her to root-fry. Elli could not CLEAN these.

SAVE THEM

to have and to hold. Hold them up and RE-LIVE!

Live

head up

HIGH

. . . and there would be the old armchair, restuffed and comforta-bly-vibrant. Holding his books, his translations of most strange and wonderful events. Reading them and him—Sir Galahad. The book/the writer/the reader, the plentiful marathon of communication, the tango of fingers and pages joining. There would be hello and the potent thrill carved of spice-pleasure—(inside) blossom smothered naked—his math had never missed a beat—and he'd let her sleep.

. . . There was a night with ee's burstings in her hands and Marcus at her feet and he smiled with the heart of an animal. Holding no when he turned, looked up starrily and the ship of his kiss touched her knee. "'we'll make yes.'" April swarms in the joy of nearness as Elli climbs to floatfull with the bells, thoughts of limber flowerfulous blooms her best ripe smile.

EMANCIPATED! Won't be banged in TERROR's ropes again! Can't—WON'T send his magicks to dark damp blackness

WON'T give BACK pistol and pistil and pastel her heigh-ho will rub with MAY—

Stings out, *"Won't!* I will be a lioness drinking from liberty's glass."

Am.

Reads another of his kites. . . . only to sweetly unfold your tomorrows, Love . . .' Puts her heart (every frisky tail and syntax flutter-ing better) in the maker's hands—

As only the persuasive paws of her stardevil could, he'd press the button of her worn/flat with depth & VIVA, turn her this*woman*-dial to luxuries primed with COMING SOON and every gear and zeal of her internal galaxy would be shaped by the sunlight of her in-dulge, luminously-tasting NEXT& NEXT and next *fresh* as a round trip with her discovery-basket surging with plump rememberratives born in coffin-seed . . .

breathing / hurrying with the scents of

"Yes." To his yes—

evening—with   their   milesOFF—a bulge,thickly,slowly,hopping,landscapes   of   giveaway   loveli-ness,along,silky whiskers stroll fluffmoist tunes, plucking—roof to any~WAY,tangerinecolors to unwrap&lipsmet swallow mouthside to propping,eager buttoning—smooth as fistsofsugaredcandies—of bend and dance,along,squeezing go in,heaping-eyes raving sticky amongst clever squirming,bedstead supply of airplane legs,"That *was* some-thing.",the mouthLOVEScherryending,"Perfectly."

"Yes." When they spoke of maps and gardens and little things.

Burn down every dry levy and DAMN let the flow well.

Sun (and dizzyspells). Moon (and dizzyspells). Take the damnclocks down.

Woke up

'Yes I love you.'

from the coldest time of night—

Unguarded. Desert unfolded—dessert, anticipant breath by the bushel.

Their table would be full (again). Cinnamon and peaches. Candy jam. The taste. (again) Now serving would be serving (again). Her kettle would sing with enormous JOY. The taste. (again) Elli would sweep up any errant crumbs and remove the threadbare, snowy ta-blecloth, replace it with the robust-green of baize he so adored.

easy

and easy *and* "Bright!" Glistens *"Perfect."* with salty stuff.

After tender neck *and* oyster paradise "He will sit there and write." (new poetic succulents for her to gobble) (again). New words

(never fearstung)

(—a full chalice—a full well—keenheart awash in long-stemmed—twinkling bellies with only a zenith of scents between—gestures magnify happy—opening mangoes and summer—slow dreams float in tropical hands)

in his ringed notebooks

at his rolltop desk by the heavenvoice of fire

on her skin

wrist shoulder nipple thigh "My treat." (eyes closed she never knew if he winked.) (eyes closed when she whispered, tingling (in his ams), to her wizard, "I wish to be the instrument you hold.") and purrs as his wand, slow *and* fast, writes (inside) (knows his eyes, feeling what she feels, are burning)

Can't—WON'T send his magicks to dark damp blackness/no wind, no sound/

with the mottled/andslime/andgunk (below).

All of them (inside) her hands.

Dear wand-words bestowed upon her buttery bouquets by her Starpoet—Love's clockless-harmony, the lighthouse quiver, a suit of fires soft(inside)

Sun sinking. Her LOVE safe. RETURNED.

knees

tears of joy

(she can hear the kettledrums speak) (syncopated winged with flowers leapt ashore, carrying a basket of fair grass memories under a skylandar of fine spring)

need

to taste (again)

Gently (as any sanctuary priestess) lifts one of his lines. Reads: "You are a treat." He would say. Mean it. The song of the next in her fingers. Reads: "My treat." Wink. Then he'd repeat it, word and wink. Leaning, clings to another. Reads: "Is there dessert?"

to drown (*Meld*......luxurious.salty stuff................) in open

padlock unshut, the ill-throb of discolored monotone snapped OFF with silver

flying

Skywriting!

(*again*)

Elli makes a neat pile of his words—incense for drouth and distresses. Sighs swell; there is a fountain of inclined dancesing in her belly. Dizzy marmalade line from July's heat. Stanza of October whirls—'It was all so free.' Paragraph of January's hearth, embers glowing. ('It did glow, dearest. During *and* after!') Swirling! She's ready to sing May. April's budding yes, clothed to consume. "Gladly." Not a flaccid line. Neat stack, properly dried and preserved, parchments sprouting. To have and to hold. They—width of touch me, sky—will be at her table soon. Tea and Her Starpoet (again) alone together. "Marcus." Lost rewritten.

Her once-wisp now fleshed velvet.

She'll serve delights. Fire her hearth. Bake reels of biglyies and mostfull again. For him. Sweets. Rolls. Sugarcane and honey and buttery CONFECTIONS! Butter melting, dripping. Gooey creamy centers—

(inside) dripping

(inside) the cold clockwork of Right's heart melted. BACK TO

starshine lamps! Not antiques. Remembrance: night to spin her crazy-witchcraft, during the day with no bad or limit at all.

She'll look at the stars tonight and pick fortune because she can. BACK TO

JOY, to the FELT of kisses.

"Marcus."

Cherry pie slathered on Olympus—her skies flying!

FREE

(inside)

FIRE

(inside)

waiting eyes calling

Standing to collect herself, to run home . . . to be a brook knowing smile(insideagain)

Toofast

turns

    her ankle (the one he sat at when she read for him)(before her clothes fell off)

stumbles

        sideways

elbow

percussive
BANGS
the bucket   tide slosh/spill/drops and puddle—rivulets

                                              veins
melting
core   desperate nursling's hands swiping   spread
                            no ingredient   saved
going
trembling
once 'This fruit is yours.'   r e w o r d e   d
                          ripped from   herpage
a tear added to   swept away
dissolve / foam tide to bye
gone
excited sun swallowed senses pierced by   undone
cleaned   away   (inside)cold
as
clockwork
sun fell
         to   gone out
on her knees
weeping
(again) leveled
DARK
(inside) wilting dryness
padlock
(again)

After "Klockwerk's Heart" and built/remade/remodeled, in part, from cascades of wit and gems and petals purloined (by a bumpkin in awe) from AT's blog/poems/tales and emails. somebody say, "steal from the best"? did.

Soundtrack of ONLYIES A's: Adam Ant, "Antmusic"; Al Stewart, "Year of the Cat"; Andrew Bird, "Fitz and Dizzyspells"; April March, "Knee-Socks"; AWB, "Cut the Cake"; Association, "Along Comes Mary"; Astrud Gilberto, "To a Flame"; Anja Lechner, "Chant from a Holy Book"; Azimuth, "Till Bakeblikk"; Anita Baker, "Caught up in the Rapture"; & . . . America, "Muskrat Love"; Annette Peacock "The Heart Keeps," Arild Andersen, "A Song I Used to Play"; America, "Lonely People"; Argent "Hold Your Head Up."

Catch Tomorrow

for the Portland–Northwest Crew

Lines of funeral rain that won't disappear, blemishes that only the weathered eyes in the mirror see, another face. Moving alone. No longer corn-fed by sunshine and brimming 8. Another voice out of befriended, sick of crybaby threatened by poison.

Tucked safely in the narrow history of her handbag, Lena has a postcard she bought in Klein's Pharmacy, a beach and a baronial retreat for Ladies and Gentlemen.

"Rivera paradise with some esteem draped in sunshine. Halls that please me." No more crying when blue Monday calls.

"Walking on a beach with at last . . .'

"That's not silly."

Another dreamer heart set on not to die in LA—

This is the street to The Stars.

Right there—5 blocks straight-thataway. In the neutered footsteps of a dozen Alisons and many Kates, Susans and Heathers, and last week a Lois (rejecting loins and tears and the doom of careless scissors), each changed their names to fit the stage and hoping to adjust their shapes left the context of boring, blended-cotton blouses and waitress culture. Each failed at the first step of livin' easy and never got a look at the stairway.

No green.

No warmth.

Bobs and Mikes tried on traveler's shoes too; they ran, episode to episode, but never made it around the bases. Nick contemplated, day after Philip played poor little lamb on a wildride to Nirvana. No grove of shiny things and PEACE, Nirvana turned into the fall of Troy. Nick still works in the bar, smokes some dope when what he didn't obtain starts pacing around the walls and ceiling and floor of his one room apartment. Sam's arabesque, trying to sing ALIVE, hit skeleton. Justin couldn't find the rail.

Robin got there.

A Lana, every petal aimed at springtime, shined her way to applause and cheers from the movie-going crowds too. No tears in her Xanadu.

JD, believing glitter and ignoring the expletive-fortified renditions of nutcase-unbearables asphalt disease tosses out like handfuls of free candy, stopped short. Grabbed, but couldn't work out of the same old blues a fifth time. In nothing but his underwear, stared in the bathroom mirror and only saw fool. Didn't shave that day.

Thursday morning it got spelled out by the new studio VP: "Fuck you." Ellen cried in a half-gallon of ice cream for an hour. Washed her wine glass, put the bottle in the recycle bin. Then she stopped throwing linguistics at the grit and removed her disguise in the tub. First cop on the scene looked. Walked out of the room. Said, "Blood, and roses."

5 Blocks. The line that does not flex.

5 blocks. Lena looks down at her shoes. Tells them you can. Even tries to mean it.

Lena looks back up.

The Street.

(Black doesn't need oxygen. Don't speak *L'amour.*)

Walls and doorways smell of things that couldn't be chewed, or swallowed, the hustles and arguments hardluck couldn't get a sparkle out of.

(no sweeper with a wide broom to tidy up the brittle wincing)

(no Batman)

The line: drug, dope, booze, sex, dope, thief, error, rupture, dying, FUCK, dope, scab—fracture—scar, booze, GREED (that doesn't mind grim or gore), dead.

Smeared light on the steps of the hotel. Smeared sounds, voices that don't understand this light. Faces blurred by the where am I they set in the gravity of difficult's difficult gamble. Faces afraid of what sings on the other side of the blackness.

(without a mourner) a face (slashed from summer) in trouble on the newspaper's exhausted bark. 2nd floor window: one gives its tears to the ghostly snow of a TV screen.

A large flicker: HOTEL
R
I
E
N
T

A space between twisting parts.
Gain, or get pushed out of the loom's reef, bring your ready-made
vice or the gears of your confusion to the tightrope for maintenance,
turn and boil until process dissolves.

Hotel entrance. ROOM AVAILABLE (the one minimum-wage
maid that comes on in the AM doesn't say clean rooms). Quick by
the flop, quick in hopes its odors don't saturate her. Lena carefully
steps around the bum whispering about the smell of garbage and
passed the black-within of the adjoining alley . . . A few steps . . .

Time doesn't like this street.

Lena's tears don't like this street. She tries to tell them it won't be
much longer. And it's not so far. Just looks like it.

Darkest before the dawn. They say it's true.

But her shoulders and skin didn't count on it being this dark.
Some rain might rinse away the screams, but—

Nervously sucking on her lip.

And still standing still. STOP. Stay. Stuck.

"No."

(Sound of a saxophone from an open window. Narcissus crying
over the new cracks in his mirror.) (Blues bleeding black.) (Black and
blue face to face a match.) (One wins.) (One's gotta fall.) (There can
only be one.)

Barebulb streetlight crumbs—keep pecking; maybe you'll see
yourself and the way from here to tomorrow if you don't runaway or
get murdered, or wind up in a shitass hotel room screaming through a
dirty window, screaming for someone to unlock yesterday.

10 steps to the next corner.

Junk. Shards the ants dropped. Spent tigers edged with cocaine,
caught thigh meat, straddled the bound dream, cut with the speed of
war, tossed when the spurt was over . . . Particles that couldn't en-
chant fallen when your big mistake ran off another color . . . The tang
of sweat and garbage and soot, all right there buzzing in the neon.

10 steps

and you're choking on the dark. Wishing you believed so you could pray for a nice little room with a strong lock and thick dark covers to pull over your head.

Lena, trying to summon grit. Wants a locked door and those covers . . . Sink back to 8—8 that was a gateway to 9—9—Mom's cancer. The rotten planks beneath a world of happy sparks, wasting her breath. The subterranean fox, 10 months slow, took away the hands that put sweet fluffy magic on graham crackers, the laughter that transformed the kitchen into Wonderland. Cancer that did not celebrate love when it swallowed the woman who defended her roses.

Dad began to drink. She began to doubt, and forgets the kiss of safety.

Lena is looking at her grey hands. At the clouds and murmurs that stained the translations she once held.

10 steps.

Just passed the eyes of the hooker (red hair blue eyes like Tori before she got crucified by the dope)(before they found her in the tub, all the silver linings cut out of her tongue). Passed her questions about locks and relations and erasures. About clarity and the absolutely of nostalgia . . . Why doesn't God remember you? Why are all the faces talking about the thing? It was so great after you said yeah and you laughed, then it wasn't. Not when you were crying. Like you are about to.

Afraid to open your eyes.

Afraid you'll see something strange.

Just get passed her. Close your ears to any oracle she tosses at you and go.

She's as scared as you. Seen what you've seen, and what, 16? Don't look at her and don't smile.

Don't speak to strangers.

Never trust one.

Not even one that looks like Tori.

Looks like she's from Massachusetts too . . . And you ought to know what Boston puts in you.

The girl. Hooker. Kid. She ever picked up a chunk of broken glass and stared at it? Ever tried to tell herself it would end the violence?

Don't look at her.

Don't.

She'll mutter something ghostly.

Or beg.

Like her eyes do.

(How many times have yours? Just like hers are. How many? And what did it get you? Fucked. Beaten by swelter. A short fuse—Simon's was the worse. His Devil's magnet slammed. Shredded any chance for a ceremony of bliss. Hoped this time would be different then took two steps back and prayed. Gun still went off.)

Girl's got a face a step away from a field that won't have a moment of remember in it. Pale—could still be pretty, if a chance was unlocked. Too young to be bled out of heaven. Too young to arrive at deserted lunatic. Too young to have a face that's a bleak tragedy map of after the powder keg went off. Entity—close, but not stone cold yet—without imagination or retrospective. Too young not to hear the color of change.

Don't you dare recognize there was a flower in there. Nothing quiet and soft once sat by her feet. She's no niece, or sister you resent, and love—screw history. Don't go there damnit. Don't fall into it.

You're not Crazy's sister.

Takes her eyes off the galaxy of thirst. Her shoes don't look like ruby slippers.

Don't think about maybe she liked cute stuffed penguins like you did, or learned macramé, or laid in bed on her back and wrote poems with a pen that wanted to fill the page with I Love You whispered by gallant highwaymen while the quiet flame of moonlight smiled on the hem of the curtains . . .

Fuck that.

Her shoes, ashen and despoiled walking in the noise of these black roots, look like chalk that will never be kissed by birds.

You're here to save you.

Don't screw it up by answering her silence.

All those fangs she has piled so high. *Don't look at them.*

5 blocks. Lena glares at her shoes. Tells them you can.

Please.

Take the step. Left right left repeat and repeat, simple if you do it right, do it smart. Quick might be good too. And then just a little more, and maybe . . .

C'mon, do it.

Keep repeating it; try to stretch it until the frisson becomes reverie acclaimed as scripture. Go ahead, make it compelling . . .

Or maybe you get broken?

Maybe.

Don't focus on it.

The Street giveth and the Street TAKES!

Every dewdrop whisht to spread as particles of thirst eats dreams. Eats stars.

Seedy binging on miserable. No math. No bee-swarm. You blink it's there. All the BLACK teeth childhood and holy can't run from.

5 blocks.

No it's-just-a-mile when you just stand still.

Still.

Struck.

Lena. Not crazy. Ready. Even though the pawnbroker—all his faces lied—only gave her 65bucks for the bracelet and the rings.

5 more blocks from Simon and his safe kinks she once thought cute and kinda fun. 5 blocks from the 2 years of new scars and her albino angel turned MONSTER PERV. 5 blocks from the werewolf's spiked-flogger. And Dorian Grey's rack . . .

You can see it from here. Don't let destroying catch your heart . . . And don't trip over your fear.

There.

Gates. Gold. Sighs. Over the flux of odds.

There—

       step

       into—

       step

She could be, *Grace.*

A new name. New directions without the claws fastened to BACK. Light measured in someone adoring, not exhausting stains. The wounds could stop bleeding in the mirror.

No more sold and owned.

No more digesting the insufficient unspooling till break.

Not to wake up with a ticket stamped RED. Or a new bruise.

"Grace."

Me. Bright.

New.

Over there.

No more half or none. No lefts. Right.

A flair of "Yes!" in her eyes.

Only rights.

Screw uphill.

There . . .

Beyond—

Cold mesh shop-grill steel . . . All-night pollution. Neon, tone of dead flower truth and wounded elegies uncoiled . . . Cold writes the prose here. Cold doesn't lose here. Cannibals clang, claw, burn. No tarot of forward dancing. No God thick as a bed of sun.

No rain and no rain. Same street same street.

Summer mounted on sharp roughHEAT.

No bargain.

No RENTmoney, gin.

"I KILL YOU!" "Fuck you." Again and again.

Beer

and tragedy.

Funhouse California-dreaming sags—bluesman or Goth would sidestep delicate and say laid down low—it doesn't wake from the downpour-madness of anvil-cannot.

Weather here, but it comes into focus as dust, never roses . . . One dead whisper from devoured, hopeheads, crazy as the Crazies that can't hide from occur—spitting "Jesus-*fuck*."—push their wobble-wheel carts of sand castles at the surface notations of light . . .

Weather in Lena's eyes.

"In a hurry?" A portion of thick blackness gives up its shade.

Weight of heavy blackboots and hellred-eyes snarling maddog-thick. Pockmarked dementia set on CRUSH. Bastard and Demon. Black coats and big hands. Overstimulated predators controlled by whirl. Scars for mouths. A steel dominant and a full-force prowler jacked to damage. A thing uncoiled. A thing out to paint Death's stage with hard fun and screams.

"In a hurry?" repeated.

They needed to be refilled.

"Date, Missy?" Coldest smile that ever raped her. Smile elevates on the itch of a 5-minuteFUCK. No condoms come with the bruised.

Wants to be running now.

Skip gold if the out is safe.

Wanted ruby slippers that could spring from suffering's furnace to balm. Wanted to remember the current of a holy name condemned by her lips. She looked down at her feet. Wanted them to move.

And she wanted John Wayne with a .50 cal roaring.

WANTED—

Not those hands.

Not those eyes.

Not that knife, snorting its hungry, ready to trim and final.

BAD (talking to her tits): "Not bad."

SIDEKICK: "Not at all. All warm like that . . . Like it."

"Will. If it shakes it up good?"

"You will. *Won't you?*"

She looked down at her feet. Wanted them to move away from won't move.

Ankles almost feel off the heels.

She only had 65bucks and 2 quarters. They could have it. But—

Bad wanted his something else.

It was in his eyes. And he said it. The overcome in his jaw was an instrument of maul.

Her ready-scream knew the word his eyes fed on. Pussy.

Split.

Debone.

Spit.

The filth on his lips was ready to torrent her intimidated curves—Her eyes plead, no they're for Hollywood. Lust heroin. Punish heroin. Fit his hunger in a violent slung of keep. No sun. No bed. Mount, scalp, WHAM her little frailty.

She'd been in this cage before.

Lost.

Bled—Nursed the fractured wrist.

Her legs weakened. Right here. Right now. No slow no heart not a single kiss to live on her belly.

Sidekick. Eyes wild with split—wanted to open it up and FEEL it. Light it up. Then walk away just as hungry.

Without a creak forward or away, her legs sap. All the times she thought they were nice legs—(How many in bars and shops and in the strip clubs had admired them?), good ones. Not good for what she needed now. Stems of lies. Not good, strong and its panther gone.

Her coward gazed from hand to rotten mouth, its taste scalded. Hollow, she had no unshakeable to raise as defend.

Wants to crawl away before her shy understands torn to dead. Wants. But her tear-stuffed mouth won't beg. Wants.

She looked down at her feet. Can't even summon a, Fuck, move!

Bad's knife smiles in the flash of a match pressed to the tip of a cigarette. Wants to open its wolfkiss and grasp.

Exhaled with the smoke: "Some nice *warm* pussy."

A new essence reaches into the center of the billowing.

"Trouble?"

The shape-shifting expressions of Lena, Bad, and Sidekick, turn and touch emerge.

Passing through a demanding smile the song of an axe traveling. "Some *snag* I might assist you with?"

The Black Man who owned the cavern-voice looked like trouble. Burned with centuries of it, saddle-leather skin survived some black-smith shop, tooled over a skull mixed with medicines roasted in deathbed recreations as quarry tongues unfolded in the palms of bury.

Lena tries to say yes . . . Thinks maybe he'd help.

But he said *assist*—

Lena pressing her knees together. Suffocating in faint. Squeezed. Conscious of hysterical simmering on grim's flex. No riddle to it, sweat covered in threatened. Wants to board up and part right out of gnaw's canvas before topple hikes up sumptuous and rips.

Maybe he'd join in? What happens if she begs and receives NO from his lips?

Three faces stare at The Black Man's smile. A void it was.

She opened her hollow mouth. Couldn't take in air.

"Well, gentlemen, that is an interesting blade. I fancy a drop point to a clip point myself, yet, even I have to admit, it does have a lovely curve to it." His tone stings their ears.

"Works." Blasted by the harder of the pair.

"Indeed." Adds a wink as punctuation. "A very hard worker that one."

"Huh?" A slow-second wondering.

"It's been quite a busy boy."

It had.

But how did he know that?

And who was he?

"I beg your pardon, how thoughtless of me to forget presenting you with a proper introduction. My name is, Mr. Phoenix. I am a traveler, and historian of sorts. A watcher, yet tonight I find myself engraved by another voice, and here I am, merely a solitary night-walker out for a leisurely stroll." Black bald-skull leans that-a-way. "One never knows what tongues may be open and waiting."

A slow turn, Bad looks down the street. Broken bottles. Dented cans of all fall down still smudged with doubts about the cure that was hoped for. Litter.

Numbness.

Bottled whispers.

Sour.

Unreceptive glissandos.

Blank

and diminished.

Sheets of unwisely. The flung paint of maxforce raw.

"Just out seeing what there is to be seen.'

"You?"

Bad drawn back to the magnet. "Collecting what's mine."

"Really? I've been known to do the very same. That is to say, in regards to the long-stemmed opportunities one chances to discover. Some sing, some boil, the dialogues occasionally prove fascinating. And there are those which, though rare, encourage laughter."

Bad looked right at him. *Strange-ass shit.* In some ways he was vague, almost not there in a creepy monster-movie way, and in others, all thrust.

Adjusting city-eyes, no dull in verbatim's conflict=kill, Bad frowns at the distinct chill of the old black man. Bad's survey quickly readjusts; the old are stale and often raggedy, dreary tongues of over and over, but not this figure. He's dressed in a blood-red, felt round hat and the tribal robe of some desert-infested Mohammed, and he's much too tall. Not basketball player tall, taller, and he's oddly cut offputting. Some aboriginal turbulence ribbons from the space he occupies. Head to expensive shoes the man is a painting that brought the wrong voice to this glare of Bukowski desolation. Bad finds him theatrical, piercing.

His face, more skull-mask than face, is spooky, some island, flag, or mystery of burnt constellations. Not ugly, just not right, unbelievable. It's elongated—something in it suggests reptilian, the teeth too perfect, too white. Deep-set eyes and no eyebrows to raise or use to detail sagas. And his eyes keep nothing stored away—their resolve is disturbing and what they devise comes from distant places. They're the dark eyes of an animal that won't tolerate, hard and locked they cry for bloodletting.

Bad is certain his eyes don't blink. For a few seconds he wonders if that is one of those "effects one in every 100,000" medical conditions, and if it is, how does he sleep if he can't close his eyes. Hard stare leveled is a short dance, something of steel and fire unbuckles secure, sticks in Bad's throat, fear feeds on his balance.

"It seems you may not be as familiar with the finer points of casting productions, but I am, shall we say, an old hand in diversion's game of happens." Mr. Phoenix, his hand thrust forward like the confession of a lance, gestures to Lena. "Now in regards to this young woman."

Bad's sidekick barks. "We were here first old man. Might wanna just move on, or some hard and nasty could point you at the ER . . . Or some other dead spot. Get it?" *Stupid old fuck.*

"A dead spot. Yes. From there, perhaps you are aware of it?" A knowing smile. "No? No need to fret over it, dear boy. As I was saying, from right there."

Sidekick and Bad stare at the bewildering seize of ill Mr. Phoenix indicates with a blackthorn finger. He is pointing to a sarcophagus of blackness that the pair find terrifying. As they stare they feel blind.

Without a watch closely, his finger suddenly turns into an illusionist's sweeping gesture of allow-me-to-present. "To this untidy spot."

They follow the arc of his hand but their thoughts remain clenched by the blinding darkness they know is not empty. It's the cold-blooded duo's turn not to understand, not to understand how a patch of utter blackness can hold and swell with that much pure dread. Cooped and emasculated, their security claimed by a sudden rising nausea, a cigarette falls from a hand tattooed with scars. The knife shrinks back a few inches.

"So we do understand each other." Mr. Phoenix brings his hands together, not to clap or pray. The act rings with a child's ready in eyes climbing the tone of snacktime. "How lovely."

No discernable snake of motion or shift in the Black Man's shape. But it possesses and amplifies the shafts and webs and pillars of harms tremendous. The blackness behind him expands with the fullness of spread wings.

Bad remembers a cartoon about a sorcerer's apprentice, sees something of that in this, but this isn't comical like his memory of Disney's animation, there's unseen here. Evil. And this man-shape conducts it.

Years ago Bad followed an arresting Scandinavian-blonde in a silk scarf and matching exotic-print, 1,200 dollar dress into Tut's visit to LA. He wanted her opened, her mouth undressed and mangling YES, wanted her belly chanting vows and thighs frenetic—he had the pre-scription for her map, looked for ways to get near her and get the blonde with the perfect ass out of her world and into his. Watched as she stood standing there. There was something else in the exhibition's galleries, it caught him. Something old, from times that didn't fit logic, something from the vast country common has never tread.

The thing that had watched him that day. Wanted him. Clutched. The old man had the shape of a man, but he felt like that thing.

He didn't get the blonde, she wound up on the arm of a power-broker in an Armani, but he got out. Got drunk while the thick lips of a hardlooking slut in a tube-top he picked up after a few beers in the Ten Dimes became an integral part of the craving he needed rubbed out. He never forgot the other desire in that museum that day. There are many nights it's in his dreams.

Fucker's sick and cold as that thing.

Am I broadens the Black Man's crow-scenting-victim smile.

Bad caught by the snip of no whiskey-hot spirit or muscle to lean on. Adrenalin wounded all the way to scrawny. Out of spit. Some nonsense has turned the doorknob of his mindset; rubber legs and its tapestry of occur nosedives into the brutal of tombstone dead.

Bad wishes his knife was a gun.

Shivers.

How'd it get so fucking cold?

What goes up must—Lights are going out—Posture clutched, volts break the lock of reason . . . No fight left in his garments, assembly loses the color of its parts . . . The inkwell of breathing, shipwrecked, loses its part in the show. All the sand in the Black Man drinks his sun. Dead without a burial. No bleedout. Bad crumbles without a thought of was or happened. Knife clatters on the curb.

Aim can't hold its place sinks. Face does about into flaccid. Disbelief is a weather of scalpels. Sidekick stunned until his self-preserving KILL conquers the thick wut-the.

Fuck. Reaching for his .9.

Two seconds later loses the pit bull-current that fueled his capacity. Spine shorn of the will and brute of his cohort, trying to rebound from the pressures of a-little-too much whiskey. Takes no step forward. Hit. In cold unrelated to familiar weather (and no last smoke or request), squeals, sounds like a winded speech of never learned.

Sways.

Woven of eclipses not subject to theology or science Mr. Phoenix's laugh wanders the inward cloaks and curses of the plaything. The Black Man takes . . .

city to shotgun . . .

the face in the backseat of the Chevy and what Ali Baba drilled with the articulations of the .9 . . . Mrs. 1941's red pen, the drag, SAID, SAID (pushed from that Sinai-carved God-face) and SAID again . . .

Haulin'

crates-haulin' boxes. Minimum wage sweat line . . .

Rollin' . . . The Boys. Party!

Under BREWS and a nest of nameless-faceless limbs in sheets, the snap of colors and crime— RISKandprison without reggae and the untamed passports of heavy thighs . . . MIDNIGHTwildside loaded . . .

(pimples and learning to shave) . . .

CONFUSION standing next to the drumming mountain of ENOUGH—he had a heart.it would give up secrets and EVERMORE for a bankable YES.he'd pin two absolutelys to it . . .

stealforfun. stealforthrills.
stealtofitin.

dry-

ing BLOOD . . . Pot. Eat. Lie.

Pot's good. Coke's better. Lot better.

23 and 10 days, parked on the steps
chewing WANT and Alicia—hooked him with that 1st wink!—
walked by. Undisguised and no sleep, and Alicia wildASS(packed
with volleys of writhing) off the domestic chain and KICKin' the coast
of his history from smelter-boomed story to MAKE IT, BABY.
Alicia—golden belly, moist perfuming the YESofFUCK, electric
devil-fingers rubbing the fevered wasp of his vortex. Alicia velvetsin
Paradise-thighs to bring him to his knees to pray. Alicia (lights turned
low): "Ever see one shake like this, Baby?" Forgot to say no when she
unzipped him . . . . "Baby." Everytime she said it. Did it beautiful!
Every time—tables fattened with platters of brisk, until the bonfire
turned wreckage . . . dropped his coins of worth, made a fist . . .

playground arousal fails . . .

Mr. Phoenix reaches
down in the jigsaw wash-layer of popsicles and pinball and comics,
down to baby and cry,

no white light

. . . Under the jeweler's eyes probing his blemishes.
Headed down. Vanishing, little pieces and the clock-machine that
runs the duties of regular life. No key or string of offhand exclamations to fix RUNquick. No artillery to
slap the battering emphasis . . .

Into—without red chalk or a table covered with a cloth
black as ink, and fire words falling from a crone's conjuring mouth. . .
(if he had a tongue that worked, or a classical education,
or any discernable sense left, Sidekick would call it, impossible
weather)

Into—without stepping forward . . .

                                        Smoldering   black
hand raking the wings of a universe where there's no breathe
                        and begin again . . .

                        to root.

Boiling in cold panic. Sidekick no tongue or will to compel it. As easily turned as a screw, trembling, looking grey. Eyes in anxiety's zig-zag, a crisis-strained rat (with bare hands) before a snake.

Mr. Phoenix enjoying numb violating brouhaha then booming ENOUGH! with his fist—Fixture dismemberment.

Lungs out of storm collapse. Not Sidekick. Litter. Consciousness galloped from where it fell. No thread of wet left in its err.

Husk for the compost.

Lena awash in fear, and ready to breathe, at the exit of leave.

Kicked.

Possessing no blessing groomed with acres expressing perfect gladness, she doesn't want to be dislodged and spilled, null, void. Liquidated.

Can't put a finger on cute and fluffy 8 shining with spring, or where it was safe. Can't re: It's just not there.

Bare.

Lena's bowels plead runaway. Fear as spasms out of the cupboard . . . Meltdown unconsoled by future.

Alone. Holding on to the next breath in the ice age.

Here.

(Street don't hear your voice.)

Cornered by the non-refundable hounds of TRUE. Can't turn away from grizzly's tear-swarm.

He killed them. Didn't touch them—but.

Staring at the emptied shells. Trembling then rigid. Cold snapped by the pressure-heat trajectory of her hammering-blood. Her lips move but she can't even whisper.

Like he spooned the meat out of them. That's like—Fuck, I don't know what it is.

Flies will come to feed. Eggs will be laid. Cops will look at this and speculate. They'll echo her how the hell?

It's like nothing she's ever seen or heard of, and she can't pull her eyes away.

How did he deflate them?

She'd watched them squirm and didn't understand.

Do they do autopsies on things like that?

She's staring at the radiant white teeth of his smile.

He killed them. Ate them to the bone . . .

Lena wonders if he's going to burp. Her stomach churns.

And enjoyed it.

The Black Man glows.

His eyes soften.

Less void. Less cold. A soft branding. Therapy. Ancient black fingers having left the lifeforce-game, attach to a new geography. Lena feels like an illustration being filled with embraceable colors.

"Ssssh." Tongue of flute music: "Quiet your fears, Child."

She looked down at her feet. Less thunder on the dark mat of street. The snares clothed in grave-treacherous dim. Lena looks at the lights at the end of the street. Her eyes are full of hours on another street, there was day and children on Aunt Shirley's porch, and all the hands and feet of God is good.

"So you hope the stars will be your destination. That my dear, Lena, can be arranged. I'm well versed in such alignments."

She turns into his smooth voice. "I was hoping for . . . *That.*" Points to neon flags of glamour and fame painting the end of the street. Wants to look in his eyes, ask about easy.

"Many hope they might catch tomorrow on the other side of easy's gates. Alas, Dear Girl, easy is not often simple. It, more times than not, comes with efforts stuck in the explosions of unattainable. Many lean . . . Most never step upon that shore." Holds out his soft hand. It carries the scent of smoke and horizons not greased in hindsight.

Lena stares at the gates less than a mile from her fingers. Sheds a tear. Electric doesn't blink, doesn't taste it.

"I have an acquaintance in the Hyades. Has a retreat, a canvas, in a vale of autumnal quietude under the Place Where the Black Stars Hang. He's not much for glitz and applause, but he's thrown many galas. You'll fit in perfectly."

Gently grasping her hand. "Shall we?"

The unveiling of embrace . . .

Unstitched from stone . . .

The thrust of a boat without a
tail . . .

all   the
sides of the river . . . . no longer hovering . . . . felt
sad   and   scared   not   with   her
. . . . the delta to the snapping ink gives up planets
. . . . and slaughter and hopes . . . .
tied to awful wings woe cries out from the darkning
flair of abyss . . . .   doors . . . . nests . . . .
the turbulent warfare of ebb and flow inscribed in unstable rifts
glittering cinders—the word botanical pops up
vessels of carrion sand.   a globe of
fountains.a table of jackals.sudden claws.

heave

shudder

shook and shook and shook

peeling

spiders gather in the wolfbush—sifting for taste they boil. a black
stream hisses an awoken song.

tips of layers uncovered

lanterns of spinning dust . . . . tangible   . . .
without quality

sun awake with RED.

moons sown with abandoned.

fire spreading. Flash image of Mom's chandelier in the dining room.

black leaping.

arcs

and thirst simmering.

shine roars . . . .   blossoms calm . . . .
newly awaken stars sweating quicksilver arcades
perfumed in the bonekiss of perishing sounds—they bring to mind
wildflowers lightly strummed by a breeze, something warm in Lena's
mind that feels like her mother's smile . . . .

abundance rises to dwell in a cluster of born . . . . thirst as
FURY yonder swift . . . .

A sea of celestial faces . . . .

No tears.

From the black river churning with voided and shredded dreams
to night's vast sea
to here. . . . .

Lena looks down at her feet. toes. not ruby slippers. she does not
stop on how or where her shoes have gone. The Black Man is taller
here. he was tall there, but here, so much taller
. . . . and his hand is warmer, comforting.
Nothing purrs.
Or shimmers.
The empty years lift her body

—beyond blackness is not as cold and empty as she would have
guessed

"This is Carcosa."
Lena's eyes leave the smoldering hand that has released her.
Meeting his eyes she asks.
His answer is a whisper. "You don't bring words here."

After a comment that brought T.E.D. Klein's "The Black Man with the Horn"
and Wilum Hopfrog Pugmire's "The Hands That Reek and Smoke" to mind.

The Clash, "London Calling"; Sam Roberts, "Detroit 67"; X, "Soul Kitchen";
Laura Vane, "Steam"; N.R.P.S., "Portland Woman"; Elbow Bones and
the Racketeers, "Take Me for a Night In New York";
Josefus, "Dead Man"; and Poco, "Barbados."

2nd draft: David Lynch/Chrysta Bell, "Polish Poem";
Iron Butterfly, "Iron Butterfly Theme"; Al Di Meola, "Egyptian Danza";
Pat Metheny, "Betcha by Golly, Wow"; and Steve Roach & Roger King,
"Snake Eyes" looped of course . . .

When a Sigh Visits Skin

No moon in Moontown tonight. Neon . . .

Neon to paint the bruised groupings.

Night for day.

NEON . . .

and scabs . . . and canticles . . .

. . . fields of get-it-all dreams . . .

Fossil-city—

one—I AM, manufactured and published that it might flex a MIGHT?

three (solid as essays of pulp)—chilled to small, shivers running, coats fighting the damp spilled on this neon-hide-&-seek fire of non-sense

Situations of identity and done[half a bottle long] so tight you know for sure.

Pulse and mire and grime the moon—when it shows—can't laugh away.

Carnival ride of again without help, packed new-order tight.

another mouth, enlarged, corridors and staircase open like drawers Trill/burble *a mouth opens within another mouth* Little side conversations [close up and loaded with crumbs] Squeak *another mouth subject to metamorphosis* Nymphomaniac echoes as jazz-low tide trouble can afford or delegate. In this house they shoot the piano player.

milk & honey? Not in this alchemical opera, shaded by enfants terribles and deathbird stories

the horde of pocked coffins, pieces stitched from pieces of this-and-that and scrapes of so on, and the little things of pray and comfort struggling-thieves can take away from the battle of HERE & NOW, splashed on the street

consulting eyes of audacity and whim fixed on sores and deliriums and To Catch

Bucket empty, a momentary eon of sadness . . .

Not Jack or Ray or Teddy. Bile—Haywire-sharp. Fingers uncoiled for creation. His toady, a choreography of whiskey-spit and piss and impacted pain, tagged its lump of bones, Spleen. Black hard-eyes, gutter-draped lanes of grotesques, gates to hissing REDWANT, open. Steel-limbs ready to blossom o'er dream-craters and alleys of nightmare fables between the puff and swells of surfacing layers.

No orderly arrangement to their kosmos. With streetlamp-Greek chorus flickering as it wraps the cold-scaled air in hues dim, the blood-glue scribes sniff, disorient every fact, every chart and scale, imagine blasts of unbounded proportion peppered with teeth.

Their only strategy quicksand purpose.

Watching the tarantella of slave, lips and chains and ink—garden. Black and RED . . . Silk and leather push. Flowers camouflaged in electric and despair. Fire exclaiming storm. Fire as enthusiastic inquisition, as hurricane machine—Creatures made litter. Hands parading, rubbing, thinning the available human factor. Lash of lionface—Thou shall hold no shield. Thou shall have no life. Presence. Flash. Futures bend. Violins with the voices of dawn doves smashed on leviathan eyes. Clock bays. Tourists lock their locks and check them twice. Chewing a kink of infamy-crooning ardor, Bile's reveries steam. Spleen, a column of impulse, begins to dream of the candy-filled adventures behind windows . . .

All the faces to taste.

The sea of uses thickens.

Not a wind chime or a leaf on this night-tide street of singsong hatchet-hymns. Birds? Not hardy. No pleasant is born here. No radiance of stars above.

Not here.

Expect tiny. Not paradisal strung with chorded flows of honeysuckle star-ivy. Its sparkling purpose would sour here.

Ash . . . tomb-centuries without the light of day . . . Dreams to fracture and burn. Storms soar o'er RED and the mendacious fuse-dance of NO/corpse/bleeding. Sad dreams, on their faces ash. Dreams, out of Bibles, not shielded from the war, eat Blackness, are split and milled into garbage overcome by the BANG of CERTAIN . . . BLACK—Tongues—Landslide sea—Wolf's-mouth herdsman.

BLACK the fingers of the desiring drain. Last grinning, spinning its matinees of anticipation, its sin-lit thunder mines the black-tingle drama. Its unfurled snake is harder than the language of light . . . run . . . wish, for a next line that won't slip from hands . . . run . . . talk about praying before Too Late . . . run

Scabs & canticles/

run

possession/

territory/

stronghold/

CAN and its texture of I AM beheaded by discontent/

language & imaginary expressed as equations that lose thrust, that no one dares to push through difficult only to have FIX, spattered with exhaustion, end on the cliff of DEATH . . .

instant forced to account/

NO intervention cross, NO ransom of meaning available in this dominated NOW—The Serpent swallows all Christs, all magic however limited . . . titanic gravity/rabies/insomnia diaries/angel noir and roses

&MORE

/more fate

/more MAX

/more skin, frank and special—spectra, frontline, assembled

victim

to touch

to ingest

victim, herb of dream, pulse, bed, attraction, and fact to have, and to hold

The tiered shadows smolder and knit lurid rites. The shadows, suspending lives in their roaring filigree beaks, beckon, shift; ribbons and verses blindfolding, soak the darkness in narrow and infant moods of be gone; fleck, touch and taste, and skin in plazas lowered to tremble. The shadows, thick and cold as iron, export reason's steps . . .

. . . Storm—ELECTROSTORM, blue angel perfection to form and command . . . golden hair . . . Near. The damned. Near. The rattle, and the children and their little books of prophesy. Victim, near storm.

In this whirlwind Nothing, no history with capable, no inflection, no marriage or mark, is covered with stars.

Clouds leak. Tongues clumped with assumption expand, express storm with confrontation woven with mindrot extremes . . .

Dreams sting.

Bodies.

Bodies. Pink. And soft. And tender. Pink. So pink . . . So sweet and fine. Sweet, yes-yes. To sing . . . JOY (to pulverize) (flayed) (resonating in intervals chaotic) . . .

Wings beating. Hearts in the jaws of WANT-WANT-WANT! Hawks to BLOOD . . .

Bile.

Spleen.

Balls—racing with crave—prowl. Frank as sin, exclaiming a cunning lie. Sharp and head-on damage, wearing hours that have much to say to mistakes. Fearless as teeth that walk away from the burden of sunset, backs laughing at the black perfume that covers lawns.

Bile

& Spleen

a flood of gnarled hazards these rocks snowing. Vivid as the steel of soon-to-be and unwilling-to-be-without

Top-billing in CREATION

(every cell—swift and natural—rising.)

The butterflies, dressed in hesitation and feeble, breathe their perfume in the flood-tide cage, but they are of no importance. Their expressions are forgotten towns of unarmed ghosts.

Bile is a dagger, a pirate, a voyage of eats and wings and uneven in wild skin. Spleen, a pin at the entrance of a butterfly.

Dark Friday. Ants. Matches blink and roar, quick their form dies. Blind symphonies. Scent and exchange. Roles wait. Coin, and Here To Take. Tread of mired-feet, Muse, now shut from the flip of gain, comes out of the Kit Kat Club. A barking stream of tormented isles adorned in alarm, the dynasty's players (powder-burned and trembling from the post-Beast caress) tumble forth . . .

Storm eyes, raking aesthetic-black and pink and years . . . lips lick swan necks . . . the shape of heads . . . Faces. Faces, the glow of curtains yet to be drawn. RED. To touch, to taste. To take. Faces. Constellations. Brown. Yellow. Washed in pain. The shape of heads . . .

You . . . or You . . . (eyes scrape) or You . . .

The countdown to ZERO.

Little winds, irregular swirling the details of the telescope with their own rush and grasp. Spheres and windows . . . the giddiness . . . RED . . .

RED

Or You?—(flare loud!)

Fingers tap sigils on blade . . . Eyes itch with time's wretched tricks. Eyes clattered with tips shining out I GIVE. Tips of permitted—Come, Rueful Thirst! Rare quantities and that sort of thing to garner.

The sigh, "Oh, Fire."

Commence. Commence.

With coughs and fireworks, truth struck in the black-drama decor. The stones roll. Unfiltered racket . . . prime-evil stroked. Weak—on its knees, wounds salted by wartime. Alpha-strong, standing ready for the kiss of ovation . . .

Hotel alley, rat house, licked by flames unspeakable. Cigarette litter. Grim scrapped shoulder to root. Black loaded with fret . . . and the blind, lunatic breath of tempestuous rims, where mortal awash in unholy, drowns in sour's fancy.

Some thing, its spells to screech and croak, churrs.

Some thing moans.

Wings from an ancient mouth laugh lightly.

Ankles—of one astray—on the boards. Glue for vulture eyes. The slope of shoulder. Calve TO TAKE. Theater of glimmering decoration calls. Two heads, one thought. Ass, fine to wrap and twist in shame, flares. The stormdance unrehearsed, but well practiced . . . Passenger Alanna. Tomorrow, some light Dajana-candy, eyes to ply, or incense-beckoning Penelope, gates to no longer sing.

Bile and Spleen flare. Grins wide open. Eyes chewing fat whore-purse. Bile's tongue drum rolls. Eden to scar, the oven boils . . .

"Nice."

"Fuck yeah."

"Appropriate ecstasy."

"The jam and suck sublime."

"Fuck yeah."

Twin smiles.

"Oodles."

"Chewy spiced with boo-hoo-hoo."

The nod yep. "A-Club-cum-laude with a lovely glass to fill." And a wink. "Fest?"

"Fest! *Of course and please.*"

"While we can."

Twin "Fuck-yeah" smiles.

Crosshair target, the stir of marks "Hark!"-ripe with castle-purses, and gallons of slippery leisure. Each planet of party calls their names, strokes the Satan-bricks of their armor. Storm.

Storm. Bristle. Master and doom in the hall of inmate. Shadow to herded white-throat, heart to empty. Years drawn in the disappearance-hole of snap-joyless. Guardian angels out to lunch or turned away, unable, or unwilling to gaze on the spontaneous evidence.

In the beginning, blood weather. Blazing.

Storm. Lionface flame. Breathing white hot. Voices high and hard, singsong tight. Hands, an influx of indulgent yards raiding flesh, visit the bill of fare, smash the tiny "I am" of stars.

Under murder-hats toxic eyes teach void to the hopeless, fending shout amidst afflictions. Moving mouths of teeth care not for names, of dim pleas of NO! Licking. Licking. Fire-monsoons milk time, plow, lace greed to the sticky machines of their wired-buzzing. Trapped, the bucket of "I am."-space shivers under the lecture of the grave-merchants' fingers.

Radiation . . . loam—the upturned eye reaches, but no hand comes to waken it . . . the page tears, syllables split . . . split-second/light trickles . . . Dark crashing . . . Pouring . . . white bone on the way to Will Be . . . Steam. Each drop of lush brazed in news of war not opposed. For-ever distilled . . . NEVERagain.

"Art."

"Toil."

"And *Trouble.*"

Hot. The tip of a tongue. A drop of sweat. Simple as stone, a summit of smiles.

The builders complete. Corners of mouths flicker with laughter. Cigarettes, tips smoking, are inhaled. Money counted. Cocks adjusted. Coin jingles.

Limitation returns.

Spleen spits.

Bile's eyes smear the engraved field he has left barren of heat, laugh upon hill fallen to landslide.

Trick of knife retired. The burning, now ashes . . .

"Drink?"

"Of course. Please."

Sadness.

Frost.

No ghost traces the air.

After a restless sigh, Spleen yawns.

Bile, licking a drop of candy from his finger, "Please."

. . . No moon in Moontown tonight

NEON

and the glimmer of a prowling rat's eyes

(for tonight, THE END . . .)

After Alan Moore and David Tibet . . . dancing . . .
with a nod to the Goblins in the Sky.

By the Light ... of

for Robin Spriggs' diabolical oratorical weather, undeniable and historic

—Crying, "Nobody, nobody, nobody knows
How much I love the maiden as I tear off her clothes"—
Michael Hurley "The Werewolf"

Gnossienne no. 1

    Lyricless joy. A melody of sighs—openly; fingers with no divide.
No words. Feel. Tango.
she loves . . .

        his Idylle

                        ". . . veils and roses . . ."

        his Meditation

                        "Chalice eyes."

        his Reflections

                        ". . . warm and sweet . . ."

a canal of New. perfectly. Face
(inhabiting the scaffold of nuzzle)
she opens her mouth
he thrusts his story
The flowers she selects and counts, nine curved skies—seamless
as kings wearing knowledge in their margins

    Her tongue is a page of paper, open—aflame.

    disguise freefall, he is a jolt, truly new accelerating

    coarse

    confusion—Hold comfort? Two together—face to face?

    meat—

    blood—golden cup yielding to chemistry swollen with its pres-
ence

    his sorcerer's death-eye sears

Vexation: his luminescence.

turn it down.

Rüegg—Werewolf. H~o~w~l~

just because her breast is a perfect moon.

she bids his eyes welcome.

nipple. Mare Imbrium.

That sea—Her bra came off in his hands. Pleased hands awash in raw know one another.

Sweet juice breathing starts.

One charming night. Freedom

jazz dance—

           Beeline hand—"Hello." "Like." Smooth. Vital organ. Season/era—Throat.

hallucinatory TEETH

           c~i~r~c~l~i~n~g

   &

     skin

Gnossienne no. 2

Echo. Where I fall. His eyes asked. Asked to be converted, whispered, salvation?

Vexation

raw scar explosion—Why . . .

Again . . . Too hot. Too fast.

"I bite back."

Pushes the rim and plain of his wildlife hand

away.

Grunt in his shining throat.

Too fast. Blood desire. his gleams

hers aches in her throat

           The letters and colors of the compass grow, gather.

the song of bones stretches—the touch of nerves/CLOSE UP

—silk cascade, lifting Apollo's honey

—bride phrase, moist, lace-touched kissed twice (fantasy phosphorous—sizes swarm)

she licks the clump of his hurry. Leans

into the long tassles of his warm pages

CLOSE UP—her mouth

             (glued to carnal action-curve and its fresh language of
                                             fairy tale fire—)

ajar

the crest

of

THAT

bright scarlet reserves—

faith/starvation/THROAT—THROAT—fruit, thread hissed–the
rhetoric of lifetime scratched on lips/Nervously's incandesce waylaid

drums, steady, overcast/influence/consequences.crossing, double-
hearted

bare throat/bruise rushes in/balance disappears

a dark action of bliss

kiss to bind dissolves/sky-prisoner—BLOOD/life pours . . .
o u tDEAD A terrible door. An empty bowl—"Too soon." . . . Anguish is a thief, he weaves nothing as he rides night and his mouth
staggers home to its desert of low . . .

what was

LIFE

(bargaining on the carousel-quest) dangling from her lips. Un-
fillable eyes moving over borders—Perfect madman genius, volumes
of indiscretions . . . and abruptly, composed. His bouquets of ink clear
as grief.

A flat path. No more, "Once." . . .

light was.

a crumb, a door with no aspect of gold or touching.

less

human.

Reflections on Aubade

Mound. Cold. Dark.

                   Dirt. Shadows cast by bare branches. Pale sunlight
dawn. Winterlight.

A magpie calls his mate.

She looks at her hands, simple windows.

b l o o d

b l o o d

cold. Dark.

Dirt. Under her red nails, guillotine. Hullabaloo-flash

dreams—solitary triumphs—divergent. anguish as truth and mystery—Further, arrows that will not shut, opens veins and trembling
heart, speaks without disguise/racing pulse bleating—qualities, lovely
to breathe, docked to her unrestrained mouth, slaughter

                                                    emerges

Hopes, beach—lovely to see and hold—liberate what roots

                                                    and

                                                    scalds

in hearts

bloodshed

          fixated on the errors spread

          lilies (desperate as a tongue—bathed in fire and ecstasy—
with no false meaning)

die

Torpor.

her lips are red. No fervor rustles where desire swarmed.

his warm blood in her stomach has turned cold.

Magpie's moaning saxophone call of after rides . . .

Not even the restless ghost wind replies.

Her eyes touch his spirit-handled things—the fruit he practiced,
the bells he roasted

—you will need them—

simple things.

Pale mulberry paper interior: There's a note in his notebook.

*I came from the grey meatmarket street and the blood it spills to
paint its dumbness . . . As if it could color yesterday with a heart of
light . . . Seeker. Escapist never tortured by careful, tricked by the
touch/prick of brindled-damage—painbite with blood in it . . .*

*There were little drops of lonely. Signals, flanks—sweet lust open
smothered my mouth. She took her panties off, then when my knees ran
away with heatwave hard and the moon leaned in and gave her a different species of emotion, she—over white fangs—barking some cheetah-
quick laugh of predator-metal, left me a rabbit, sprawled, slaughtered
. . .*

courtyard of nightsky

I didn't understand what I had entered. Couldn't categorize this new décor—the tension of time and space, the resources . . . I looked at citations, at what was scattered on rugs, at the interchange of you & I on my lips . . . at the Other Place . . .

Looked in a hundred mirrors for invitations that did not ferment So Are You. Lost every single argument.chunks of life

feed

feed

Ghosts traveled in my diaries . . .

Bellies. Lovely legs in my bed—courtyard of nightsky, moon leans in—shift from anonymity to Devil.

courtyard of nightsky

marry death and fantasy and the orgasm of no history—couldn't mitigate honest

Did I want to?

feed

Human shape understood as animals. Clash of mythologies—luscious-spinning. Personality/symphony of questions. Map/surface as a test.

I was reading Patchen—(What are we to teach?) Or Levertov?—ants, acropolis, plunge from native lands to moon on flesh and hair. Dusk—first note of all night . . .

Faces (above, fathomless gem, no thine or seeds to connect mind), mine, worn away by shadows, parting and shifting rhythm and description—memory(room tamed by color/pleated with a ceiling)shortening—Horizon wall. Time casts its shadow on my mouth. No alternative. The wall split—moon throbs in my teeth. Bitter bolt/clustered perceptually. Shirt/boot—absurd gestures. Brillo-pad skin—hurry arrives brightly. Teeth—muzzle—meat urge—Sharp teeth, rush to cut, to splinter and swallow. Stiff, slow. Bristling vigor, proportion made visible. Hands that were leashed charge. Fist breathing true. Animal act.

Guiltless tomorrow—Extreme clarity of imperatives. The rejoicing form, cheek and cock drums of truth and thunder, raised from the ripples of hunger . . . rearrange the legends by painting the sky.

I met her at a border of flowers and graves. She spoke of having another side.

Some union of unfinished haunted us
tree(confused out of reward) in a world at large
half dressed.

A drop of blood on her sharp fangs of o-taste-and-see . . .
Blind.alone. Her protests of sorrow echo in the dark.

Above troubles, the thinning moon laughs.

The fumes of drought. Tragedy affixed to the bitter she opened
"The werewolf . . . The werewolf."

Big nightsky talk ebbs: inscription, tears on trembling breasts.
Dance now hard-luck trash—no prayer embraced—lust screwed,
paradise devoured. Winterland screams instead of pleasure

Shutters. Bare longing
                        dancing on her
sickness

"shame." Means, *fool.* Eyes bent with fury

Loathsome monster-hunger laments nothing—won't sleep or surrender its borders/wings, wolves tearing for other roofs/wants more
devilnight drums/outlaw-sourmouth OPEN [in six-foot tall letters]
re-fuel/SUCK—*W!A!N!T!S!*

no bread or
siege backtalk. No
history of the knight's lost causes prayer

Near sundial ruin. Her cabinet of black shades—large enough for
her red mouth and the razor—is not far. Soaked in impassable, its
death-mouth hours will be silent. Her dreams of night and ash and
night and ash and night and the moist beginnings of and touch will
not

Bill Evans, "Turn Out the Stars"; Cat Power, "The Werewolf"; and
Erik Satie, "Gnossienne No. 6—Avec conviction et avec une tristesse rigoureus."

Her Lips Were Wet with Venom

Rolling,
tumblin',
bad,
nothing changes.

Circumstances and treachery damn homeless bare bones.

Broken stays broken.

The enemy god dances on the littered affairs and fortunes of what it sucked dry yesterday.

And it rains.

Been rainin' for days. Rainin' a river of tears.

Call it blues
or suffering.

Whatever it is it came right on in. And it's staying. Gonna sit right there in yer easy chair like some fat possum predator lickin' its painted, ripe-hot cherry lips. Just better keep the gravy and honey comin' honey. Or it gon show ya a thing. A mean, drunken, thick manic thing swelled with greedy.

It's never satisfied.

Never.

Can't fill that hole.

No way.

No how.

Just cain't.

Never has.

Never will.

Cain't.

Won't.

So you shout and search the universe for things to fertilize your frying pan, give the vexations clamoring at your door a thorough once-over and find nothing in the mousetrap but the scrapes of ballyhoo gone flat and none came back.

Another night in another bar. Circus games. Fireworks. Little skies tremble and carve horizons with absinthe tongues, blackworm eyelids flash, courtships upholstered in rust sting of not this . . . collisions of solitude fly from brow to brow . . . It's all scars, no halos.

She sits in the Crystal Lion waiting. Little round table of scratched and erosive possibilities at the shadowed back—*hurry to it.* Stroking her crystal ball with long onyx-ringed finger. What she sees, what she'll tell ya, if you open your mouth and ask, is uncensored.

She'll whisper about the faces and the masks and the cold winds blowing in off the lake. Whisper of choirs of silent things that have their places in the cold blindness between the stars. Whisper of the labyrinth of verdant flesh and pleasures to be had by two sitting alone in the dark . . .

And filled with beast-adrenaline and desire—yours and hers, and the sanctified-in-hardcore blues scrape pounding off the walls of the club, you'll follow her down any hole. Hoping it leads to mouth and ankles and breasts and perfect round ass pushin' and pushin'—cookin' with gas and scalding bed and one long uncompromising—PLEASE-PLEASE-PLEASE, overheated burst.

But what it leads to is a hell.

And you do not get to choose.

And you do not get to choose.

Sound cruel?

Tough.

This is where you were meant to be . . .

Right here.

Right now.

With this dead creature, this Feaster of Living Sin. She cries your name . . . Her cloak unfolds . . .

You dance.

Happily in the first moments of the sham . . .

Then, amid her silence, the graveyard of your questions, your noisy questions of mud begin to burn.

Root to Christmas tree you follow those hips, sensuous as any language of animal-muscled taboo, follow what they offer . . .

Her windowless rooms are dark, appointed with the unique. Old books written in tunnels under basements in nameless places by souls with unblessed fingers, her fever-books are a jungle, a secret world cloistered about you.

She brings you tea. Sits beside you.

Smiles as she removes her clothes . . .

Watch. TAKE IT! Eyes—all your *WANT*—seizing yours, pretending the heat in her flower pot is feral caviar for the tray of your pavement-smeared lips. Her mosaic in your orbit, your fingers map the curves of FELT.

And you, a devil that would destroy answers or sabotage any plan for a taste of the pie, reach out, throw yourself at her . . .

And her scorpion arms of fire take you in. Her smooth, cold hand is on your face . . .

And she whispers, "I will take you inside."

You fly to her mouth—

She has no need for fangs or blades to cut and rend for her dead lips are wet with starmilk-venom and when she sings her silent psalms give birth to shadows so foreign they bloom from lifeless buds in the black shades of the darkest, unknown places of nothingness.

Can you see it now—Before the earth and all its stains and marks are hidden from you by her alluring night-skin . . . the sunset pales . . . and the endless fugue of blackness spills over the costumes and accoutrements of this hoedown of living sins . . . Do you, small sad dreamer, bitter, tired and confused, stare into it? Do you think anyone, or anything cares, or stares back?

The blackness is blind . . . and cold . . . it cannot lie for it cares not for the disenchanted puppets who dance in this thin, scarecrow reality of huddled trends . . .

Blackness. From the beginning to the Last. Everything.

Something there and not there, this is the enigma. This is the Truth.

In your fatigue of fear, crowds of rancid lies and dust, all the mistakes you stole to try to unravel the spell of fire, collapse . . .

Silently her eyes laugh, shine with a blackness pure and solid . . .

It is done . . .

For you—this moment and for-ever, the stars won't open

Soundtrack: Emerson, Lake, & Palmer, King Crimson, SunnO))) &Boris.

Now (a parade)

for Robert Bloch and Oscar Wilde

—gone . . .

    launched syringe numb. Qualities that blundered over the accent sleeping in the dark. Rain wants in and out the cold. It would settle for the book of matches and a dry cigarette. But I keep no quicker in the house since the train left.

    No shrug of might to replace . . .

    Near what still believes today. Near. Not close enough to moor the fever of displaced. Not. Can't speak of yet.

    Fade. Pulls. Pushes the gift of the wine . . . near her silent hand. Offered honeymoon after the evening of rain . . .

    Shift. No melt away.

    No crash.

    Wreck. And evening's orchestra, slow as lost tourists, discusses bare.

    My mouth offers no ready. No sorry that moves hurdles . . . There are no pangs in my chair.

    Not now.

    Spent where the laughter whispered. All the little colors that fit in-between doubt . . . Anxiously fit well, so nicely. It's sudden, shaded, waited for the absurd parts to pass . . .

    This row of acquaintance. Sounds like an old postcard. Shame there are no tourists to astonish. Shame. None to side with the hymn.

    And the minutes can't imagine any. I wonder if the telephone might fetch some?

    Would they rush with sir and names? Would their cigarettes wink with satisfaction?

    Bother

    and trouble . . .

Hour—after dark without pause . . . long with other and bridge and no goodbye . . . hour . . . no care for gone . . . arms open wide . . . once . . . twice . . . staying like a laugh . . .

No longer blind with elsewhere, radio on the table opens the book of friends . . . Brel as surgeon reports circumstances as his mattered moves to the street. Sylvian, every formidable hallucination a rose the clock has passed, opens amnesia. Walker designs closed . . . Oh Scott, this outcome inside me; I met it in your halls.

Perfect hat trick of blue. Glad for their anyway, close enough to an answer and not as hostile as the crash of whiskey . . .

inside

As I read it desire leaned. "Might offer depth." My boots disconnected from fog in the overspill of rain-colored hours to look.

What did the specter at my shoulder say? FOR MADMEN ONLY.

If you insist.

"*Yes.* Escape common's loud." *To be singed by marvels . . .*

"Something fresh."

Entrance bell dropped a pattern. Worn hands behind the crisscross meshing with chipped polish waited for remit. I read the fading menu selected a flavor. Wondered about a face, but there was no light to go with the voice. "257545. You will be greeted." Just ennui's dry voice.

Ticket in the soiled tray. Paper hardly the size of a stamp. Rosy? Or plum? I came in for color, picked rosy. Soft velvet.

A masked man holds the door open for me. Have I seen that sallow countenance before? There was that night of roving, colonnades, the piazza—faces hammered with same place, experiments, brown skin—she said, "We will be friends tonight, Signore."—in the mirror, the moment she changed her tongue, pieces of a vase, and laughter in his Arrivederci . . . I nodded my greeting and withheld my comment.

Autumn wallpaper.

Voluptuous room cloaked and scented in oriental possibilities. Weary, blue lovers in their long-stemmed dance touch thee. Warm side effects.

A soothing corner table away from explanations and any flow of interruptions. Sitting with my cigarette.

There are women who offer maps and little red palaces and umbrellas and means to be looked over and if flash stings, plucked for sport. Legs, and round bottoms that will ping when properly placed. Sighs toot. Directions wave. The stage is a moment of breasts, firm sources of pleasure waiting to be christened.

On the bandstand the blue velvet of the singer, her shoulder pleasure-bent, is involved in conjecturing. It's an old song about belonging to you. I've heard it, sang it, many times ... But this one, her contours are clever prescriptions.

Eyes searching the dance for any misspellings. Twins with jovial curves and opposites who will without a moment's hesitation. Names. Breasts. The pressure of lips designing value for the gambler's bundle. An ass that has never danced its tiger's dance on the streets. Promises and speed, gossamer knots. Silk-draped. The orbit of tobacco. A lisp. Whiskers waiting to bind the myth it's caught. Gilt, but not a single clock. Jaded-looking. A sour man with considerable proportions of error bows. Red gloss, rope and black bra straps, all to lift and repair. Heaven. Hell. Pride. Scarlet—with a mind to be drugged with poppies. Platinum. Plum-colored. Cigarette studying the follies of an amateur, a Robert, ever the hungry heart, sits with a physician and a judge. It is not hard to determine which hand is responsible for the black bag under the table.

Grape. Whiskey. Troops of coded messages. Gin.

Spin.

Nibble.

Cascade as needed.

How delicious it all is! My tourist walks.

Soft—and an athletic ass—*The caprices I would give to its prow of sudden.* Serving two ladies. They laugh. Drink their drinks. They are wild for the modes of luxury, their naked souls, this night not to be refused or poisoned, touch no shame.

A strategy in my fingers scrapes a route to her. I beckon for her influence at my table.

"Simone."

She is graceful, her qualities fashionably quicker. My true fluffs as fiery's terrain expands. She offers me easy.

"I am a guidebook of magic, a cathedral of roles opened, if the sleeves of your game search evening for a holiday? Lift the lid of your coffin and I will blend light to remove your boat from the projections of these mired complexities and give it the mouth of breathless shores."

The saddle. Her arms. Her red hair and rosy nipples. A bottle— red and heady—and the bedroom. I am no fool to deny ripe temptations. "Tonight, as we lose the minutes to our venture, you will be, Cynara."

Smiles and nods. Procedures concluded.

On my arm of wanderlust, ready for our between . . .

The bedroom—a room of antiques and fine qualities undulating in the flickering candlelight. It takes me back . . .

Red and lace, no restraint in the bottle's reception.

Cynara pours.

Her hands—I encountered dove-versed baubles like these in Venice . . . The bite of perform on every page.

Stallion swept with overindulge, I laugh a conquistador's laugh.

Breath, "*La peur. Peur.* "

Smile. "*Ne crains pas, mon enfant.*"

She, on this night, my Cynara, comes to my opium peaks in a black-mesh string bikini with no gridlock, shape-shifts, blows upon the briny notes of my worn hieroglyphs.

Close. Cheeks of desire and sin. An ivy of limbs. I cling to her breasts . . .

Gravity. Flanking her pleasure. Gliding in entangled . . . Feverish liquid colors. Wings flex . . . Apex. Mouth flexes—

Sauté . . .

Singe . . .

Some sudden meddling thought in her is the destruction of everything. Fluctuations manifesting some demon of mannered and proper, afraid of libertine lecheries broadcast—

In a rented toy? Blasphemy!

I am a titan. My thunder reaches and I put it to her.

The gong strikes.

"No?"

Torment.

stretching my   arm
stretching her

"No?"

Break.

Ripples. Oh, how they echo ... *No well of solace.* Pretty little thing. All I asked was a little originality, allow me to tap open dazzle.

And all she would do is flicker, let fear dim and tatter the spirit of the boudoir's lesson. I've seen that movie. Looked in their eyes, saw patches of flaming fear, saw the toxin-face act—

She gave me limits.

"No?"

Bonds.

turning my
            head
                    to her condition (the invading fissures of cal li g ra p h y)
                                        there on the bed

            curled

"No?"

Filled my spoon with thin and common.

I asked for no safe word!

Sought to push aside my velvet blade. Sought to deny my red kiss.

"It said *inside*. For madmen only. I read it. There was no wrong, no inattention to its address."

Her red mouth—like Juliette's. Curled on the bed. Her red blossom—like Juliette's. Curled on the bed. Flung roses—like Juliette's. Curled on the bed. Breath shed—like Juliette's.

Again.

Like Juliette. Heedless of the pleasures, denied my virtues. Like Juliette.

This anatomy of stronger shadows.

again

This nightingale came to sing, traveled across time to find hospitable, there was no look back on my brow.

My stare smeared in moon splashed its chalk on the sparkle of her stage. I was swimming in flowers. They were a pool, a gift, I gave all to the hot flush, climbed the phrases of her ladder—ate—revamped—*twirls and wider* ... All.

All.

And she offered my hourglass that end?

For all I gave?

For all I offered? Helping her undress, leading the bloom of her rose to do things . . .

Earnestly swayed with her allurements, let her kiss it, stroke it, lick it. I fed her. Showed her gold's obsessed—*my incense burned.* All I braved, my poetry in her ass, her quim. I offered her a chalice to drink from.

And she offered my hourglass end—

"I would have been faithful to thee, Cynara."

empty blows over my tray

Feet travel the hall. A jangle and jingling of keys at the lock, one finds its home, brings light into the room. "Mister Gray." Voice does not argue about danger and trouble, it carries ways.

I look like Then. The frame, no flat constellation that hunger, vibrating with narrative is a warped crowd of NOW and when and suffer and the moods of underbelly.

My wallet is open.

Madame Archer smiles. "I believe that sum will supplement delivery requirements. I'll have it cleaned."

Back to the pavement and the fog . . . On the steps I light my cigarette . . .

The rain has ceased.

A barking dog. A drunken tin cup . . .

. . . Feet.

The fray. Parade gestures

(holes in oversize/and cracks in fear of creases unfolding/eyes wishing they had another set of hands, watching the clock . . .   whine/anger/sick/sinner/of course controlling the needs of yet/eyes out for a tide . . . bones . . .   lips that lick keyholes

and black-shadow rotations . . . and that little magpie bitch . . .

efforts toward another try, another small portion they can leash to the other depressions of memory in their small rooms . . .)

exclaiming NOW

Ankles—glue sings to my blue roots . . . degrees of clarity as I follow this Eugenie to her lyceum . . . her shore sprays my poetry . . .

My mask off—no fox between . . . Wine. Warm Dionysian heartbeat . . . Parked at her heel—the scent of her temple . . . pressed . . . a live thing . . . whirling . . . Her clothes are almost off . . . I see her rose ... swoon plunges into sweet delirium as the skylight frames crazy moonrays—

My fire is out. Remembrance in a curl of blue smoke. The days when Juliette—her urgency to tantalize and titillate pressed me toward the bed and deep into the well—was queen will not return for me.

Yesternight the moon came down—

to gaze upon my portrait of ruin

In The Nursery selections from *Anatomy of a Poet*, Hector Zazou, "First Evening," and various Marshall Tucker Band songs.

After Plath's "Goatsucker"

The things of yellow are closed now. Gone. Surrounded by the
    Black Country.
The night jar is open.
The corpse-foul churrs,
And seeking the coin of deathbird stories
Begins a conversation of witch-cloth wings.
The unmasked burring and whirr,
That knavish fever of ill,
Wakes the moon to its ebony bristle.
The night jar is open,
And in the silence of decay
The corpse-foul—fat and full of fire—churrs.

Tark Left Santiago

for Karl Edward Wagner

Tark left Santiago and its stalkers to their experiments of felt. Left behind his bike. Brought his scissors (always) (seems to) (rusted in the endeavors of his ice-white chapters he has to). Wanted to see her legs. In those black stockings. Sheer. Thin. Lovely. The ones with the run in them. The run that ended with a hole at the knee.

He didn't fit in with them. Wasn't a stalker, or low, pitiful, wasn't a thief, or a mirror, wasn't the Anti-Christ spilling statements of distance and damn it all on the broad veneer of abstraction. Let them say what they wanted. Let them. They would anyway.

But what would she say?

Hi and smile?

Hiss?

Try to bite him?

She might have a gun. Might still look like the woman in the black and white film. The one who didn't smile. Not ever. Not even After.

Another After.

One more for the line. One more road to push it out on. Let it walk. See how far it would go. And if it lead anywhere.

Did they ever?

All those skies to get lost under. All those trees to wind through, some like devil-brutes, some a concert of angels, pushing green like it was hoping fingers. Half with cracked rotting branches. Pushing before the speed of autumnal brought the knife . . .

3 cigarettes left and still an hour to go. He took one out. Considered it. Odd. An odd thing. Strong as a drink. Quiet as a thoughtful friend. Lit it. Watched it burn.

Smoke. Like a carnival—not a big one, not one that you glee over body and soul, moving, swirling—whirlpool no crossroads, no pre-views. Dancing. Smelled like success. Another illusion.

Didn't preach. No.

Wasn't a fairy tale.

Just a cigarette.

Watched it burn. Smoked it slowly.

Still had time.

Time before her scene and the tension it might release.

59.

Right there on the page of his thin little volume.

No entry between page 40 and page 59. Odd.

Not eerie odd. Strange. No blank pages either. All filled. But with the smoke closing doors he was having troubling seeing the shape of the black marks as whole and present.

Odd.

Then again the whole week had been. The afternoons stormy. The twilights uncertain. Nights were not too cold, more detours than lost highways.

Detours.

"You think my legs are detours."

"Did I say that?"

"You're eyes did."

Didn't laugh. Never laughed at the stars. Or the faces. Didn't laugh when they came right over to the porch and sat there with stories to tell. Love. Hate. Light and what it means. He never got to pick. They did. Didn't smile. Never started like that. Gave him that look and before a second breath out came the consequences.

Deal.

Nothing to win.

No card to play.

Handle it. And move on.

She did.

Watched her. Then watched her walk away. The hole in the knee of her black stocking. Knew it was there. But didn't get to see it.

Wanted to.

Wanted.

Wanted to ask her what she wanted.

Just lit a cigarette and watched the carnival.

Cigarette burned out and she was gone.

Page 40 (long as playing footsy with a hookah loaded with un-stoppable flavors) was Santiago. Afternoons in the bar, not searching, just waiting for things to fade. Nights—here, there, busy, even if you didn't agree with the venue. Didn't deal with daylight when he could sidestep it.

Day was like jail, or a job posing as an execution. Took a long time. Didn't give you much. Mere pennies or some water. Not much.

Much. That was night. Like a railway station. Going, going, going. Stops everywhere. Slow to desperate to polar. All you had to do was watch.

Maybe smile here and there. Maybe smoke a smoke while things burned. Didn't have to hold up your hands for it to stop. Did that in its own time. Watch. You weren't needed as cinematographer. Just smoke your smoke and watch.

He did.

Page 40. Wrote it down for later. Older, he needed reminding.

She told him he did.

He believed her. She was not to be overlooked, or disregarded. And one could not accuse her of reasonable doubt. Not when she was as clear as the siege of the clock's big knife.

Here. Clock? Interlocked with some gesture by one's fear. Blue as ink endowed, extended, chewing the calm. The lid of an eye, unpack-ing the suitcase lost in the moat . . . (fear a chilling music)(something tight in the amnesiac lines of the curtains)(a ferry of loopholes, a sticky shakedown dragging some pitfall, begging for punishment and mercy to stop peeling unfettered black)("We catch fire in the solar-fire.") unpacking . . . another (count out the past) and another (count the stills and the chase) and another (the constellations connected to her neck, like you're some detective who can confront the verbs and colors under the crust of flesh) . . . All in there, the silt on it, tempo-rary, preventing . . . But it can slide, mid-sentence; all the meanings, moving crows painting the lawn of shadows, and the clouds, unfold-ing the maps, making doors—leaning in . . .

Blackening(no soft isolated trumpet up in it). Gut captured on the platter(no crying sax or snare-shot to frame it) . . . Melting, a fraction of a ripple(anger that was banked comes out of the scrap-book—monkey on a knife or gun bender, spinning Joe Frazier particles at your heart and ribs), the opposite side and its unborn dust an ice of ghost-wings—a delta of veins—spilled on the black and white canvas . . . 10 digits of madness grasp a hollow spot of language, a circle . . . Eyes like the perfume of a sea . . . A coitus of sundown . . .

 . . . leaning in . . .

Elsewhere

the ghost-house, leaning in, splashing yesterday wall to wall

Cry.

(for Mother)(for bye and bye)(and windows)(open)

ash

dust

Words

a door

the season after The Crossing . . .

The circle, traces of stormy in the sand, salty air says it needs Forever.

Cry. (sister full of sour lunar illustrations cries, "There!")(on the battlefield with the fire in brother's "You'll fall hard." eyes)(every word blooms)(every speck—root to fable—picks at the years)

Words in the bedroom,

the crack in the sky,

the speed of the bed,

the calligraphy of the electric-light moon perched

diffusing

nebulae . . .

Page 40. A one way street named To-morrow. A weathervane hour swaying with names that never orbited golden. Something about a scarf that didn't make a good shield. A big hole in the footnote you could fall through, some error without a pearl yes. All there. Overturned, and rubbing on the bottom of the echoes. Are all those signs you touched melting?

Somewhere in the night illusions are sleeping on a staircase. Drank their fill of rain, drank them right down to undone. A dim fugue of a sonnet swerved in the roots, lost its stitches, the auctions of sugar went Outer, whirled in the collision. Shriveled.

Boots impersonated miles. Santiago. Seemed like the highway to hang the verdict on.

Page 40. Frisson. Secrets. With make-up on it looks like a poem.

Nice little hill—folded in prayer to the mountain, nice little halo, you don't see the wedding of torn wings and the gun. (Arm reaches out)(longer) No evidence in the disturbing illustration. (middle dropped)(no coma)(no period). Sidewalk and city end in sleep.

Window's open. No witness in it.

Night's a good canoe in the FURTHER game (if your chemistry doesn't get stuck on "But the thing is—"). You move, not independent, mouse (with no scissors) in an occult game of drain. Move . . . before Emptiness dyes the light DEAD.

The waves come, the waves go; jealousy, reckless, time is strange, words bleed and multiply with error and a circus of commas, sounds likes a blues for Monday, got some dead mixed in with the stormy. Repeat performances; night, big town, jungle. Fingerprints of pretenders with nocturnes to kiss to-morrows that decide not to come. Heated core in its error suit, the censor that doesn't care what light it leaves on the floor after the interrogation.

Rowing. Rowing . . . lighthouse in Poe City burned out of dim, bellied-up to off . . .

Dulled doesn't change much on the way south. Grey skies. Murmur, no surface bursts -rustle -feathers -feel every raindrop . . .

Rowing . . . all the rinds of the old poets are dirty, littered with exhausted vowels.

Rowing . . .

Hard enough might avoid the pendulum . . .

Till the wild wind blows.

And cold dances.

The horizon starts like a pinprick, a pitchfork erupting on the eye. No blur, no commentary. Not there to take a sworn statement of the disaster. Just there. Opening. Opening a spot labeled run. Could be a guide, or a hatch, but there's no net.

No chase after a crime wave—the blood and tears over there, back there, offstage (ACT III—newly penned—an asylum/winter/deadfall/diamondback ripple ending on a scream), but caught just the same. Framed. The obsessions of dust seem to take over the room.

Ruin had the same margins as *Macbeth*. Eyes can't stretch it out of their possession. Why can't a pen, ink responding in WILL words, make a scene of "there is still time" there?

Page 40

(just before the last paragraph—PAIN-sorrow-press on, find redemption thin as a dead dog's picked-over carcass. try not to worry
about the toxic seams in the back-half of the 4th sentence . . .)

more tears ahead

other words about the other thing that spoke on the other page,
spoke about gone, told you with harsh bells

Santiago.

Slow and lazy. Nice current of blue. Plenty green, a sea chemical-
rich with metaphor. Entrepreneur could work with this if he stashed
the bundles of rash and rowdy.

Little this and little yellow flowers. A soft district, no fog, no
thrash, smiles you can hear in the glass windows. The bright one,
simple as an escape, cut into the scene—Ankles. And fragrant knees.
You like her shoulders, scrubbed gently. Nice, with a little fire. You
like the arrows of ready her mouth clasps. Nice how she reads. Slow,
one dab at a time, every summit a gateway. Nice little yellow print
dress. Her legs make sense in it.

Slow and lazy. Bit of this, pieces of feast on her Scheherazade fingertips. Moments a little less chopped here; might be the cotton of
her pulse; she twirls, her silk doesn't bruise the secrets in your spoon.
She's a bird content with the threads you weave. Not love, but it
glints with the same colors.

Slow and lazy.

Not writing it in the book. Not on the opulent paper. Not measuring disorder with light. Just enjoying how soft and yellow it is this
time.

For a time. (stopped rowing)(didn't reach out)(let longer stay
Over There)

But then there were words. Fast as the isolated thing on the bed.
Sleek yellow thing shaking her head no . . .

That river . . .

Before's Night becomes Now.

Again.

(returns with The Face)

(and the sound of words that stand right next to you)

Tark left Santiago . . .

2 cigarettes left. Took one out. Considered it. Odd. Strong as a

drink. Quiet as a thoughtful friend. Lit it. Watched it burn like a carnival—not a big one, not one that you paid the price body and soul
for. Moving, swirling—whirlpool, no crossroads.

Didn't preach. No. Wasn't a fairy tale.

Just a cigarette.

Watched it burn. Smoked it slowly.

Slow and lazy. Not hit by the imbalance of the scriptures. Not
meditating on the soil of intricate. Crayon doesn't have to play saint
to the puzzle pieces. Don't care what couplet came first. Just a cigarette, not death valley, not a home behind the damn.

59. New page, but it burns 98.6 on its way up.

(Hotel. Well lit.) (The end starts—the worm of fear big as a
Humpty Dumpty all-splat)(No one switches off the lights)

Just sneaks in.

With another

now

no memory

just this

huge lonely place

in

naked moontide-o'clock. She crossed the sea. Lotta nerve, all
those horns of wrong punctuating the risk. Made it out of the past all
the way to no way out. You get to see the clots you wish you didn't
line yesterday with. Got to give her credit for it, carrying that tongue
without swallowing it.

Nice hand, touching Once . . . Nice hand. (the length)(all the way
from there to its wrist) Always was, mostly. Nice gun it in.

Too bad it's covering the hole in her stocking.

. . . Summer ends in Knoxville . . . *In their castle of Night* . . . the
wind sounds like the measure of a cello that's slipped back into a
map of rebuked lantern light . . . Escape the day . . . (as if you could
choose) *That Day* . . . Didn't know each other. Not well enough to
know what stepped off the page—could have been there wasn't
enough light, or not enough warmth in your veins to open the floor
to START . . . Shadows in motion on the ladder, eyes a family portrait of me and you out of tune, cold blue steel loaded with eagerness
. . . then . . . was . . . fear . . .

Then it

is . . .
again fear . . . what should be . . .
here
Someone does not say what should be . . .
Nothing
good
in her eyes
—not even the flower you brought here for her . . .
nothing
here
Now.
nothing . . .
the joy of the other words
someone else's words
of
Night ("withered the sun")
Night (is always)
Night
(that tells you not to ask for a door out of over and over)
in
a
lonely
place

Here.

Now.

Lights the last cigarette before this is all over

inhales "you can't remember the morning"—it had water on the horizon—on the other page

Maybe the jury of bibliophiles meant mourning? Maybe he shouldn't have mentioned the emotional trauma caused by her un-buttoned blouse in his disposition? Her being nearly naked and hold-ing him open like that as her eyes scanned what he had translated, didn't that count? Her blushing when her nipple brushed his vocabulary was not his fault. If they'd bothered to read the italicized passage in his volume and not focus on that single damning annotation regarding "Hildred de Calvados, only son of Hildred Castaigne and Edythe Landes Castaigne, first in success," they might have, should have, understood the effect of *that light* on honorable human qualities. . .

Leaving Santiago. All because she'd misunderstood the typesetter's error—

Weather Report, *I Sing The Body Electric.*

How I Survived the Cowboy Movie
[or When the Barron Opened His Eye]

Portland, OR: parking lot of a centipede-infested motel. No sun. No beautiful. Procession of black—one Price, one Shelly, one Hopfrog, a Myers, a Shea, and a bEast.

And The Barron.

Opened his eye, spoke, "Damn pussyfooting . . . I've never."

Lot of nodding in agreement. Same as yesterday's panel, *The Dream Quest of a Lovecraftian Writer*. No one disagrees with The Barron. Might if Lee Marvin was around and holding an .8 gauge. He sure as hell wasn't.

Didn't drop any other words on us. Left. We looked at each other, shivered a-might, felt we'd just made it out the apocalypse by the skin of our teeth. No, I'm not sayin' our underwear was still clean.

5 hours later: I sat by the jukebox w/ the Judge. Played some old JT's tunes, and the b-side of a Seeger hit, "Makin' Thunderbirds." We were on our 5th cup of tea, Earl Grey, and almost done w/ our pizza.

The Barron sat 3 tables away. Deep in his black notebook, mutterin' and hissin' sharp as a pack of madass hopped-up on blood, as he scratched away. Stopped sudden-like. Got up walked passed us. On the way back he muttered something about, "Designer food is shit."

Classic Italian, peppers, onions, double cheese, hot sausage. Maybe yer not susposed to cook the meat? Too each his own I guess.

He sat there for a while. Smiled. Spit some more fire into his notebook . . . Still don't remember why we didn't bug outta there . . .

Barmaid came over told him he had an important call from Mr. Ellroy. He left. Stupid, but I went over to see what the hell he was writing.

Dear Cormac,

Hell, Jack was right. The battle of the fangs is a love-tale redwritten on the snow. These listless cattle just don't get it. Death's head rings, pours out 6 glares, the white-lumpen magpies fold. They stink of urine and sweat. Makes you want to bulldoze the whole zoo—

There was a thrak and 2 b'booms by the bar so I hot-footed it back to my table, played dumb real good. He came back, snapped his notebook shut. Left.

Only other thing I'd seen was SLOTHS in caps, with a hard line drawn through it. Yeah, scared me pretty good.

Next day—Hollywood Theater 2 pm: Panel on *Put A Little Death's Head Blues in Your Contemporary Lovecraftian Fiction.* One Price, one Hopfrog, a Myers, a Shea, and a bEast. First one prattled, and then the next one took it for a spin. I was 'bout ta bleed a fever about a room of mystery and darkness and some strange white savages I'd encountered when the Sergeant waved from the back door of the auditorium. I knew the wave meant time to haul ass. I mumbled something about an emergency and split before dust and sorrows stepped aside and terror fell.

As I hit the door I heard a loud rasping howl. Knew the voice, even in the city we've got wild dogs. Where they blow upon the streets you double lock the door and turn off the lights, hope they pass thinking nobody home. One foot in the hallway, one in the grave, I turned. Guess enough was enough. The Barron opened his eye, there was a flash and his knife came out, started taking scalps.

Newspapers said the brute was a mad god, he'd applied his teeth.

These days I stay away from blood meridians and cons where the whims and fancy of the New Master lunge and whip. They say the super-max will hold The Barron. They also told me I could be President . . . Hey, feel brave, you go pull on Superman's cape if you like. Me, I'm cleaning my .8 gauge . . .

for Laird Barron, hero and one of the nicest guys 'round! ! !

In Her Forest Garden Dreaming

for Kristamas Klousch

a marble drama.

> . . . the sunset was a swan . . .

Downstairs is a graveyard. Every corpse a flag. Talons and wings, the crows come to breathe their colors. From the moon that splashes and punishes with silence the methods of the black castle spill into Hotel Noir . . .

Without a scream she hung herself. Dead her eyes are pages of a tombstone manuscript. Her brow believes the rain that knots their immigration.

She could not wait for the dreambirds.

Her lipstick does not touch the ceiling—she opened her mouth but the Raven Lake offered no totem.

She, in the end, ran out of self-made.

And the Watchbirds made a black noise~

TIME GOES COLD IN SOLITUDE

scared to the condor nightmare
the attention
of wire leather dance of cruel
Hexan-rain in the SHAMEcage~ DRUMSsssssssss
dervishstars & sand
and all her lips can do is drone

(face) In Plastic and Passion
[or When Her Finger Says YES]

321

Dawn's apple
her ghost trapped
in the wedding pump of Ouija's chant

Lash SparkSSsSS.SS.SS.SS.Sss

Tea slowly.Rhetoric habitat in a little town of hearts.Big eyes~sweet a forest banquet in YES.Ankles called to a doorstep of moon.sub.want.yes a movie of thirst.the arcade of hand designs.The Anubis kiss of softRED.eros swarm.

season painted.

the book
the secret
the mirror
a field burning with crows.

(love again) In a Circle of Trees

tango of Old Ways   September's wedding of stars in the
                           courtyard between shadows
                           the fingers kiss
                                   a farewell the knife will not forget
skulls
and apples
a hallway where leaves and the glory and chapters of a fence miss
lips

my mothlife sea is smaller this way

Her Other Face Is Moonlight

walking away from forget
                        to fit you in my mouth . . .
(beneath the tugging beeline of midnight
room licked with a discourse of bed)
you dance like Loki.
I love how your elbows laugh when my medicine curls.
mighty tiptoes with IS/the back of your knees hugging the growth of
my sky/

where I fit my jealousies in your dreams

from round
in a hard chair (where leather minds you with care)
your eyes
embracing syllables with jeweled vowel tricks
you mark me Outlaw

a bright cat confirms

stash of clocks in the sunwindow that sing hips
and courage
        that
        won't shrink when mouth goes away

strange weather fingers
            ginseng eyes dressed to climb
                        if your veins still can
            rub the pause
            with faith from your bottle of two   hush the ash nip-
        ping to escape with your bowl

                                                of frilled garlic
agreeable cut
as your cloak unfolds
            lacehour rose—I hear your skin
            muffin
            clear as a realm half-off

how pale and soft your voices are
your mouth is my table

the flow of your aroma in feathers opened by the travel I feel

pushing go as a form of sweat
I play Mingus for your Paris

the blood of my ladder sore with Medusa

born for summer
to seek

alone with her pillow of vulture clouds

The Minor King

the scrapbooks of
minor kings and losers,
rotting in the smaller of grief breeze, glued to the bridges of gull spirals

Hindemith, *Mathis*, *Der Maler*, and Marrianne Faithful, *Secret Life*.

Icarus Above...

Wind.

Free of anxiety and hunger. A poem swarming above the ground.

Scott Tullis was 8 the first time he saw the Null Immortalis of Megazanthus. First time he ran toward it, ideas and crackling glee bursting. Quixote's windmill perhaps, or the skeleton of another Trojan Horse yet to be built?

He settled on wind.

"Wind." Running in circles. Laughing. "Wind. Wind. *Wind.*" Eyes and mouth wide. Smiling and laughing.

He was counting his saved coins in his head. The yellow kite in Mr. Hülsmann's shop window. Yes, he had enough for the canary-song yellow with the long, red bowtie tail.

Great blessed wind.

Wind power to free the people.

Wind power. Clean and cheap. Cheaper than cheap. Free.

Free as a bird.

Or a soaring kite.

The boy, Scotty, when his Dad ruffled his hair and pleasantly beamed, had never heard of Old Meg and his madman magic and certainly had no idea what a Null, or even an Immortalis was. 8 and April busting out, he didn't care.

So his father let him dream. Didn't cloud him with the bad news. 8 is too young for the one-sided ticking of the cold, uncaring clock. Let him smile and dream a while longer. The dictionary and the door sheathed within could wait.

So he spent 9 and 10 and 11 outside the walls of their easy cottage in the long stretch of flat, green fields, outside Everyday's Hard Method and The Transformation. Spent the years on robots and exotic animals from The Continent, and impressing Amelia with his kite stories.

Without being arranged, morning chiseled night from the sky and Scott, fully exhibiting 12, followed his day nurse's voice to the study desk. Pen and paper laid out for him. Neatly. There was the book. Not open, but its disguise would be cast off the moment his daring fingers visited the first pages.

Megazanthus' book. Verses of flame. Doors and victories, the language of the birds. Steal the power of the hungry wind. Channel it. In the mist-shrouded long ago Megazanthus designed the device, etched his magic into the book's margins. Diagrams and sketches flourished on the pages. But he never finished it.

He never had the chance.

The lightning came and the magician and his dreams flew away.

A day with out white vapor trails scaring the sky. Yellow's fingerprint on the light-as-a-feather blue. A clean ascent into air. Rising. Circling.

Running, no landmarks, no neighborhood. The only border Summer. Running. Weaving kite stories.

His Dad smiling. Clapping.

"Wind. Wind, Scotty."

Smiling. Proud.

Running to catch up.

Then out of breath. Stopping. Suddenly. Reaching out to support himself on one of the eight trunks that supported the Null Immortalis.

45. A Saturday a million years from 8. Leaning in a doorway, watching sparrows spindle in the whispering wind.

"*Wind* . . . Catches your dreams . . ."

Scott stopped. Tears came as he thought about his father and his fatal heart attack the very second he touched the Null Immortalis.

Collected. Taken back. Gone and with him, a boy's hopes and dreams.

Dreams dead in the long grass.

The hurt. Gospel in the chapel. Flowers. Grey clouds to fill out the epic of a good man gone. 747's cruising above those standing graveside, dressed in woe and darkened by tears.

Amelia pulled in the driveway. Smiled. Opened the garage door with the remote control.

It hung on the side wall of the garage. Hadn't flown in years.

Hadn't danced in the sky since the day Amelia said yes to lacy and white and til death do us part.

He freed Icarus from the old nail.

"C'mon, Hon." Pointing to the blue sky. "Before afternoon exhausts the sun. While we still have time to laugh."

And she does. Beams and ruffles his hair.

In the field. Running, steps stretching. One more time.

Free.

Amelia catching his joy.

One last kite story.

A roaring tug of wind. Old string snaps.

Yellow plummeting. Its red tail bleeding behind it.

The Null Immortalis waiting.

Strands tangled, broken wings bound. Paper and color taken back. Collected. One with the web that weaves. As all things must be.

Running. Hoping.

Hoping he can save the dream.

Running.

Out of breath. Tilting. Clinging to old school days, the days before his father died. The landscape of a wide world collapsing.

Lightning in his chest. Terror and the heartbreak of never again free in Amelia's eyes. The null in his father's eyes.

His hand touching the Null Immortalis. It taking.

Birdsong of sun-fruit silent in the tidal green field. Amelia breaking as the calendar ends.

8 years old. Thought he could control it. Dreamed of it.

But that was before he realized, like spiders, whose banquets were living, breathing things, the Null Immortalis had eight legs too.

My Mirage

for BJ

Came in from the rain, murderous rain—the drops of rain falling off her didn't seem to be hitting the floor. Looked around. Looked at me.

Like she knew me.

Left suddenly.

I meant to pull myself away from the conversation I was stuck in. Couldn't find my feet. Sometimes I drink too much.

I kept thinking she was barefoot.

Did I know her?

All I could settle on was maybe?

I know I thought something odd about the light, but I'll be damned if I recall what. I think it had to do with shadows.

Or dust.

Happens in drunken.

Floating in that fleeing universe. You believe you feel something. Think you see something. Can't decide on what's real.

Never leaves flowers.

Or joy.

Or solid.

~*~

A little hung-over. Hazy, with an exceedingly bitchy nail deciding my temple was a roof that needed tending to. Eggs. Tomato juice. 2 cigarettes. 2 aspirin. Tea. No angels. Parts of last night almost something I could almost touch.

2pm. I'm even on time. Print Works Bookstore. Very comfortable friendly Indie. 20 copies of my new one, *Portraits of Ruin*, in the front window. Nice display, someone considered style and yearning.

David Lynch came in. Lifted one up from the front table went and sat. Had coffee. Thumbed through it.

Came over to where I was signing.

"Dedicated to ME?"

Nodded. "*Inland Empire*. Loved it . . . You might be the only guy on the planet nuttier than I am."

Two 9 year olds that shared the secret the world couldn't grasp, we exchanged smiles.

"Let's have a drink and talk about that."

We did.

"I'm working on a new film. Brandi Jording is starring. A friend of yours I believe."

"She is. Sort of. Laurence is . . . Well, we're close."

He was polite. Didn't say everyone out here knows about the killer and the conqueror and the galleons they sunk. Said, "She says you're the real King In Yellow."

Didn't laugh. Smiled. "She's a nutbag. Sweet kid, talented as hell. Smart, but a nutbag." Did laugh a bit after that.

"That's why I wanted to see you. Wondered if you'd look at the script."

"Me? I'm no movie guy. I watch some here and there. 'bout it. Comes to film, you're the genius."

"Part's noir. Part surreal."

Wanted to say, like that's a shocker coming from you. Didn't. Didn't yawn either.

"It's a *King in Yellow* film."

"I'll read it. When?"

"What are you doing tonight?"

"Whatever you have in mind."

Was his turn to smile.

~*~

Brandi showed up at 8.

Walked over like summer curves on a hula girl. Friend of the lies on the bottom of the Devil's bottle I am, but even I had solid thoughts of a slow dance with a fast girl.

We sat by David's pool.

Me with my back to it.

I don't like looking down in the depths.

Waves make it worse.

David: "Starts as a cartoon, not sure what it's comprised of yet. Leaning toward an old train platform in the desert? There's a woman's hands, she's holding a hatbox and you can see the hem of her dress, her shoes . . . 3am noir/dub music in the background. A slow surf guitar too. Some effect and we cut from animation to film and see bare feet walking in a foggy vale—strange lighting, dead moths litter the ground. Then we cut and see her feet on a damp deck around a pool. Stone work of the deck is the color of sand. Toying with the wet footprints she leaves being letters or changing into them. Neon maybe, red or orange with blurry green borders? They may spell vacancy?" He shrugged. Smiled. If anyone ever looked 9 years old.

"And the water dripping off her never hits the ground. Maybe?" He looked at the cement deck around his pool but his expression said he wasn't receiving the answer.

"The pool's lit by torchlight. Not Bright. Just a few torches. Moths are fluttering. Brandi's feet descend the pool stairs and her night gown rises to her knees. There's blood in the water, not a lot, and it's slowly drifting toward her. Might be faces, or a face, in the water too? A woman's face. But we wouldn't see her eyes. Her hair covers them."

"Her name is Gil Brewer. She's a writer who's acting now. Her new book and the film she's making are called, *Lady's A Walking Heartbreak.'*

"Throughout the film we'll keep seeing a dark-haired woman kissing Gil's Yellow Sign tattoo. Just the lips, nose, never the eyes, not open. Very pale skin. Blood red lips."

Brandi flashed a smile. Very pale skin. Blood red lips.

I looked at her tat. I wouldn't have minded just taking in her shoulder, but with the tat on it, kinda became something I wanted to sip. Many's the time I've seen pics of her, but sitting there breathing that's something else. Lady glows and you know her slightest touch is pure heroin. Told myself to behave. Started by not staring. Not an easy thing to do when your skull's dreaming of stretched out on the bed with her and her eyes are softly brushing you and you can feel the moonlight on her knee.

At least I wasn't panting.

"Next scene is a train station in some old and out of the way place. Night. Foggy. We see a ticket and the red hatbox in her hand. You can see the letters CA on the ticket, the rest of the word is covered up by her fingers. Could be Carcosa or California.'

"She's barefoot, steps onto the train. She may have cut her foot and it leaves a red imprint? A woman with black hair and blood red lips blows her a kiss. It's slow and soft, but still it's an incinerator. The soundtrack of dub/noir jazz kicks back in. A liquid guitar loaded with reverb plays a spare single-note waltz over it."

David smoked what he smokes.

I sat in a moment of departure.

"When we see the woman again, she's standing there in a pale cotton dress, one sleeve's been ripped, and it's nearly see-through, almost off one shoulder. You can kind of make out her skin and it's cracked and peeling like an old mannequin that's been left out in the weather too long. But you can't see her eyes."

Brandi set down her coffee cup. "The woman on the platform is a touch Dorian Grey in reverse."

I thought she added, "Lost summer dreams."

I wanted to say I thought I saw you last night in a bar and you didn't have shoes on. Didn't.

Lynch's phone rang and he excused himself.

She excused herself too.

Watched her walk away. Steambath of wow that pull any man from dry dock.

I smoked what I smoke.

Slow coils . . .

The fragrance of my cigarette smoke tested the air for stems and blooms . . .

Butted it.

Waited.

~*~

Bare feet. Not much else on.

Shivered

in the damp air. Air that drifted like it was lost.

Tragic is the sign above the blue light cobbles here.

Three floors up the roofs and the pallid clouds lean away from the grime and blisters below. The rags know they won't get far.

The street lantern reveals the depths of sour and sunken . . .

A rat that lost its property squeals—springs away in disgust.

The one cold detail she has to spread she's dragging along.

The door—robber—syphilis—dangerous, opens with a calm perversity.

She holds out her hand . . .

but not even the gaslight will take it . . .

~*~

Waited.

Pushed the butt in the ashtray away with another cigarette.

Didn't light it.

"A walking heartbreak." Low. A drowned voice behind me, miles away.

There was a splash behind me. I turned to it. A little blood in the water—looked like little red roots reaching, adjusting. No one was in or around the pool.

I looked at the blood.

Reaching for me. Could have been hungry for some endless dream of feathers my margins were too weak to tread beyond.

Hearing shit.

I heard Brandi coming back. Stood.

When I went to sit back down I looked and the pool was clear.

Seeing it too.

She smiled. "Odd we haven't met before this."

"Not so odd. You guys have been going out for what, 6 months? He's always so busy, you're a rising star. Cannes really turned up the heat for both of you."

"True."

"I thought I'd heard you were going to work with Aronofsky. *FLICKER* or—"

"You know how it is. What if, maybe. Deal's done then it's gone. Puff of smoke. I was going to do that robot picture and play Anubis Loki. Looked like fun with Snyder attached to direct, but we bumped into David in Cannes and this was too good to pass on."

I lit the smoke I was holding instead of laughing. Engaged to Laurence Amiotte it would be. He was almost as big on the King In Yellow as I was. We'd even talked of doing something with my last book. But he got sick and then busy and I got drunk. Some say I lost my mind. I called it a vacation.

Livia left me too. Took her engine of desire back.

The liquid on my 2nd liquid vacation flattened me. Went and played a small speck in the high desert. Finally found a lantern that would talk to me. Came back, wrote about magnetism, youth, and the air in a sepulcher.

"After Del Toro's hit with Lovecraft, David said it was a good time to do something from an old weird fiction writer, but he didn't want horror-horror. You know how he loves to get in people's heads."

David came out. Left the door open. The radio or stereo was playing War's "Spill The Wine."

Brandi starting singing it.

"Take—That—Girl." Laughed a little.

David smiled. Was talking but all I could hear was

Take—That—Girl

"You think that's ok?" David asked.

"Huh?"

"There's a murder. Montages of the same murder. Framed in different ways. One commonplace, one a keyhole. Maybe as the formalities of a detective? You see capable, decisive."

"OK."

"We'll see crime scene photos and paintings of the dead woman framed on a red wall. Not mixed."

Brandi. Sitting there. "Different colors. Different angles. Once or twice we'll see the photographs framed in neon."

David lit a smoke. "We only see them over Gil's shoulders. Pictures at an exhibition. A gallery. A real cheesy organ and piano will play a noirish version of Mussorgsky's "Promenade" every time she walks the gallery. That's all we see. The pictures, Gil's shoulder, the red wall . . .

It's a flat wall but like the folds in a curtain it's a maze too."

"I like that."

David flashed that 9 year old boy smile again.

There was more coffee and more talk of the film.

"Scenes . . . Reason is, ah, in the eye and heart of the beholder. Let the experience unlock the motivation."

And the song was still playing.

For an hour?

Same song.

"Your stereo is messing up."

~*~

Rectangle. Rectangles. Brown and brown and brown. Luggage. Stacked. I wouldn't call it neatly. No white. No black. I would have called that odd.

Breeze.

Dialed up to wind.

Woman's hand in a red glove drops a brown suitcase.

Pops open.

A red curtain inside.

It opens a little.

A grey sky . . . plumes of smoke here and there . . . on top of the rectangle stack of brown a birdcage. Antique. The door is open . . . a thin current of smoke in the shape of wings . . .

The seats on the train are boards, they're really worn. Outside the window the bottom of the clouds are rust colored. Some are black.

It's a chess game . . .

. . . No sun. Ever. Dead leaves. A woman with a ghostly face and the eyes of a wolf . . . and she's unbuttoning her blouse. Showing her nipple.

The heat from it caresses my face . . . her fingers flutter . . . the heat from her nipple makes me feel crazy . . .

She's whispering fast.

But I don't speak French . . .

All the heat.

Her nipple is like a mandala . . .

its heat is a crown . . .

Her voice is some math or sonata I can't understand . . .
her nipple is a wave and a church window . . .
I can hear the needle lift from the groove . . .

~*~

Mini-bar was open.
Curtains weren't.
My function was drenched, chaos had taken my umbrella. I was in disarray, or just distorting.
Babel's TV was on.
Rear Window was examining the feelings in my hotel room but I won't lie, my appetite really didn't care.
The script sat in a chair like an old tramp too tired to walk over to the bed and cry.
I felt clever. Hadn't let the mirror look at any of my schemes.
As payment for my vigilance mini-bar door said, "Next."

~*~

Woke up in my clothes. Thought someone was lying beside me. Someone soft and naked.
Felt hungover.
But I hadn't been drinking.
Not that much. Not really.
No woman there.
Sighed. Told myself I was relieved. No one there.
I'd thought it was Brandi.
Wasn't.
Part of me wanted it to be.
Showered.
Dressed.
Looked at the bed.
No woman there.
No signs of fire.
Left my hotel room.
Had an appointment with my agent.
Short drive.
Snapped on the radio. "Spill The Wine" on every station.

I could hear the needle set down in the grooves.
On every station.—Take—That—Girl
"You listening?"
"Huh?"
"Listening?"
"Yeah."
"Did he ask?"
"Sort of."
"You call him. Could be your biggest break yet."
"I will."
I called Brandi.
Laurence was still out of town.
She said yes.
8 o'clock. FABRICE. Drinks. Something light. She had something
to show me.
I wondered if I should go out and get new shoes.
Wondered if she'd wear shoes.
"Yeah. Sandals."
Knew they'd be new.
Stopped and picked up a new pair of shoes.
Stopped and had a drink.
Took a nap. Might be a late night.
Had an itch.
Wanted it to be.

~*~

Brandi looked just like Brandi. Young. Vibrant. Beautiful.
But she was black.
Spoke.
Something in French.
Her voice. But she was speaking French.
Fast. Not many words.
Can't say what they were. I don't know French.

~*~

7:40 FABRICE
Didn't want to be late.

Not tonight.

I felt the heat coming off the front door.

Red door.

She could be sitting in there right now.

Hoped my suit was ok.

Shoes too.

They were new.

Black man at the door.

Big man.

Times like these I'm happy I carry the gun. Guess it feels empowering. Maybe it's like I control the fever . . .

~*~

crazy. just spilled there.

like it meant something . . .

it was there

it had to be

~*~

She always wears 6 or 7 necklaces.

Long.

Colorful.

They hang between her breasts.

Her nipples are boudoirs.

Perfumed.

If my tongue could sing, they'd dance.

Waltz.

Ballerinas . . .

~*~

"It's a spider web. A beautiful, beautiful spider web. And music flows along the web."

David's fingers were knitting, thinking. The burst of witnessing. A fever of image uncovering flesh, removing the mask. His face, every naked shift of context, every lark of so, was taking in the dance.

~*~

Ballerina.

There were stories in her hands. Arcs. Wings that had escaped the wasteful paws of the pyramids, sculptured bowls of feathers in search of liberty and berries . . . Graceful, the kind of graceful that hadn't been frozen by trivial lips. Hadn't been hurt by snowbird storms or kept low with the salt of yesterday's ceilings. She cupped her hands like she was carrying water.

She turned. Her back was beautiful . . .

Her shoulder arm outstretched. Leg slowly coming up. That one finger pointing at me. Its words by lamp sigh . . .

Beautiful.

My Apollo could not turn away from the breath of the medium . . .

Beautiful.

The narrative of her torso . . . Maybe she should have been nude—pure.

Her shoulder . . .

Her back . . .

Muscle and flesh, definition suspended in rhythm . . . the delicious spilling of breath and devotion . . . no one could resist . . . Maybe?

Her back as I touch it . . . a horizon of redemption . . .

It would have been beautiful.

Beautiful.

It was so slow.

All, so slow. So slow . . .

~*~

Her nipples seduce me. They're something between life and death. No. *Birth* and death. They're real. Maybe the faces aren't?

White face.

Black face.

Some are mad, angry. Red.

Color is the devil. Color is a lie. How it laughs. It's a floor or a mirror. It splits the world. It's unpredictable and it loses the dreams of darkness.

Her nipples are like that. In color. They make me lose my place in darkness.

~*~

I could have just looked at her eyes for an hour. Could have watched her lips move.

I would have been happy to be an overwhelmed stone existing under the singing stars.

I didn't need moonlight.

~*~

David: "I know a great little train station up by Bakersfield. Old. Worn. It's like a dream. Lots of sand. Dust . . . Wind comes up . . . There's coyotes."

I lit a smoke.

He lit a smoke.

"Brandi in a red dress. Dead. Sand starting to cover her.'

"Let's take a drive."

~*~

Later: Radio losing the signal.

David: "I should have brought my CDs. Ah, something nice that has the fever of September."

He played with the knob, like he was able and zealous—he was, you could see it. There was no rage to finish. It was like he was preparing it, or tuning in the color. Made the awful noise disappear.

"Spill The Wine" comes on. I can hear the needle settle in the grooves.

Me: "No. A yellow dress. Pale . . . Faded out. Maybe torn?"

David: "Yes. Makes sense. Good. Good."

I'm getting a headache. We pull into a gas station. Place looks like something from one of his films but I skip telling him that. I buy aspirin from a cashier that looks like Brandi. She's on a cell phone hissing about spilled wine on her living room carpet. Red wine. Said the carpet was the color of sand. I don't laugh.

Wine.

Blood.

"Christ."

I was slightly pissed they didn't have any unsweetened green tea.

Came out and got in David's car.

Saw a coyote across the road by a dumpster the Methodist church didn't seem to want.

It looked at me. Then looked at the road. Toward where we'd come from. Back that way was Hollywood and civilization.

Eaters of the dead. That's what I thought.

Back on the highway, black road.

Sign.

Signs.

Sign.

Something that passes for plant life.

Sign.

Sand . . .

Windows open.

Heat don't want a beer or the wind, enjoying its own gusto.

On the drive we've talked about the solar system . . . Bela very briefly . . . Hollywood generally—most not too nice . . . Mexico . . . color, decay, and some trees and a red house we passed . . . even the weather, which was very warm without being overly hot . . . He's interesting, and sharp-witted. I really like him.

Not having brought his CDs he spoke about sound design a lot too.

David: "Gil has a theme song. Some 3 am, whiskey-laded Brubeck kind-of thing. But no piano. No sax. Bass, drums, oboe, and surf guitar. The oboe is Desmond, everything is shot from a distance at a high angle when it plays. The guitar, haunting single note lines, is Brubeck. Maybe use "Turn Out The Stars."? Got to have one Bobby Darin tune in the soundtrack and maybe Mel Torme's "Too Close For Comfort"?

Bit of slow motion and grainy here or there when her theme plays. Call it hued in guilt or shame maybe. A swamp of dream and hallucination that convulses more than unfolds."

"That shot in black and white?"

"Yeah. Mostly. But I think some bumpy orange coloration, like say neon on the fritz, gets in there too."

The road was very straight. The hood of the car was very red. For a moment I wondered if I turned away from the machine-gun fire of the broken yellow lines would I see Jim Morrison . . . Would he wave to me? Would he hold up a book of poetry?

Sand.

Desert.

White clouds. Wind pushing them like rootless boats.

I didn't see an Indian.

I also spent time thinking of Brandi. I'd like to take her to City Lights and show her around.

Knew she'd love the poetry.

I wondered what she'd wear.

~*~

That's her bed. Big enough. Not for 3 . . .

My gun.

Her nipple. Looks like a mandala . . .

My hand.

Her hand. Near her nipple. Pretty as a mandala . . .

The gun goes off.

The curtains are red.

~*~

the texture of her open mouth. the opening is like a mandala . . .

I'm trying to remember does David like Hitchcock?

Do I?

Was there a mandala in *Vertigo?*

Was there?

she's all in white. like a wedding dress.

did David say something about getting married?

did Laurence?

must have.

I think she was laughing . . .

I don't think she was wearing shoes.

~*~

She's unbuttoning her blouse.

It's red.

~*~

The radio is on.
—Take—That—Girl
I want to put my lips on her lips
I want to look into the mandala
the trance
the kisses /werewolf kisses
my tongue twirling /my lips on her throat, burning, conversant
my eternity in her ear
the crest of fingers on her molten heart

~*~

Her hair is yellow—wind blown—the hem of her yellow dress is
above her knees
There's water—waves
A balcony
She's smiling
Her face is black
She must have been dead a long time
She's wearing a mask of flies
There's lights around the bed.
A camera.
The sheets are silk. Red silk.
The bellies of the clouds are rust colored
and black
stormy
Her dress looks white in this light
like a cocoon

~*~

I'm naked. Wet.
There's blood.
Red.

~*~

there was a red curtain

~*~

little brown train station near Bakersfield
she was wearing red shoes
I took her overnight bag
it was red

~*~

red
/
a caress on my face
/
true sight
comes to my naked heart
/
legs—a crazy river
a fire burns
/
my ambition, its flaring spider instincts, sips her shoulders
kisses her tattoo
no reverse in her "not letting you go" she burns
gnaw on her piper skin
"Shearer, deep inside . . ."
yellow, curved and permanent, drags me

~*~

my typewriter sits on the brown desk in my hotel room
I'd stopped typing
    /does life spring eternal?
    can a still, somnolent heart ink
    technicolor lines?/

prey in the mouth of a cave . . . I could see . . . true . . . the shape
of the darkness . . . there was a scroll, the image of a character, a face
with a point of view, atoms of flesh, I wanted to count her names . . .

~*~

She could laugh
melt you with a smile
break your heart with a sigh

or a tear.
Did to a lot of people.
Moviegoers . . . and real people too.

~*~

her thighs were wrapped around me . . .
I could feel the heat of her nipples on my thigh
if she was being graded for poetry or angles
A
she looked perfect doing it
stroked me until I forgot depressed and what colors the sky came
in
her mouth was open
—Take—That—Girl
pretty girl
yellow hair
sweet
her nipple feels like a beautiful knife on my tongue

~*~

she stepped onto the platform
she was not wearing shoes

~*~

she was very pretty

~*~

the light was dangerous

~*~

her eyes were a speech

~*~

her posture was a speech

~*~

there was music

~*~

she was dancing for me
a sumptuous evening sky of honey
I wanted her to slip her bra off and slide into bed

~*~

(Reaction shot)... her eyes were closed. But she could see.
              ... her mouth was open. I could smell
every flower of its poem.

~*~

David was dead. There was blood in the water.
He was wearing my new shoes.
There was a white moth fluttering above his lips.
I wondered if it had breathed in all his poetry.

~*~

Brandi was from the South. She was young. Pretty. The kind of
pretty that occupied you. You'd kill for it.

~*~

Nice pool.
Rectangle.
Sand colored.
I wondered if he ever had pretty young girls over.
Did they wear their watch when they went in the water?
Did their eyes sparkle? Did they say yes?
I can't remember.
I wonder if they understood.

~*~

She had four brown suitcases by the door of her hotel room.

~*~

I had two brown suitcases by the door in my hotel room.

~*~

His pool was the color of my suitcases.

~*~

I was holding on to her wrist. Tightly.
"Just say yes."
Didn't add still could be.

~*~

She handed me the script.
"Have you read this?" I asked.
Her mouth was open. Open the way a door's open.
But this is not my room.

~*~

The moon came down. A parade over the blue of the hotel pool.
She sat on her balcony and read the script.
Dreams and personalities.
Peel away time and deceit.
The moon was fishing on the canvas.
The words were playing with her.
One page said drab, clouds, and fetched.
Daughter said, "Yes, ma'am."
Made her think of Southern belles, moonlight, flirting, and grow-
ing up in the desert outside Vegas.
Made her miss soft afternoons of rain and leisurely whiskey.
The guitar on the radio cried on the shore of isolato.
Looked up.
Didn't see a ghost ship.
But she expected one.

~*~

```
Brandi in Gil make-up and wig [sitting there
naked in her hotel room on the floor / script
in her hands/ some pages are ripped out and on
the floor around her / a few are shredded
/she's wearing a black wig / under the wig her
real hair is wet--the wig sits unevenly - some
```

of it is flat and sticks out like crow feathers / the make-up she's applied looks like a
drunken freakshow.]

Pan down to her knee on the floor. It's wet.
From dripping water or tears?

DISSOVLE TO: Bare feet. Not much else on. Blue
light cobbles. The door--robber--syphilis—dangerous, opens with a calm perversity. There's
a red curtain at the end of the hall . . . She
holds out her hand . . . but not even the
gaslight will take the stain it echoes . . .

CUT TO:

small [old] train station platform board floor-
ing says PORTERVILLE [worn/weathered/painted in
yellow] bare feet on it a dim lagoon of light /
dead moths littered on the boards near the wall
camera pans slowly up we see her knees, the hem
of her dress is soiled and shredded and her
hand, she's holding a red hatbox wind comes up
presses her dress tight between her legs--it's
like it's glued on / the dress is very thin almost see through / camera pans slowly up from
her knees, pan slowly closer to where her sex
would be, where we see CLOSE UP the impression
of a HOWLING tortured FACE under the dress

CUT TO:

A WHITE ROOM flashing with a rapid "weird yellow" STROBE LIGHT effect--might go green to
red, to orange too?

CUT TO:

CLOSE UP on something like Jena Osman's The
Periodic Table As Assembled By Dr. Zhivago,
Oculist on the wall. It's slightly tilted. 12
to 16 words or so on the table.

[Possible words: Seizure. Sky. Next. Just
stars. Watch. Fidelity. You can't. Ribbon ship
flag. This is love. Portrait of a Head. Coils.
Scar. Contagion. Passenger. Gas food drama.
Lawn.]

CUT TO:

A nippy series of double exposures of shears
on the floor.

The sound of a match being lit.

CUT TO:

Cigarette smoke, then: "Gil's Theme" (Always
played largo) (We've heard it, some variation
of it, every time we see the Yellow Sign tattoo) starts. Circling. Gull-voice oboe cries
(a cry from the past). Liquid surf guitar bubbles, it's a bed of tidal sea-foam under the
ghostly colors of the oboe.

CUT TO:

Gil standing [wearing a black wig / under the
wig her real hair is wet--the wig sits un-
evenly--some of it is flat and sticks out like
crow feathers / the make-up she's applied
looks like a freakshow] naked /sweating
/breasts heaving /belly heaving /eyes blasted
wide, barely blinking

All the wires--clamps biting nipples--clamps
chained to head and cunt and veins

crow laughter--pain as BLACKmadness spitting
FUCK YOU

Cut to CLOSE UP of a dial needle in the RED:

11
12
13
14

crow laughter because it cannot cry
lightning strips away the mask
naked--RAPENAKED and you cannot go back-cannot
go awayRAPENAKED
NIGHT again
     growling
     coughing

TEST

     light
     climbing
     running
     bitter wind
     vision
tongues flash--parts--angles--shot--there's no
NUANCE in BLACKNESS
     sparks
     swimming in your own banshee-stupid
bitch cunt
     snapping vows--"this FACE"--"that Face"-
-"that BITCH"--"that whore didn't"
     "YEAHHHhhhhhhhhhhh--FUCK"
     "DID"
     "DID!DID!"
     "yeah"
     "FUckk"
     secrets punctured by worms
     "I'll fuck yoo if yoo make it STOP"
     "I am telling the truth mommy"
     learning ten years in one day
RAPENAKED-burning up-going somewhere
blind
"fiv-shi-plo-baby-givmebab-y-givemeplea-FUCK-
fucKKKK
NoNO-no-NOnowwwwwwwww"
"I'll FUCK if yoo WANoww"
"anyTHING--confess-will--anyYESYES-What you
wa-WILL"
blind

```
the anvil drum of you cannot GO
the anvil drum of YOU CANNOT go
"I do not want to feel the mouth of the grave
splitting my cunt
nonoNO-pleas-no-owwwwwwwwwWWWw"
"I'll FUCK YOO if you STOP thisriver"
crow laughter because IT cannot cry
        learning eternity in one second

CUT TO:

Lower left leg of a man in black dress pants
and "new shoes" sitting on the corner of her
hotel room bed. CLOSE UP of his knee, hand
with a Yellow Sign ring comes into view and
moves left over the knee. It drops the page it
was holding on the floor.

Unnamed man: "As you're laughing-screaming.
Reach down and touch yourself."

CUT TO: her hand moving up her thigh toward
her sex.

CUT TO: BLACKNESS [a SCREAM--not a loud
scream/exhaled pain--the scream is an exten-
sion of the one we were hearing.]
```

~*~

There was a party.
We were drinking red wine.
"Spill The Wine" came on the radio . . .
"Live."
The clarity of a soul experience.

~*~

She had bought new shoes. Sandals. They were in a red box on a chair by her hotel room door

Eric Burden & War, "Spill the Wine," and
Iron Butterfly, "Iron Butterfly Theme."

And this is where I go down into the darkness

for beelzeBOB & Tom Ligotti, titans BOTH!! !

I sat in the Days Between the Years. Darkness whispered to the corpses in the palm of my hand . . . and I planned my escape.

I am not a learned man. I am an escape artist. Was when I started.

Poor. Hungry. Inner-city caught, small—walled in, all men are. Here in the grey rain they are. Mired with learning disabilities I took the route I could afford and held the most appeal, or coulda been no option is the only option. The poor care not, an open door is an open door.

Books were my road. Thinking is the best way to travel for a needy—grasping—dreamer and I took to it.

I learned to read and feed the dreams in comic books. Loved superheroes; Dr. Strange and Batman, Thor and Captain America. The boat of Dr. Strange and Thor sailed to long ago and far away, I stood watch in the crow's nest, saw Huginn and Muninn's wings chart the weight. Strained to see Out There too.

At eight the public library became my haunt of choice. Books. Shark at a chum convention my primary diet became the ingestion of animals, dinosaurs, robots, cowboys, birds—wings to escape, and Vikings. At 11 I upped the ante, discovered novels. Thick, deep, whole worlds you could make a meal of. Characters and color, journeys that lead outta here. *DUNE, LotR.* Holmes as a single volume of intrigue and wonder. Five volumes of Lankhmar, two in Cora-monde, three in Gormenghast. Melniboné. Callisto—lot of places Lin Carter and his company of flashing swordsmen stormed. Dumas and Dumas and Dumas. 14–16 my love affair deepened; words are pure China White and I had a Jones. Fowles. Fowles. Slipped in Lolita and some pale fire. Hesse—'I felt my fate drawing me on . . .'

Hesse.

For madmen only; had my hand raised, pick me, pick me! I could escape further. Get more deeply lost. And I did travel.

Words. As horse, and canoe or pirate ship, and airship or jet.

Words—in my glutting mandibles, under my skin. Mountains I hoarded like some dragon of old. Built my castle walls of books.

New books—a night gallery full, new words, new vistas. Each to escape the grey. Wanted to find a nice city to live in.

Collections. Anthologies. Visions of speculation and impregnable daring-do, save the day or lose. Didn't matter.

And a darkness crept in.

It would come and sit with me as I read; hold my tethers enabling me, the escaping puppet, to turn the pages. I took a sword to it, but the steel in my arm was weak.

Poe. Conan. Mars. If it had a sword or a monster on the cover I read it. Heinlein, Seabury Quinn, Doc Savage. I was a junkie, a lost dog looking for a master.

My library didn't howl and didn't have the biographies of Miss Destiny and Tralala, yet, so I returned tossed out beer bottles and did odd jobs to buy books. Junkie hoarding, stashing what little he can amass for dry and stormy nights.

Clockwork word viruses. Last exits. Cities of night.

Went from Mayan splendor to tainted words. Ancient exhumations.

Books of occultation.

Satanic works, cold print.

Found time for the stars (stars and isles, oh my), tough guys and street corner blondes and hardboiled hardcore.

Went to the Doubleday, shelled out $1.50 and entered the Theatre of the Absurd; I didn't need a hall of mirrors to see the incurable. Gave Vintage $1.95 to get a glance at Democritus and Camus—Yeah, took a chance, felt it was a necessity. Extending my imagination by forking over a buck and a half to Old Man Hinshaw for a black-bound volume of wounds, I attended a tea party with Sartre, de Sade, and Pavese. There was talk of suicides and the desire to be a man. I had a fix on both subjects.

Fantasies and wonder and pain, dropped the chunks in the caldron, let things steam, roil, and stew.

The gothic tales of dead dreamers lost in noctuaries of ill frost
that was a yes. Spent bitter black nights in the shadows at the bottom
of the world reading what the worms remember. Did. Makin' my
way in the Darkness. Crawlin', climbing. Kept my security bottle
close.

Darkness and more darkness to try to understand my own. Played
with drugs and more booze, dreamed of girls, avoided the mirror
when I did. Looked at art, listened to music, heavy and not. Somewhere sat a key. If I turned enough pages I would discover the map.

Somewhere was a far piece when you're low on ready cash or
friends with Daddy connections; jobs at the post office and the power
company were few, not many opportunities for the backalley bred.
Somewhere wouldn't be the warehouse. Boxes of real, not a dream in
the place. Spent the shifts clawin' to get to the 5 o'clock world, even
if I didn't have the shelter of a girl's arms to soothe me when I got
home to my three-room box. I heard about Sugartown on the radio.
My nine year old rust & dent oil-burner didn't ever seem to have
enough gas to get there; maybe two working headlights would have
helped . . . Didn't waste two fuck it's on *c'est la vie*.

No one 'round here did. Not a single shadowjack. Here, well, was
a place all you see is taillights forgetting the blocks, place's a sledgehammer of lonesome, old games of skin squashed by blasts of collapsing. Dogs wounded by chalk, bait afraid of breathing, figured and
feared someone would see it as neon advertizing take out, they rang
on every corner. School on Palace St. was right across the street from
The Vine, no hustlers outside, not during the day. Night, sitting in
there you'd see the eyes curled up with something in a grave, some
are wet, remembering. I sat in here and there. Mostly I drank alone.

Mostly.

Or read. To

escape

Moon came downtown brought some beer, we sat on the roof
talked Kant and Hegel and 'bout tush. Lot about long legs. Even if
they were only one-night long.

Billy Joel sang about drinking a lot of take-home pay. I did.
Mostly in bars that never heard of stardom, or 3D. Old ghost behind

the bar walks past, you point at the dead soldier, he acts startled. You'd think you'd screamed NEXT. I'd laugh quietly. Think Brel was sittin' there with me. Then I'd hum a bit of "Jackie" and head to the jukebox and play "D.O.A." or "13 Questions."

There were times when I was close to flat-out of everything and sat in while the eagle soared o'er someone else's Friday night. Many were the Saturdays I did not go out to play. Stayed in, sat on the floor, cheap whiskey (free ice cubes) and words. When the demons came down off their throne of bones to dance I tried to hide in fantastic stories; Vance, Tuttle, Niven, Anderson, Malzberg. Sometimes it sort of worked.

Whiskey too, sort of.

Never could get over my under and out to kneel to pray Sunday mornings. The mouth of beautiful wings calming my crescendos of endless holes of empty and desperately, I wasn't fondling that fuck you.

Saturated my blues by sending my horses through narrative windows that weren't thinned in dullness. Tried to. Friday. All day rain. I set out to find lights.

Rain took a powder.

In a rathole-bar on a Friday night after the used bookstore next door closed. Neon licked the worn faces. Despair sat on the bar with watered-down draft and near empty packs of smokes. Elbowed me, smiled, no highway to the Promised Land that. Bottle of Genny and a nail. Looking at my old friend, wishing for a new one, long legs would be nice.

Isabel had long hair and magic eyes. Gentle hips and a nasty scar on her shoulder. Nice legs too. Very nice.

She turned, smiled. Bought me a beer.

Isa looked in my small bag of books, liked the two I had bought. Told me of others that would bite my feelings and imagination.

She liked the record I'd bought too. Tchaikovsky's *Serenade Melancolique, Op. 26.* Smiled. "I have the same one."

My vacancy was drawn to her smile. It was a cascade of lyric, had the scent of gravity. My heart loved her eyes, her legs too—a lot.

We left together that night.

As we did the next Friday and the next.

In a bed, naked, we talked of books. She unspooled mythologies for me. Between kisses and the passport clasp by our bellies, she promised to show me where enlightenment waited.

Did. *Essays on Alienation* as Lou Reed's records played. Reread Fowles and Hesse. Shook hands with scarecrows and beautiful losers as Weather Report sang the body electric. Leaned toward Eastern Europe. Foreign towns. Foreign lands. A stranger, rarely grazed by conviction, disturbed by identity—a blizzard of fatigues, but traveling under a sky lit by the torches of Kafka and Kubin . . . I went to other places to experience Night and what lay under her dungeon skirts.

Reading, riding. Silent. Old dark roads. Long dark roads.

So our nights began, my nights tasting the apple she hand-fed me. Friday, drowning. Out. Food, pizza. Chinese or Italian on 2-for-1 feast night; she loved the spicy meatballs. Sometimes pool, always plenty of beer. Some blues band in Marty's. Whiskey; beer when our pockets were leaning on thin. We drank we laughed, or tried to. Then we took our cravings to her bed. Drowning. Ate flesh, Seger's night-moves. Then came the talk of books, of dreams and *escape*. Saturdays afternoons we haunted used book stores.

Rushed home with our cheap treasures. A six-pack, or a bottle and we read. To each other.

Isa was 15 years older than me. She dreamed of writing, settled on teaching, came with tears and an epigram from Nietzsche. I was her great experiment. She was my light. A blue light.

Long ago sadness had filled her chalice. I drank from it. Hoped it would wash away my dust. Prayed to drown in what she gave me, tried to meet it, sometimes I could get halfway.

She tried too, permitted my impatience and limits to explore. Gave me poetry—Patchen, Levertov, Wakoski, Lamantia, Rimbaud—'Her clothes were almost off' (no tree tapped on the casement to my window, but the moon came, leaned in, watched Isa drop her clothes)—books of luminous things and the extraordinary tides of her body. A naked palace of comfort and wonder she'd sit there in bed and read to me. Gave me medicines and new time. There were moments where her eyes laughed. She'd move borders and I walked into her voice.

Her voice alto-grey. Lonely or something deeper, in the moonlight, in candlelight, her clothes almost off, its sonata of autumnal syllables never slept. I took the embers as psalms for my lonely. I might close the curtains on the rain for a minute or a night, two if I were momentarily harder than downbound. The perfume of sunlight came, let me sip, but the candy melted and darkness and its rhapsodies of pain came home.

In and out of the room . . . in and out of the room . . . in afternoon's yellow light, in the labyrinth of thin, lingering night shadows . . . like a sentry patrolling, a silent sentry . . . or a detective reexamining clues . . . The black cat, its kiss, not gentle, not sweet, came in and out of the room. Just sat there. Waiting.

It was the same for her. Same downbound train. Same cold eye savoring our plump song.

Midnight. The living room. What passed for curtains open on the street. No light. Had her coat on. Was silent. The air between us was a puzzle.

Not the first time our mouths were shut. Not the first time you could hear the tick-tock-tick-tock over the ice in our whiskey glasses.

I did nothing to correct it.

Blue valentines. Should have pushed away that weight, made miles out of the ebbing sigh of moonlight. Not the first time we stayed grey, didn't try to avoid the epidemic of darkening, just couldn't grab a hurricane of intrepid. Didn't try. Just weeds. Mostly. Hard-pavement weeds struggling for glimmer, but shut out. Lack of capacity? Disappointed?

When we could we tried. Wednesday. Drunk. Naked. When the frantic wind churned and we could squeeze something from the loneliness. A kiss. A laugh. "Wanna?"—thirstily. But not enough?

One day, without a word, Isa's apartment was dark. Her landlord told me she'd moved out.

"Gone?"

A simple nod. He knew nothing else. But he handed me a wrapped-up book and an envelope.

I took it back to my cramped apartment and threw it all on the chair. Afraid to look. Maybe not afraid? Just didn't want to stir the dust in the corral. If I could help it.

Couldn't.

Drank. Swam in a bottle as if it was full of words.

Pulled out blues records, raw blues, wallowed in the autumnal dash of zigzag tears. Darkness screamed, made me a peasant, stripped me naked. Hooker could not heal the trouble I had in mind.

Middle of the night it was still there, old demons pissing on my scars. Most of the whiskey was not. Threw it across the room. Cried hot mad tears.

Looked at the book, the envelope. Tied up. No pretty ribbon. Twine. Frayed. Used. Maybe to cover a slab of meat.

Her hand applied my name to the envelope. Funny thing the letters in my name looked like they spelled, Anubis calling.

Smoked my smoke. Hissed. Glowered. Cried.

T-shirt ash-wounded, cigarette, glass of whiskey from the fifth, stood at the window, didn't see magic, no infinite. Looked like same old greyass street wrapped in unfocused suffering, all the shuffleboard pain the newspaper splatters just waiting for another shell of sick to crawl by. Stood at the window starin' at the street grinnin' with garbage. Grey tattoos and spiders of black and garbage and nothing. Might be a hundred years of darkness out there. Might be dust. Might be knife peeled dreams down to white bone. Might be time didn't care to spent flowers on this funeral. Cigarette steaming, worse just scratching for am or crust.

Thought of afternoons. Isa sitting on the sofa. Ice tea and a book. Maybe a laugh. Eyes holding me. Looked out the window once, saw birds. Was glad I was me.

Birds.

vast

bitten and pulled

—all the gears and pounds—

—the wash of wet coils—

choked

stuck rubble

birds of the iron slum, scared—rain of heartbeats now chimneys of stone

       i [empty beer can]

  b   r

         d [crushed soda can]

           s

[something color of rust]

    litter . . . their stained wings rejected by the carved blue theater of the sky.

sc rap s

   s

      s   s

broken by experience. tied to shock. the weight. having your skull measured. studied. your head split open. your hands chopped off. reduced to a scape. autumn/ragged surfaces/embedded in CRUSH
chiseled
NOT alive.

Glad then. For a moment.

Now. Whiskey cause I couldn't brush away the tears.

Streetlight halfway down the block losing interest.

Slug. Burn. Slug—want, wish, cry. Look.

No afternoon.

little sunlight . . . afternoon out here can rain confusion. or stones. or a riot. of one. or three. it can divide struggling by harrowing. can. does. it can drag the threatened face to face inferno. and often does. flesh—tingling with jackhammer touch. flesh—consumed in a turbulence of reckoning.

sunlight loses itself. evening into later on Mayor Lindsay's words ring—'What crime and poverty have created is a riot in slow motion.'

is. is. even quiet and slow

*   it sears.*

Look out that window, the necropolis swells a few pores. I know I don't have a monopoly on suffering, but it feels like it. "Fucked up."

fucked me.

Twist agony's knife, kill what's left of the bottle of self-pity.

Sadness kills brain cells.

Breathing the cemetery factories. Washed in the cleaver.

Tang erupting

    strands/cut up/cut up/cut—cutting/sour night open/gathering whorls

pocked &

    growing/gathering—this—and this—and another—coiling and churning—eating all—and no John Wayne with a blazing fist holding 6 chambers of sanity or ambulance headed this way.

Alone. Scared as the days when I was seven years old and unable to accomplish in the Land of Filth. Scared of being another jackass-nobody that never obtains. Overpowered by the terms of decay's hellgame.

Pissed.

Smoke in my fists.

Look at that street.

My hometown . . .

closed down

never to come back

Gone. Gone

out of weekend chance to breathe and lay back and shining, all the effervescent lyrical states of spiritual with their bursts of love

gone

Shade, no Brando moanin' for a grail—no Mission words gripping Mercy, moved. Might-a been up all night, (after the cheap wine and the rats vanished another picnic of crushed) played dance with the crossfire. Might have death in its eyes, if it had eyes. Thin—almost see-through, in a conversation of slow pills, thin that couldn't find a knob, leans, pisses on the phone pole. Nothing out there in broken dreams gets to reach for the sky.

Stepped from the curtain.

Grimy dark.

I listened to the street doing nothing.

Wiped my cheeks.

Made a ball out of an empty pack of cigarettes.

Tried not to look across the room. Cain was in my hands.

Fire bit and deranged.

I looked at it. Trapdoor. Wire. Both sides thirsty. Before I could catch my breath it yanked me. Ran to it. Wanted. Wanted bad.

Cut the twine. Unwrapped it.

Thomas Ligotti THE CONSPIRACY AGAINST THE HUMAN RACE

Opened. Read—*I have gone traveling and I leave you the map. Should you care to follow. I hope* Isa's hand.

Isa's Dear John words.

Unwrapped. *The Conspiracy against the Human Race.* Scanned the back cover. 'The worst and most plentiful horrors are instead to be found in reality.'

Fucking-A. Wanna tell me something I don't know. Got to love these geniuses with 3½ PhDs. Wondered if he ever even saw a rat let alone eight or nine tearin' up garbage cans, ever had to step over a cat carcass to get to his front dead. Ever get popped in the face by hate on a madass-bender, or lose his job and his girl and the crumb of self-respect he struggled to hang on to? Ever get kissed by empty so full of hollow you choke on it? Ever had to climb moonlight while black, deformed by contaminated chaos, moaned, just to find another desolate place? Didn't. Fuck no. Nice parents, nice street—shade trees—lawns, had a nice bike—maybe a new one, went to nice schools—Fuck no. He didn't know SHIT. Never walked in it. Never had it shoved down his throat by a gang of laughing hands.

Night is a highway, no fair or right in it. Busts you up. Day's a tunnel of savage, a grinder. A book? Paper and glue and ink?

Isa escapes with my heart, leaves a hole, an isolation that crunches on my marrow, sends me a book? A god-damn book?

And a cryptic note?

"Where's the damn map, Is?"

But idiots and the desperate cling.

Brand new. Hardcover. Not cheap. Cover did not give away much. Black. Black. It glared at me. Sent wind. Tasted like a hammer and a pry bar.

Her fingers had touched it. Saw the prints, smeared. Absent fingers. Sorrows staining my dust. I needed to sober up a bit and I needed to read this.

I have gone traveling and I leave you the map . . .

Isa.

"Isa."

In this?

It needed to be read, to be explored.

BLACK coffee. Cold water on my face. BLACK coffee. BLACK coffee.

Read—

'THE NIGHTMARE OF BEING ALIVE'

'What should we say about being alive?'

"Sucks." *Breathing equals fucked, Asshole.*

It's an assembly of punches. Hell with a razor-sharp double-shot of homicide, power company and the street says turn it off. That's how I had it eyeballed. One puppet's theory is another's tunnel of shit.

Had the taste in my mouth. Mouthwash whiskey didn't change no fact.

Turned a few more pages.

'Could there be anything to this pessimistic verbiage, this tirade against the evolution of consciousness?'

Lot of beyond me. But there was a film on my fingers. A universe was correcting future. Congealing in my mal. Offering seizure, dark sky. Stick hissing at my eyes. Swallow the periods. Swallow the commas. Page. Paragraph. Page. Black word ivy. Page, phrase, syntax. Logic. Structure, agitations. Poetics. Caught fly, swallow what it ploughs, swallow the ships it disrupts. Ride the sorrows of weak. Starting to insist train gathers my inches. Swallow.

Cold shit. Hard. Cold fire on the streets inside. Points out lies. Calls my name. Slips a wire noose around my tired. Blood slows. Not to relax . . .

> not to that season . . .
> this wind has eyes, eyes of harvest,
> eyes wanting birds to burn,
> wanting consume in their furnace . . .

Wanted out. Back. Some safe. Wanted another shot of cheap burn. Poured one. Splashed two more. Sat. Drifted in the chain of darkness.

Left space for lights out. Left . . .

Undoing gushes . . .

And I'm losing my grip. Not my first time. Not. But that was not like this. And Isa, my North Star, not here to save me. And I'm out of numb medicine.

"Isa."

Went to bed my lips kissing her name.

Rusty dreams scabbed with BLACK.

Hoofbeat, funeral, the book talks . . .

> 'omnipresence of the *infernal*'

'the vastness'   'a world that is wholly evil, desolate, and doomed'

'overtaken by the horror of feeling he was a human puppet' **'Unpersons'** 'the curse of conscience'

'bleakness'   'sick to death'

'full bloom'   'chaotic and meaningless' 'autopsy'

Rolled into Saturday morning's circus of decay, the anvil riot strapped to my feathers of consciousness.

Ate. Slice of cheese. Slice of bread with bargain margarine. Instant coffee, out of creamer. Out of sugar. BLACK. Drank.

Stumble to sofa.

Shut my eyes.

Isa's hand holding the book. I see her eyes, her lashes now Night's peacock feathers. A scroll of despair reaches for me.

"Is—" My lips reaching for

cello-soft skin /art /prayer /bells ARE EYES-two tongues sad /bars /stories—lips—hard mouth open, words from words /milk tones /RED her skin—belly—belly—sweetness-lacquered eyes—arrows flutter throat to feet vernacular—inhabit the glad of waist—mouth desire on my mouth—mouth calling ribs and fingers /the sphinx is not blind /I—I—I—yes breath—as lie /breath—as veins /coming /blood—the itch—the hole—the nail /NIGHT—scream and scream BLACKtime /time—time—split lie—spider on skin of you— thread NO NO NO—stroke of past /past/ cracked old /old crone scurry close /eyes /island /close /I

am shown a page

skin

skin—clown host

page/skin—takes—erase—unlists—breaks fluent returns funeral

skin page—takes hand—doors—heat—I know

Isa—cold blood without a hand in its hand needed the arms of these words

"I."

"Fuck." Trying to tell myself to breathe.

"God-damn."

Return to the book.

'The Weight.'

'Isolation.'

'Rhetoric.'

        Line after line of woven words, death row words.

'As penetrable as it is cheerless, it rests on taboo commonplaces and outlawed truisms while eschewing the recondite brain-twisters of his forerunners, all of whom engaged in the kind of convoluted cerebration that for thousands of years has been philosophy's stock in trade.'

        'a mindless and untiring master of all being, a directionless force that makes everything do what it does, an imbecilic puppeteer that sustains the ruckus of our world.'

The maze to find Isa's map.

"What the—?"

Left the curtains open. Mistake. Blinding light. Burns. Crushes.

Some warmth but it's a tightrope of razorwire. 2 flies come in the open window. Even their buzz is a slap. And they bring a maelstrom of humidity.

Back to the casket. Page 31 300+ words, black marks on white paper, black marks. Shadows, patterns. Maze. Tastes bitter, truth does that. Here in the squalor it does.

'And a puppet is only a plaything, a thing of parts brought together as a simulacrum of real presence. It is nothing in itself. It is not whole and individual but exists only relative to other playthings, some of them human playthings. That support one another's illusion of being alive.'

not. whole.

i. am.

Not.

Isa. Not

here to affirm my

need, my illusion.

"Isa." Humid as the air the flies brought to my squalor.

Her hand—eyes-so soft, so bright—all the nights I drank from her chalice—all the nights I sipped tenderness on her pale shoulder.

"Isa."

I could hear her voice. Parts of it. wings—waves—suffering the torture rack of flesh. But I could not see the Begin Here of her map.

"Where's the X?"

Got to be a spot. START HERE. *Got to.*

Page 35—
guidelines
suicide
decide
'the Will to die'—'The Undoing'—No! She could not have
38 became 42—
Isa had *touched* this book—

43
'Composed of the same dross
    (outside my window—within these walls—BARS)
as all mortals, the pessimist
    (Isa, my dear)
cleaves to whatever
    (me, another puppet-thing, pessimist)
seems to validate his thoughts and emotions.'
Puppets.
The dance of the blind. The dance of the weak.
Null.
the pages turn . . .
'there will be an end of the line' Null.
BLACKness
'there will be an end of the line'
NULL
'THERE WILL BE AN END OF THE LINE'
Nothingness.

No God. No compassion. Decay, no bracing to slow it. Self-
pity—whiskey—flesh—open a heart, cling, share lyrical, while you
can, if you can.

Isa. Her fingers tracing Nietzsche and Kierkegaard and Cioran.
Leading me on. Hesse. Schopenhauer. Camus. The salve of her lips on
my heart. Her fingers parting the thicket of briars . . .

Whiskey . . . and more whiskey . . .

The dross outside my window . . . birds trapped in rust . . . 'there
will be an end of the line'—wings stained in garbage . . .

The puppet weathers, cracks, peels,—'there will be an end of the
line'—get bumped, gets dropped, nicked,—'there will be an end of
the line'—dent here, chip there . . . 'there will be an end of the line'—
the tether snaps—

ALL FALL DOWN

Madness. "Shit. Another crazy fuck, world's full of 'em."

How many times did we talk about this. Hide in the bed and try to blot out that black hole of caustic. Close the curtains and try to find safer in each other's arms. Disconnect from ALL THAT. That crazyass shit out there.

"This is nuts."

The empty bed says, "Is it?"

pain

no human purpose, time. no touch. share

no—no

dead man reading, crying

I remember you kissing me and telling not to worry, what else did I need, I had your arms. That's what you said there in the dark. I knew it was true. Was. Was. You said it was.

Told me a lot of things. Said a lover loves and I came around— tried to, tried. Laid in that bed and wrote in me as you sailed the boats of our flesh to tropical comforts—you gave me flowers and sugar, quivered, pledged, made my paper lantern a star.

No stars outside my window. No stars in Ligotti's Coffin Book, a thing of DEATH poems, **MALIGNANTLY USELESS**, but there were more pages and a map to find.

Blossoms, the rain of isolato . . . Words, black dog words, some special plan for this world, for the Clown Puppets and their nonsense . . . Professor Nobody lectured and I listened, had his hand on my heart. Had to listen to his one way ticket. He made my puppet fingers turn the page.

Hissed, "You must! You must."

Did.

MALIGNANT—the life outside my window was, had always been. **USELESS**—life within these walls was too. Without Isa it was nothing, worse, Hell, ripping and slashing, slicing the blind, tearing at what little high I had.

More than my need was in me now. The Coffin Book, its touch, corruption, its words lived in me. The BLACK marks etched like death's ivy on white pages alive. The current of my blood flowed where the corruption dictated. Tethered to the undercurrent, that gale of cold—all the exhausting holes, cold catastrophe-deep, the knot that circles, spews its stubbled-hard. A puppet of words, dis-robed, jarred, danced as they played, beckoned—psst-psstpsst-hey, nemo, c'mer. They did not ask me to take this waltz of gloom-night frost, they, leaning with their pikes of grave, demanded it. Come to my tree, dove, there's a place for you in my cave of jaws.

A street of nothing. A shell of nothing. Ashellofnothing. Iamnoth-ing. Nothing. Nothing. Wretchedgreynothing. Iamnothing.

"Isa."

I need your reflection to slip my gaze into. "Isa."

Not this BLACKsoul yelling a grease of GONE.

This damn book. I cast it across the room. Ran to my whiskey. Sought burn. Let it burn this malignancy of vehement monsters from me. But the book would not rest. Its words shuffled in my surfaces. Hellhound on my trail, coal-black dog elongated, sang in the dead air, hissed wrongness patterns of DEADcell at me.

USELESS. USELESS. puppet—some poor bastard lost in the piti-less order of things—coward, no prodigal of gentle and elegant—puppet, bound, waiting for cure or word, prisoner, bound, waiting, pleading for a comment or an exchange with gain or godot

USELESS USELESS. and self absurd

Spiderblur-BLACK poked desperation . . .

Grimscribe hand, hungry black ink overflowing, hissing nothing-ness. Terror-scribbling hand held a pen and wrote this down. A hand that was directed, controlled. A hand that was nothing. The puppet's hand—depletion—darkness midnight-wide—oblivion danced. And I held its BLACKNESS in my rattling hands and it unlaced me. Found the guilt and flounder of my Inmost. Words that do not save. Accusa-tion words that purify with loaded-BLACKNESS. Down and narrow, digging thick . . . down . . . the fragments of my imagination hunched over a dead cavity, the words sing of the forest of NULL. I was bread, it insect . . .

"Dance, Puppet, dance." *Fuck that. Fuck you.*

I can walk away.

"I can walk away from nemo."

couldn't. drowned. BLACKNESS around me. in me.

cold. Touched with the Grimscribe's black ashes—dead—dead—dead—singing like scraping black   gulls   circling

      grave cliffs.

  down . . .

"bleakness' "sick to death' 'full bloom'

  'chaotic and meaningless'   'autopsy'

    down . . .

I put my whiskey down and was taken back to the black pages and the nightmare of TRUTH. Held the book Isa touched—*touched*. BLACK cover burned skin. It put its key of fever in me.

The pages of scar and fire wing—

their sound, this dredge of crow salt, chokes me

    seized in a storm of nails

      the winter grave

      the black hole

'Schopenhauer's a great pessimism'

'Mainländer, a Will-to-die'

'For all others who suspect that something is amiss in the life-blood of being, something they cannot verbalize, there are the malformed shades of suffering and death that chase them into the false light of contenting lies.'

Its turbulence pulled my strings—made a nightmare of the nightmares of my Reality. Damn this coffin builder and his deft worm-tongue—Damn the thrust of his disaster-sight!

Worse. Yes he delivers worse—shovels HIS Thunder on my island of chaff. Marks me! Why will you not let my ghosts lie dead, Ligotti?

You couldn't put out your fucking hand and offer me an angel, or a lantern?

Why must you hand your weight to me? This is your lot! Your curse. Not mine. Not mine.

I am small. Nothing. I shutter, hobble about. I am plain. A mere thing. Carry your plague of black angels to another famished throat. I did not cry out to you for meat. This is your feast. I did not ask to borrow your burning hornet. This is your luck. Let it be YOURS. I did not invade you. Did not even whisper in your direction. Why?

Are you listening, Demon? This is your life Thomas Ligotti—your cobalt frills, your stains and hollow. Take back your torturous serpent, I have no use for this crown of thorned-weeds. I am no priest or poet or occultist to receive manifestoes. Let your ship lost on razor-tears meet the rocks. Be gone, damn you!

I am not some Adam to take the apple you offer. This is your lot! I am small. nothing

iamnothing

Then I see, or begin to, he too is a puppet, a mere mouthpiece for the power behind this chaos-hive of violent life. It forces him to dance, to write—to erase. He is small. Nothing. The infection will bleed him dry too. He smells of fear. Loathing tugs him. Another sucker. Another fool, tragic, but a fool. Hollowed out. Forced to scream, Gone, Baby, GONE!

My eyes and fingers tear at the pages—layers and layers of soot, BLACKNESS nothingness—The BLACK dog howls and his infection taints me as it must have tainted Isa.

Where does his cancer-map lead?

"Where, Isa?"

—telling me early of her love of Holmes, his doubts, his complications, the company of despair he sometimes kept, all she felt kin to. Darkness. Young. Unhappy with her looks—the embarrassment, in silence, when she bought her first bra; married to the blood that lit her womb that 1st time; the crazy stripes of heat when she cradled desire of his flesh, then the dark dance of fear and the horror—her station, unhappy with her fears and desires, drawn to the soft darkness, its cloak of deep quietude.

Darkness to escape bitterness. Whiskey to escape The Thinker that discovered and then pronounced. Darkness to cure with soft medicine her anguish and the irrationality of a puppet existence.

Isa—a fascination—Mine!—in and out of bed—a lyrical joy, hand, eyes dancing, eyes cottages with no winter—Isa. Round. Smooth. A wreath of warm for my knife.

So I read the damning book.

the map . . . the map . . . my need . . . words and whiskey altering my state . . . fueling the whiskey with whiskey and my rain . . .

47—

downbound

'Disenchantment'

I know why—RAIN. Wind blows . . . Clock scrawls jagged on the bell tower, Church is a horse outta milk and bullets; folks have withdrawn their spoons. Puppetshow, creepshow, bone horizon, cardboard faces, slaughterhouse has cardboard walls ... ephemera herding goats ... someone said man needs to be what he is even if it kills him, how's that work when the resume says Puppet, To Go ... when's the last time you heard phew 'round here? Cigarette butts no valiums ... blank wall ... drunk/screwed/steaming with endless regret hold out your bowl you inherit yelling ... dogs here don't bark, attracts attention and kicks, you bleed get flies ... RAIN. Wind blows.

Blunt drunk, sometimes I forgot to close my windows ...

'Disenchantment'

the slaughterama is dialed up to overload

'The Anatomy of Negation'

the blundering puppet. naïve. Thinking. Feeling.

Fool in his empire of

crypt.

'the tumult is indescribable'

stupid

Turned back. Had I missed anything? Must have. Old news. Missed a lot. A whole life's worth. Must have missed the X?

'And a puppet is only a plaything, a thing of parts brought together as a simulacrum of real presence. It is nothing in itself. It is not whole and individual but exists only relative to other playthings, some of them human playthings that support one another's illusion of being real.'

not. whole.

i. am not

Isa. Not here to affirm my need, my illusion.

"Isa."

—her hand, eyes, so soft, so bright ... all the nights I drank from her chalice ... all the nights I sipped tenderness on her pale shoulders ...

"Isa."

demons ... disease ... living in this scream of hair and skin ... the book is a siren song and an assault on my species ... a predator. .. breaks dreams ...

break its grasp with whiskey

reach

out of sunshine and feel and hope

Out of whiskey. Out of beer. Not even a joint. 4 Kools left. I had
to go out. Out there. In it. Let the stain claw me again.

The street. Another stained bird with broken wings

Four cop cars in front of the liquor store. Robbed. "Shit." Dia-
mond Liquor was seven blocks away.

Walked across the street. Figured a couple of beers would help
the trek. Sea Horse Inn, closet five steps wide barto-wall, 65 years of
dour and grime pain in some frozen char. Grabbed a stool. Smoked
my smoke. Drank my first. Wasn't ice cold, never are in here. The
blonde, 40 and a couple/nice hair/good build, on the corner stool
smiled, wanted one if I was buyin', maybe a fuck too. I almost
thought about it. Might have, but some big-brain professor, Robert
Price, wrote *The Reason Driven Life: What Am I Here on Earth For?*
came on the TV. Was talking about the Coffin Book, held it up,
called it a major work. Damn book was some kind of big news.

Expression was a cold phrase: "God is not on their side.'

"In the literature of the fantastic, in Robert W. Chambers' "The
Yellow Sign," anyone who attended the decadent play *The King in
Yellow* or even read it was at once plunged into suicidal melancholy?
Well, this new book by Thomas Ligotti is *The King in Yellow.* The
real one."

Cut to the opposing talking head, some fundamentalist-
throwback from Oklahoma waving his Bible. Had a few holy words
to push at the brimstone, boiled down to God would punish the Coffin Builder. God would fix this—"I can do all things through Christ
who strengthens me.' The Pure have nothing to fear. God's light cannot be turned off, or down. Certainly not by the lies of The De-
ceiver's coffin-monger.'

"This is America. God lives here. In II Chronicles 7:14 it says, 'If
my people which are called by my name will humble themselves,
and pray, and seek my face, and turn from their wicked ways, then I
will hear from heaven, forgive their sins, and heal their land.' God
lives here and we, His Children, will not accept this reign of darkness
to spoil our land."

OK. Right. Assbag for Jesus. God? Whole place was a mess—
God wasn't fixing shit. Congress either. They might as well be as dead
as God.

I watched, fuck I was glued to it. Book was selling and it was infecting people, that's what the shrinks said. There were assertions people were reading it and killing themselves. Some were killing their families too. Mini Jim Jones shit in suburban kitchens.

Anchor woman said:

CATHR was a winning Lotto ticket for the tabloids

Nostradamus + Ligotti - God =

The END is Nigh—You Pick the Date

I was not alone. I was not the only prisoner, the only puppet. I ran out of there. Crossed the street to the Hadji-mart.

"Global Weekly Report" had a chimp holding a burning copy upside down while it scratched it head. Magazine cover said Wal-Mart had two "Wal-Mart exclusive" Ligotti is Satan's mouthpiece books; word was they were selling well. But not as well as *CATHR*. Bought four magazines and a sixer. Smokes too.

Went back to my walls. Turned on the TV. CNN. They were on CATHR. Talking heads and some celebs. A former Suicide Girl, TragiDi, started a cult she was calling a church. Saw her get interviewed. Some shit about decay holds the puppet's strings. Right then she lifted her skirt a bit, showed the puppet tats she had on her knees. Get off your knees. Free yourself from the tethers she said. Quoted 15 and ½ nihilists and said she hoped to be recording with David Tibet. Hoped to spread the holy word of the Ladder Down with music. For more news join her church. Near the end she held up her membership card. $59.95 + S+H. Or if you're in L.A. just stop in. Yes, they take VISA.

HOOKED

Them.

Me.

It got in my seams. Stuck. Stopped dreams. Closed future. Called it no good. No good. Said fabulous was a lie, a poison dart.

Dry whisper: "Sure is."

This writer had looked at the puppet—me, at his absurd nightmare-dance, his reality, his grim vision of life was as hard as the street. Doom, fierce or some waxy film of Beinglessness, ain't fair.

Looked in the mirror, saw a ghost lookin' out at me. Dead, just hadn't laid down yet. Wanted too. That's what scared me. Wanted to change my face.

Murder book said even constellations change when they read CRUSH. Losing my head. My speech and river shut from muscle shimmering human. No Jesus-dope in my spoon. No hope

stripped

by the black-oracle bloat

        even the twisted stream of my howl

abandoned me

   in

     the getaway

Thing got in and ate. Guess the BLACKNESS always does. Did in the cave. Same now. Old scene of scar-grey swirl. Same old smother noble. All that greying is nothing more than a cave. Unknown is out there, waiting.

Book said null was open all the time. And it was gonna come in. Hell I can see that. It's on every street, chewing. Wearing. Taking back. BLACK is chaos, chaos won't allow structure. Thought why try to reach for the sun, bone-palace ballet was going to lay a last night on you if you spit and cursed or not. Sift the madness all you get is more madness. Build and chaos comes and leaves BLACKNESS.

I'm not a genius like this Ligotti fellow, and I'm sure no philosopher, but I can tell when weather's coming. Storm is brewin'. BLACK storm. Sweeps clean.

Book was a storm. Like I said, TV. Talk shows and talking heads. Late night and Saturday night. *SNL* did two skits. *The View*, Jon Stewart, everyone hit it. Papers decried it. Internet burned, Facebook buzzed. Came, slapped trouble on everyone. Butcher. Baker. Soldier. Sailor. Coffin maker.

Reverend whatever the hell his name in Tuna-sandwich-on-white, Ohio held a public book burning. Was on TV, every channel, top of the hour, shoutin'—"Scripture says, 'Without a vision, the people perisheth.' Well, Mr. Ligotti is a thief. He is stealing the vision of hope from people everywhere. They are lost souls, and we weep for them. But as for this thief, well, you know what the Bible says, 'Temptations are sure to come, but woe unto him by whom they come.' Woe, then, woe unto Thomas Ligotti!" His anointed wore T-shirts against the Coffin Book. Lasted a few news cycles. Only served to fan the flames.

Critics and columnists chewed on it.

'We do not belong. *We*, and not some pantheon of gods or ghosts or Great Old Ones, are the intruding blasphemies against the natural order. How so? In what sense? Simply that human consciousness is an aberration of evolution, creating a brain too big for its needs, so it manufactures artificial needs, i.e., for answers to questions which are inappropriate and have no answer. We create delusions and illusions such as the very notion of meaning, not to mention fantasies like a hopeful future, gods, and life after death. Our consciousness, unlike that of the blissfully sleeping world of beasts and stones around us, and trampled by us, makes us aware of the eventuality of death and the acuity of suffering.'

'The earth has become unchained from its sun and wanders now through the coldness of space. God is dead. The category of "truth" is empty.'

Fire's dangerous. Some run from it. Others step closer. They have to see. Lot stepped up to see. Bought it. Read. Let its madness in.

Hollywood grabbed spiking sales numbers, was making a movie. PBS had a documentary in the works. Networks smelled trouble from advertisers whose blood closet-to-sleeve was a sea of traditionalist, ran like hell.

Berlin 'bleakness'   "sick to death'
NY NY "bleakness' "sick to death' 'full bloom'
Tokyo 'bleakness' 'full bloom'   'chaotic and mean-ingless' Paree 'bleakness' 'and meaningless' 'autopsy'

London. Blazin' hot; hell, you'd have thought the book was free. Vatican wanted it banned. Bible-belt took a steamroller and torch to it.

Goth bible. New age sensation. The Coffin Book. Madison Ave tagged it—

Euthanize your torment

All hail the new philosopher! Except those who wanted his head on a pole! The publisher went into hiding on a South-Jersey beach.

Couples uncoupled. Dancers heard no song.

Eyes went black.

Disillusionment that wanted to be a prisoner of love, that had tasted fire and entered the lyrical state, crashed, its aspirations and any hope of consolation or friends or release from the convulsions of poverty burned in the listless madness of NIHIL's abyss. Weathered to nothingness the puppets shed their final tears.

Downtown. Roof of a seven-story grey office prison. Grey sky. Grey street. I saw him with his copy. Saw darkness scraping him. Watched him leap.

Out of geography.

All the flies of misery. Death scenes the maggot detectives pasted in their scrapbooks. Hands in a puff of out.

Tin cup with no monkey to yell direction.

Broke.

The news said it happened to others. The new age had opened; people were reaching for a way. Some way around or out of darkness. Finding the secret.

Flower power world got tore up by grit and information—INSTANT, hard times snatched up all the plenty, nostalgia grabbed hearts & minds that gazed up or gazed in, folks wanted Back, MY Glory Days or soft, even a bit. Got their minds set on religion and herbs, on promises, any sense or season of LOVE and Light. Wicca, crystals, tarot, feng shui, snake-energy if it had the right pitch. Magic, hell yes, if it solved distant and loneliness. Pills for stress. Pills for insomnia. Blessings for health, herbs just ain't enough. Fortune cookie blessings for fulfillment, for financial enrichment. Blessings that pushed the Apocalypse into the lap of the next generation. If it sounded lyrical they let it in their prison. Tack IMPROVED on any old scam and it got swallowed, with everything NOW they never look twice. Anything.

Hungry world was feeding. Frenzy was feeding too.

Was eating me.

Finally went back to the book. Had to. Had to find the map. Had to find Isa before—"Where does your map lead, Isa?"

To nothing? All this shit and at the end will I only find hollow shadows and a vast pit of shit? *This is the world of shit.*

And you, Coffin-maker, you would cast me down—lower? Lower?

Why couldn't you have played with lies? O Wormword-engraver, slapping the weak with your deluge of ashes, you sing far better than most, you could have granted escape, a few hours of wonder with your tales, but you choose to render to Nothing.

"This has to be a lie. A fiction."

Has to be.

Please?

Sat with his vulture-book.

Trapped in three tight rooms with the vampire book, its bleakness feeding off me. Sat. Read. Drank.

Cried.

I had read dark tales before. Poe and Lovecraft, Bloch and King. Enjoyed King Death and the torsos and throats that faced the blood test of fang and the butcher. All the quests, the ritual evil, the seduction of witches, the deadwalk of shadow men, serial killers and Hell's sirens, read, escaped in the dark hollows. I had been beyond the Mountains of Madness and stood at the crossroads where the fingerpost said Carcosa. I had been to Drakulon. And now the weapon of the blackscribe touched on tales I'd escaped in. Blackwood, Lovecraft, Chambers, they too were fellow conspirators, inching me closer to the birth of this End of humanhood w/ their haunting and horrors. But this, what Ligotti put in my hands was darker than night and I had no sword, and no fire, no latch or door for my cramped cave.

The pen is mightier than the sword, it is!

BLEAK has a name—

Ligotti.

Bleak—

I call it the death of life.

Awash in the Coffin-lord's dyspeptic declarations I could not find anger. I crawled as he hissed DESPAIR. Cried.

Drank.

Tore at the words for the key to this cartographic illness.

Distortions smolder.

Dismay replaced the illusion that life was worth anything. Self—I AM—was nothing. Myth. Trickery. The Dance of Maya indeed. Life is not bullshit as you're a mistake, a freak. I live in bleak squalor and he calls me a freak.

iamnothing

a puppet

And the world was discovering they too were mistakes. The Coffin-maker had opened his black lantern—'there will be an end of the line'—and a plague of black angels came forth. They hissed. 'there will be an end of the line' They howled. 'there will be an end of the line' They sowed all with sadness, and all were brushed and scratched by madness. It was an epidemic of black sand. It fastened itself to the dark sky of consciousness and no drink or holy words or medicine or river of tears could lessen its control.

The puppets danced. Right over the cliff. One
right after
      the
other.

Disruptions. Cut. There was muttering. Scrambling. A revolution. Took over notions and the stock market. It was in music and poetry and in bedrooms.

This was no 16-year-old-schoolgirl offs herself when Mr.-Hot-as-a-Nova-Today marries, this didn't care about bends of gender or age.

An open fire that ended and the carnivorous mass quoted it, made burrows and walls before they, often without fuss, concluded succumb.

Fire. It scorched. Some even burned away their pain with gasoline and matches and it was on TV. I drank and tried to hide from it. Tried to find the map in the book. It was there. Isa said so.

But where?

Some dreamland she had not told me about? Some vale she may have mentioned but I didn't pick up on? *I have gone travelling and I leave you the map. Should you care to follow.*

Was that all there is, the decay that infects the consciousness and drives its host over the cliff?

'there will be an end of the line'

Sirens come. Sirens go. Emergency in batches. E.R.'s are flooded; knife wounds, the I'm telling you bullets make. Moonlight bursts through my windows. No warmth in it.

I skipped back, recovering old ground. Had I missed something. I must have. I must have. Skipped ahead, hoping to connect dots that made secrets codes to this maze. There was a way out. There had to be.

Cold lonesome ground. 'autopsy' Sky of fire. 'autopsy' No kiss, no stars . . . Nuthin' you want to swallow. Did she?
     f a l l
. . . this field
        forget the kiss, how it felt   to have
            heart

give

all

to this empty sky with cloud-skin of evil . . . . . .   stop

            hoping

                   for a chance   the   dust   is   a
mountain

               —black line no alright   can't shut the door—no lock
       cold

no sleep nothing in a white robe no euphoria not even a lovely postcard or the fit of a nocturne

   cold black ground not a window no hands to pray

     no Eric John Stark, no John Wayne, no God, Moses ain't, no phone call from the Governor

There is a shadow man dead by the phone pole. Dead. Propped right there. Knife. Blood. Sat down on the curb. Slit his wrists. No wind. No flies yet. But they will come

'autopsy'

I don't need the weatherman, I know He opened the Coffin Book, nailed to a terrible place, danced his dance—did not live to a ripe old age, silenced the slow motion riot with a rite of soft black spring

Ligotti, the Conductor of Bleak, choreographed it.

Puppet sprouting melancholy and puppetmaster steered by un-bearable, damned and doomed, mastermind, trapped in the galactic array of downpour, insistent worm-whorls of this sewer of black-foaming, black ditch gloom, this factory of nightmare-confetti . . . and longing.

Undone no bells

'there will be an end of the line'

no mourners

'THERE WILL BE AN END OF THE LINE'

Undone

'. . . will soon find himself in the twists of a labyrinth from which he will not be able to escape . . .'

Yes I was an idiot. And I was poor. And—

Undone

no red eyes still on the movement of the beat . . . stilled by BLEAK—all GONE . . . to bottomless—the weight of no star

       no move

no signals

or griots or balance of dear world or even the long of just another day passing

The virtuoso's hieroglyphic operations—word—phrase—crypt ('. . . will soon find himself in the twists of a labyrinth from which he will not be able to escape . . .')—his turf hurling effect ('. . . will soon find himself in the twists of a labyrinth from which he will not be able to escape . . .')—stirring view ('. . . will soon find himself in the twists of a labyrinth from which he will not be able to escape . . .')—I was reading his secret language . . .

Solar's eager crushed by Ligotti's black-finger hysterias of nega-tion manifest from demons of anxieties, plunged in cold-morgue cel-lar dimension—

'It will go on and on until it stops. And the horror will go on, with generations falling into the future like so many bodies into open graves. The horror handed down to us will be handed down to others like a scandalous heirloom. Being alive: decades of waking up on time, then trudging through another round of moods, sensations, thoughts, cravings—the complete gamut of agitations—and finally flopping into bed to sweat in the pitch of dead sleep or simmer in the phan-tasmagorias that molest our dreaming minds. Why do so many of us bargain for a life sentence over the end of a rope or the muzzle of a gun? Do we not *deserve* to die?'

Last word.

DIE

'there will be an end of the line' die

and her hand had a few to add. Inside the back cover—neat. soft. flowing

My Sweet Doubter, I did love you. Needed you. I have always tried to give you what joy I could. Tried to show you Truth. This is my last gift . . .

*A map to the soft **BLACK** truth.*

nothingness

It can be the only peace, the only rest.

I have escaped—Come, step out of the flame "Isa."

She talked of rope once. We were watching Hitchcock on TV

. . . And she could make knots, nooses from twine or string.

Did.

Laughed. Poison is for poets. "Not for one such as I." The coils . . . throbbing timpani . . .

Burning, my soul folds in the blizzard. No melody of Eve with harmony fruit luminous in my veins, no Eurydice to bring out of the underworld. I know what I know.

No whiskey to brush away the tears. No howling. Just the searing in my chest. The napalm shredding my thoughts . . .

all the things that don't last . . .   city living . . . apart . . . no explanations—disputes—rushing—scab doors—nowhere touching cracks—perspiration replying to questions . . . fire and shit and slaughter, no CPR . . . thieves and whores and grim and

grey . . . catching the spurt of worthless . . .

DOOM, here, black angels, cash in hand, with black lies . . .

air and tears . . . consequence and ghosts . . . sleep full of sand, the drowning. . locks to cross . . . stop . . . scar . . . tiny voices . . .   ghost blank as might have been . . .   dirty flags of flesh and blood sold to madly . . .

tables turned.dead city . . .

full force funeral, end of a dead man, his lines, feelings and things, buried seed, logic and shimmer deflowered,   no prayer,

no after dinner conversations that measure home or thank you, yes . . .   crowd rolls down its blinds on shocked . . .

problems in last week's underwear . . .

pantomime . . . alone at the window . . . no peacock interlude . . . glances that slip away before something feral laughs or they have to respond . . . innuendos of shadows and smoke . . . endgame with flies . . .

no great revelry of rainstorm spitting signs—shit piled on shit piled on shit piled on filth and THERE IS NO EXIT. It's 12 o'clock. Night'll come. Another sick man will sigh, bark in whispers of down here in the grey dredges. Drenched in blended sweat won't fight the lapping undercurrent of the sewer river. Scarecrow bones reduced. No ten feet tall. Drinking with the jukebox. No ten feet tall. Flesh. 'there will be an end of the line' Shut up. 'there will be an end of the line' Flesh. 'there will be an end of the line' Don't know sleep. 'there will be an end of the line' Dim. Dim. Bloody. Frank. Mary. Sitting at a table—a life sentence of sweat. Dead. Bodies rooted in not. A facade from some hall of vodka gurgles , "Again?" Zombie with an hourglass of expletives. Gloom comes blows away the sun.

                 the weight.   zero.

nothing
covered up
     factories closed
hopes
     closed accounts
     closed
pictures you don't want to see in color
                   blues ain't a healer. the promised land worked and worked, dug, took, harvested, the promised land wounded, raw
     this dragon's lair . . .
               30-ought six 3rd degree
                 sucker no shore leave
             no work small change blues
                 bastards
                   orphans
           the 18th time
                 no lost souls howlin' SALVATION
                 all stripped down no emotional spare parts
                 temptation
     hometown broken night
     rise and fall of murder
     poet's kiss staggers

Thomas Ligotti

THE CONSPIRACY AGAINST THE HUMAN RACE

Thomas Ligotti. Butcher. Baker. Coffin maker.

I don't think I need whiskey anymore. Don't clean these bruises. Don't clean these streets. Don't hurl grey from my soul.

Got the book. "It's got my number."

'It will go on and on until it stops. And the horror will go on, with generations falling into the future like so many bodies into open graves. The horror handed down to us will be handed down to others like a scandalous heirloom. Being alive: decades of waking up on time, then trudging through another round of moods, sensations, thoughts, cravings—the complete gamut of agitations—and finally flopping into bed to sweat in the pitch of dead sleep or simmer in the phantasmagorias that molest our dreaming minds. Why do so many of us bargain for a life sentence over the end of a rope or the muzzle of a gun? Do we not *deserve* to die?'

Book. Pages of black earth with a grave tattoo. Sentence, mausoleum-wisdom skyline. Ligotti, nightwalker, BLACKstalker, standing there on the dead end street with his art of coffins waiting. I don't think I need whiskey anymore. I think I got it. No. No, its got me. Yeah. Its got me. Snapping at my heels. Its got me. Calls. Dead day dawn.

All wild bark—'finally flopping into bed to sweat in the pitch of dead sleep or simmer in the phantasmagorias that molest'—louder than Bible—'Do we not *deserve* to die?', like a gang seeded with rags and words that stop the sun, calls.

My sin. My blindness.

"The whole fucking shitstorm. All of it."

'Do we not *deserve* to die?'

hurt

pride took back its invitation

siren in the hole of disorder

sorrow bitches

scene

decays

"Lot of people leavin' town. Turned off the sound of the siege. Didn't bend things with goodbye, not even once." *Not a one.*

"Didn't yell no. Just succumbed to dust. Worm freight."

Everything's got a season.

black wings

sore   s o r e

head hung down

blind

sore

bullets

         sin, no somewhere no hot water nuthin' puttin' flowers on the flower's grave no Jack & Jackie no sea of love no young at heart not a head turns

                     no downchild getting to the

             point

                        tired neighborhood with a

            dirty face wolf

won't

      survive

                    cryin'

              rain sore and tired, sick

               of the poison

      stained, crumbling facades—lies that skin you

             if you're looking or not . . . graphic—

repercussions—knife—underbelly,

                soft, white, the reaper—mouth and teeth

and knife, stalking the collective—nameless faces in the dim-stain
shadows of seedy bars looking for lipstick, looking for lights, looking
for a dreamscape to spill out of the jukebox . . .

    soft black truth

    Did you find quietude?

    No demons to tear at sleep?

    I laughed.

    Sleep?

    Whatever his name was in *The Godfather* sleeps with fishes.
Down in the BLACK deep bottom. Cold.

        COLD

        quiet

    "I love you, Isa."

    Coffin-maker, are you out there? Waiting, struggling? Thank you
for the map. In this mad sewer of a world, this hungry permanent
midnight, whirling with chaos-teeth and rotten fangs and brittle tedi-
ums, I wish you peace. I wish you

    quiet

    It's a short walk past the broken eyes of the abandoned locomo-
tive factory to the Stockade, to the tiny lot of 3 trees and a picnic
bench they call a park. Green St. Park with the nameless bronze Indian. Green St. ends with this park. Dead end. Right under the
sculpted steep cliffs of Riverview, grey cliffs right here where the

river bends before it rushes 8o miles south to the ocean. They say it's deep here. Very deep.

Watching the river run ... looks like little hills rolling along ... the hills flow ...

The nightmare of being—head full of false imaginings, the cravings the blundering puppet paints, being handed the scandalous heirloom ... The surface of the river is graced by soft lights, a trance

and this is where I go down into the darkness

After Thomas Ligotti's *The Conspiracy against the Human Race;* bunch of songs by Bruce Springsteen and some by Scott Walker and David Tibet/Current 93

Acknowledgments

Thanks to my weirdo Facebook friends—you post fact/info, fancy, crap, tunes, pics, kind and WEIRDaSS comments, and some parts stick and often, one leads to nExt and suddenly I have ideas in my pencil; ;;;;;~;:: ;;; & MUST run w/ them. Thanks for putting up w/ me.

THANKssssssssS to Derrick for being insane enough to do this 3 times! !! HugsSSSSSss, My Brother!! !

To those who folks I dedicated tExts to, you are a gang of WONDERFUL {& plenty-Wacked!} sweeties. Thanks for the fuel and inspiration, and saying, "GO AHEAD! TAKE IT!"

Robert Bloch & Robert W. Chambers—I love you both more than my lacking words can ever convey! !!

My deepest thanks to Matt Cardin for the intro.

THANKS!! ! to Tom Ligotti, Bob Price, Anna Tambour, and Kristin Prevallet, for allowing me to cite and quote from their exceptional work! !!

Thanks, LOVE! !!, & bEastly hugSSSSSSSSSSSSSSSSssssssss to Lena Griffin for going along w/ my wacky ideas, allowing me to—, (and for posing)! !!

Thanks to my pal, J Karl Bogartte, for another wonderful cover! !! Loves ya, Bogo!! !

Thanks & hugSSssssssSSSS to LL for all the red pen readin' &—

Thanks to David E. Schultz for (another! !!) wonderful job of setting my s;tuF:F: on the page! !!

Thanks [again] to S.T. for keeping an eye on the dials and levers behind the curtain.

vewwy humbly,
a bEast [unmasked]

www.ingramcontent.com/pod-product-compliance
Lightning Source LLC
Chambersburg PA
CBHW060926030726
47503CB00003B/493